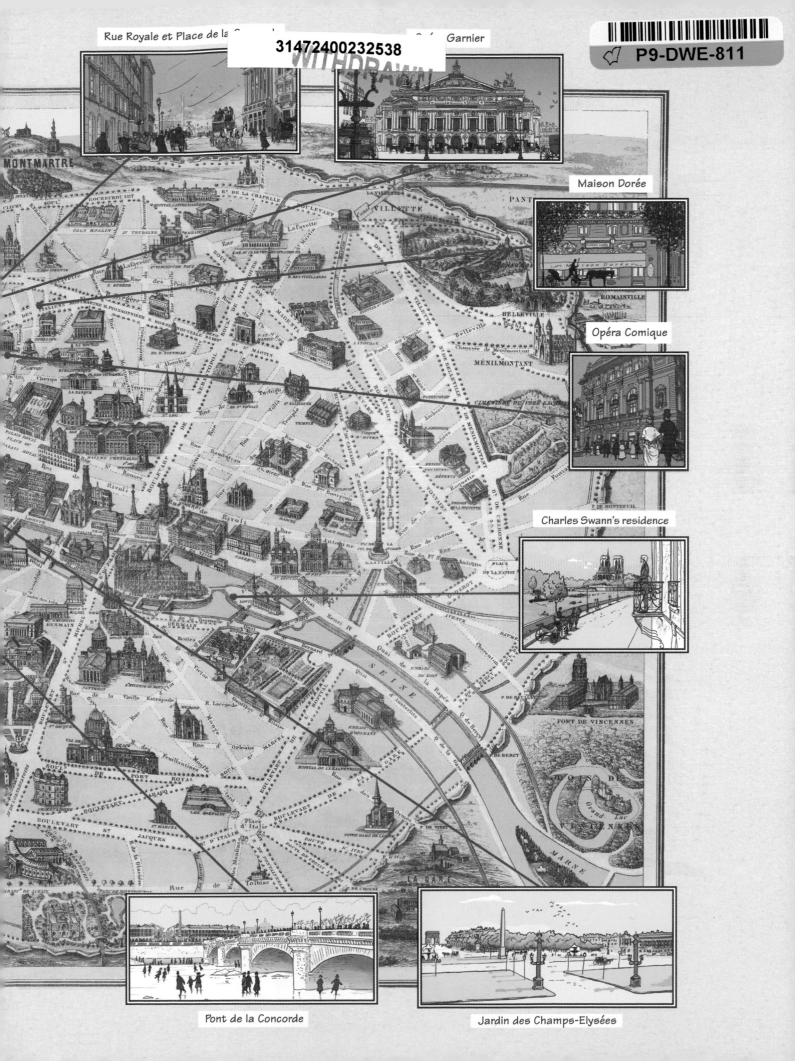

Rue Royale et Place de la Concorde

Opéra Garnier

Maison Dorée

MONTMARTRE

Opéra Comique

Charles Swann's residence

Pont de la Concorde

Jardin des Champs-Elysées

DATE DUE

			PRINTED IN U.S.A.

In Search of Lost Time

Swann's Way

Marcel Proust

In Search of Lost Time

Swann's Way

Adaptation and Drawings by
Stéphane Heuet

Translated by
Arthur Goldhammer

LIVERIGHT PUBLISHING CORPORATION

A Division of W. W. Norton & Company

NEW YORK   LONDON

Originally published in French as *Du côté de chez Swann: Édition Intégrale* from
À *La Recherche du Temps Perdu* by Marcel Proust, adapted by Stéphane Heuet

For information about permission to reproduce selections from this book,
write to Permissions, Liveright Publishing Corporation,
a division of W. W. Norton & Company, Inc.,
500 Fifth Avenue, New York, NY 10110

For information about special discounts for bulk purchases, please contact
W. W. Norton Special Sales at specialsales@wwnorton.com or 800-233-4830

Manufacturing by RR Donnelley, Shenzhen, China
Production manager: Anna Oler

Library of Congress Cataloging-in-Publication Data

Heuet, Stéphane.
[Du côté de chez Swann. English]
In Search of Lost Time : Swann's Way: a graphic novel / Marcel Proust ; adaptation
and drawings by Stéphane Heuet ; translated by Arthur Goldhammer.
pages cm
ISBN 978-1-63149-035-4 (hardcover)
1. France—Social life and customs—19th century—
Comic books, strips, etc. 2. Graphic novels.
I. Goldhammer, Arthur, translator.
II. Proust, Marcel, 1871–1922. Du côté de chez Swann.
III. Title.
PN6747.H48C6813 2015
741.5'944—dc23
2014048982

Liveright Publishing Corporation
500 Fifth Avenue, New York, N.Y. 10110
www.wwnorton.com

W. W. Norton & Company Ltd.
Castle House, 75/76 Wells Street, London W1T 3QT

1 2 3 4 5 6 7 8 9 0

TRANSLATOR'S INTRODUCTION

To adapt *Swann's Way*, the first volume of Marcel Proust's masterpiece *In Search of Lost Time*, as a graphic novel? As they say in French, *c'est pas évident*; it's not obvious at first blush that such a feat can be pulled off. Proust is famous for his long, complicated sentences and his philosophical ruminations on the passage of time, the nature of art, and the elusiveness of memory. He is a painter in words, whose verbal artistry is bound to outshine any attempt at visual representation. Yet when I was approached to translate the text of Stéphane Heuet's adaptation of Proust, I hesitated for only a moment. To a lover of Proust, the appeal was obvious.

But what about the reader? Who will want to read this book, and how should they approach it? In a review of the French version of Heuet's adaptation, the critic Michael Wood imagined that the typical reader would be a person who had always dreamed of reading Proust but had been put off, perhaps, by the author's daunting reputation for difficulty or by the sheer magnitude of the undertaking. I expect—I hope— that new readers will be drawn to my favorite writer by the promise of the gentle introduction this text offers. But gentleness is not the only virtue of Heuet's adaptation. The ruthless compression required to squeeze Proust's expansive sentences into the confining frames of a graphic novel yields an unexpected benefit: it sheds a revealing light on the book's

armature, on the columns, pillars, and arches that support the narrator's resurrected memories as the columns of the church in Combray support the stained glass and tapestries that transport visitors into the past they represent.

Proust's regained time does not unfold in chronological order. Memory is cunning. It doesn't disclose what it knows all at once. Even the involuntary memory by which Proust sets such great store refuses to unveil its truth straightaway. It tantalizes, as the view of an enticing landscape tantalizes the traveler discovering it for the first time: the beauty of the whole can be taken in at a glance, but the particular aspects that the whole encompasses must be explored patiently, sequentially, one by one, and then knitted together again into the composite whose alluring unity motivated the search to begin with. Proust likens the memory of the town of Combray, which the narrator often visited as a child but which has "died" for him until he dips the plump cookie known as a madeleine into his tea, to one of those Japanese paper novelties that blossom when immersed in water: "And just as the Japanese amuse themselves by taking a porcelain bowl full of water and dipping in it small, seemingly shapeless bits of paper, which, the moment they touch the water, expand, assume new shapes, take on color and variety, and turn into flowers, houses, or people, substantial and recognizable, so, now, did all the flowers of our garden and of Swann's estate and the water lilies of the Vivonne and the good people of the village and their little homes and the church and all of Combray and its surroundings take shape and solidity, a whole town and all its gardens emerging suddenly from my cup of tea." But for us, Proust's readers, Combray would remain a mere novelty, a Japanese water flower rather than an object of art, if Proust didn't walk us through the memory of his aunt's garden and Swann's estate and the water lilies and the "good people" of the village step by step, taking us by the hand and introducing us one after another to the people and buildings and even the flora and fauna, the water lilies of the Vivonne and Mme Sazerat's stray dog.

As we discover Combray through Marcel's eyes, we find that his life there as a child is centered, as most children's lives are, on his family, but we also find ourselves repeatedly taking surprising detours. In order to explain why he no longer enters a small sitting room formerly used by his uncle Adolphe, the narrator jumps backward in time and several hundred miles in space, and we are introduced to Uncle Adolphe in the company of a beautiful denizen of the demimonde, whose presence in his Paris apartment leads to a break between Adolphe and the rest of the family, thus accounting for his banishment from the house in Combray. Adolphe then reappears in the next section of the novel, "Swann in Love," when he is enlisted as an intermediary between Swann and another disreputable beauty, Odette de Crécy, with whom Swann is obsessed and on whom, we learn, Uncle Adolphe has tried to force himself. We recall having previously met Odette

back in Combray, though at that point she is introduced only as a woman whose scandalous past and compromising relationship with the Baron de Charlus make it impossible for the narrator's family to receive her as the wife of Charles Swann, their neighbor of many years. In Combray we merely glimpse Charlus, who reappears as a younger man in "Swann in Love," where he is the one friend whom Swann thinks he can trust with his lover. We also catch our first glimpse of Gilberte, who will become the object of the narrator's obsession in the third and final section of the novel, "Place Names: The Name."

Similarly, we meet the Duchesse de Guermantes in "Combray," only to find her again, years earlier, in "Swann in Love." We might easily miss her reappearance, however, since in that section she is still the Princesse des Laumes. The composer Vinteuil, whose sonata will play such an important role in creating the bond, or bondage, that is the subject of "Swann in Love," is first encountered in "Combray" as a censorious fellow parishioner of the narrator's family who disapproves of the slovenly manners of the young and fusses over his mannish daughter.

Clearly, then, the reader new to Proust must attend closely, even in this compressed rendering, to the novel's circling rhythms and abrupt cross-cuts between different places and times. But this necessary attentiveness is abetted and facilitated by the compactness of the graphic format. The patterned bass repeats at more frequent intervals here than in the original novel, so it is easier to keep the overarching structure of the great symphony in mind. Even the reader already familiar with the novel may make new discoveries thanks to the clarity of what might be likened to a piano reduction of an orchestral score. For what is sacrificed in variety of color and dynamic range, there is compensation in the prominence given to the major themes. And Heuet's careful selection of certain extended passages of Proust's rich prose ensures that enough of the color and range and contrasting timbres of the principal instruments is retained to suggest the depth and breadth of the composer's conception.

In using musical metaphors I am following Proust's lead. The "little phrase" of Vinteuil's sonata for violin and piano that is at the heart of *Swann's Way* poses a challenge to the visual artist. What pictorial representation of the music can convey the power it has over Swann's emotions? Music for Proust is art in its purest form. It works directly on the emotions. The narrator's feelings about works of literature are shaped by what he has heard about them from people he admires: from his friend Bloch, from the engineer-aesthete Legrandin, from his elegant neighbor Charles Swann, from his teachers. Even his feelings for Gilberte and the Duchesse de Guermantes arise from names he has invested with significance before actually perceiving the people those names designate. But the little phrase from Vinteuil goes straight to Swann's heart, unheralded by prior reputation or authoritative advocates. Its origin, Proust tells us, is "supernatural," so in order to represent its effects on a natural being like Swann, the writer is forced to associate the playing of the music with certain coincidental events, whether Swann's search for Odette on dark Paris boulevards late at night after the gaslights have been turned out—a search that Proust compares to Orpheus's search for Eury-

dice among the shades of the underworld—or, evoking pathos (or bathos) of another order, the Comtesse de Monteriender's comparison of the music's power to the mysteries of table-turning. The latter incident exemplifies another characteristic of Proust's prose: its corrosive humor, its scathing satirical portrayals of a vast range of ludicrous and pitiable human types, from the witless would-be wit Dr. Cottard to that anti-Semitic snob, the Marquise de Gallardon, inconsolable because her younger cousin the Duchesse de Guermantes will not have her as a guest in her home despite the family tie that is at once the marquise's greatest pride and greatest shame.

Translating this adaptation of *Swann's Way* presents challenges similar to the challenge of adapting it in the first place. Speech that is reported in the text as free indirect discourse is here put in the mouths of the characters themselves and represented as speech by being enclosed, as in a comic strip, in "balloons." Of course Proust also reports some of his characters' speeches directly in the text, so not all the lines in the balloons are transformations of the author's original words. Another change from the original is the truncation of some very long sentences, which, if they had been presented in their entirety, might call for a different translation, since rhythm is an important aspect of any prose style, and the rhythm of a sentence is necessarily affected by abbreviation. In other places sentences are telescoped to adapt to the visual representation of the text, or, conversely, lengthy passages are broken down into shorter phrases and distributed over many frames. Such passages might well be translated somewhat differently if set in their original context.

Nevertheless, the fidelity of the adaptation to Proust's own language is remarkable. To be sure, there is a good deal less of that language than some Proustians might like. Readers who know Proust may find that some of their favorite passages have disappeared, that some of the finest images have had to be sacrificed, or that the pacing of the narrative is not as they remember it. Those discovering Proust for the first time should therefore bear in mind that this book is not *Swann's Way* as Proust wrote it. But both Stéphane Heuet and I have tried to preserve the "flavor" of Proust—or, as they say in Combray, his "fragrance"—as *un ménu de dégustation*, or tasting menu, tries to give a full sampling of the dishes in the repertoire of a great chef. Those who find the taste to their liking will want to return often to savor fuller portions.

Finally, a word about existing English translations of Proust. I have looked at all of them but haven't "followed" any of them, except insofar as any two translations of the same text will inevitably overlap here and there. Still, there is remarkable "entropy" in language, in the sense that the various elements of style—meaning, rhythm, register, diction, connotation, imagery, and so on—can be ordered in more than one way. Each possible arrangement of words on the page has its good qualities and its flaws. As the writer Marguerite Yourcenar once said, translation is like packing a bag: you can't always get in everything you want or need to get in. Different translators will have different ideas about what is essential to bring along and what can safely (or silently) be left out.

I hope I've packed enough to make your journey comfortable and haven't left out anything necessary to your enjoyment. In my own case, my love of Proust, which first blossomed some forty-five years ago, was a major reason for wanting to perfect my French, and I have returned again and again to the places where my love first revealed itself, much as the narrator Marcel is obsessed with the places associated with the most powerful emotions he has experienced. Inevitably, "working on" Proust has proved to be a very different experience from simply enjoying him or even studying him or writing about him. I've had to contemplate not just the effect of his words but how they produce their effect and how the devices he uses might best be carried over into English. But following my path back and forth among the sentences of *Swann's Way* is surely less interesting to the reader than following the narrator's path back and forth among the hawthorns of Combray or between his home in Paris and the park in the Champs-Elysées where Gilberte gives him as a souvenir an agate marble the color of her eyes. It is therefore time to end this introduction and invite you to proceed directly to the text and the art that Stéphane Heuet has created to accompany it.

[A glossary at the end of the text explains some references that may be unfamiliar to contemporary readers. There is also a map of Paris indicating some of the places that figure in the narrative.]

—Arthur Goldhammer

In Search of Lost Time

Swann's Way

COMBRAY

For a long time I went to bed early.

... and when I awoke in the middle of the night, not knowing where I was, at first I didn't even know who I was;

... but then memory (not yet of the place I was in but of several places I had lived and might now be) would come to me like help from on high and rescue me from nothingness ...

... my memory engaged ...

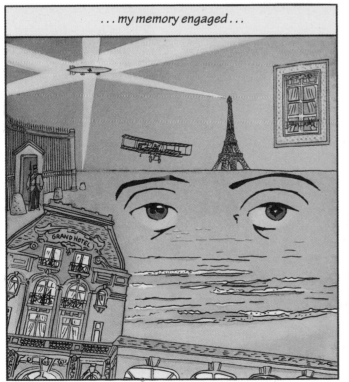

... I would spend most of the night remembering our former life in Combray at my great-aunt's house, in Balbec, in Paris, in Doncières, in Venice, and other places ...

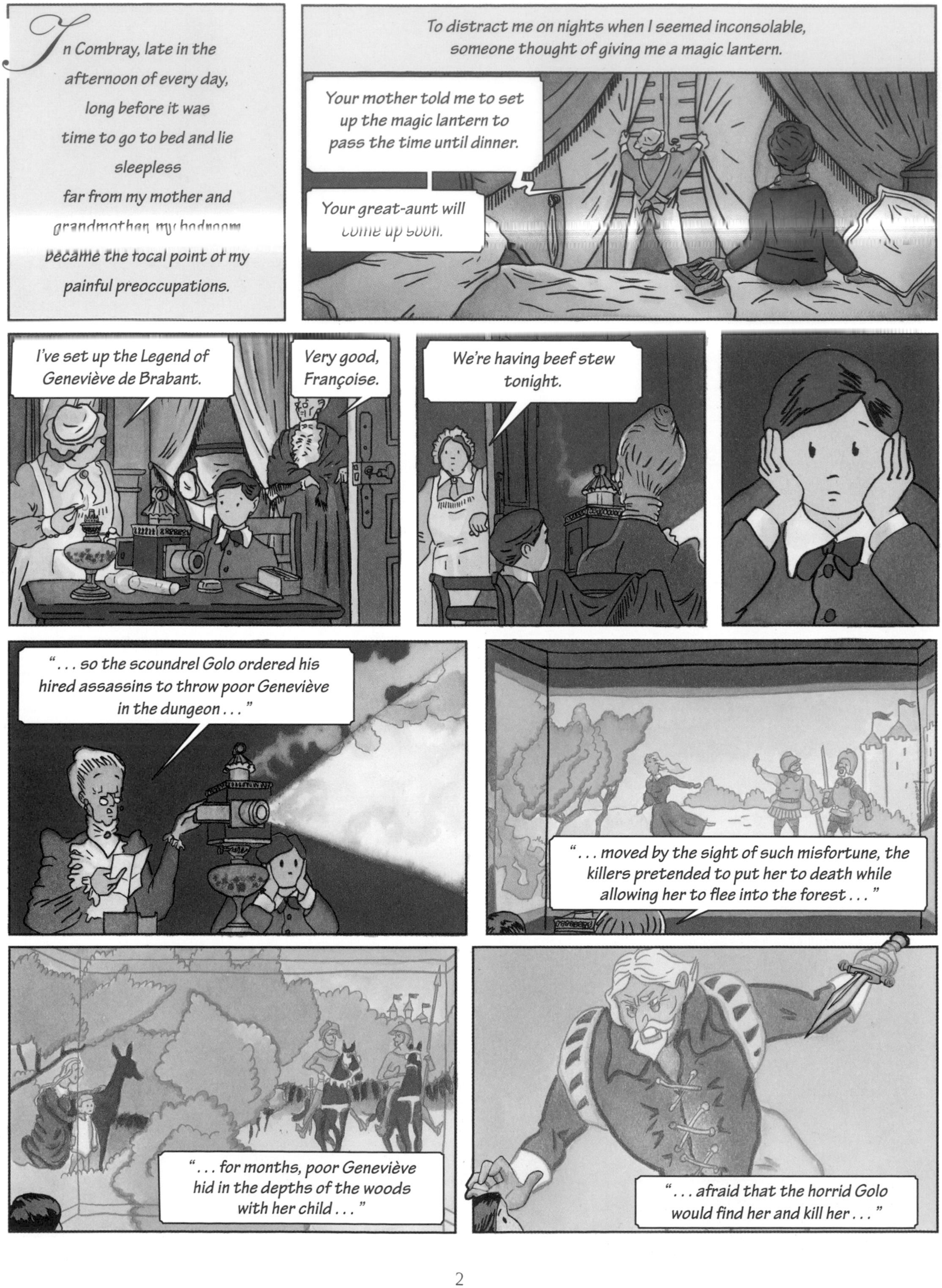
In Combray, late in the afternoon of every day, long before it was time to go to bed and lie sleepless far from my mother and grandmother, my bedroom became the focal point of my painful preoccupations.
To distract me on nights when I seemed inconsolable, someone thought of giving me a magic lantern.
Your mother told me to set up the magic lantern to pass the time until dinner.
Your great-aunt will come up soon.
I've set up the Legend of Geneviève de Brabant.
Very good, Françoise.
We're having beef stew tonight.
". . . so the scoundrel Golo ordered his hired assassins to throw poor Geneviève in the dungeon . . ."
". . . moved by the sight of such misfortune, the killers pretended to put her to death while allowing her to flee into the forest . . ."
". . . for months, poor Geneviève hid in the depths of the woods with her child . . ."
". . . afraid that the horrid Golo would find her and kill her . . ."

DING DING DING

"Dinner is served!"

After dinner, alas, I was soon required to leave Mama to chat with the others, in the garden if the weather was nice or in the small salon to which the company retired if it wasn't.

Ah, it's raining.

Françoise, please serve the liqueurs in the small salon.

Everyone except my grandmother, who, no matter what the weather, even if it was raining hard, would go for a walk on the soggy paths.

It's a pity to shut oneself indoors in the country. At last I can breathe!

When she took these turns about the garden after dinner, only one thing could compel her to come back in.

To tease her, my great-aunt would offer a few drops of liqueur to my grandfather, who was forbidden to drink spirits.

Here, Amédée, have some.

Bathilde! Come stop your husband from drinking cognac!

Alas! Little did I know that what worried my grandmother on these perambulations, far more than her husband's dietary indiscretions, was my weak will, delicate health, and the consequent uncertainty about my future.

3

My only consolation when I went up to my room was the thought that, once I was in bed, Mama would come give me a kiss.

But that good night would be over so quickly . . . I began to hope that it would be delayed as long as possible, to prolong the time of respite during which Mama had not yet appeared.

But the nights when Mama stayed in my room only briefly . . .

. . . were still sweet compared with those when company came to dinner and she did not come up to kiss me good night at all.

Usually the company was limited to our neighbor Monsieur Swann, who, other than a few occasional guests, was almost the only person who came to visit, sometimes for dinner (though more rarely after he made that bad marriage, because my parents did not wish to receive his wife), sometimes after dinner, on the spur of the moment . . .

DING DING

A visitor? Who might that be?

Stop whispering. Nothing is more unpleasant for a visitor than to hear whispering.

SLING

I recognize Swann's voice.

M. Swann, though much younger, was very attached to my grandfather, who had been one of his father's closest friends.

For many years, especially before his marriage, during which the younger M. Swann visited us often in Combray, . . .

. . . my great-aunt and grandparents never suspected that they were receiving one of the most elegant members of the Jockey Club, . . .

. . . a close friend of the Comte de Paris and the Prince of Wales, . . .

. . . one of the most sought-after members of the high society of the Faubourg Saint-Germain.

If the conversation happened to turn to the princes of the House of France:

. . . people you and I will never know,

and we can do without them, can't we?

So my great-aunt took a haughty tone with him . . . handling this elsewhere much sought-after guest with the naïve clumsiness of a child who plays with a collector's item as carelessly as if it were a cheap toy.

Our social personalities are the creations of other people's minds. We invest the physical appearance of the person we see with all the notions we have formed about him. . . .

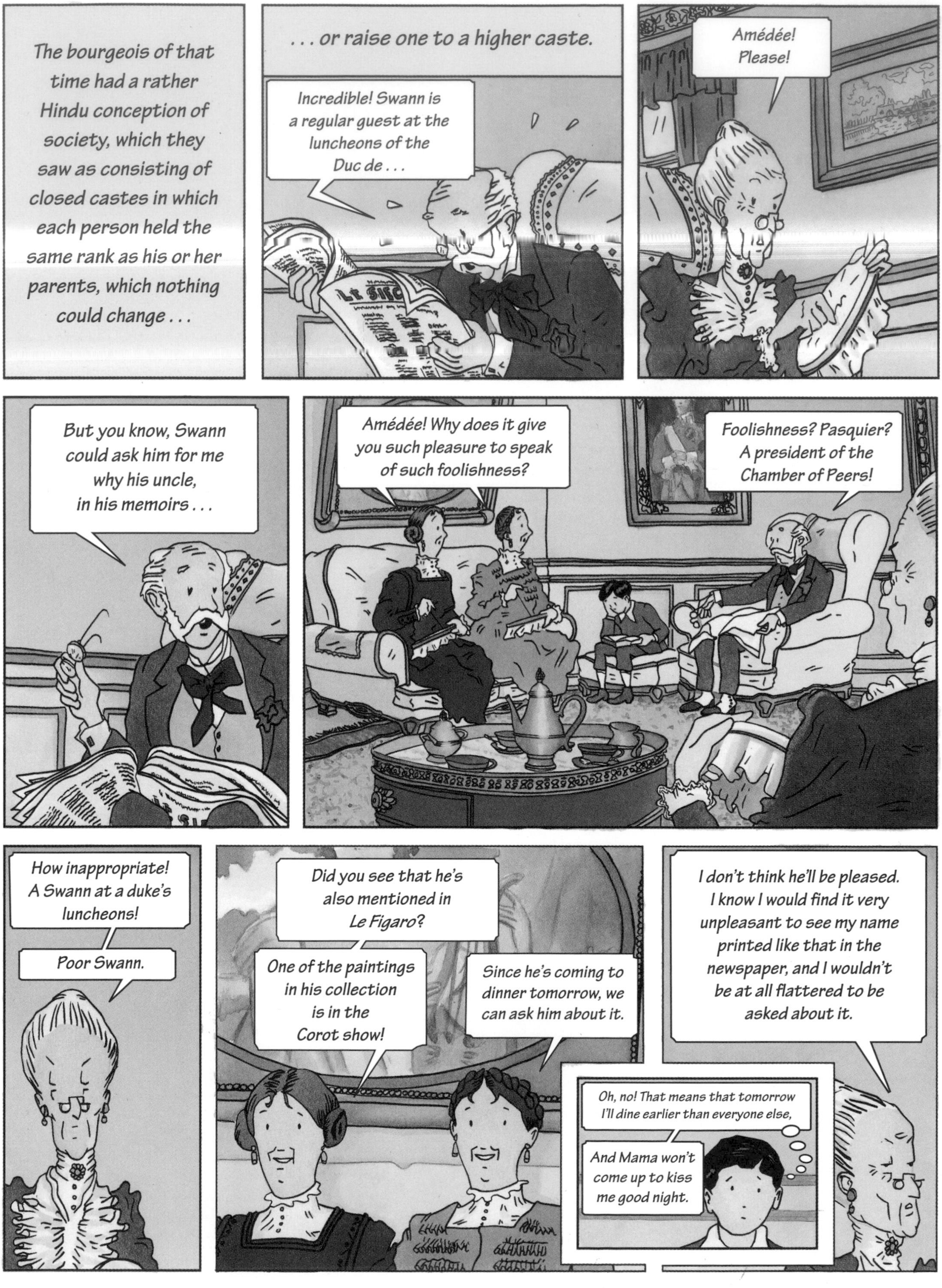
The bourgeois of that time had a rather Hindu conception of society, which they saw as consisting of closed castes in which each person held the same rank as his or her parents, which nothing could change . . .
. . . or raise one to a higher caste.
Incredible! Swann is a regular guest at the luncheons of the Duc de . . .
Amédée! Please!
But you know, Swann could ask him for me why his uncle, in his memoirs . . .
Amédée! Why does it give you such pleasure to speak of such foolishness?
Foolishness? Pasquier? A president of the Chamber of Peers!
How inappropriate! A Swann at a duke's luncheons!
Poor Swann.
Did you see that he's also mentioned in Le Figaro?
One of the paintings in his collection is in the Corot show!
Since he's coming to dinner tomorrow, we can ask him about it.
I don't think he'll be pleased. I know I would find it very unpleasant to see my name printed like that in the newspaper, and I wouldn't be at all flattered to be asked about it.
Oh, no! That means that tomorrow I'll dine earlier than everyone else,
And Mama won't come up to kiss me good night.

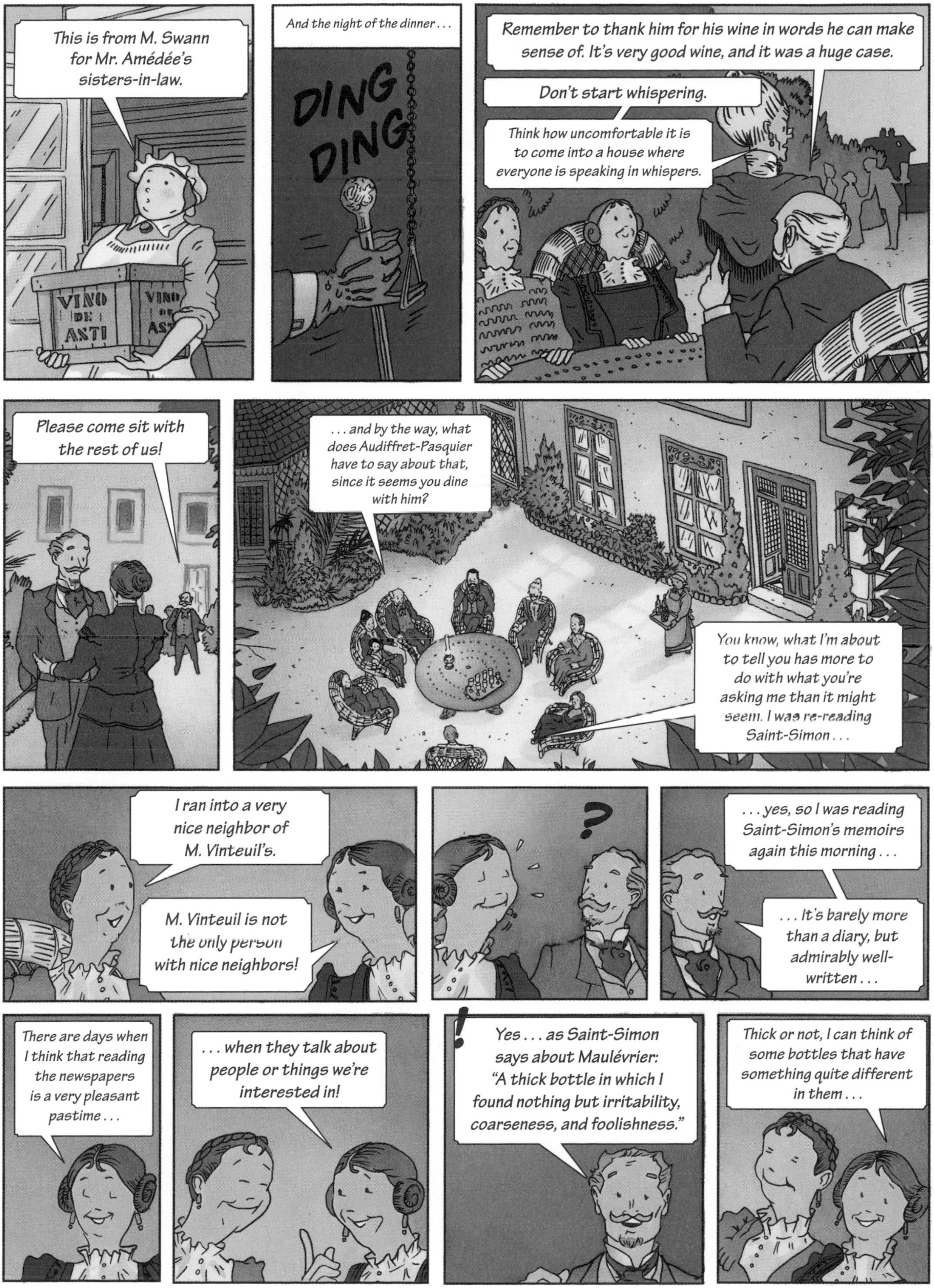
This is from M. Swann for Mr. Amédée's sisters-in-law.
VINO DE ASTI
And the night of the dinner . . .
DING DING
Remember to thank him for his wine in words he can make sense of. It's very good wine, and it was a huge case.
Don't start whispering.
Think how uncomfortable it is to come into a house where everyone is speaking in whispers.
Please come sit with the rest of us!
. . . and by the way, what does Audiffret-Pasquier have to say about that, since it seems you dine with him?
You know, what I'm about to tell you has more to do with what you're asking me than it might seem. I was re-reading Saint-Simon . . .
I ran into a very nice neighbor of M. Vinteuil's.
M. Vinteuil is not the only person with nice neighbors!
?
. . . yes, so I was reading Saint-Simon's memoirs again this morning . . .
. . . It's barely more than a diary, but admirably well-written . . .
There are days when I think that reading the newspapers is a very pleasant pastime . . .
. . . when they talk about people or things we're interested in!
!
Yes . . . as Saint-Simon says about Maulévrier: "A thick bottle in which I found nothing but irritability, coarseness, and foolishness."
Thick or not, I can think of some bottles that have something quite different in them . . .

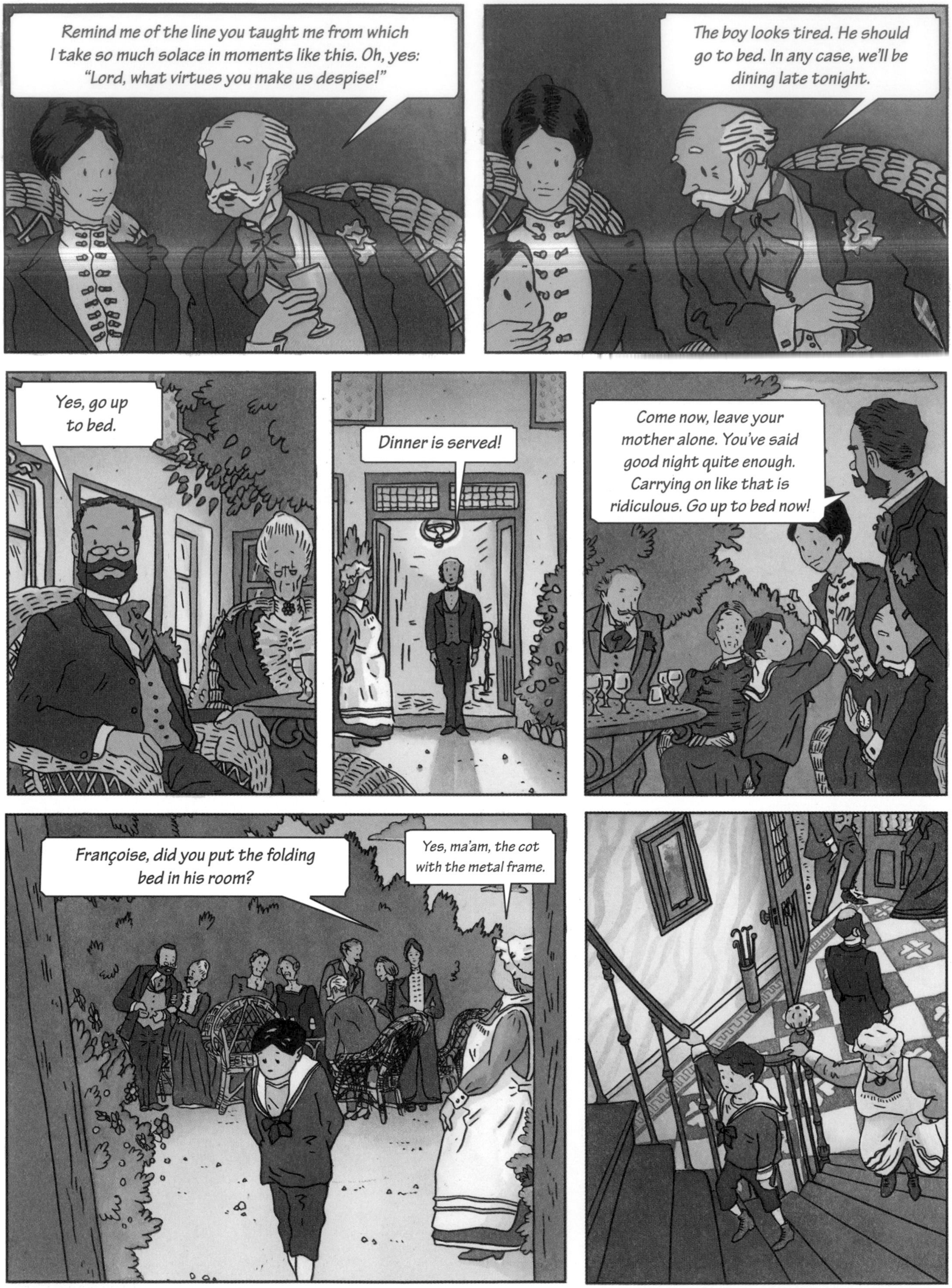
Remind me of the line you taught me from which I take so much solace in moments like this. Oh, yes: "Lord, what virtues you make us despise!"
The boy looks tired. He should go to bed. In any case, we'll be dining late tonight.
Yes, go up to bed.
Dinner is served!
Come now, leave your mother alone. You've said good night quite enough. Carrying on like that is ridiculous. Go up to bed now!
Françoise, did you put the folding bed in his room?
Yes, ma'am, the cot with the metal frame.

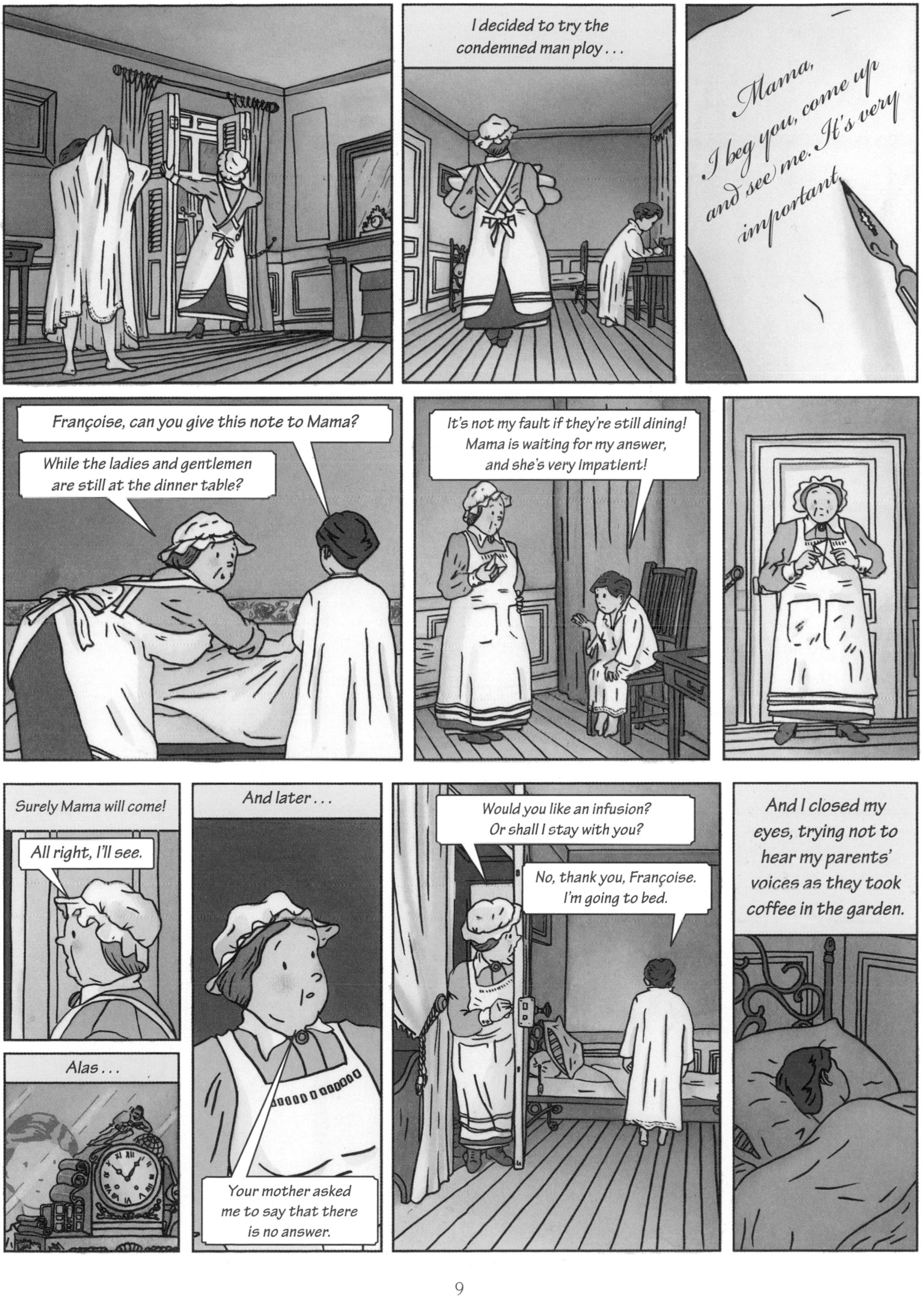

I decided to try the condemned man ploy . . .
Mama, I beg you, come up and see me. It's very important.
Françoise, can you give this note to Mama?
While the ladies and gentlemen are still at the dinner table?
It's not my fault if they're still dining! Mama is waiting for my answer, and she's very impatient!
Surely Mama will come!
All right, I'll see.
Alas . . .
And later . . .
Your mother asked me to say that there is no answer.
Would you like an infusion? Or shall I stay with you?
No, thank you, Françoise. I'm going to bed.
And I closed my eyes, trying not to hear my parents' voices as they took coffee in the garden.

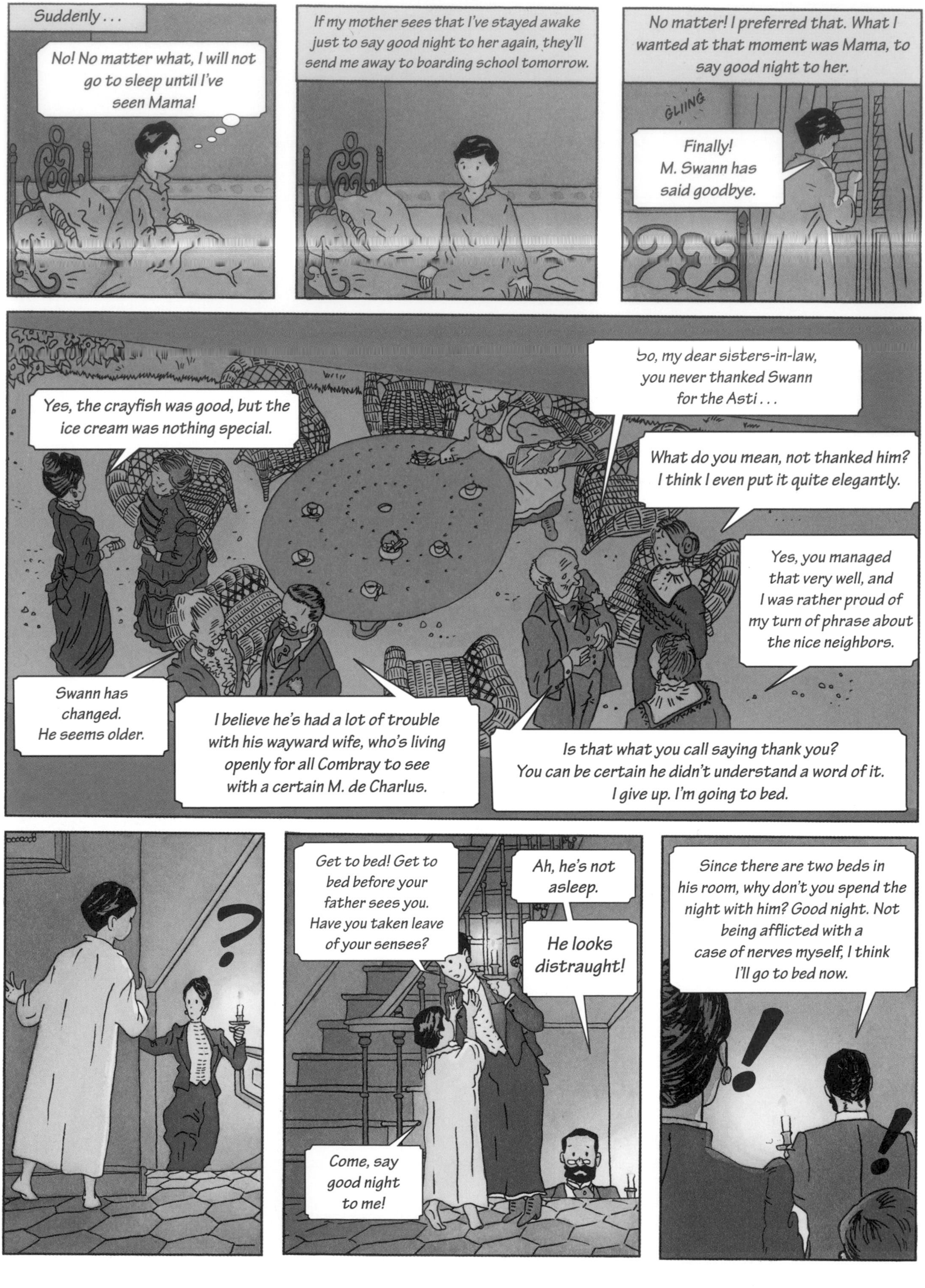
Suddenly . . .
No! No matter what, I will not go to sleep until I've seen Mama!
If my mother sees that I've stayed awake just to say good night to her again, they'll send me away to boarding school tomorrow.
No matter! I preferred that. What I wanted at that moment was Mama, to say good night to her.
GLIING
Finally! M. Swann has said goodbye.
Yes, the crayfish was good, but the ice cream was nothing special.
So, my dear sisters-in-law, you never thanked Swann for the Asti . . .
What do you mean, not thanked him? I think I even put it quite elegantly.
Yes, you managed that very well, and I was rather proud of my turn of phrase about the nice neighbors.
Swann has changed. He seems older.
I believe he's had a lot of trouble with his wayward wife, who's living openly for all Combray to see with a certain M. de Charlus.
Is that what you call saying thank you? You can be certain he didn't understand a word of it. I give up. I'm going to bed.
?
Get to bed! Get to bed before your father sees you. Have you taken leave of your senses?
Ah, he's not asleep.
He looks distraught!
Come, say good night to me!
Since there are two beds in his room, why don't you spend the night with him? Good night. Not being afflicted with a case of nerves myself, I think I'll go to bed now.
!
!

Mama stayed in my room that night. I should have been happy, but I wasn't.

If I had just won a victory, it was over her. That evening, which opened a new era, would remain a dark date on the calendar.

So for a long time afterwards, whenever I awoke during the night and remembered Combray, I saw only a glowing slab of light amidst vague shadows.

As if Combray consisted only of two floors linked by a narrow staircase, and as if the clock was stuck at seven.

Concerning Combray, I had no wish to recall anything else or any other time. To me it was in reality all dead.

Dead forever? Possibly.

It Is wasted effort to try to remember the past. Intellectual effort alone is futile. The past is hidden beyond the ken of the intellect, in another realm, In some unsuspected material thing.

And whether or not we encounter that thing before we die depends on chance.

any years went by during which nothing of Combray existed for me apart from the drama of my bedtime, until . . .

12

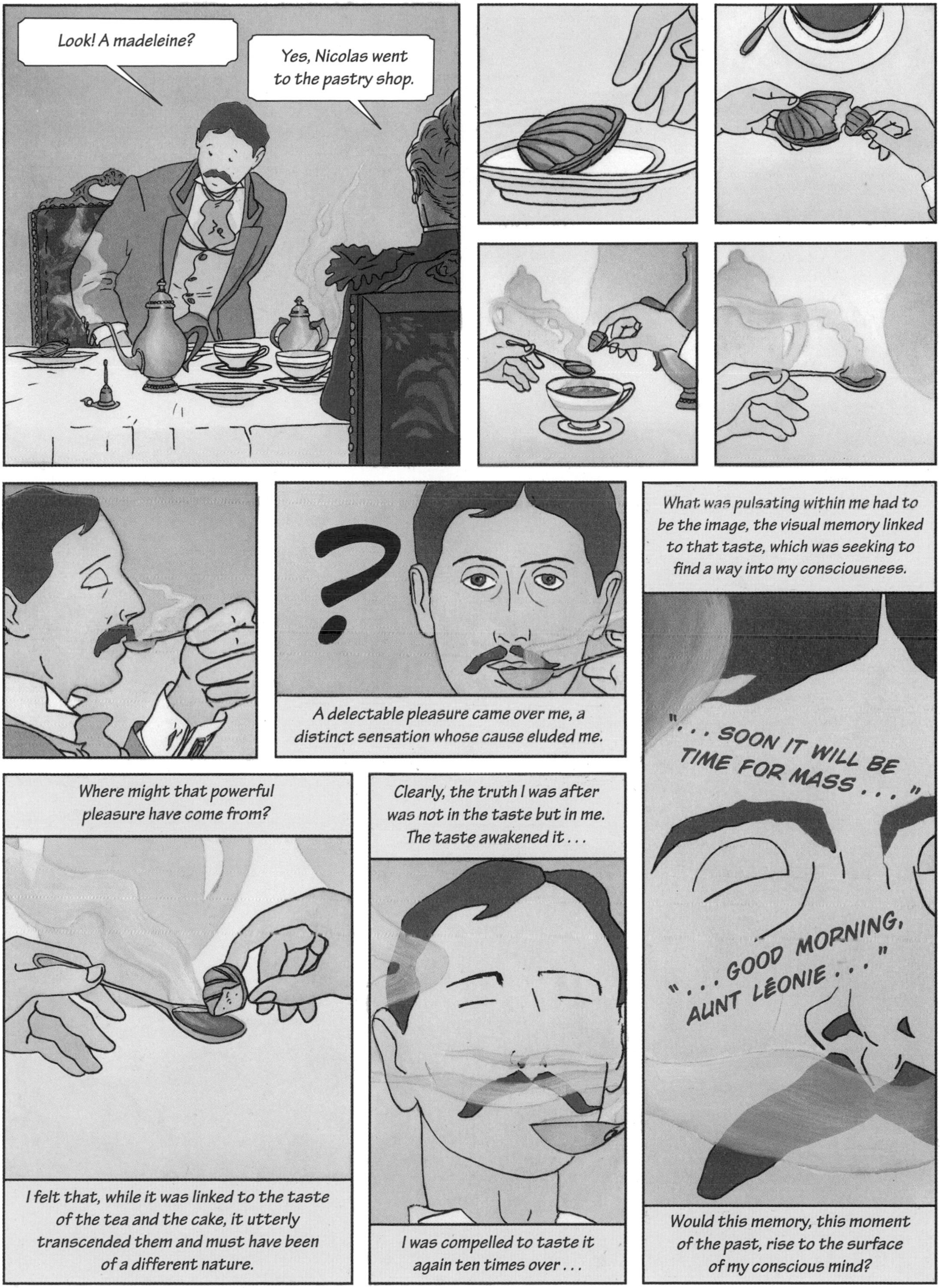

Look! A madeleine?
Yes, Nicolas went to the pastry shop.
A delectable pleasure came over me, a distinct sensation whose cause eluded me.
What was pulsating within me had to be the image, the visual memory linked to that taste, which was seeking to find a way into my consciousness.
". . . SOON IT WILL BE TIME FOR MASS . . ."
". . . GOOD MORNING, AUNT LÉONIE . . ."
Where might that powerful pleasure have come from?
I felt that, while it was linked to the taste of the tea and the cake, it utterly transcended them and must have been of a different nature.
Clearly, the truth I was after was not in the taste but in me. The taste awakened it . . .
I was compelled to taste it again ten times over . . .
Would this memory, this moment of the past, rise to the surface of my conscious mind?

The taste was that of the morsel of madeleine Aunt Léonie gave me every Sunday morning in Combray after dipping it in her tea or lime infusion.

GOOD MORNING, AUNT LÉONIE!

And just as the Japanese amuse themselves by taking a porcelain bowl full of water and dipping in it small, seemingly shapeless bits of paper, which, the moment they touch the water, expand, assume new shapes, take on color and variety, and turn into flowers, houses, or people, substantial and recognizable, so, now, did all the flowers of our garden and of Swann's estate and the water lilies of the Vivonne and the good people of the village and their little homes and the church and all of Combray and its surroundings take shape and solidity, a whole town and all its gardens emerging suddenly from my cup of tea.

To live in, Combray was a rather sad place, as were its streets: Rue Saint-Hilaire, Rue Saint-Jacques, where my aunt had her house . . .

Mama, I'm going up to kiss Aunt Léonie before mass.

My great-aunt, whose home we lived in, was the mother of my Aunt Léonie, who, since the death of her husband, my uncle Octave, had lost all desire to leave first Combray and then her house and after that her room . . .

You may go in now. Madame Octave is ready for you.

. . . and finally her bed, so that she no longer "came down" but remained in bed in a vague state of sorrow, physical debility, illness . . .

Here, have a bite of madeleine.

. . . obsessiveness, and devotion.

Go now and get ready for mass, my poor child. And if you see Françoise downstairs, tell her not to play with you for too long and to come up soon in case I need anything.

My aunt resigned herself to giving up a little of Françoise's company while we were there.

She had the street before her eyes and, to distract herself like a Persian prince from the tedium of life, would read in it from morning to night the immemorial chronicle of Combray, which she would later discuss with Françoise.

Françoise, Mme Goupil was so late for mass that I wouldn't be surprised if she arrived after the Elevation.

Hmm! It wouldn't be surprising!

Françoise, Mme Imbert just went by with some asparagus twice the size of those you get from Mother Callot's. Since you've been serving us all sorts of asparagus dishes this year, ask her maid . . .

It wouldn't be surprising if they came from the curé's garden.

Ah, I'm sure you're right, Françoise, from the curé's garden! I swear those asparagus were as big around as a person's arm. Not your arm, to be sure, but my poor arm, which has shrunk even more this year.

Françoise, for whom were they ringing the funeral bells? Oh, good heavens, it must have been for Mme Rousseau, who passed away just the other night. It's time for the good Lord to take me, my mind is gone. But I'm wasting your time, my dear.

Not at all, Mme Octave, my time is not that dear. He who made it didn't sell it for a profit.

16

Sometimes these events took on such a grave and mysterious character that my aunt . . .

DING DING DING DING

But Mme Octave, it's not yet time for your pepsin. Were you feeling faint?

Why no, Françoise . . . or I mean yes . . . Would you believe that I just saw Mme Goupil with a little girl I didn't recognize . . .

It must have been Monsieur Pupin's daughter.

Why yes, of course! But still, I wouldn't have recognized her!

But I'm not talking about the elder child, Mme Octave, I mean the little one, who was in boarding school at Jouy. I do believe I saw her earlier this morning.

Oh, yes, of course. She's probably home for Easter vacation. That's it!

Poor Françoise, I made you come up for nothing.

But my aunt knew that it was not for nothing . . . Because in Combray, a person "one didn't recognize" was as incredible a sight as a mythical god would have been. One knew every creature in Combray, animals as well as people, so well that if my aunt had by chance seen a dog "she didn't recognize," she would have been unable to stop thinking about it . . .

That would be Madame Sazerat's dog . . .

As if I wouldn't recognize Madame Sazerat's dog!

Ah! It must have been Monsieur Galopin's dog.

Oh, that must be it.

It's apparently a very friendly animal.

Mme Octave, I must be going, my oven is not even lit, and I still have to peel the asparagus.

What's that, Françoise? Asparagus again!

But you've plagued us with asparagus all year! Our Parisians will have tired of it!

Not at all, Mme Octave, they love asparagus. You'll see how they'll gobble it all up when they get back from church.

The church.

How I loved our church, and how clearly I see it now!

...I entered the church and advanced toward our seats as a peasant in a valley inhabited by fairies is amazed to see...

...palpable traces of their supernatural passage in a rock, a tree, or a pond.

For me, all these things made the church entirely different from the rest of the town: it was, you might say, an edifice that occupied a four-dimensional space, the fourth dimension being Time, a vessel plying the centuries, with bay after bay, chapel after chapel, seeming to vanquish and traverse not only a few yards of space but one era after another, ultimately emerging victorious.

DONG

DONG DONG

DONG DONG DONG

The steeple of Saint-Hilaire shaped, crowned, and consecrated every occupation in the town, every hour of the day, every view.

In some mysterious way, my grandmother found in that steeple what she valued most in the world, an air of naturalness and distinction.

Children, make fun of me if you will, it may not be beautiful according to the rules . . .

. . . but its queer old look pleases me. If it played the piano, its playing wouldn't be dry.

And still today . . .

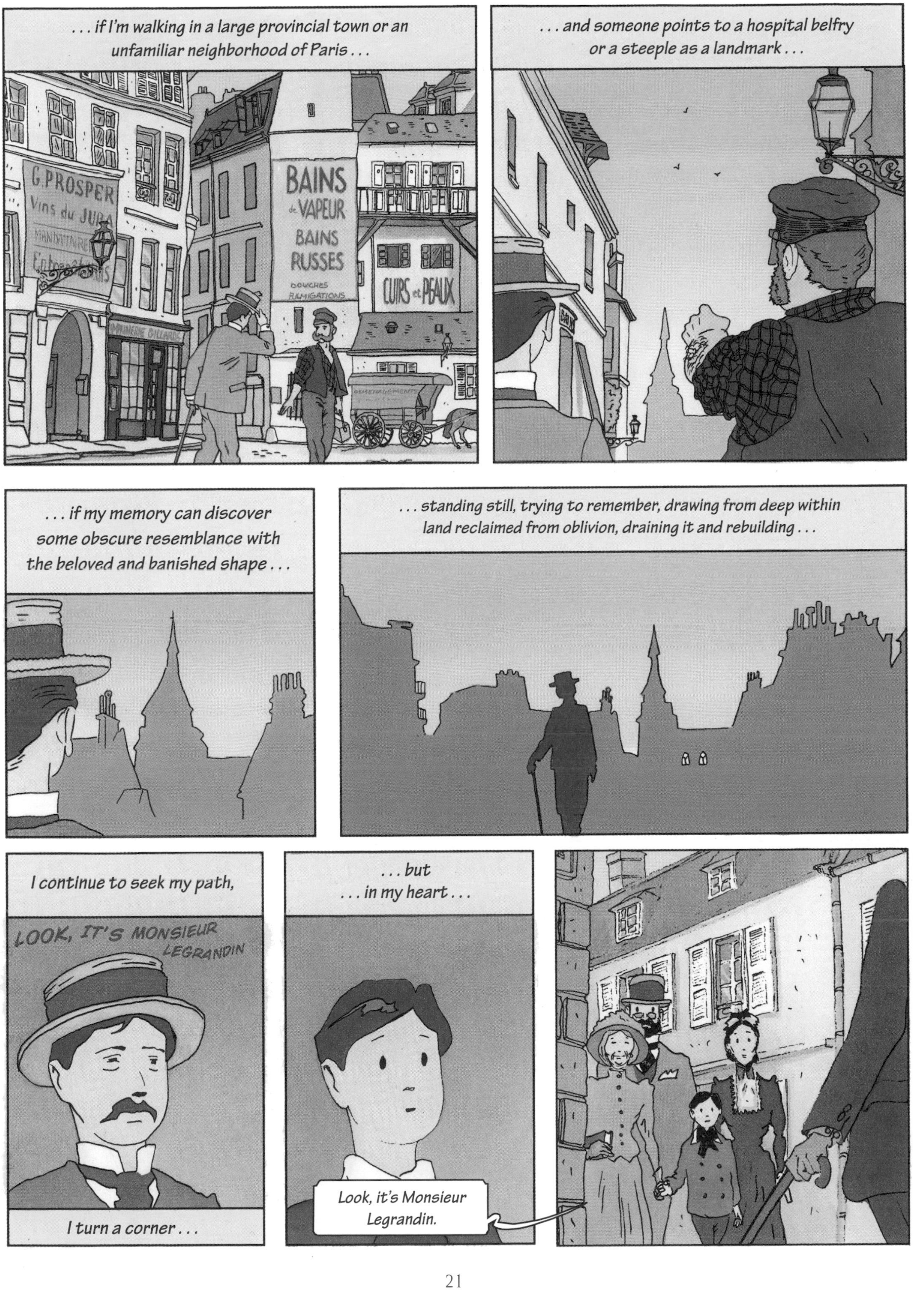
. . . if I'm walking in a large provincial town or an unfamiliar neighborhood of Paris . . .
G.PROSPER Vins du JURA
BAINS de VAPEUR BAINS RUSSES
DOUCHES FUMIGATIONS
CUIRS et PEAUX
. . . and someone points to a hospital belfry or a steeple as a landmark . . .
. . . if my memory can discover some obscure resemblance with the beloved and banished shape . . .
. . . standing still, trying to remember, drawing from deep within land reclaimed from oblivion, draining it and rebuilding . . .
I continue to seek my path,
LOOK, IT'S MONSIEUR LEGRANDIN
I turn a corner . . .
. . . but . . . in my heart . . .
Look, it's Monsieur Legrandin.

Monsieur Legrandin, tied to Paris by his profession of engineer, could, outside of long vacations, visit his property in Combray only from Saturday night to Monday morning.

He was one of those men who, quite apart from achieving brilliant success in a scientific career, also possess a totally different literary and artistic culture that goes unused in their professional specialty but from which their conversation benefits.

Hello, friends!

...tomorrow I must return to my nest in Paris.

The only thing missing there is what's necessary: a great slice of sky such as one finds here.

My grandmother criticized him for one thing only: speaking too well, a little too much like a book.

She was also taken aback by the angry tirades he often unleashed against the aristocracy, high society, and snobbery...

...Surely what Saint Paul had in mind when he spoke of the sin for which there is no remission.

She thought it not in very good taste, moreover, that Monsieur Legrandin, whose sister had been married near Balbec to a nobleman of Lower Normandy, indulged in quite violent attacks on the nobility.

...the Revolution should have guillotined them all!

Try always to keep a patch of open sky over your head, my boy!

Mme Octave wants you in her room, Madame.

Yes, Françoise, we're going up now.

You have a soul of rare quality, an artistic nature. Don't deprive it of what it needs.

So, tell me about mass. Mme Goupil must have arrived quite late!

That I cannot tell you, Léonie.

Did you know that an artist has been painting in the church?

A painter? How can that be? Tell me more.

All we could see was that he was at work copying the window of Gilbert the Bad.

Oh! I wish it were time for Eulalie's visit.

She's really the only one who can tell me what I want to know.

Eulalie was a spinster, deaf and lame but still active, who had "retired" after the death of Mme de la Bretonnerie, for whom she had worked . . .

. . . since childhood, whereupon she had taken a room next to the church from which she emerged frequently to attend services, say a short prayer, or lend a hand to Théodore.

The rest of the time she visited the sick . . .

Her visits were my aunt Léonie's main distraction, since, except for the curé, she had driven out all other visitors, including both those who advised her not to take herself so seriously and recommended a short walk in the sun and a nice rare steak . . .

. . . and those who evidently believed she was as sick as she said she was.

. . . when two nasty swallows of Vichy sit in my stomach for fourteen hours!

. . . Ah! When your health is gone! But people in your condition live a good long while.

. . . such as my aunt, to whom she recounted everything that happened at mass or vespers.

In short, my aunt insisted that you approve her diet, pity her suffering, and reassure her about the future.

Eulalie excelled at this

The end has come, my poor Eulalie.

Knowing your illness as well as you do, Mme Octave, I know you'll live to be 100, as Mme Sazerin was saying to me just the other day.

Sazerat, Eulalie, Sazerat.

Her regular Sunday visits were such a pleasure for my aunt that the prospect of Eulalie's arrival kept her in an agreeable mood.

It's Sunday. Eulalie won't be long.

But if the wait went on too long, the pleasure of expectation turned into torture...

Eleven o'clock and Eulalie isn't here yet!

On Sundays she thought of nothing but Eulalie's visit.

Mme Octave rang?

Françoise, I think... I feel faint... uh... still no Eulalie?

And as soon as lunch was over, Françoise was impatient for us to leave the dining room so that she could go up to "occupy" my aunt.

But (especially when the weather was nice) we were often still at the lunch table long after the proud hour of noon had struck...

Lord, I can't take it anymore. We've been at the table for two hours! And this heat...

24

Our menu somehow reflected the rhythm of the seasons and the vagaries of life, because in addition to the permanent fare of eggs, cutlets, potatoes, jams, and biscuits, which she no longer even bothered to announce, Françoise added the bounties of field and orchard and sea, the whims of the market, the kindness of the neighbors, and her own genius.

The fishmonger promised that this fish was really fresh!

I found this beautiful chicken at the Roussainville market . . .

The country air gives you an appetite, no?

I've never made you cardoons in marrow before . . .

At this time of year, these are still rare, you know!

Some spinach for a change . . .

M. Swann came by on purpose to give us these raspberries . . .

Two more weeks and there will be no more red currants.

It's our turn to give.

The child is fond of this . . .

And you thought the cherry tree had stopped producing after two years!

I ordered it yesterday.

And to top it all off, especially for Madame's husband . . .

Now, you don't have to sit here all afternoon. Go up to your room if it's too hot outside, but first get a little fresh air instead of going directly to your book after eating.

CRÈME AU CHOCOLAT!

You can eat it even if you're not hungry.

In earlier years, before going upstairs to read, I used to go to the sitting room . . .

. . . that my Uncle Adolphe, one of my grandfather's brothers, a retired major, occupied on the first floor, which invariably gave off the kind of dark, cool fragrance, redolent of both the woods and the Ancien Régime, that fills the nostrils when you enter a certain type of abandoned hunting lodge.

But I had not entered Uncle Adolphe's room for many years, since he no longer came to Combray on account of a quarrel between him and my family of which I was the cause, for the following reason:

In Paris, once or twice a month, I was sent off after lunch to call on my uncle.

You haven't been here for quite a while! They've truly given me up. Here, my boy, have a tangerine or some marzipan.

I'll take my coffee in the study.

Yes, major.

We sat together until:

Major, the coachman asks when he should hitch up the carriage.

. . .

2:15.

2:15? Very well, I'll tell him . . .

The answer was invariably and infallibly "2:15."

In those days I adored the theater, although I'd never been to a play.

All my conversations with my friends were about actors: Got, Delaunay, Febvre, Thiron, Maubant, and Coquelin . . .

Yet while actors filled my mind, the sight of a woman I believed to be an actress threw me into even greater disarray.

I ranked the most illustrious in order of talent: Sarah Bernhardt, Berma, Bartet, Madeleine Brohan, Jeanne Samary. My uncle knew many of them . . .

. . . as well as tarts, whom I didn't always distinguish clearly from actresses.

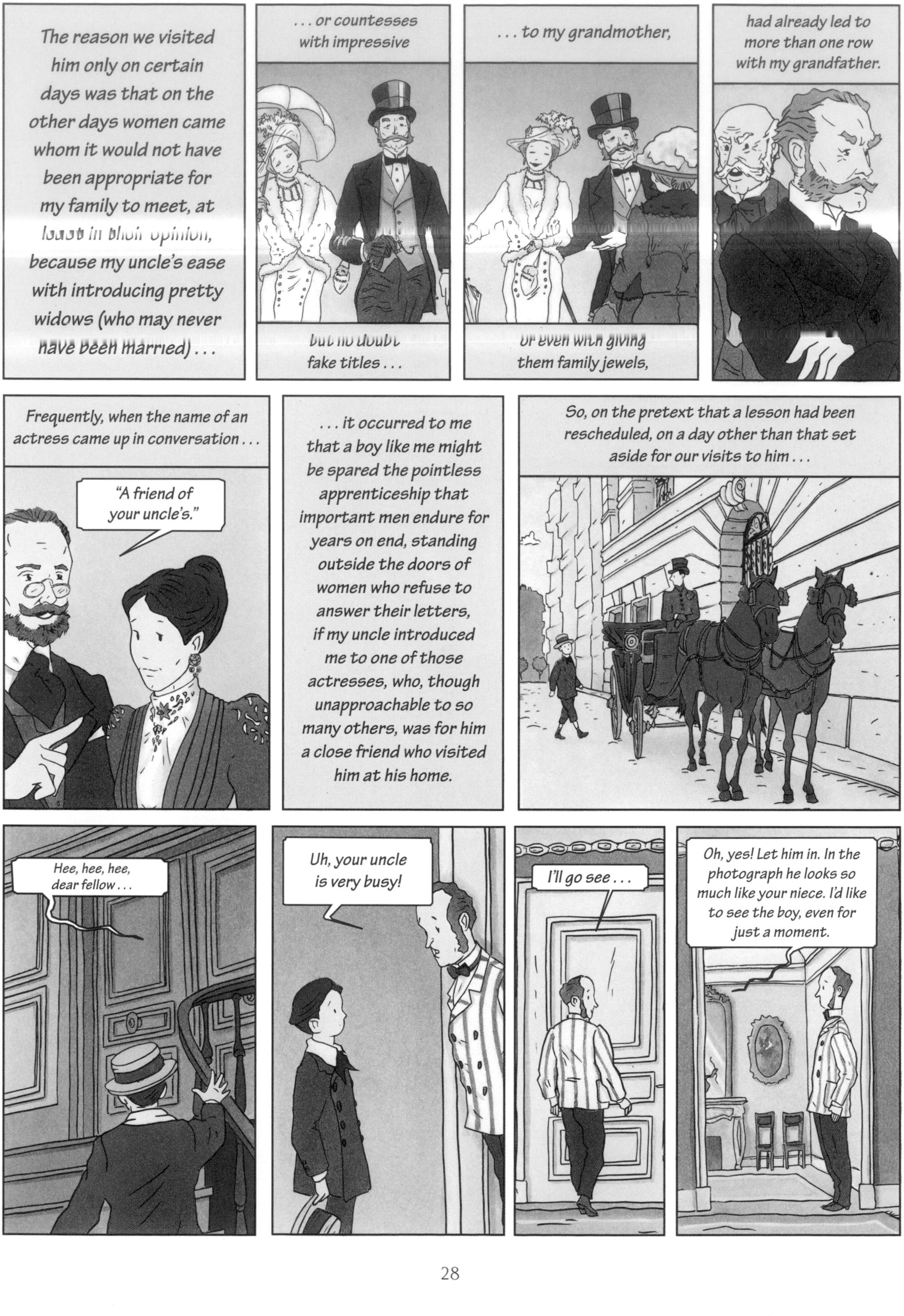
The reason we visited him only on certain days was that on the other days women came whom it would not have been appropriate for my family to meet, at least in their opinion, because my uncle's ease with introducing pretty widows (who may never have been married) . . .
. . . or countesses with impressive
but no doubt fake titles . . .
. . . to my grandmother,
or even with giving them family jewels,
had already led to more than one row with my grandfather.
Frequently, when the name of an actress came up in conversation . . .
"A friend of your uncle's."
. . . it occurred to me that a boy like me might be spared the pointless apprenticeship that important men endure for years on end, standing outside the doors of women who refuse to answer their letters, if my uncle introduced me to one of those actresses, who, though unapproachable to so many others, was for him a close friend who visited him at his home.
So, on the pretext that a lesson had been rescheduled, on a day other than that set aside for our visits to him . . .
Hee, hee, hee, dear fellow . . .
Uh, your uncle is very busy!
I'll go see . . .
Oh, yes! Let him in. In the photograph he looks so much like your niece. I'd like to see the boy, even for just a moment.

My nephew.

He looks just like his mother!

But you've never seen my niece except in a photograph . . .

I beg your pardon, my dear fellow, but I crossed paths with her on the staircase last year when you were so ill.

He looks more like his father. He's the spitting image of his father, and of my poor mother as well.

I don't know his father, and I never knew your poor mother, my friend.

I felt a slight disappointment. She had none of the theatrical look I admired in photographs of actresses nor any trace of the diabolical expression appropriate to the life she must lead. I had difficulty believing she was a tart, and I wouldn't have believed she was a fashionable prostitute if I hadn't seen the two-horse carriage, the pink gown, and the pearl necklace . . .

. . . and hadn't known that my uncle frequented only the best of that class of women.

No, dear, you know I'm used to the ones the Grand Duke sends me. I told him you were jealous.

Why, yes, I must have met this young man's father in your apartment. Isn't he your nephew? How could I have forgotten? He was so nice, so exquisite to me.

She had taken some insignificant remark of my father's and delicately transformed it . . . into an artistic jewel, something "exquisite."

Later it occurred to me that one of the touching aspects of the role of these idle, attentive women was the way they used their generosity and talent, their image of approachable, sensual beauty, and their gold, which costs them very little, to create a precious and refined setting for the rough, unpolished lives of certain men.

Come now, it's time for you to go.

My God, how dearly I would love to kiss her hand.

Should I or shouldn't I?

What a nice boy! He's already a ladies' man. He has an eye for women . . .

He takes after his uncle. He will be a perfect gentleman!

Couldn't he come sometime for "a cup of tea," as our English neighbors say?

He would only have to send me a "blue" some morning . . .

No, it's impossible, he's very busy. He works a lot. He wins all the school prizes. Who knows? He may be a young Victor Hugo or another Vaulabelle, you know!

I love artists. No one else understands women.

. . . Artists and elite gentlemen like you.

Uh . . . listen, boy, it would be just as well if you didn't mention this visit to your parents. It would be of no interest to them.

Uncle Adolphe, you know, one day I'll find a way to repay you.

You're so kind, so very kind . . .

30

So powerful indeed was my memory of his kindness that two hours later I recounted the visit to my parents in the most minute detail. I had no intention of causing my uncle any difficulty by doing so. How could I have, since it was the last thing I wanted?

My father and grandfather had some rather heated words with him . . .

My parents unfortunately judged my uncle's actions according to principles entirely different from those I suggested to them.

I learned of this indirectly.

A few days later, when I encountered my uncle in the street . . . I felt a mixture of pain, gratitude, and remorse, which I would have liked to express to him. Given the immensity of my feelings, I felt that a tip of the hat would have been inadequate. I therefore resolved to refrain from such a paltry gesture and turned my head to avoid him

My uncle thought I was obeying my parents' orders and never forgave them.
He died many years later, and none of us ever saw him again.

That is why I no longer entered my uncle Adolphe's room, now closed.

I'm going to let the kitchen maid serve the coffee and bring up the hot water. I need to attend to Mme Octave.

The year we ate so much asparagus, the kitchen maid responsible for "cleaning" it was a poor, sickly thing who was already in a fairly advanced state of pregnancy when we arrived at Easter, and we were surprised that Françoise let her run so many errands and do so much work . . .

As M. Swann pointed out, the folds of her ample smocks were reminiscent of the cloaks worn by certain symbolic figures in Giotto's paintings.

What do you mean, Giotto's *Charity*?

She also looked a lot like those stout, manly virgins who personify the virtues in the Arena Chapel.

And I now see that those allegories of Virtue and Vice in the Padua chapel resembled her in yet another way:

Just as the girl's image was enhanced by the symbol she carried in her belly without seeming to grasp its meaning, while her face reflected none of its beauty and spirit, as if it were merely a heavy burden . . .

. . . so, too, did the stout woman portrayed under the label "Caritas" in the Arena embody that virtue without seeming to suspect it, without the slightest hint of charity in her vulgar, energetic face.

For a long time I took no pleasure from contemplating the Giotto figures that M. Swann had brought me: that uncharitable Charity, that Envy that resembled an illustration from a medical book, that Justice with the dull, narrow-minded look of certain pious, desiccated townswomen of Combray . . .

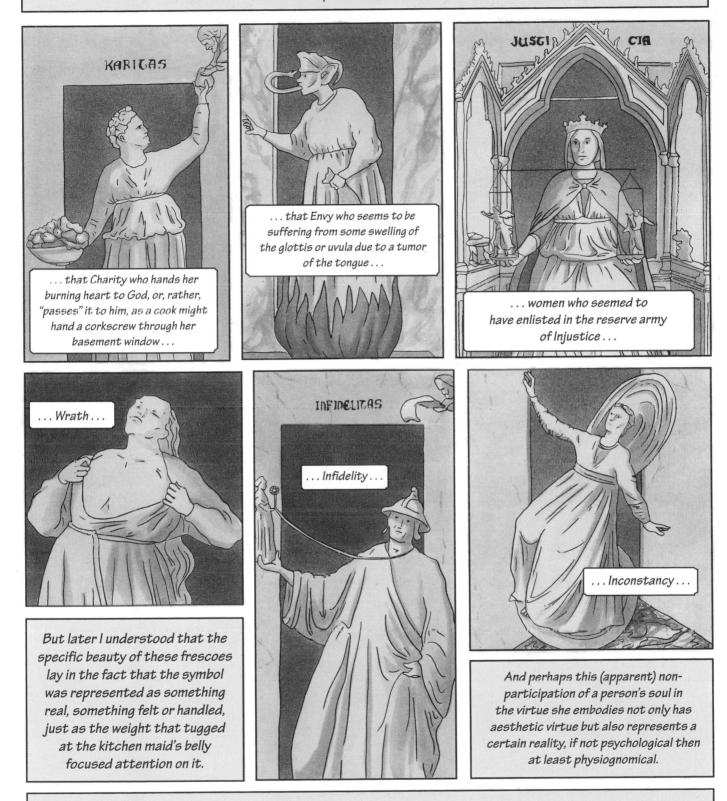

KARITAS

. . . that Charity who hands her burning heart to God, or, rather, "passes" it to him, as a cook might hand a corkscrew through her basement window . . .

. . . that Envy who seems to be suffering from some swelling of the glottis or uvula due to a tumor of the tongue . . .

JUSTI CIA

. . . women who seemed to have enlisted in the reserve army of Injustice . . .

. . . Wrath . . .

INFIDELITAS

. . . Infidelity . . .

. . . Inconstancy . . .

But later I understood that the specific beauty of these frescoes lay in the fact that the symbol was represented as something real, something felt or handled, just as the weight that tugged at the kitchen maid's belly focused attention on it.

And perhaps this (apparent) non-participation of a person's soul in the virtue she embodies not only has aesthetic virtue but also represents a certain reality, if not psychological then at least physiognomical.

When I later had occasion to encounter truly saintly incarnations of practical charity, they generally had the cheerful, positive, indifferent, and brusque look of a hurried surgeon, revealing no commiseration or tenderness toward human suffering and no fear of encountering it: this is the unsentimental, antipathetic, sublime face of true goodness.

Did you ask about the noise?

Yes, Camus, Françoise said you could go ahead, because Mme Octave is not resting.

I felt the splendor of the light only thanks to the blows struck in the Rue de la Cure . . . which resounded through the air on hot days and seemed to send scarlet stars flying in the distance . . .

. . . and also thanks to the flies, which performed their little concert of chamber music before my eyes.

The cool darkness of my room was to the broad daylight in the street what the shadow is to the sun's ray—just as luminous—and filled my imagination with the full spectacle of summer, which, if I had been walking outside, my senses would have been able to enjoy only piecemeal . . .

. . . and was thus well suited to my repose, which (thanks to the adventures recounted in my books) was subjected, like a hand at rest in a swiftly flowing stream, to the shock and animation of a torrent of activity.

Oh, you're still enjoying your reading! Come down and breathe the fresh air in the garden for a little while.

Unwilling to give up my reading, I would go and continue it in the garden, in a small canvas-hooded chair . . .

. . . in which I sat, thinking I was out of sight. . . . My thought was another hiding place in which I concealed myself, even when I remained attentive to what was happening outside.

What was deepest in me, the constantly moving core that governed all the rest, was my belief in the philosophical richness and beauty of the book I was reading, and my desire to appropriate it, no matter what the book. Even if it was a volume I had bought in Combray, I recognized it as a work whose remarkable qualities had been pointed out to me by the teacher or friend who at that moment seemed to me to possess the secret of truth and beauty.

On top of that were the emotions I derived from the action in which I took part, for those afternoons were more filled with dramatic events than many a lifetime . . .

. . . happiness and unhappiness that would never be revealed, no matter how intense, because it comes about so slowly that we cannot feel it.

Then I saw, as if projected in front of me, the scene in which the action unfolded. . . . And so it was that during two summers in the heat of the garden in Combray I longed, because of the book I was reading at the time, for a mountainous country traversed by numerous streams.

DONG...

DONG

Every hour it seemed to me that the previous hour had struck only moments before:

Sometimes, the premature bell even struck two more times than the preceding one.

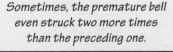

DONG...

DONG...

DONG...

DONG

So there was one I did not hear: something that had taken place did not take place for me.

As magical as a deep sleep, my reading was so interesting that it deceived my hallucinating ears . . .

Fine Sunday afternoons under the chestnut tree in the garden of Combray, which I diligently emptied of the mediocrity of my own existence and filled with a life of exotic adventures and aspirations in a land of raging rivers, you still evoke that life for me whenever I think of you . . .

There they are! There they are!

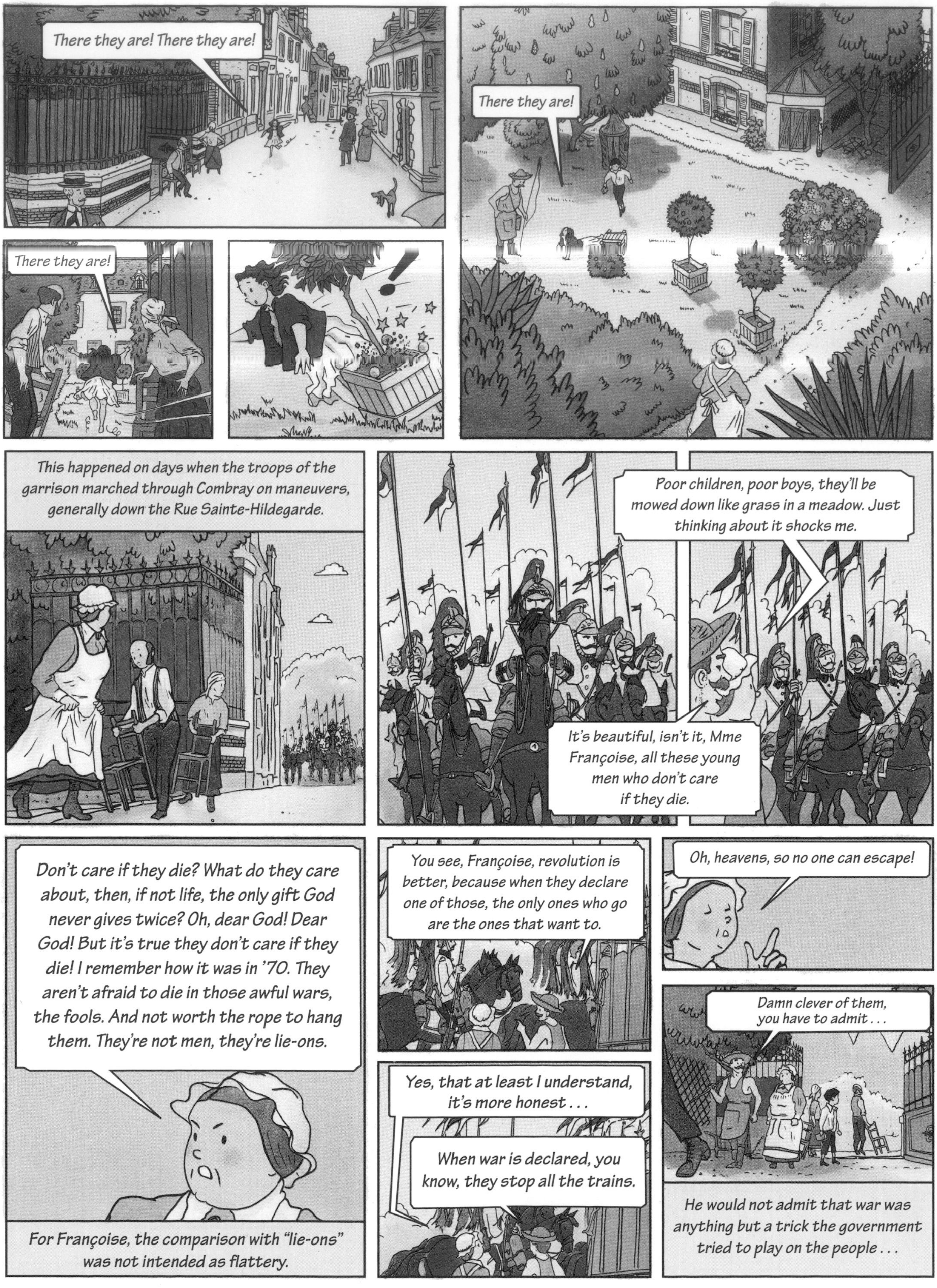
There they are! There they are!
There they are!
There they are!
This happened on days when the troops of the garrison marched through Combray on maneuvers, generally down the Rue Sainte-Hildegarde.
Poor children, poor boys, they'll be mowed down like grass in a meadow. Just thinking about it shocks me.
It's beautiful, isn't it, Mme Françoise, all these young men who don't care if they die.
Don't care if they die? What do they care about, then, if not life, the only gift God never gives twice? Oh, dear God! Dear God! But it's true they don't care if they die! I remember how it was in '70. They aren't afraid to die in those awful wars, the fools. And not worth the rope to hang them. They're not men, they're lie-ons.
For Françoise, the comparison with "lie-ons" was not intended as flattery.
You see, Françoise, revolution is better, because when they declare one of those, the only ones who go are the ones that want to.
Yes, that at least I understand, it's more honest . . .
When war is declared, you know, they stop all the trains.
Oh, heavens, so no one can escape!
Damn clever of them, you have to admit . . .
He would not admit that war was anything but a trick the government tried to play on the people . . .

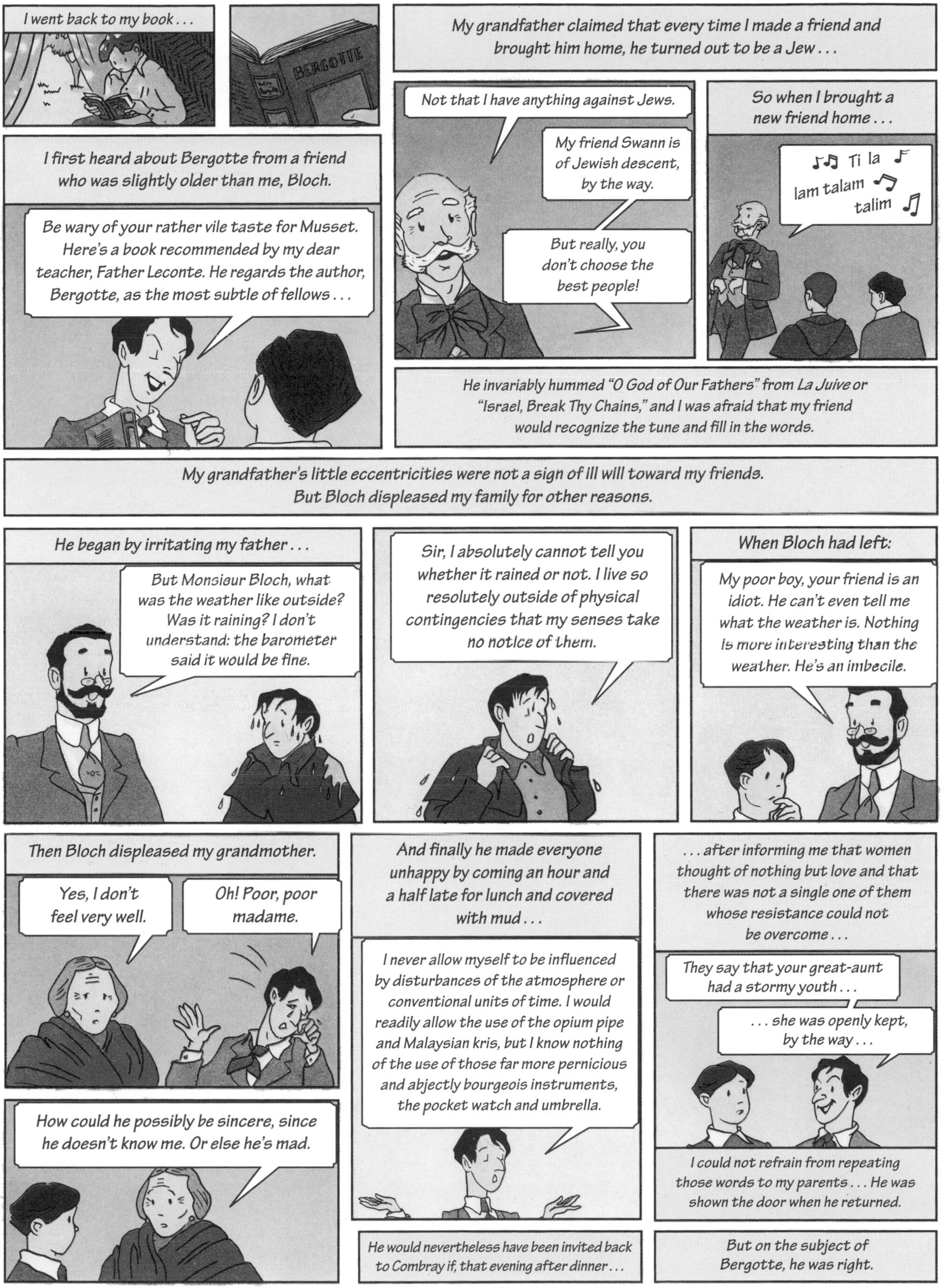

I went back to my book . . .
BERGOTTE
My grandfather claimed that every time I made a friend and brought him home, he turned out to be a Jew . . .
Not that I have anything against Jews.
My friend Swann is of Jewish descent, by the way.
But really, you don't choose the best people!
So when I brought a new friend home . . .
Ti la lam talam talim
I first heard about Bergotte from a friend who was slightly older than me, Bloch.
Be wary of your rather vile taste for Musset. Here's a book recommended by my dear teacher, Father Leconte. He regards the author, Bergotte, as the most subtle of fellows . . .
He invariably hummed "O God of Our Fathers" from La Juive or "Israel, Break Thy Chains," and I was afraid that my friend would recognize the tune and fill in the words.
My grandfather's little eccentricities were not a sign of ill will toward my friends. But Bloch displeased my family for other reasons.
He began by irritating my father . . .
But Monsieur Bloch, what was the weather like outside? Was it raining? I don't understand: the barometer said it would be fine.
Sir, I absolutely cannot tell you whether it rained or not. I live so resolutely outside of physical contingencies that my senses take no notice of them.
When Bloch had left:
My poor boy, your friend is an idiot. He can't even tell me what the weather is. Nothing is more interesting than the weather. He's an imbecile.
Then Bloch displeased my grandmother.
Yes, I don't feel very well.
Oh! Poor, poor madame.
How could he possibly be sincere, since he doesn't know me. Or else he's mad.
And finally he made everyone unhappy by coming an hour and a half late for lunch and covered with mud . . .
I never allow myself to be influenced by disturbances of the atmosphere or conventional units of time. I would readily allow the use of the opium pipe and Malaysian kris, but I know nothing of the use of those far more pernicious and abjectly bourgeois instruments, the pocket watch and umbrella.
He would nevertheless have been invited back to Combray if, that evening after dinner . . .
. . . after informing me that women thought of nothing but love and that there was not a single one of them whose resistance could not be overcome . . .
They say that your great-aunt had a stormy youth . . .
. . . she was openly kept, by the way . . .
I could not refrain from repeating those words to my parents . . . He was shown the door when he returned.
But on the subject of Bergotte, he was right.

For the first few days, what I would come to love so much in his style eluded me, like a tune you eventually become crazy about but at first can't make out.

Then I noticed the rare, almost archaic expressions he liked to use at moments when a hidden wave of harmony, an inner prelude, elevated his style:

" . . . vain dream of life . . . "

" . . . the inexhaustible torrent of beautiful shapes . . . "

" . . . the sterile and delicious torment of understanding and loving . . . "

" . . . moving effigies that forever ennoble the venerable and charming façades of cathedrals . . . "

it was . . . this same melodic flow, these old expressions, and some other very simple and familiar ones that he placed in such a way as to reveal a particular taste of his; and finally, in the sad passages, a certain brusqueness, an almost gruff accent.

I knew those passages by heart.

I was disappointed when he resumed the thread of his narrative. Whenever he spoke of something whose beauty had previously remained hidden from me—a pine forest, hail, Notre-Dame de Paris, Athalie, or Phèdre—the images he used caused that beauty to explode in my mind.

I would have liked to have his opinion or a metaphor of his about everything . . .

On the basis of his books I imagined Bergotte to be a feeble, disappointed old man who had lost children and never gotten over it.

So I read, I inwardly chanted his prose, more dolce and lento perhaps than it was written, and the simplest sentence spoke to me with a tender intonation.

I loved his philosophy more than anything . . . It made me impatient for the age when I would begin to study philosophy in school.

. . . and if someone had told me that the metaphysicians I would care for then would not resemble him in the slightest, I would have experienced the despair of a lover who hopes he has found the love of his life, to whom one speaks of the mistresses he will have later on.

One Sunday . . .

What are you reading? May I see?

Well now, Bergotte! Who suggested that you read him?

My friend Bloch.

Oh, yes, the boy I saw here once who looks so much like Mehmet II in the portrait by Bellini. In any case, he has taste, because Bergotte has a charming mind.

I know him well, so if it would please you to have him write a dedication in your volume, I could ask him.

Can you tell me who his favorite actor is?

That I don't know. But I do know that for him, no male artist can equal Berma, whom he ranks above all others. Have you heard her?

My parents don't allow me to go to the theater.

That's unfortunate. Berma in *Phèdre* or *Le Cid* may be only an actress, but you know, I don't really believe in the "hierarchy" of the arts . . .

When Swann employed an expression that seemed to imply an opinion about an important subject, he was careful to set it off with a special, ironic intonation, as if he did not wish to speak in his own name . . .

Until then, this horror of seriously expressing one's own opinion had struck me as something that must have been elegant and Parisian, in contrast to the dogmatism of the provinces. . . . But now I found this attitude rather shocking. It was as if he did not dare to have an opinion . . .

Oh, the Princesse de Léon's balls are of no importance.

Yet he spent his life seeking this sort of pleasure. I found it quite incomprehensible.

For what other life was he waiting to say seriously at last what he thought about things, to formulate judgments he would no longer place between quotation marks, and no longer waste his time with things he thought ridiculous?

I can also ask Bergotte anything you want. Not a week goes by that he doesn't dine at my house. He's a great friend of my daughter's. They go together to visit old cities, cathedrals, and castles.

When I learned that day that Mlle Swann was such a rare creature, immersed in such privileges as if these were her natural element . . .

. . . I sensed how crude and ignorant I would seem to her and was overcome with both desire and despair.

When a person partakes of an unknown life that her love would allow us to share, love is born: this is all it requires, what it wants most. That is why women love soldiers and firemen: their kisses are directed beyond the armor, toward the heart they think lies beneath, more tender and adventurous than others.

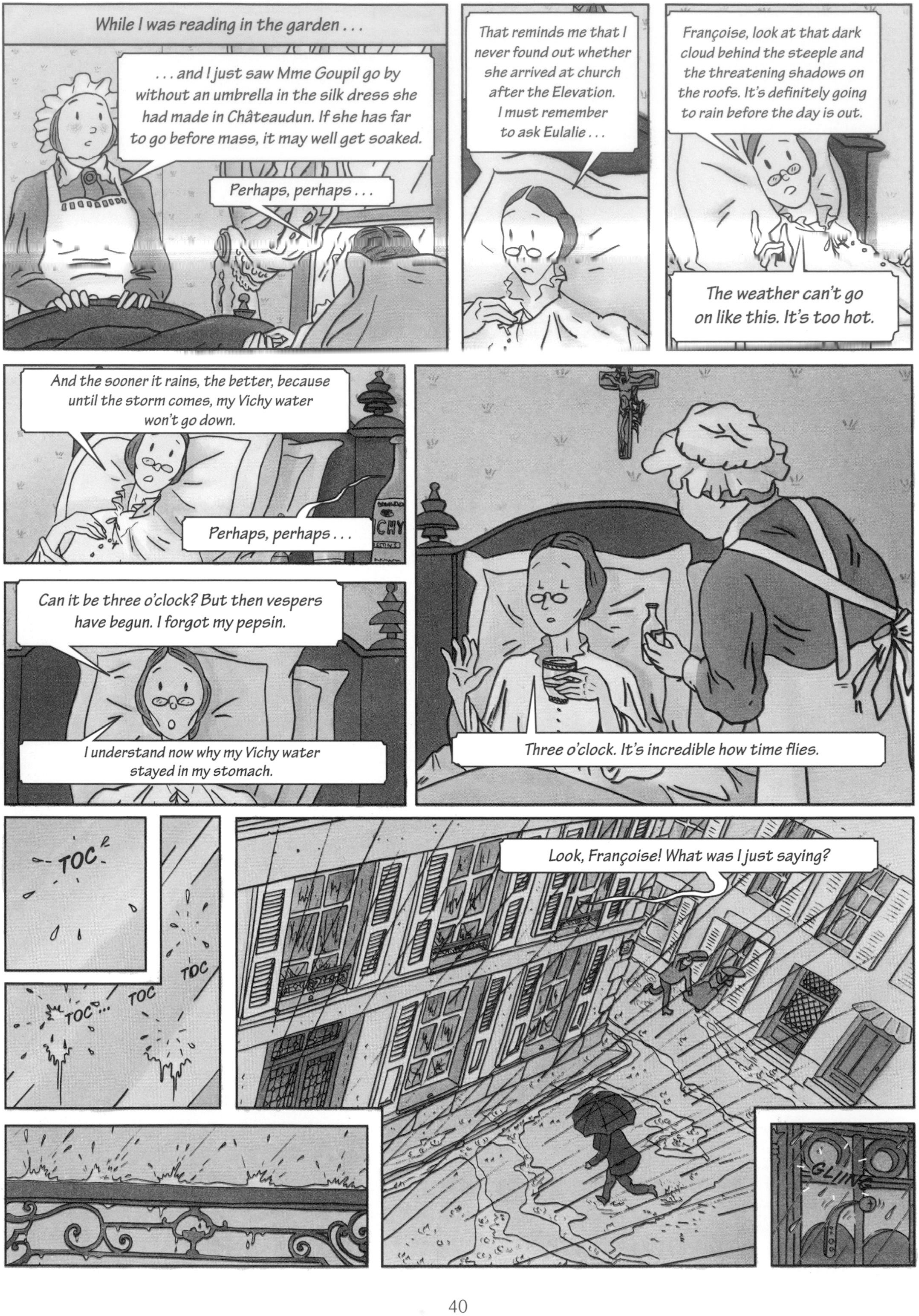
While I was reading in the garden . . .
. . . and I just saw Mme Goupil go by without an umbrella in the silk dress she had made in Châteaudun. If she has far to go before mass, it may well get soaked.
Perhaps, perhaps . . .
That reminds me that I never found out whether she arrived at church after the Elevation. I must remember to ask Eulalie . . .
Françoise, look at that dark cloud behind the steeple and the threatening shadows on the roofs. It's definitely going to rain before the day is out.
The weather can't go on like this. It's too hot.
And the sooner it rains, the better, because until the storm comes, my Vichy water won't go down.
Perhaps, perhaps . . .
Can it be three o'clock? But then vespers have begun. I forgot my pepsin.
I understand now why my Vichy water stayed in my stomach.
Three o'clock. It's incredible how time flies.
TOC
TOC
TOC...
TOC
Look, Françoise! What was I just saying?
GLIING

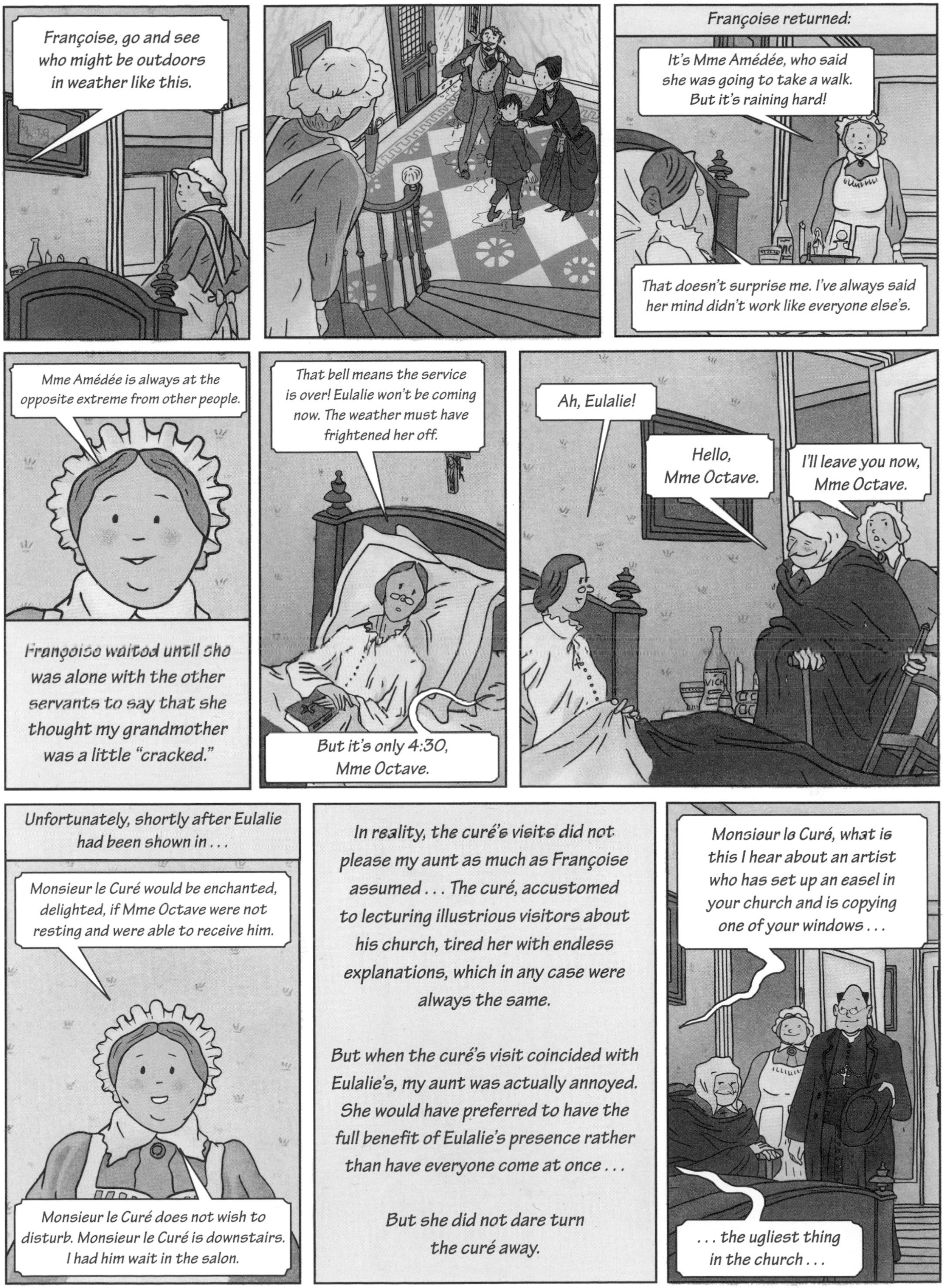
Françoise, go and see who might be outdoors in weather like this.
Françoise returned:
It's Mme Amédée, who said she was going to take a walk. But it's raining hard!
That doesn't surprise me. I've always said her mind didn't work like everyone else's.
Mme Amédée is always at the opposite extreme from other people.
Françoise waited until she was alone with the other servants to say that she thought my grandmother was a little "cracked."
That bell means the service is over! Eulalie won't be coming now. The weather must have frightened her off.
But it's only 4:30, Mme Octave.
Ah, Eulalie!
Hello, Mme Octave.
I'll leave you now, Mme Octave.
Unfortunately, shortly after Eulalie had been shown in . . .
Monsieur le Curé would be enchanted, delighted, if Mme Octave were not resting and were able to receive him.
Monsieur le Curé does not wish to disturb. Monsieur le Curé is downstairs. I had him wait in the salon.
In reality, the curé's visits did not please my aunt as much as Françoise assumed . . . The curé, accustomed to lecturing illustrious visitors about his church, tired her with endless explanations, which in any case were always the same.
But when the curé's visit coincided with Eulalie's, my aunt was actually annoyed. She would have preferred to have the full benefit of Eulalie's presence rather than have everyone come at once . . .
But she did not dare turn the curé away.
Monsieur le Curé, what is this I hear about an artist who has set up an easel in your church and is copying one of your windows . . .
. . . the ugliest thing in the church . . .

I wouldn't go so far as to call it the ugliest thing, because if there are parts of Saint-Hilaire that are worth visiting, there are also some very old parts of my poor basilica, the only one in the diocese that hasn't been restored.

God knows, the porch is filthy and very old but in the end quite majestic. Leave aside the Esther tapestries, for which personally I wouldn't give two cents but which connoisseurs rank just below the ones in Sens.

But don't talk to me about stained glass.

Does it make sense to leave up windows that admit no daylight and deceive the eye in a church where no two slabs are on the same level, yet they refuse to replace them for me because they are the tombstones of the abbés of Combray and the dukes of Guermantes?

I'm sure that if you asked the bishop, he wouldn't refuse to put in a new window.

But in fact it was the bishop himself who made an issue of that wretched window by proving that it depicted Gilbert the Bad, a lord of Guermantes and direct descendant of Geneviève de Brabant, a princess of Guermantes, receiving absolution from Saint Hilary!

But I don't see where Saint Hilary is.

But haven't you noticed a lady in yellow in one corner of the window? That's Saint Hilary or Hilaire, also known as Saint Illiers, Saint Hélier, and even Saint Ylie. Those various corruptions of "sanctus Hilarius" are not even the most curious that have occurred. Do you know, my good Eulalie, what your patron saint became? Saint Eligius: a male saint. Do you see them making a man of you after your death, Eulalie?

You're a great one for keeping us in stitches, Monsieur le Curé!

But the most remarkable thing about our church is undoubtedly the grand view from the steeple. I would not advise you to climb the 97 steps, especially since you must double over if you don't want to hit your head. In any case you must bundle up, because there's quite a wind once you reach the top.

Still, there are always groups that come from afar on Sundays to admire the panoramic view.

42

When the air is clear, you can see all the way to Verneuil. The main thing is that you take in all at once things that you normally see separately, like the course of the Vivonne and the moats of Saint-Assise-lès-Combray, from which the river is separated by a curtain of tall trees, or the various canals of Jouy-le-Vicomte.

Whenever I go to Jouy-le-Vicomte, I see a bit of one canal and then, on turning a corner, a bit of another, but then I can no longer see the first. Even if I put them together in my mind, it never really makes sense.

But from the steeple of Saint-Hilaire it looks very different. You see the whole network of canals in which the town lies ensnared. Only you can't make out the water, just what looks like large slices dividing the town in quarters, so that it looks like a brioche that has been cut into pieces but somehow still hangs together.

The curé had so tired my aunt that the moment he left she was obliged to send Eulalie away too.

Here, my poor Eulalie, a little something to make sure that you don't forget me in your prayers.

Oh, but Mme Octave, I don't know if I should. You know that isn't why I come!

. . . said Eulalie with the same hesitation and embarrassment on each occasion, as if it were the first, and with a look of unhappiness that amused my aunt and did not displease her, for whenever Eulalie seemed slightly less vexed than usual on taking her coin, my aunt would say:

I don't know what's wrong with Eulalie. I gave her the same amount as always, but she didn't look happy.

I don't think she has the slightest cause for complaint.

Not that Françoise wanted for herself the money my aunt gave to Eulalie. She benefited enough from what my aunt owned, knowing that the wealth of the mistress enhances the servant's image in the eyes of others . . .

She was greedy for my aunt alone;

yet she wouldn't have minded much if my aunt gave more away, provided it was to the rich . . .

Perhaps she thought that the rich, who did not need my aunt's gifts, could not be suspected of liking her because of them.

Flatterers know how to make themselves welcome and gather up the crumbs. Patience! God will punish them someday.

Mme Octave, I'm going to let you rest. You look tired.

BOOM BOOM BOOM BOOM

Has Eulalie already left? Can you believe that I forgot to ask her whether Mme Goupil got to mass before the Elevation? Run after her!

But Françoise returned

without having caught up with Eulalie.

How annoying. That was the only important thing I had to ask her!

Such was Aunt Léonie's life, always the same: what she called her "quiet routine," which everyone protected . . . even in the village, where three blocks away the shipping agent, before nailing shut his crates, would send someone to ask Françoise if my aunt was "resting."

On Saturdays in May, we would go out after dinner to attend the services celebrating "the month of Mary."

Make sure there's nothing amiss in your attire. M. Vinteuil will be there, and he is very severe in regard to what he calls "the deplorable ways of today's unkempt youth."

I remember that it was during Mary's month that I fell in love with hawthorns . . . which were inextricably linked to the mysteries of the celebration in which they played a part . . . as well as a holiday decoration, festoons of leaves made lovelier still by the clusters of dazzling white buds scattered over them as over bridal train.

Though I dared only furtive glances, I felt that these formal decorations were alive and that nature herself, by drawing the outlines of the leaves and adding those white buds as a crowning touch, had bestowed beauty on what was both a popular celebration and a mystical rite.

M. Vinteuil and his daughter took their places near us.

Born into a prominent family, he had taught piano to my grandmother's sisters, and when his wife died and he inherited some money, he had retired to Combray, where he often visited the house. Being extremely prudish, however, he stopped coming in order to avoid running into Swann, who had made what he called "an inappropriate marriage, as seems to be the fashion nowadays."

On learning that he was a composer, my mother mentioned in a friendly way that when she visited she hoped to hear something he had written. M. Vinteuil was probably overjoyed, but he was so scrupulously polite and kind that he always put himself in the other person's place and was afraid he would bore them or seem selfish if he gave in to his desire or even allowed it to be glimpsed.

The day my parents went to visit him, I went with them.

May I stay outside and play?

Yes, stay if you wish, but don't wander off too far.

Because M. Vinteuil's house, Montjouvain, stood at the bottom of a hill covered with shrubs among which I hid, I found myself on the same level as the salon . . .

When the servant announced my parents, I watched as M. Vinteuil hastily put a piece of music in a conspicuous place on the piano.

But when my parents entered, he removed it and placed it in a corner.

Please play that piece.

But I have no idea who put that on the piano. That's not where it belongs.

His sole passion was for his daughter, who looked like a boy, so robust that it was hard not to smile at the precautions he took for her health . . .

On leaving the church, I smelled the bittersweet fragrance of almonds emanating from the hawthorns . . .

I was very glad to see you.

Careful, now, dear, you must put this on.

And both returned to Montjouvain.

One Sunday, when both the curé and Eulalie came to visit my aunt at the same time, after which she took a nap, we all went up to say good night, and Mama expressed sorrow at the bad luck that brought all her visitors to the house at the same time.

I know that things didn't go well this afternoon, Léonie. All your company came at the same time.

Embarrassment of riches . . .

I want to take advantage of having the whole family together. . . . I'm afraid we may have offended Legrandin. He barely said hello to me this morning . . .

. . . since M. Legrandin had passed near us as we emerged from the church, walking alongside a woman who lived in a nearby château and whom we knew only by sight, my father had greeted him in a friendly but reserved way . . .

. . . I would be especially upset if he was angry because amid all those people in their Sunday best . . . he seemed rather simply dressed and unpretentious, which I found quite endearing.

But the family council unanimously agreed that my father was imagining things, or else that Legrandin had been preoccupied at that moment with some thought of his own.

In any case, my father's fears were dispelled the next evening. As we were returning from a long walk . . .

Ah, it's M. Legrandin!

So, Mister Reader, do you know this line of Paul Desjardins: "Already the woods are black, but still the sky is blue"? What a fine way of describing this hour of the day, don't you agree?

May the sky always be blue for you, my young friend. And even when you reach the hour of life that I will soon reach, when the woods are already dark, console yourself as I do by looking up at the sky.

Farewell, friends!

The sight of the asparagus delighted me, with their stalks dipped in ultramarine and pink and tips finely daubed with mauve and azure that faded imperceptibly from head to foot . . .

I felt that those heavenly shades revealed delicious creatures that had amused themselves by turning into vegetables and which, beneath their guise of firm, comestible flesh, chose these colors of early dawn, wisps of rainbow, and late evening blues to disclose their precious essence, which would persist through the night after I'd eaten them, as they played, like Shakespearean fairies in a crude poetic farce, at transforming my chamber pot into a bottle of perfume.

Françoise was late.

I would have preferred it if Françoise had been dismissed on the spot. But then who would have made me such nice hot-water bottles, such fragrant coffee, or even . . . such chicken? . . . In fact, everyone else had had to make the same base calculation. Aunt Léonie knew that Françoise was extremely hard on others.

Françoise's virtues concealed certain kitchen tragedies, just as history reveals that the reigns of kings and queens who are portrayed in church windows with hands clasped in prayer were marked by bloody incidents.

The torrents of tears she shed while reading in the newspaper about the misfortunes of people she didn't know dried up quickly if she could form a fairly concrete image of the person in question.

One night, shortly after the kitchen maid gave birth, she came down with an acute case of colic. Mama, hearing her moans, got up and woke Françoise.

But Madame! It's just play-acting. She wants to be mistress of the household . . .

The doctor, who feared these attacks:

I put a bookmark in your medical dictionary.

Françoise, go find the medical dictionary in the library, and be careful not to lose the bookmark!

An hour later, Françoise still had not returned.

Oh my! Oh my!

My God, my God!

Oh my! Holy Mary, Mother of God, is it possible that the good Lord would want any human being to suffer so miserably? Oh! The poor girl!

But after I fetched her and she returned to the bedside of Giotto's Charity, her tears immediately ceased to flow, and at the sight of the same suffering whose description had made her cry, she merely grumbled or made scathingly sarcastic remarks.

Well, she needn't have done whatever she did to end up where she is! She had a good time, you can be sure! She'd better not put on airs now.

God must have given up on any boy who went with that girl. As my poor mother used to say in her dialect,

"Fall fer a dog's ass and ye'll think it smells like a rose."

Many years later, we learned that the reason we ate asparagus every day that summer was that their smell caused the poor kitchen maid who had to peel the stalks such terrible asthma attacks that she was eventually forced to quit.

I dined with Legrandin on his terrace. He had explicitly asked my parents to send me over one night to have dinner with him. Nevertheless, at home, there was a discussion about whether or not I should go.

Come keep your old friend company . . .

Come with the glorious silky raiment of the lilies, worthy of Solomon, and the polychrome enamel of the pansies, but above all come with the cool breeze of the last winter frost, which will prise open the petals of the Mso Jerusalem rose for the two butterflies that have been waiting since this morning outside its gates.

. . . But my grandmother refused to believe he had been impolite.

The silence is very pretty, don't you think? . . . In everyone's life there comes a time . . . when the ears can no longer listen to any music but that which the moonlight plays on the flute of silence.

Sir, do you know the ladies of Guermantes?

The rings around his eyes darkened, and his eyelids drooped. His mouth, briefly marked by a bitter crease, quickly regained its smile, though his eyes still brimmed with pain, like the eyes of a handsome martyr whose body bristles with arrows:

. . . No, . . . I don't know them.

. . . No, . . . no, I don't know them. I've never wanted to. At bottom, I've the mind of a Jacobin.

In truth, I no longer care for anything in the world but a few churches, two or three books, scarcely more paintings, and the moonlight when the breeze of your youth brings me . . .

I understood, however, that Legrandin was not being entirely truthful when he said he liked nothing but churches, moonlight, and youth; he very much liked people who lived in châteaux. . . . He was a snob. And if I asked:

Do you know the Guermantes?

Legrandin . . . suddenly resembled a Saint Sebastian of snobbery, his body slack and studded with arrows:

Please stop! You're causing me great pain by asking me that! No, I don't know the Guermantes. Please don't remind me of my life's greatest sorrow.

Around Combray there were two "ways" to walk, in such different directions that depending which way we wanted to go, we left by a different gate: there was the direction of Méséglise-la-Vineuse, which we also called Swann's way because we passed M. Swann's property when we went that way, and then there was the Guermantes way.

The Méséglise way? The most beautiful view of a plain I know.

The Guermantes way? A typical riverscape!

Thus, "take the Guermantes way to go to Méséglise," or vice versa, would have struck me as an expression as devoid of meaning as "head east to go west."

One day . . .

Do you recall Swann's saying yesterday that since his wife and daughter were leaving for Reims, he would take the opportunity to spend a day in Paris? Since the ladies won't be there, we could walk past his property. It would shorten our route.

To be sure, we'd avoid a considerable detour.

. . . and it was Swann's parents who had the pond dug . . .

Because Mlle Swann was not there, the contemplation of Tansonville left me cold the first time I was allowed to look.

I hoped that by some miracle Mlle Swann and her father would materialize so close to us that there would be no way to avoid them and she would have to be introduced.

. . . Nothing has changed since the death of Swann's mother. Those plantings, on the other hand . . .

So when I suddenly saw on the grass a sign of her possible presence . . .

Hey, there, are you coming?

To catch up with my father and grandfather, I had to run up the narrow path that climbs toward the fields . . .

. . . I found it abuzz with the fragrance of hawthorns.

Since you like hawthorns, look at this pink one! How pretty it is!

It was indeed a hawthorn, but a pink one, even prettier than the white. . . . "In color," and therefore of higher quality to judge by the price list in the "store" on the square or at Camus's, where pastries with pink filling also cost more. I myself preferred pink cream cheese—cream cheese into which I was allowed to crush strawberries.

A little girl . . . was staring at us, lifting up a face spotted with pink freckles.

Her dark eyes gleamed, and . . . for a long time, whenever I thought of her, the memory of their glow came immediately to mind in the form of a brilliant azure, because she was blonde.

She allowed her gaze to shift in my direction without seeming to see me but with a steady feigned smile I could only interpret . . . as a sign of contemptuous scorn.

. . . and her hand simultaneously made a vaguely indecent gesture.

Come, Gilberte!

What are you doing?

Poor Swann! What a miserable role they make him play: they send him away so that she can be alone with her Charlus. That's who that was, I recognized him at once! And the little girl, mixed up in such a dirty business!

Gilberte . . . I loved her. I was sorry not to have had the time or inspiration to offend her, to hurt her, and thus force her to remember me. I found her so beautiful. . . . And already the charm her name had imparted to that place beneath the hawthorns had begun to perfume, imbue, and embalm everything associated with it.

That year, on the morning we were to leave for home, after my hair had been done up for a photograph and a hat had been carefully placed on my head, my mother found me in tears on the steep path adjacent to Tansonville, where I was bidding the hawthorns farewell by taking their sharp rambles into my arms.

My poor little hawthorns! It's not your fault that I have to leave this place! I'll love you always . . .

Wiping away my tears, I promised them that when I grew up I would not imitate the senseless lives of other people, and even in Paris, when spring arrived, instead of calling on people and listening to stupid talk, I would head for the country to catch a glimpse of the first hawthorns.

The wind was a constant companion on the way to Méséglise. . . . I knew that Mlle Swann often went to Laon . . . and when on hot afternoons I saw the wind blow from the horizon, bending the stalks of wheat in waves . . . the plain we shared seemed to bring us together, to unite us, and it occurred to me that the breeze had passed close to her, that it was a message from her whispered in my ear . . . and I embraced it as it passed.

M. Vinteuil lived in Montjouvain, on the way to Méséglise. On the road we often encountered his daughter, who liked to drive her buggy at breakneck speed.

After a certain year, whenever we ran into her she was never alone but always accompanied by an older friend who had a bad reputation in the region and who eventually moved permanently to Montjouvain.

Well, now, it seems that she plays music with her friend, Mlle Vinteuil. You look surprised. What do I know? Nothing but what old man Vinteuil himself told me yesterday. And that girl has every right to love music, doesn't she?

I wouldn't dream of thwarting a child's artistic vocation, and neither, it seems, would Vinteuil. And anyway, he makes music with his daughter's friend too . . .

They make one hell of a lot of music in that house! But why are you laughing? They make altogether too much music, that lot. The other day, I ran into old man Vinteuil near the cemetery. He could barely stand.

Anyone who saw M. Vinteuil at that time—avoiding people he knew, growing old in a few months, wallowing in sorrow, and spending entire days at his wife's grave—would have found it difficult to avoid the conclusion that he was dying of a broken heart.

But the fact that M. Vinteuil may have known what his daughter was up to does not mean that he adored her any less.

But when M. Vinteuil thought of his and his daughter's reputation in the eyes of the world, he saw both of them among the lowest of the low . . .

One day we were walking with Swann in Combray . . .

Oh! Uh, hello.

And Swann, with the proud charity of a man of the world who, amid the dissolution of all his moral prejudices, finds in another man's shame nothing but a reason to show him a kindness that flatters his own self-esteem all the more, the more precious it is to the person receiving it, spoke at length with M. Vinteuil, to whom he had previously not spoken at all . . .

. . . And why don't you send your daughter to play some day at Tansonville? My daughter Gilberte would be delighted.

Two years earlier, such an invitation would have incensed M. Vinteuil, but now it filled him with such feelings of gratitude that he felt obliged not to commit the indiscretion of accepting it.

After Swann had left us . . .

What an exquisite gentleman! What an exquisite gentleman! How unfortunate that he made such an inappropriate marriage!

And then . . . my parents joined M. Vinteuil in deploring Swann's marriage in the name of principles and proprieties which they pretended to believe were not being violated at Montjouvain.

M. Vinteuil did not send his daughter to Swann's, and Swann was the first to regret it, because each time he left M. Vinteuil, he remembered that he had for some time wished to ask him about a person with the same name, someone he believed to be a relative of his . . .

We had to go to Combray for the reading of my Aunt Léonie's will, because she had finally died, vindicating both those who believed that her meager diet would eventually kill her and those who had always maintained that she suffered from a real rather than an imaginary malady, as the skeptics would be forced to concede when she finally succumbed to it.

Françoise did not leave Mme Octave's side for a single moment. She didn't change her clothes or allow anyone else to care for my aunt. She left the body only after it was buried.

That autumn, my parents were preoccupied with formalities and discussions with notaries and farmers, so they allowed me to go for walks without them in the direction of Méséglise.

You're not properly attired for the occasion . . .

You know, Françoise, if I miss my aunt, it's because she was a good woman despite her foolishness, not because she was my aunt. She might have been my aunt and still seemed odious to me, and her death wouldn't have upset me at all.

OH !

You know I'll have no answer for you, because it's hard for me to put my feelings into words.

But she was one of your skinfolk. . . . You must respect your skinfolk. . . .

How good of me to talk to an illiterate who makes such incredible mistakes!

It was perhaps from an impression I had near Montjouvain . . .

. . . an impression that remained obscure at the time, that I much later formed my idea of sadism.

The weather was very hot. Having walked all the way to the pond at Montjouvain . . . I lay down in the shade and went to sleep. . . .

I saw Mlle Vinteuil, who had probably just come in, opposite me . . .

. . . in the bedroom where her father had received mine and which she had turned into her private sitting room.

I could see all her movements without her seeing me, but if I had tried to leave, I would have rustled the bushes, and she would have heard me and might have thought I had hidden there to spy on her. She was in mourning, her father having died a short while earlier.

As a wagon could be heard rumbling down the road . . .

57

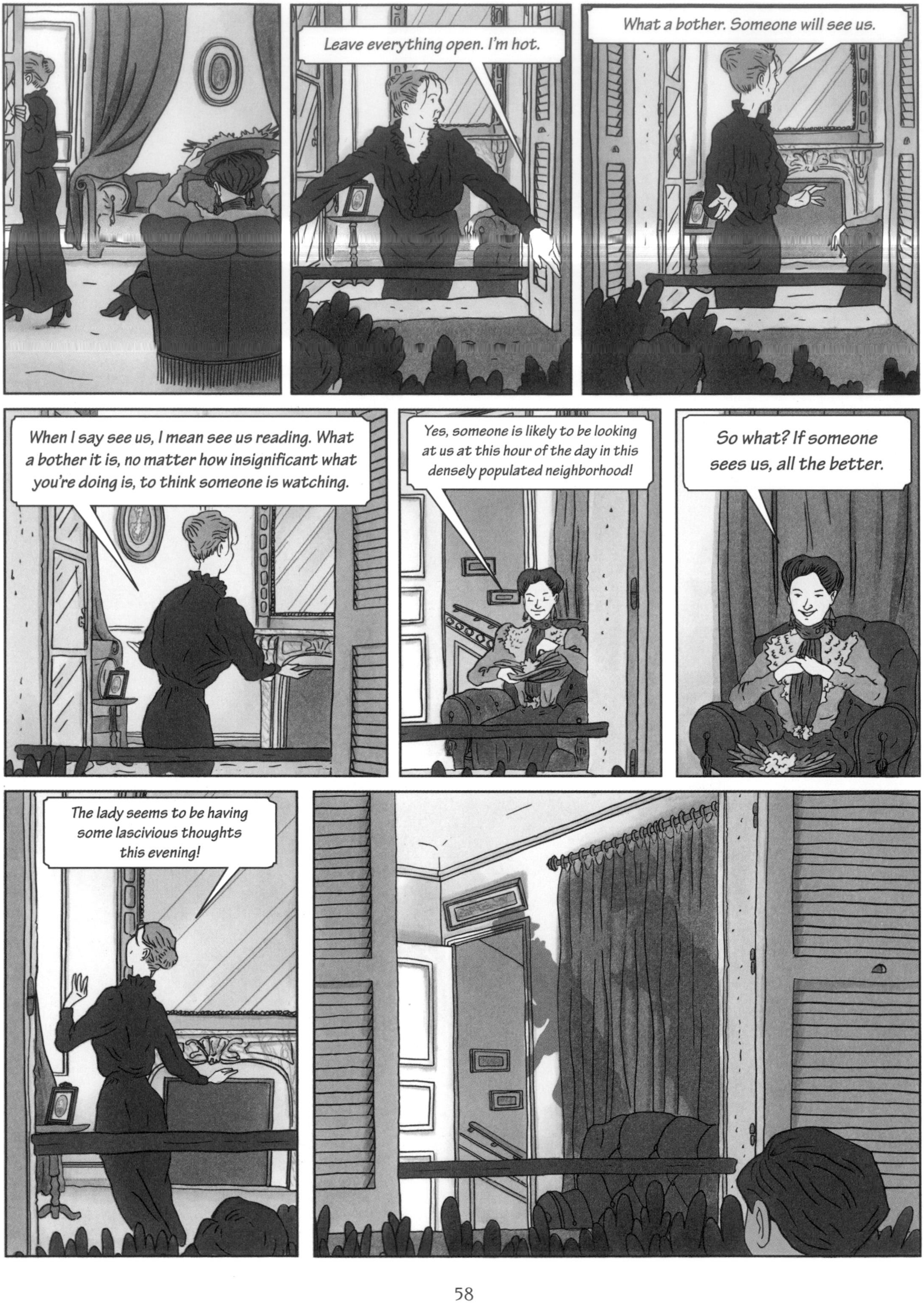
Leave everything open. I'm hot.
What a bother. Someone will see us.
When I say see us, I mean see us reading. What a bother it is, no matter how insignificant what you're doing is, to think someone is watching.
Yes, someone is likely to be looking at us at this hour of the day in this densely populated neighborhood!
So what? If someone sees us, all the better.
The lady seems to be having some lascivious thoughts this evening!

Oh !...

I have no idea who could have put that portrait of my father there. I've said twenty times that's not where it belongs.

I remembered that those were the words M. Vinteuil had spoken to my father in regard to the sheet of music. They were probably in the habit of using that portrait for ritual profanations, because her friend answered with words that must have been part of a regular liturgy.

Leave him where he is. He's no longer around to get in our way. Do you think the old goat would snivel if he saw you there with the window open and tell you to put on your coat?

Now, now . . .

Do you know what I'd like to do to that old horror?

I wouldn't dare spit on him? On that!

I now knew what M. Vinteuil, in return for all the suffering he had endured because of his daughter while alive,

... ...

Oh, you wouldn't dare.

That was all I heard.

... was paid back after his death.

Sadists like Mlle Vinteuil are such purely sentimental beings, so naturally virtuous, that they think even sensual pleasure is bad, a privilege of the wicked. And when they allow themselves to indulge in it for a time, they try to imagine themselves in the skin of the wicked and to bring their partner into it as well, so as to savor for a moment the illusion of escaping from their scrupulous and tender souls into the inhuman world of pleasure.

It was fairly easy to walk toward Méséglise but quite another matter to take the Guermantes way, because that meant a long walk and you needed to be sure of the weather.

Tomorrow, if the weather holds, we'll take the Guermantes way.

The most charming thing about the Guermantes way was that you had the Vivonne alongside you almost the whole time.

The Pont-Vieux led to a tow path, which in that place was shaded by the bluish-green foliage of a hazel tree, under which a fisherman seemed to have taken root.

Papa, how does that man . . .

Shhh! The fish!

. . . That fisherman was the only person in Combray whose identity I never discovered.

Broad meadows stretched along the other bank of the river all the way to the village.

Half-buried in the grass were the ruins of the château of the old counts of Combray, who in the Middle Ages had the Vivonne as their defense against attacks by the lords of Guermantes.

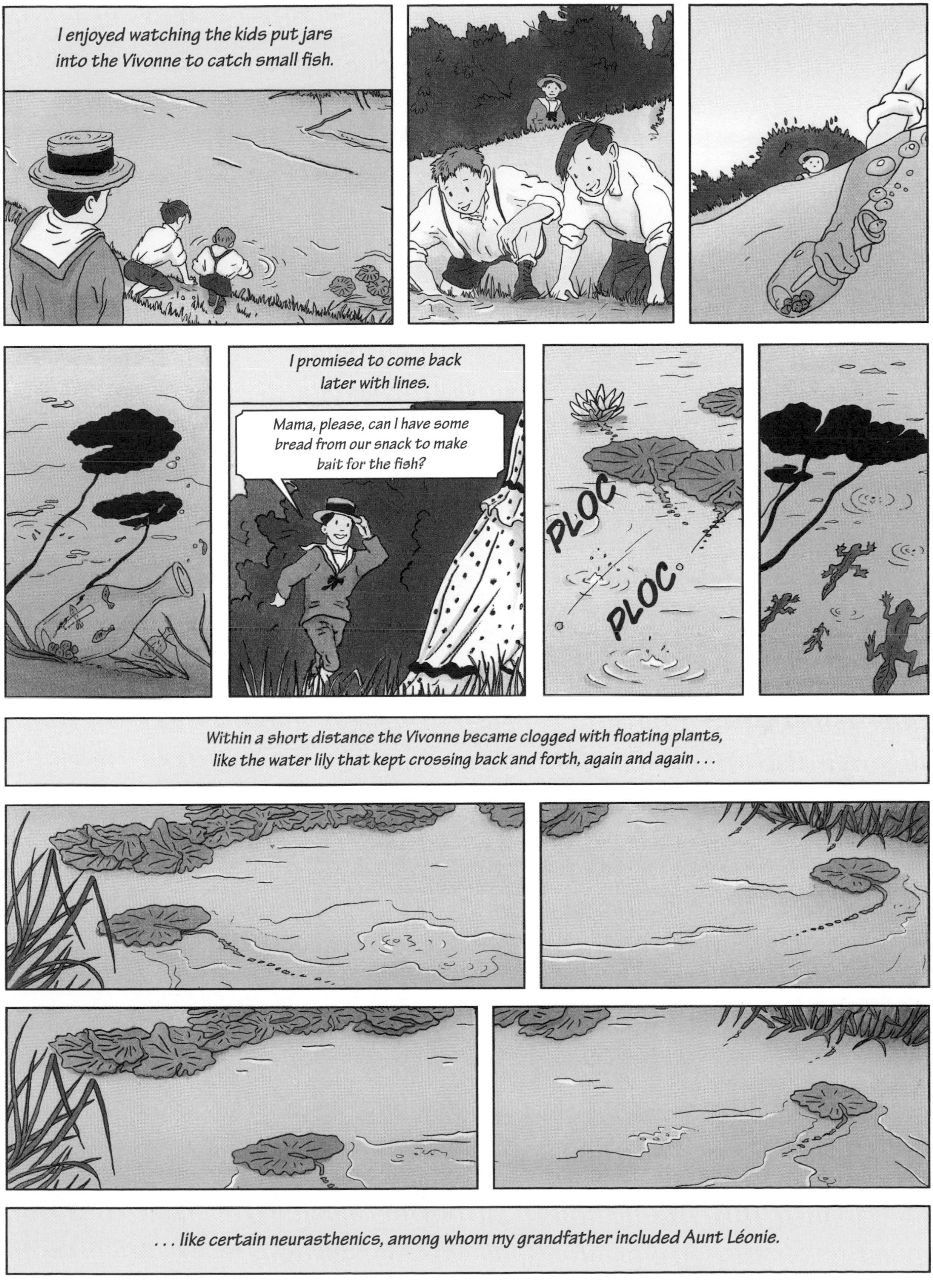

I enjoyed watching the kids put jars into the Vivonne to catch small fish.
I promised to come back later with lines.
Mama, please, can I have some bread from our snack to make bait for the fish?
PLOC
PLOC
Within a short distance the Vivonne became clogged with floating plants, like the water lily that kept crossing back and forth, again and again . . .
. . . like certain neurasthenics, among whom my grandfather included Aunt Léonie.

Sometimes we'd happen upon a forlorn, isolated country house . . .
a young woman who, as the saying goes, "buried herself there" . . .

. . . One had the feeling that in her retreat she had voluntarily left the places where she might at least
have seen the man she loved for others where he'd never shown his face.

When we took the Guermantes way,
we were never able to continue all the way to
the source of the Vivonne . . .

Nor were we able to go all the way to
the place I so much hoped to reach,
Guermantes.

I knew that the Duc and Duchesse de Guermantes lived there. I knew they were real people who actually existed, but whenever I thought about them, I imagined them . . .

. . . sometimes as figures in a tapestry, like the Comtesse de Guermantes in the "Coronation of Esther" in our church . . .

. . . sometimes as subtly shaded figures, like Gilbert the Bad in the stained-glass window . . .

. . . sometimes as utterly impalpable, like the image of Geneviève de Brabant, the ancestor of the Guermantes.

The grounds of the château . . . I dreamed that Madame de Guermantes, suddenly taken by a capricious fancy for me, had invited me there and spent all day with me fishing for trout.

She would make me tell her about the poems I intended to write. And those dreams alerted me to the fact that, since I wanted to be a writer, it was about time I decided what I wanted to write.

I felt that I lacked genius . . .

. . . or perhaps that a cerebral malady prevented it from manifesting itself.

Discouraged, I renounced literature once and for all, despite the encouragement I had received from Bloch.

63

One day my mother said to me:

Since you're always talking about Madame de Guermantes, it may interest you to know that because Dr. Percepied took such good care of her four years ago, she'll be coming to Combray to attend his daughter's marriage. You'll be able to see her at the ceremony.

So that's Madame de Guermantes! Nothing more than that!

I was greatly disappointed, because when I thought about Madame de Guermantes, I had never noticed that I imagined her with the colors . . .

. . . of a tapestry . . .

. . . or a stained-glass window . . .

. . . in another century, and different from all living beings . . .

... It never occurred to me that she might have a red face or a mauve scarf like Madame Sazerat ...

... or that her body, ignorant of the name attached to it, belonged to a certain female type that also included the wives of doctors and shopkeepers.

But ... my imagination, briefly paralyzed by a reality so different from what it had expected, now came to life:

The Guermantes, illustrious before Charlemagne, had had the power of life and death over their vassals. The Duchesse de Guermantes was a descendant of Geneviève de Brabant. She does not know anyone here, nor would she be willing to.

I saw her again, especially during the procession in the sacristy.

Is that lady really Madame de Guermantes?

Yes, sir.

She is better-looking than Madame Sazerat.

... and Mlle Vinteuil.

How beautiful she is! How noble! How wonderful it is to have before my eyes a proud Guermantes, the descendant of Geneviève de Brabant.

Her smile graced me, who could not take my eyes off her.

I think she likes me.

And I immediately fell in love with her, for if it is sometimes enough for a woman to look at us with disdain to make us fall in love with her, as I thought Mlle Swann had done, it is also sometimes enough for her to look at us with kindness, as Madame de Guermantes did.

From that day on, whenever I took the Guermantes way, how much more distressing it was than before that I had no literary talent and would have to renounce forever all thought of becoming a famous writer!

Then, suddenly, a roof or the glint of sunshine on a rock or a smell would cause me to stop to savor the particular pleasure each gave me . . .

. . . and also because these things seemed to hide something else, which they invited me to capture.

I tried to remember the exact line of the roof or the color of the rock, which, though I could not understand why . . .

. . . had seemed to me pregnant and ready to open themselves up and deliver what lay within.

At home I thought of other things, so that my mind filled with images beneath which long lay buried the reality I had lacked the will to explore.

But once, we were glad when we ran into Dr. Percepied driving his wagon at breakneck speed and he invited us to ride with him . . .

. . . I had an impression of this sort and did not let it go before delving into it a bit.

I have to stop to see another patient in Martinville-le-Sec.

May I ride in front, Mama?

If you wish.

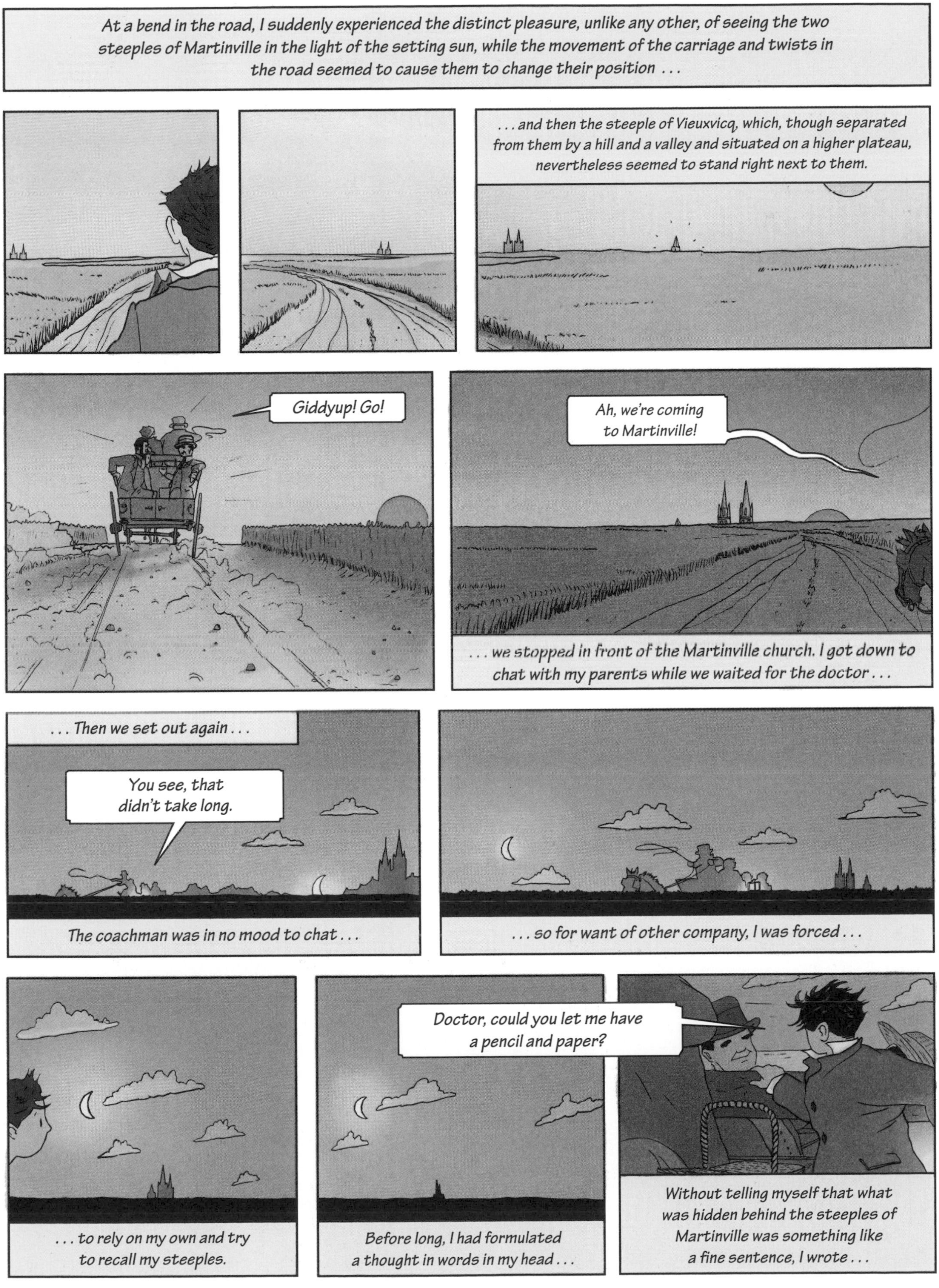

At a bend in the road, I suddenly experienced the distinct pleasure, unlike any other, of seeing the two steeples of Martinville in the light of the setting sun, while the movement of the carriage and twists in the road seemed to cause them to change their position . . .
. . . and then the steeple of Vieuxvicq, which, though separated from them by a hill and a valley and situated on a higher plateau, nevertheless seemed to stand right next to them.
Giddyup! Go!
Ah, we're coming to Martinville!
. . . we stopped in front of the Martinville church. I got down to chat with my parents while we waited for the doctor . . .
. . . Then we set out again . . .
You see, that didn't take long.
The coachman was in no mood to chat . . .
. . . so for want of other company, I was forced . . .
. . . to rely on my own and try to recall my steeples.
Before long, I had formulated a thought in words in my head . . .
Doctor, could you let me have a pencil and paper?
Without telling myself that what was hidden behind the steeples of Martinville was something like a fine sentence, I wrote . . .

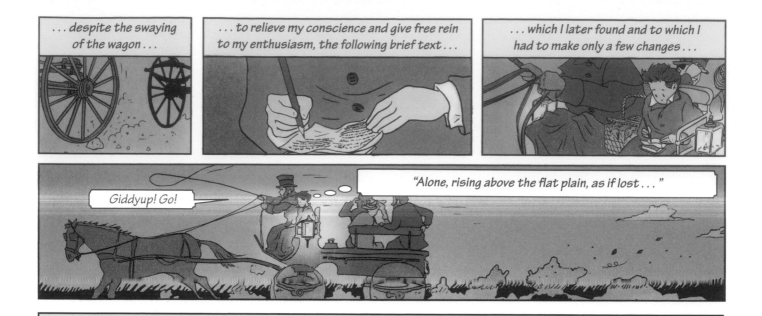

... despite the swaying of the wagon ...

... to relieve my conscience and give free rein to my enthusiasm, the following brief text ...

... which I later found and to which I had to make only a few changes ...

Giddyup! Go!

"Alone, rising above the flat plain, as if lost ..."

Alone, rising above the flat plain, as if lost in open country, Martinville's twin steeples soared heavenward.

Soon there were three: after a sharp turn, a late arrival, the steeple of Vieuxvicq, joined the other two.

Minutes passed. We were moving quickly, yet the three steeples remained ahead of us, like three birds perched on the plain, standing still and clearly visible in the sunlight. Then the Vieuxvicq steeple moved off into the distance, and only the steeples of Martinville remained, illuminated by the setting sun, which even at this distance I could see playing over, smiling on, their sides.

We had been approaching them for such a long time that I was thinking about how much longer it would take to reach them when, suddenly, the wagon turned and deposited us at their foot. They had so brusquely hurled themselves in front of it that we barely had time to stop before crashing into the porch.

We continued on our way. We had left Martinville a short while earlier. The village, having accompanied us for a few seconds, had disappeared, and all that remained on the horizon, watching us flee, were its steeples together with the one in Vieuxvicq, which waved their sunny tops in a gesture of farewell.

Sometimes one would stand aside so that the other two might glimpse us an instant longer, but the road changed direction, and all three steeples turned in the light like three golden pivots and vanished from my sight.

A little later, however, when we were already close to Combray and the sun had set, I saw them one last time, very far away, looking like three flowers painted on the sky above the line of fields.

They also reminded me of three legendary maidens condemned to solitude and shrouded in darkness, and as we sped away at a gallop, I saw them timidly feeling their way until their noble silhouettes had stumbled clumsily a few times, after which they merged, slipping one behind another, forming a single dark shape against the still rosy sky, a charming, melancholy shape that vanished into the night.

I never thought of that page again, but at that moment, as I finished writing ...

Giddyup! Whoa!

... I felt so happy, because the words had completely relieved me of those steeples and of what lay hidden behind them, that, as if I were a hen that had just laid an egg, I began to sing at the top of my voice.

Thus, for me, the Méséglise way and the Guermantes way are still linked to many small events from the one life of all those we lead in parallel that is most fully stocked with surprises and richest in episodes, namely, the life of the mind.

The fragrance of hawthorn that hovered about the hedge, the dull sound of footsteps on a gravel path, a soon-popped bubble clinging to an aquatic plant in the river . . .

. . . my exaltation sustained them through many long years, while the paths themselves have vanished and those who walked them died, along with their memory.

On summer evenings when the harmonious heavens growl like a wild animal and everyone grumbles about the storm, it is to the Méséglise way that I owe the ecstasy that I alone feel . . .

. . . as I inhale, through the sound of falling rain, . . .

. . . the lingering fragrance of invisible lilacs.

I often remained awake until morning dreaming of that time in Combray, remembering my sad sleepless nights and the many days whose memory had recently been brought back by the flavor—or what we in Combray would have called the "fragrance"—of a cup of tea . . .

. . . Of course, as morning approached, the brief uncertainty of my waking dream had long since dissipated.

I knew what room I was actually in. I had reconstructed it around me in the darkness . . .

. . . The dwelling-place I had rebuilt in the darkness joined the places glimpsed in the whirlwind of awakening, sent fleeing by the pallid sign traced above the curtains by the raised finger of dawn.

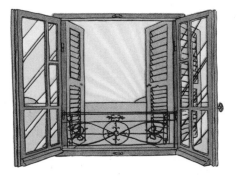

Swann in Love

To belong to the Verdurins' "inner circle," "little group," or "little clan," one condition was sufficient but also necessary: one had to subscribe tacitly to a creed, one of whose tenets was that the young pianist who was Mme Verdurin's protégé that year "trounced" both Planté and Rubinstein. and Dr. Cottard was a better diagnostician than Dr. Potain.

No one should be allowed to play Wagner that well!

The Verdurins did not invite you to dinner. Rather, they "laid a place" for you.

There is no program for this evening's entertainment.

He'll play if he fancies.

No one can be forced to play.

. . . and as M. Verdurin said:

It's all for our friends! Cheers to our company!

Any "new recruit" whom the Verdurins were unable to persuade that anyone who did not spend their evenings with them was condemned to be bored to tears was immediately banished.

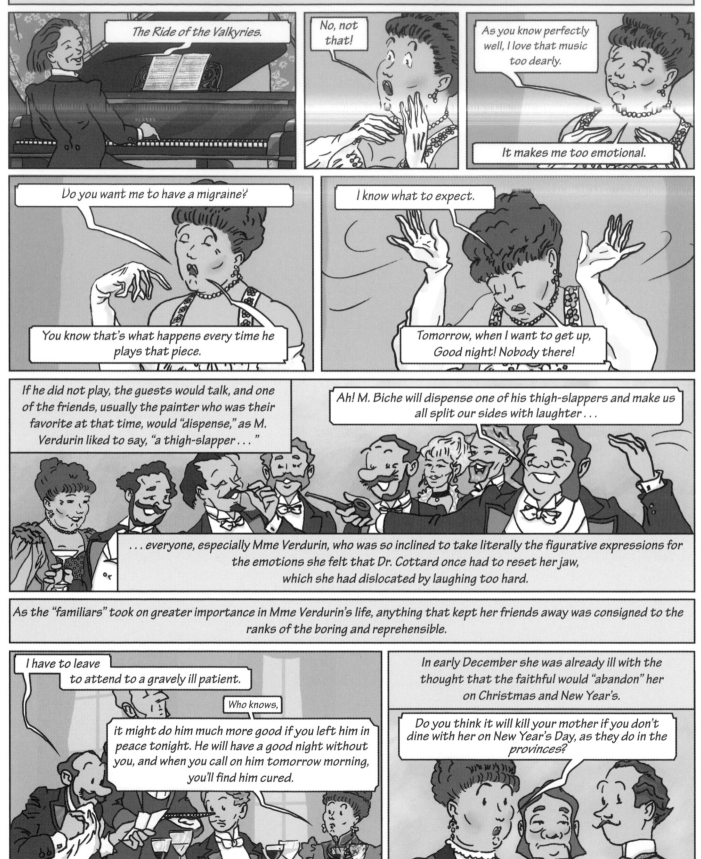

Because women were more refractory than men when it came to abandoning all curiosity about the rest of society, the Verdurins had no choice but to dismiss their female "faithful" one after another. Apart from the doctor's young wife, they were reduced that year to one woman who practically belonged to the demimonde, Mme de Crécy, whom Mme Verdurin called Odette, in addition to the pianist's aunt.

The Ride of the Valkyries.

No, not that!

As you know perfectly well, I love that music too dearly.

It makes me too emotional.

Do you want me to have a migraine?

You know that's what happens every time he plays that piece.

I know what to expect.

Tomorrow, when I want to get up, Good night! Nobody there!

If he did not play, the guests would talk, and one of the friends, usually the painter who was their favorite at that time, would "dispense," as M. Verdurin liked to say, "a thigh-slapper..."

Ah! M. Biche will dispense one of his thigh-slappers and make us all split our sides with laughter...

...everyone, especially Mme Verdurin, who was so inclined to take literally the figurative expressions for the emotions she felt that Dr. Cottard once had to reset her jaw, which she had dislocated by laughing too hard.

As the "familiars" took on greater importance in Mme Verdurin's life, anything that kept her friends away was consigned to the ranks of the boring and reprehensible.

I have to leave to attend to a gravely ill patient.

Who knows, it might do him much more good if you left him in peace tonight. He will have a good night without you, and when you call on him tomorrow morning, you'll find him cured.

In early December she was already ill with the thought that the faithful would "abandon" her on Christmas and New Year's.

Do you think it will kill your mother if you don't dine with her on New Year's Day, as they do in the provinces?

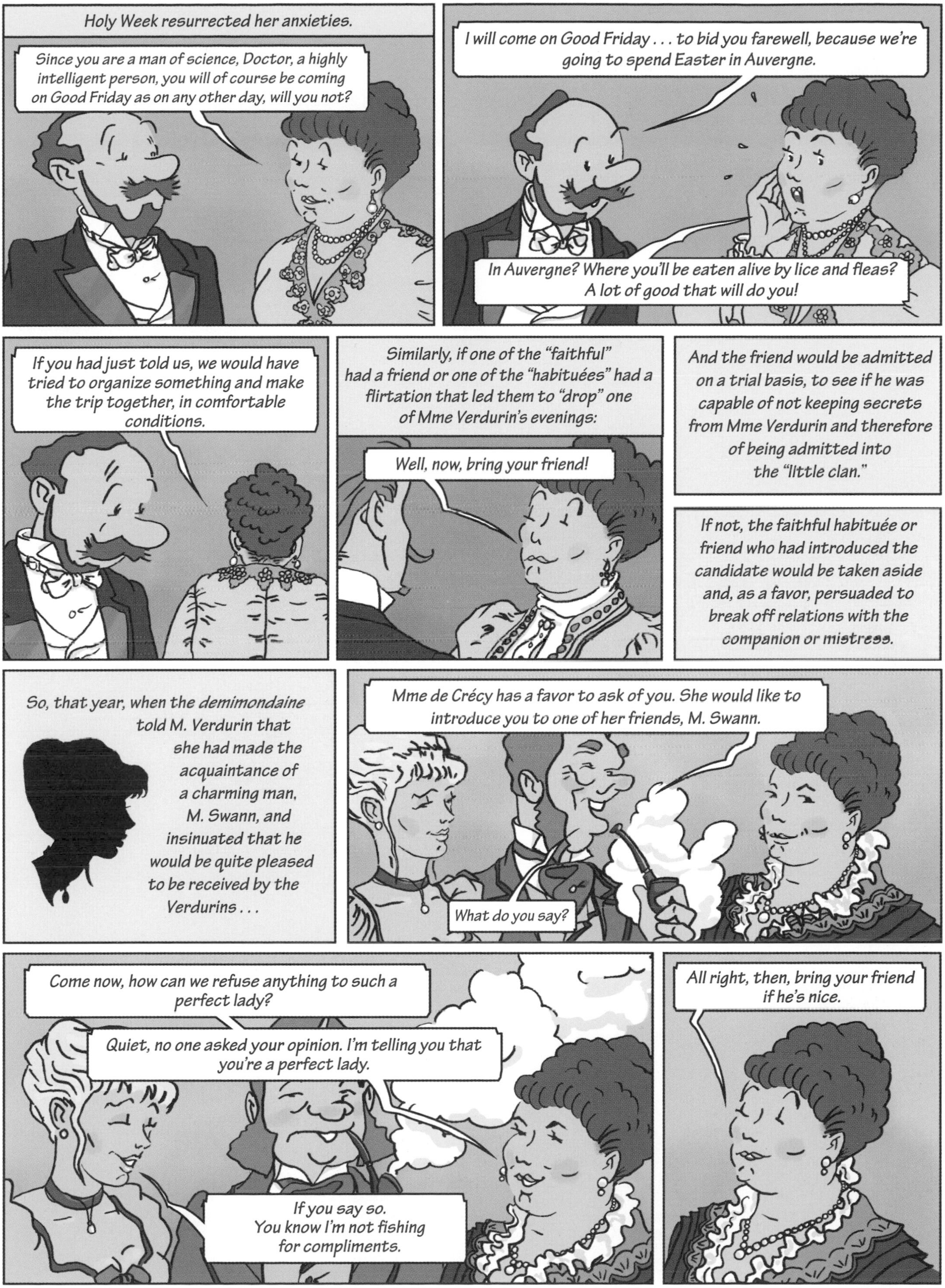
Holy Week resurrected her anxieties.
Since you are a man of science, Doctor, a highly intelligent person, you will of course be coming on Good Friday as on any other day, will you not?
I will come on Good Friday . . . to bid you farewell, because we're going to spend Easter in Auvergne.
In Auvergne? Where you'll be eaten alive by lice and fleas? A lot of good that will do you!
If you had just told us, we would have tried to organize something and make the trip together, in comfortable conditions.
Similarly, if one of the "faithful" had a friend or one of the "habituées" had a flirtation that led them to "drop" one of Mme Verdurin's evenings:
Well, now, bring your friend!
And the friend would be admitted on a trial basis, to see if he was capable of not keeping secrets from Mme Verdurin and therefore of being admitted into the "little clan."
If not, the faithful habituée or friend who had introduced the candidate would be taken aside and, as a favor, persuaded to break off relations with the companion or mistress.
So, that year, when the *demimondaine* told M. Verdurin that she had made the acquaintance of a charming man, M. Swann, and insinuated that he would be quite pleased to be received by the Verdurins . . .
Mme de Crécy has a favor to ask of you. She would like to introduce you to one of her friends, M. Swann.
What do you say?
Come now, how can we refuse anything to such a perfect lady?
Quiet, no one asked your opinion. I'm telling you that you're a perfect lady.
If you say so. You know I'm not fishing for compliments.
All right, then, bring your friend if he's nice.

Of course, the Verdurins' "inner circle" had nothing in common with the society Swann was used to. But he was so fond of women that when he had acquainted himself with nearly all the aristocracy had to offer, he attached no further value to the naturalization papers, virtually titles of nobility, that the Faubourg Saint-Germain had offered him, except as a kind of negotiable security, a letter of credit . . .

. . . which enabled him, if the daughter of some country squire or lawyer struck him as pretty, to establish a position for himself in some provincial hole or obscure Parisian circle.

At the time, desire or love made him vain in a way from which he was now exempt . . .

. . . and made him wish to stand out in the eyes of the unknown woman with whom he had become infatuated, . . .

. . . especially if she was a woman of modest station.

Just as an intelligent man will not be afraid of being mistaken for stupid by another intelligent man, an elegant man will fear having his elegance overlooked not by a great lord but by a boor.

He was not like so many people who abstain from the pleasures that come their way from outside the station of life in which they remain confined until the day they die.

Swann did not try to think of the women with whom he spent his time as pretty; rather, he sought to spend his time with women he already found pretty.

And often they were women whose beauty was of a rather common type, for the physical qualities he sought without being aware of it were the complete opposite of those he admired in sculptures or paintings of women by his favorite artists.

A profound or a melancholy expression in a woman's face left him cold, but his senses were immediately aroused by the sight of healthy, pink, voluptuous flesh.

How many times had he instantly forfeited his credit with some duchess by asking her for a telegram of introduction to her steward because he had noticed the man's daughter on a visit to the country?

This amused him, even afterwards, because there was a base element in his nature, redeemed by a rare degree of refinement.

It was not only the illustrious phalanx of virtuous dowagers, generals, and academicians with whom he maintained close relations that Swann cynically pressed into service as his procurers.

Many years later, when I began to be interested in his character, which in quite different respects resembled mine, I learned that he had written to my grandfather (who was not yet my grandfather, because it was around the time of my birth that Swann's great affair began).

I know this handwriting.

Swann will be asking for some favor.

On guard!

My grandparents dismissed out of hand even those of his requests they could easily have satisfied, such as to introduce him to a young woman who dined at the house every Sunday . . .

. . . and whom they were obliged to say they no longer saw whenever Swann brought her name up.

even though they had been asking all week whom they might invite with her and often ended up inviting no one rather than the one man who would have been so pleased to have dined with her.

My grandparents were friendly with another couple:

What a joy! You remember that we never used to see Charles Swann?

Well, he has lately been as charming as can be. He spends all his time with us.

My grandfather did not wish to diminish their pleasure, but he looked at my grandmother and hummed:

♪♪♪ What can this mystery be? I can't imagine. ♪ ♪♪

or:

Fleeting vision . . . ♪ ♪♪

or:

In such affairs, it's best to be blind.

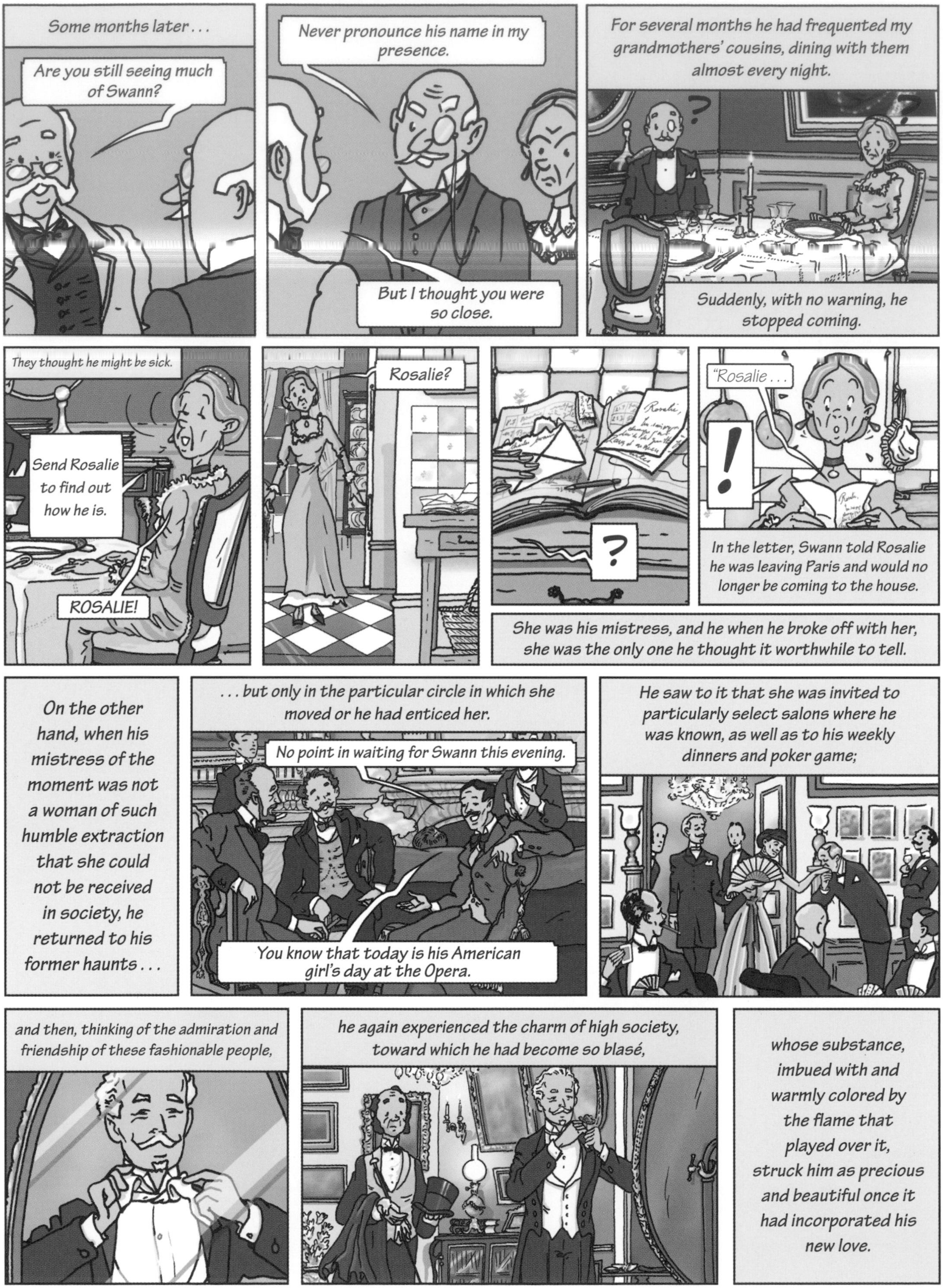
Some months later . . .
Are you still seeing much of Swann?
Never pronounce his name in my presence.
But I thought you were so close.
For several months he had frequented my grandmothers' cousins, dining with them almost every night.
?
?
Suddenly, with no warning, he stopped coming.
They thought he might be sick.
Send Rosalie to find out how he is.
ROSALIE!
Rosalie?
?
"Rosalie . . .
!
In the letter, Swann told Rosalie he was leaving Paris and would no longer be coming to the house.
She was his mistress, and he when he broke off with her, she was the only one he thought it worthwhile to tell.
On the other hand, when his mistress of the moment was not a woman of such humble extraction that she could not be received in society, he returned to his former haunts . . .
. . . but only in the particular circle in which she moved or he had enticed her.
No point in waiting for Swann this evening.
You know that today is his American girl's day at the Opera.
He saw to it that she was invited to particularly select salons where he was known, as well as to his weekly dinners and poker game;
and then, thinking of the admiration and friendship of these fashionable people,
he again experienced the charm of high society, toward which he had become so blasé,
whose substance, imbued with and warmly colored by the flame that played over it, struck him as precious and beautiful once it had incorporated his new love.

But while each of these affairs and flirtations had been the realization of a dream born of the glimpse of a face or body, when he was introduced at the theater one day to Odette de Crécy, she struck Swann as a woman not without beauty, to be sure, but a type of beauty that left him indifferent.

Some time after that introduction at the theater, she wrote him to ask if she could see his collections, which she found so interesting—she, an "ignorant woman with a taste for pretty things."...

"...I feel I'll know you better when I've seen you in your 'home.'"

"...where I imagine you living in comfort with your tea and your books, although I'm surprised that you live in a neighborhood that must be quite depressing and isn't very smart for such a smart man..."

And after he invited her to visit:

How sad I am to have made such a brief visit...

...to an apartment I'm so glad to have seen.

A young man dreams of possessing the heart of the woman he loves. Later, feeling that he possesses a woman's heart can be enough to make him love her.

Swann, being close to the age of disillusionment, knew how to be happy with being in love for the sake of being in love.

At that stage of life, a man has already experienced love several times. Recognizing one of its symptoms is enough to call forth the others.

Since we know the song, which is engraved in us in its entirety, we don't need a woman to tell us the beginning to know the rest. And if she begins in the middle,

we know the music well enough to join her in the appropriate passage, where she is waiting for us to come in.

Odette de Crécy returned to see Swann again; her visits became more and more frequent.

As he chatted with her, Swann regretted that her great beauty

was not of the sort he normally preferred.

She had a lovely figure,

but it was difficult to make out its lines (owing to the styles of the day, even though she was one of the best-dressed women in Paris).

Wouldn't you like to have tea at my place some time?

He claimed to have work to do, a study of Vermeer of Delft, which in fact he had abandoned years earlier.

I know I'm useless, a worthless thing like me, next to a great scholar like you.

I would be like the frog in the fable.

But I'd love to learn, to be initiated.

How much fun it would be to search for old books, to stick my nose into old papers.

You're going to laugh at me. This painter who prevents you from seeing me—is he still alive? Can one see his work in Paris, so that I can form an idea of what you like,

Guess a little what is going on behind that great brow, which is always at work, inside that head, which is always thinking . . .

. . . and say to myself, "So, that's what he's thinking now."

How I dream of being involved in your work.

78

Be kind. I'm afraid of new friendships. I'm so afraid of being unhappy.

You're afraid of affection? How funny, I think of nothing else and would give my life for some.

Some woman must have made you suffer, and you think all the others are like her. She didn't understand you. You're such an unusual person.

That's what I first loved about you. I sensed that you weren't like everyone else.

And what about you? I know how it is with women.

You must be very busy and not have much free time.

No, I never have anything to do!

I'm always free. I'll always be there for you.

Any time of day or night that it's convenient for you to see me, send for me, and I'll be only too happy to come running.

Will you?

Do you know what I'd like? I'd like to introduce you to Mme Verdurin, whom I see every evening.

Really!

If we met there and I thought you came in part to see me!

My grandfather had in fact known the family of these Verdurins. But he had lost all contact with the one he called "young Verdurin."

One day, he received a letter from Swann asking if he might introduce him to the Verdurins.

On guard! On guard! This doesn't surprise me at all. Swann was bound to end up with that lot.

What company!

But I can't do what he asks, because, in the first place, I no longer know the gentleman in question.

In any case, there must be a woman mixed up in it somewhere, and I make a point of keeping out of such matters.

Oh, well! We'll have some fun if Swann takes up with young Verdurin.

After my grandfather turned down Swann's request, it was Odette herself who brought him to the Verdurins'.

On the day Swann made his entrance, the Verdurins had invited to dinner Dr. and Mme Cottard, the young pianist and his aunt, and the painter who enjoyed their favor at the time. They were joined later in the evening by some of the other faithful.

Dr. Cottard was never quite sure . . .

. . . what tone to take when answering someone, or whether his interlocutor was serious or joking.

but since he didn't dare assert this smile forthrightly, it hovered in perpetual uncertainty, in which one could read the question he did not dare to ask:

Hence he randomly added a conditional, provisional smile to all his facial expressions,

Do you really mean that?

Following the advice his prudent mother had given him when he left his native province, he never allowed an unfamiliar expression or name to pass without seeking additional information.

When it came to expressions, his thirst for knowledge was insatiable.

"The bloom of youth"?

"Blue blood"?

"Carte blanche"?

"Like a rolling stone"?

"Time to pay the piper"?

"Arbiter of elegance"?

"To be floored"?

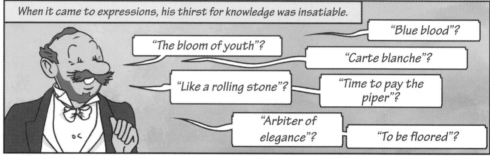

As for the names of individuals, he simply repeated them in a questioning tone, which he expected would be enough to elicit an explanation.

Since he was utterly devoid of the critical acumen he believed he brought to everything, he took everything literally.

How kind of you to have come, Doctor, especially since I'm sure you've already seen quite a lot of Sarah Bernhardt.

But perhaps we're too close to the stage.

Indeed, we are much too close, and Sarah Bernhardt has begun to be tiresome. But you asked me to come.

Your wish is my command.

You are so kind.

I'm only too glad to do you this little favor.

What wouldn't I do to make you happy?

Sarah Bernhardt is "the Golden Voice," is she not?

The newspapers often say she "steals the show." What a bizarre expression, don't you think?

You know, I think we're making a mistake when for modesty's sake we play down our gifts to the doctor.

He's a man of science who lives apart from the world of the mundane. He has no idea of what things are worth and relies on what we tell him.

I didn't dare mention it, but I couldn't help noticing.

Next New Year's day, instead of sending Dr. Cottard a ruby worth 3,000 francs and calling it a trifle, M. Verdurin bought a fake stone for 300 francs but intimated to Cottard that it would be difficult to find another quite as fine.

Tonight M. Swann will be joining us.

Swann ?

Swann ?

Who is Swann?

The friend of Odette's we mentioned to you.

Ah, yes!

Good.

Of course.

The painter was overjoyed to be introduced to Swann:

He loved to encourage affairs.

Nothing amuses me as much as making a marriage.

I've been quite successful at it.

Even between women.

Having told the Verdurins that Swann was very "smart,"

Odette had made them afraid he would be boring, but he made an excellent first impression.

Swann, when moving among people of inferior station such as the Verdurins and their friends, was instinctively attentive and put himself forward in ways that, in their view, a bore would not have done.

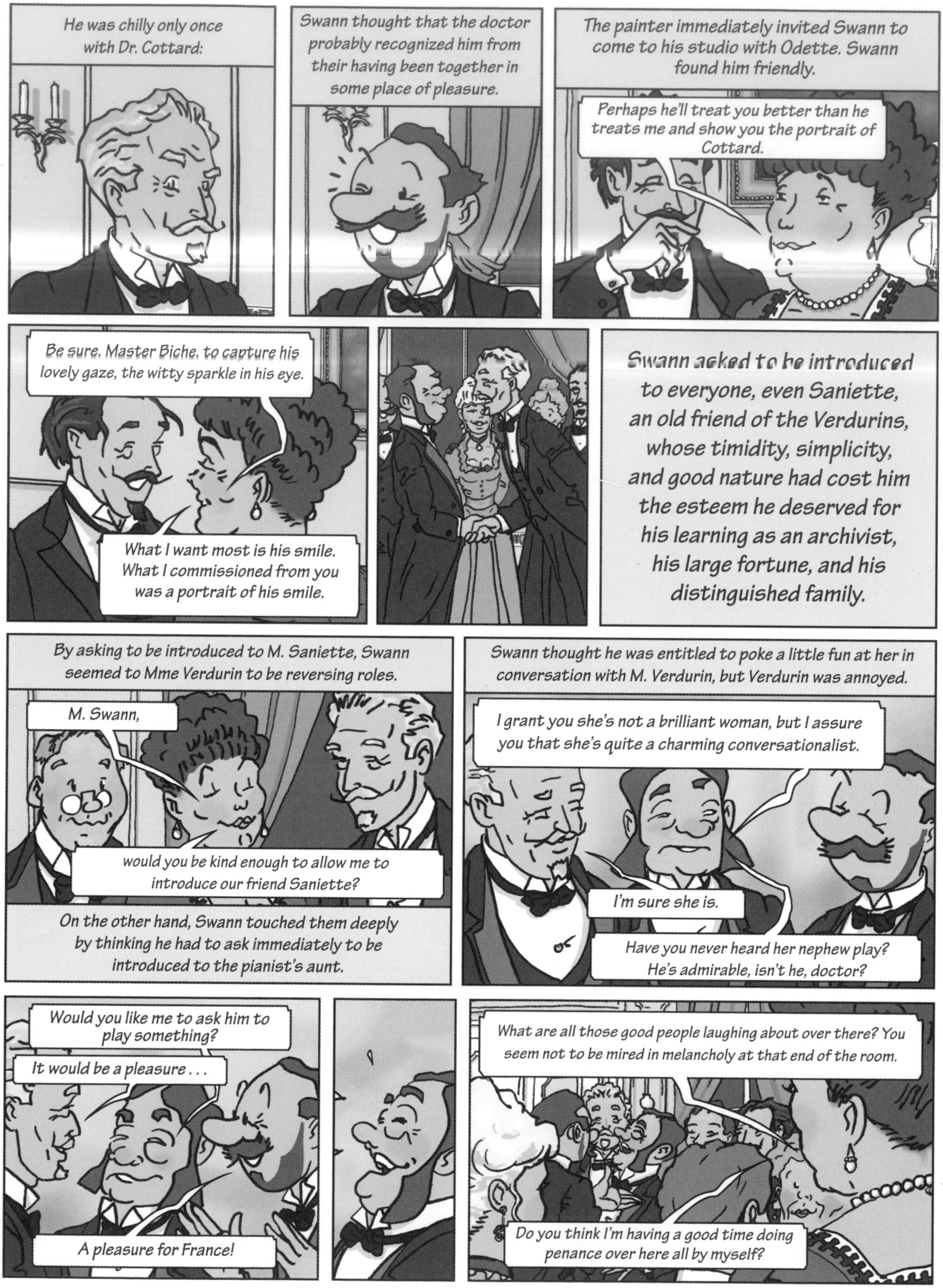
He was chilly only once with Dr. Cottard:
Swann thought that the doctor probably recognized him from their having been together in some place of pleasure.
The painter immediately invited Swann to come to his studio with Odette. Swann found him friendly.
Perhaps he'll treat you better than he treats me and show you the portrait of Cottard.
Be sure, Master Biche, to capture his lovely gaze, the witty sparkle in his eye.
What I want most is his smile. What I commissioned from you was a portrait of his smile.
Swann asked to be introduced to everyone, even Saniette, an old friend of the Verdurins, whose timidity, simplicity, and good nature had cost him the esteem he deserved for his learning as an archivist, his large fortune, and his distinguished family.
By asking to be introduced to M. Saniette, Swann seemed to Mme Verdurin to be reversing roles.
M. Swann,
would you be kind enough to allow me to introduce our friend Saniette?
On the other hand, Swann touched them deeply by thinking he had to ask immediately to be introduced to the pianist's aunt.
Swann thought he was entitled to poke a little fun at her in conversation with M. Verdurin, but Verdurin was annoyed.
I grant you she's not a brilliant woman, but I assure you that she's quite a charming conversationalist.
I'm sure she is.
Have you never heard her nephew play? He's admirable, isn't he, doctor?
Would you like me to ask him to play something?
It would be a pleasure . . .
A pleasure for France!
What are all those good people laughing about over there? You seem not to be mired in melancholy at that end of the room.
Do you think I'm having a good time doing penance over here all by myself?

Mme Verdurin was seated on a Swedish high chair of waxed pine, which a violinist from that country had given her and which she kept, even though it looked like a stepstool and clashed with her fine old furniture,

but she liked to show off the gifts that the faithful gave her now and then so that the givers could enjoy the pleasure of recognizing their gifts whenever they came.

She therefore tried to persuade them that she was partial to flowers and candy, which are at least perishable.

From her raised perch she participated enthusiastically in the conversation of the faithful and laughed at their "witticisms,"

but since the incident with her jaw, she had given up laughing outright and instead engaged in a sort of conventional mime intended to indicate that she was laughing so hard that she cried, but without expenditure of energy or risk of injury.

At the slightest joke . . .

ha !

Her head spinning from the gaiety of the faithful, intoxicated with camaraderie, nastiness, and affirmation, Mme Verdurin, perched on her high chair like a bird whose biscuit has been moistened in mulled wine, sobbed amiably.

Will you allow me?

Would you play something on the piano?

Now, now, leave him alone, he's not here to be tormented. I will not allow him to be tormented.

But why would he mind?

M. Swann may not know the sonata in F# that we discovered. He can play the piano arrangement.

Oh, no, not my sonata!

I don't want it to be like the last time, when I cried so much that I caught a head cold and developed a facial neuralgia.

Thanks very much. I have no wish to repeat the experience. You are all very kind, but clearly none of you will end up in bed for a week.

This little scene, which was repeated whenever the pianist was about to play, delighted her friends as if they had never seen it before.

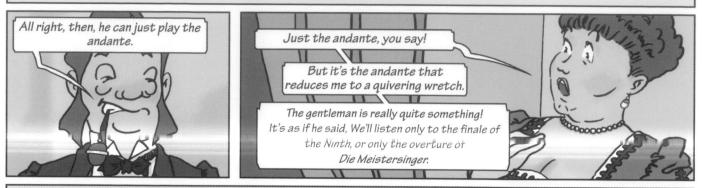

All right, then, he can just play the andante.

Just the andante, you say!

But it's the andante that reduces me to a quivering wretch.

The gentleman is really quite something! It's as if he said, We'll listen only to the finale of the Ninth, or only the overture of Die Meistersinger.

Meanwhile, the doctor pressed Mme Verdurin to let the pianist play, giving in to the habit many doctors have acquired of reducing the severity of their prescriptions when they have some pressing engagement to attend.

You won't be ill this time, you'll see.

And if you do fall ill, we'll take care of you.

Really?

I have my special place, you know.

You don't look very comfortable standing there. Why don't you sit next to Odette? Won't you make room for M. Swann, Odette?

What beautiful Beauvais!

Oh, I'm so pleased that you appreciate my canapé. Each of the bronze ornaments corresponds to one of the subjects in the upholstery. Notice the border theme. See, there, the little vine on a red background in "The Bear and the Grapes." Isn't it nicely designed?

Don't those grapes make your mouth water? My husband says I don't like fruit, but why would I fill my mouth with grapes when I can enjoy them with my eyes?

Why are you all laughing? Ask the doctor. He'll tell you that these grapes have the effect of a purge on me.

But M. Swann, you mustn't leave here without having touched the little bronze moldings on the backs. Feel the softness of the patina. Please, use your whole hand, feel them well.

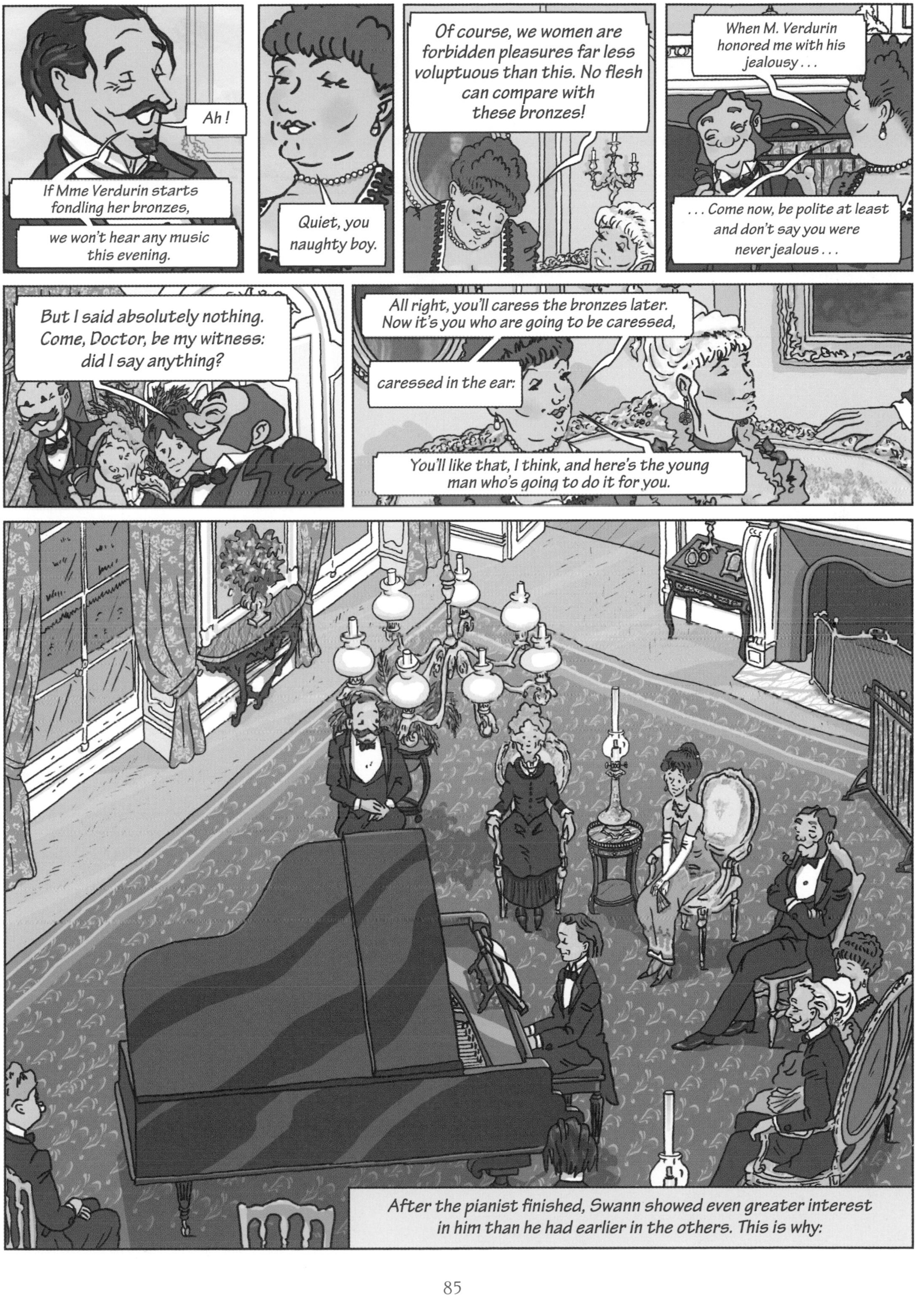
Ah!
If Mme Verdurin starts fondling her bronzes,
we won't hear any music this evening.
Quiet, you naughty boy.
Of course, we women are forbidden pleasures far less voluptuous than this. No flesh can compare with these bronzes!
When M. Verdurin honored me with his jealousy . . .
. . . Come now, be polite at least and don't say you were never jealous . . .
But I said absolutely nothing. Come, Doctor, be my witness: did I say anything?
All right, you'll caress the bronzes later. Now it's you who are going to be caressed,
caressed in the ear:
You'll like that, I think, and here's the young man who's going to do it for you.
After the pianist finished, Swann showed even greater interest in him than he had earlier in the others. This is why:

One night, the previous year, he had heard a piece of music for violin and piano.

At first, he had savored only the material quality of the sounds produced by the instruments.

But at a certain point, suddenly charmed by the music, he had tried to fix in his mind the phrase or harmony—he didn't know which himself—as it flew past, and he had opened his heart to the music.

Perhaps it was because he didn't know the music that he had been receptive to such a confused emotion.

No sooner had the delicious sensation that Swann felt vanished than his memory provided him with a provisional, summary transcription, which he could see in his mind's eye as the piece continued, so that when the same impression abruptly returned, it was no longer impossible to grasp.

This time he clearly distinguished a phrase that for several moments rose above the waves of sound. From it he took immediately a particular pleasure he had never previously imagined, a pleasure he believed nothing but this phrase could offer him, and he loved it as he had never loved anything before.

He desperately wanted to hear it a third time. And it did indeed return,

but did not speak to him more clearly, and his pleasure was this time less profound.

At home, however, he again felt the need of that phrase:

he was like a man who, having glimpsed a woman in passing, takes from her a new idea of beauty, which enlarges his sensibility, though he does not know whether he will ever again see this person, whom he already loves without knowing anything about her, not even her name.

He had long since given up the hope of finding his life's ideal, believing, though he never said so directly, that nothing would change for him as long as he lived.

But now Swann found within himself, in the memory of the phrase he had heard, in certain other sonatas he had asked someone to play for him in the hope he might hear it again, the presence of one of those invisible realities in which he had ceased to believe . . .

. . . and to which he felt anew the desire to dedicate his life.

But because he was unable to discover who had written the piece he had heard, he was never able to obtain the score and in the end forgot about it.

He had many musician friends, but although he remembered the special and untranslatable pleasure the phrase had inspired in him and could see before his eyes the shapes it described, he was nevertheless incapable of humming it for them.

Then he stopped thinking about it.

But only a few minutes after the young pianist began to play, he suddenly became aware of the stealthy, surreptitious, cautious approach of the fragrant, evanescent phrase he loved; he recognized it.

For Swann it was if he had entered a salon and run into a person he had admired in the street and despaired of ever seeing again.

At the end, it vanished in the multiple coils of its fragrance, leaving a trace of its smile on Swann's face.

But now he could ask to know the stranger's name. (He was told that it was the *andante* movement of Vinteuil's *Sonata for Piano and Violin*.)

88

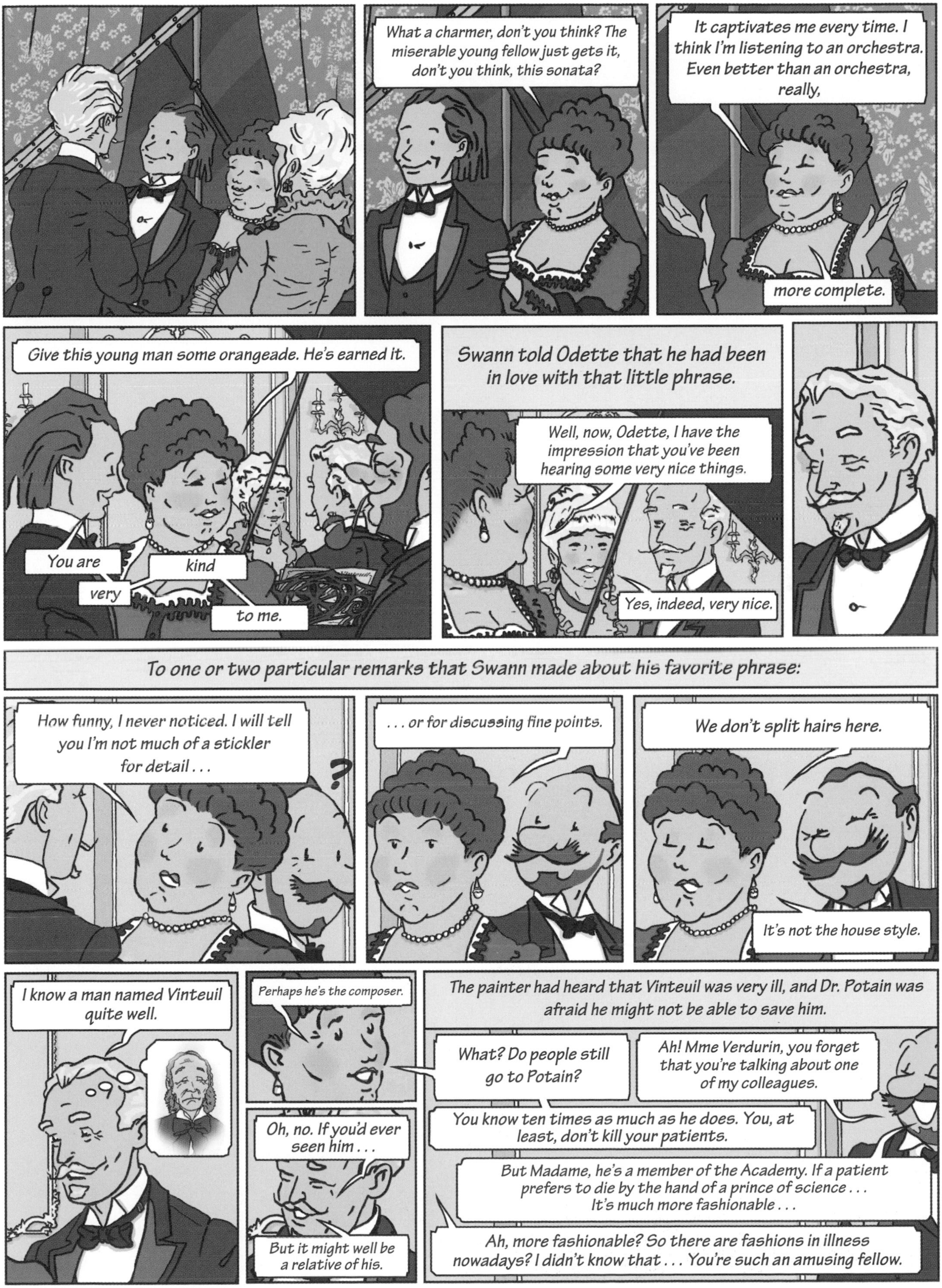
What a charmer, don't you think? The miserable young fellow just gets it, don't you think, this sonata?
It captivates me every time. I think I'm listening to an orchestra. Even better than an orchestra, really,
more complete.
Give this young man some orangeade. He's earned it.
You are
very
kind
to me.
Swann told Odette that he had been in love with that little phrase.
Well, now, Odette, I have the impression that you've been hearing some very nice things.
Yes, indeed, very nice.
To one or two particular remarks that Swann made about his favorite phrase:
How funny, I never noticed. I will tell you I'm not much of a stickler for detail . . .
?
. . . or for discussing fine points.
We don't split hairs here.
It's not the house style.
I know a man named Vinteuil quite well.
Perhaps he's the composer.
Oh, no. If you'd ever seen him . . .
But it might well be a relative of his.
The painter had heard that Vinteuil was very ill, and Dr. Potain was afraid he might not be able to save him.
What? Do people still go to Potain?
Ah! Mme Verdurin, you forget that you're talking about one of my colleagues.
You know ten times as much as he does. You, at least, don't kill your patients.
But Madame, he's a member of the Academy. If a patient prefers to die by the hand of a prince of science . . . It's much more fashionable . . .
Ah, more fashionable? So there are fashions in illness nowadays? I didn't know that . . . You're such an amusing fellow.

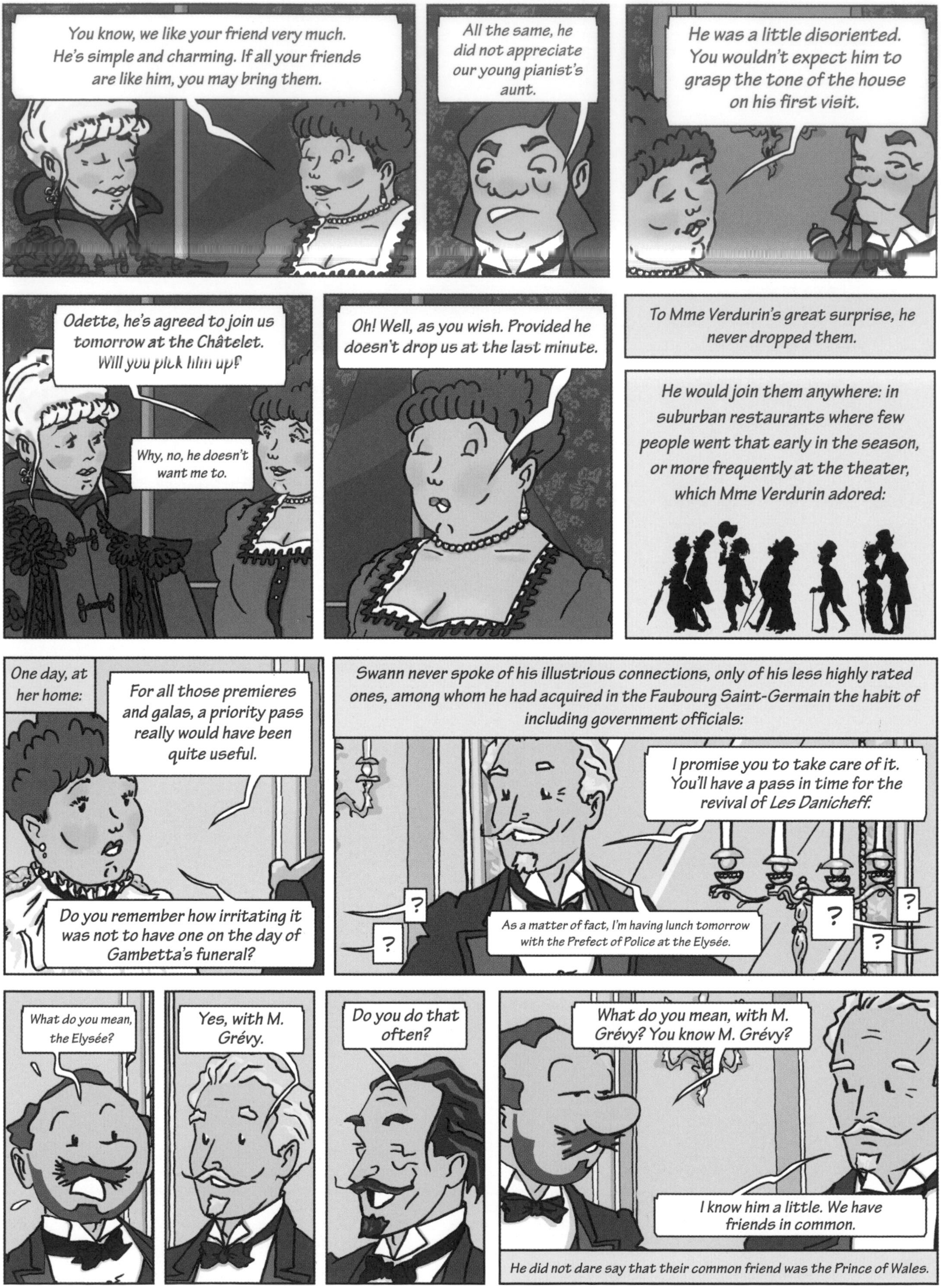
You know, we like your friend very much. He's simple and charming. If all your friends are like him, you may bring them.
All the same, he did not appreciate our young pianist's aunt.
He was a little disoriented. You wouldn't expect him to grasp the tone of the house on his first visit.
Odette, he's agreed to join us tomorrow at the Châtelet. Will you pick him up?
Why, no, he doesn't want me to.
Oh! Well, as you wish. Provided he doesn't drop us at the last minute.
To Mme Verdurin's great surprise, he never dropped them.
He would join them anywhere: in suburban restaurants where few people went that early in the season, or more frequently at the theater, which Mme Verdurin adored:
One day, at her home:
For all those premieres and galas, a priority pass really would have been quite useful.
Do you remember how irritating it was not to have one on the day of Gambetta's funeral?
Swann never spoke of his illustrious connections, only of his less highly rated ones, among whom he had acquired in the Faubourg Saint-Germain the habit of including government officials:
I promise you to take care of it. You'll have a pass in time for the revival of Les Danicheff.
As a matter of fact, I'm having lunch tomorrow with the Prefect of Police at the Elysée.
?
?
?
?
?
What do you mean, the Elysée?
Yes, with M. Grévy.
Do you do that often?
What do you mean, with M. Grévy? You know M. Grévy?
I know him a little. We have friends in common.
He did not dare say that their common friend was the Prince of Wales.

In any case, he gives out invitations quite readily, and I assure you there's nothing amusing about these lunches.

They're also very simple, never more than eight people at the table.

Ah, well, well. That's all right then.

I believe you when you say those lunches aren't very amusing. You deserve credit for going to them.

Apparently, he's stone deaf and eats with his fingers.

Indeed, you must not enjoy yourself very much.

But the prestige of the President of the Republic in the doctor's eyes ultimately won out over Swann's humility and Mme Verdurin's malice,

and at every dinner:

Will we be seeing M. Swann this evening? He has a personal connection with M. Grévy.

Does that make him what people call "a gentleman"?

He went so far as to offer Swann a ticket to the dental show.

You and anyone with you will be admitted, but dogs are not allowed.

You understand that I'm telling you this because I have friends who didn't know and were very frustrated when they found out.

M. Verdurin, for his part, noticed that his wife was not happy . . .

. . . to learn that Swann had powerful friends he'd never mentioned to her.

When no rendezvous had been arranged elsewhere, Swann met the inner circle at the Verdurins', but he came only in the evening and almost never accepted invitations to dinner, despite Odette's insistence.

I could even dine alone with you, if you prefer.

And Mme Verdurin?

It would be very easy. I'd just have to say that my dress wasn't ready or my cab came late.

There is always a way to manage things.

But Swann told himself that if he showed Odette that there were pleasures he preferred to being with her, it would take longer before her appetite for his company reached the point of satiety.

91

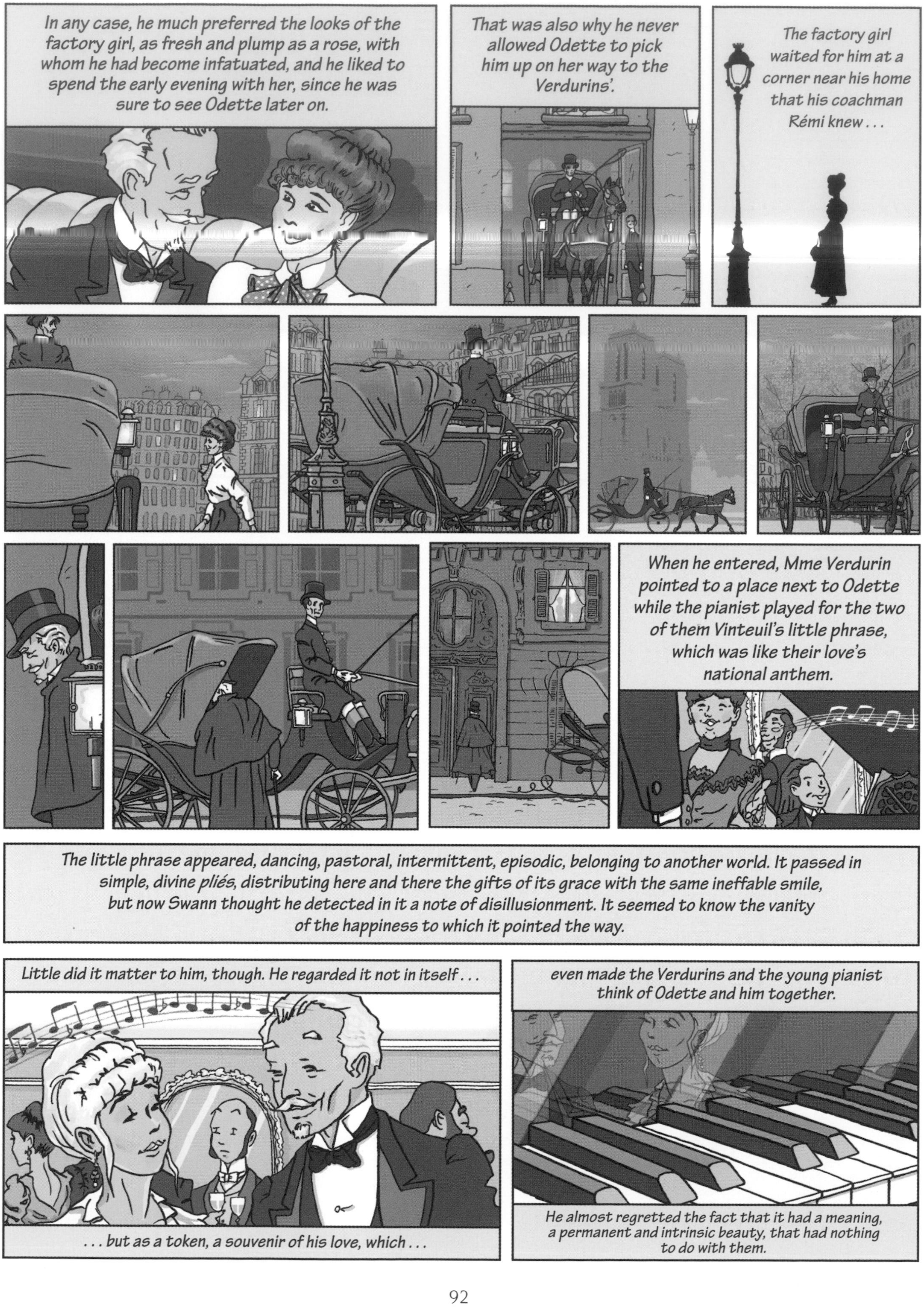
In any case, he much preferred the looks of the factory girl, as fresh and plump as a rose, with whom he had become infatuated, and he liked to spend the early evening with her, since he was sure to see Odette later on.
That was also why he never allowed Odette to pick him up on her way to the Verdurins'.
The factory girl waited for him at a corner near his home that his coachman Rémi knew . . .
When he entered, Mme Verdurin pointed to a place next to Odette while the pianist played for the two of them Vinteuil's little phrase, which was like their love's national anthem.
The little phrase appeared, dancing, pastoral, intermittent, episodic, belonging to another world. It passed in simple, divine *pliés*, distributing here and there the gifts of its grace with the same ineffable smile, but now Swann thought he detected in it a note of disillusionment. It seemed to know the vanity of the happiness to which it pointed the way.
Little did it matter to him, though. He regarded it not in itself . . .
. . . but as a token, a souvenir of his love, which . . .
even made the Verdurins and the young pianist think of Odette and him together.
He almost regretted the fact that it had a meaning, a permanent and intrinsic beauty, that had nothing to do with them.

Often, he tarried so long with the young factory girl before going to the Verdurins' that by the time the pianist played the little phrase, Swann realized that Odette would soon be leaving for home.

He would drive her back to the door of her small house on the Rue La Pérouse.

He sacrificed what for him was the less necessary pleasure of seeing her earlier

no one prevent him from remaining with her

to the exercise of the right she granted him to leave together, thanks to which he had the impression that no one could come between them . . .

. . . after he left her.

One night . . .

See you tomorrow.

After a few days, when the flower had faded, he sealed the precious gift away in his secretary.

93

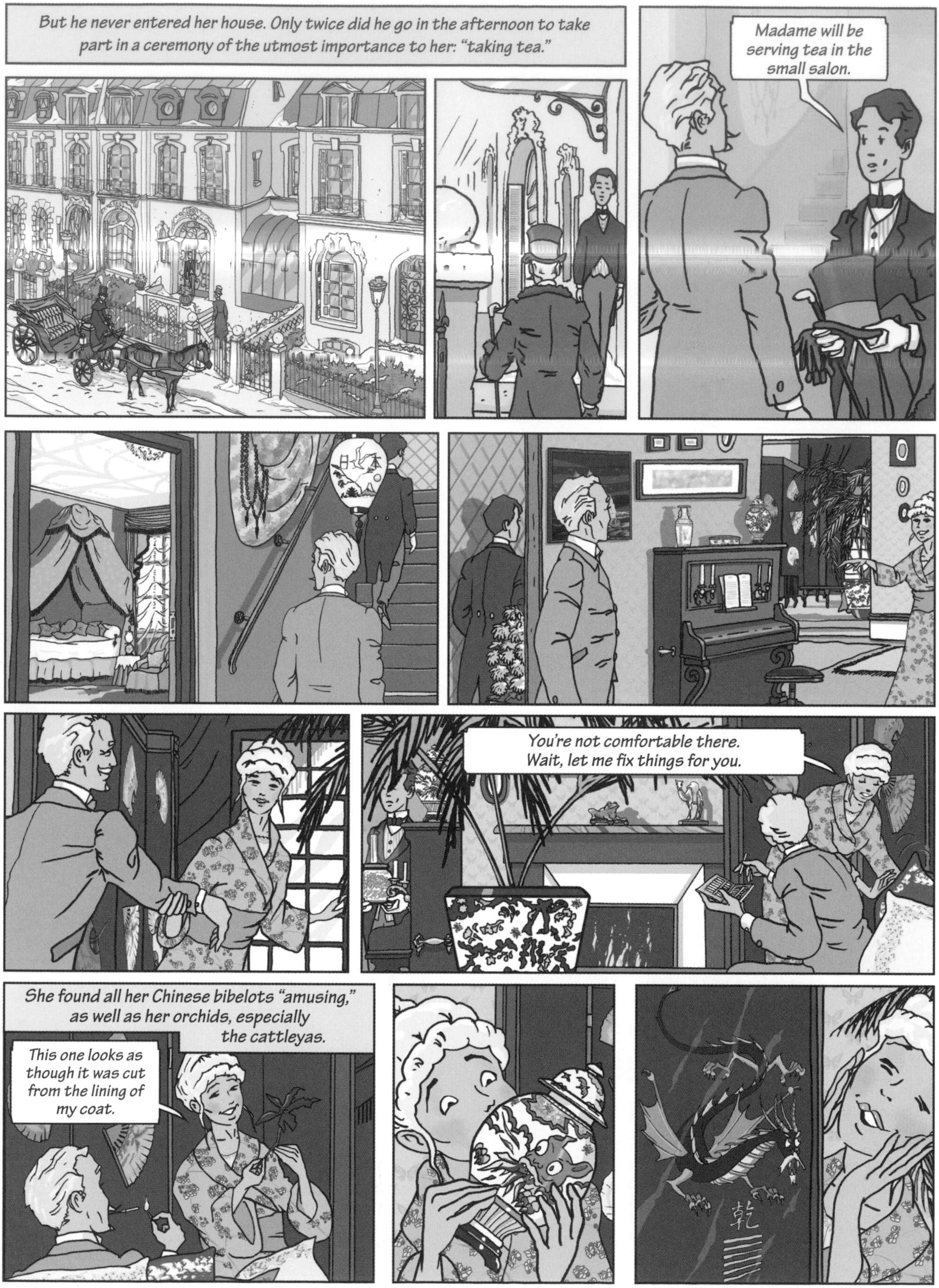
But he never entered her house. Only twice did he go in the afternoon to take part in a ceremony of the utmost importance to her: "taking tea."
Madame will be serving tea in the small salon.
You're not comfortable there. Wait, let me fix things for you.
She found all her Chinese bibelots "amusing," as well as her orchids, especially the cattleyas.
This one looks as though it was cut from the lining of my coat.
乾

These affectations contrasted with the sincerity of certain of her devotions, especially to Our Lady of Laghet, who, when Odette lived in Nice, had saved her from a fatal illness and whose gold medal she always wore . . .

. . . and which she credited with unlimited powers.

Dears!

Lemon or cream?

Cream.

A wisp of cream.

Mmm, it's good.

You see, I know what you like.

The tea had indeed seemed precious to Swann. Love stands in such need of a justification, a guarantee of duration, in pleasures that would not be pleasures without it, that when he left her at seven to return home and dress . . .

It would be quite pleasant . . .

. . . It would be quite pleasant to have someone with whom one could find that rare thing . . .

. . . good tea.

. . . It would be quite pleasant . . .

An hour later, he received a note from Odette. He had forgotten his cigarette case.

Had you also left your heart, I wouldn't have allowed you to reclaim it.

His second visit to her may have been of greater importance. He brought her an engraving she wanted to see.

She was a bit under the weather.

What struck Swann was her resemblance to the figure of Zipporah, Jethro's daughter, . . .

. . . in one of the frescoes of the Sistine Chapel.

Swann had always had a special taste for identifying in the paintings of the great masters the individual features of people he knew. For instance, in a bust of the Doge Loredan the prominent cheekbones . . .

. . . revealed a striking resemblance to his coachman Rémi;

under the colors of a Ghirlandaio he saw the nose of M. de Palancy;

. . . and in a portrait by Tintoretto, he saw the sideburns, the crooked nose, and the penetrating gaze of Dr. du Boulbon.

His deepest pleasure at that time, which was to exert a lasting influence on him, came from the resemblance of Odette to the Zipporah of Sandro di Mariano, commonly known as Botticelli.

Swann blamed himself for having underestimated the beauty of a woman whom the great Sandro would have admired.

He forgot that Odette was not for that reason a woman of the sort he desired, precisely because his desire had always tended in the opposite direction from his aesthetic tastes.

When he was tempted to regret the fact that for months he had done nothing but see Odette,

he told himself that it was reasonable to devote so much of his time to a priceless masterpiece,

which he contemplated at times with the humility, spirituality, and disinterestedness of an artist and at other times with the pride, selfishness, and sensuality of a collector.

. . . drawing a photograph of Zipporah close to him, he felt as if he were clasping Odette to his bosom.

The way the "little clan" functioned as a social organism allowed him to pretend he was indifferent to seeing her or even that he no longer wished to see her, without incurring any great risk,

. . . since he would inevitably see her that evening

and drive her home.

But one time, after he had taken his factory girl to the Bois

to delay the hour of his visit to the Verdurins'.

he arrived so late that Odette, thinking he would not be coming, had already left.

Swann felt sick at heart. He trembled at being deprived of a pleasure he measured for the first time, having previously been certain that he would find her whenever he wanted her.

Did you see the face he made when he noticed she wasn't there? I think you can say he was stung.

The face he made?

M. Swann was here?

For a fleeting moment only. We had a highly agitated, very nervous Swann. Odette had left, you see.

You mean he's "gone all the way" with her,

they've "been around the block"?

Why, no, there's absolutely nothing going on, and between us, I think she's quite wrong and behaving like a perfect fool, which she is, by the way.

Now, now, now, how do you know there's nothing going on? Has any of us got firsthand knowledge?

If there were anything, she would have told me about it. She tells me everything!

Since she has no one else at the moment, I told her she ought to sleep with him.

She says he's timid with her, and that intimidates her in turn,

and in any case she doesn't love him that way, he's an ideal person.

Still, he's absolutely what she needs.

I beg to differ. I've never entirely liked that fellow. I think he's a phony.

I doubt the problem is that the gentleman thinks she's "virtuous." In any case, what can you say, he seems to think she's intelligent.

I don't know if you heard what he spouted to her the other night about Vinteuil's sonata:

I love Odette with all my heart, but you've got to be quite a fool to think she has the slightest interest in aesthetic theories.

Please, I won't hear anything nasty about Odette. She's a charmer.

Who said she isn't? We're not speaking ill of her. But charm isn't the same thing as virtue or intelligence.

In any case, do you care all that much whether she's virtuous or not? She might be much less charming if she were. Who knows?

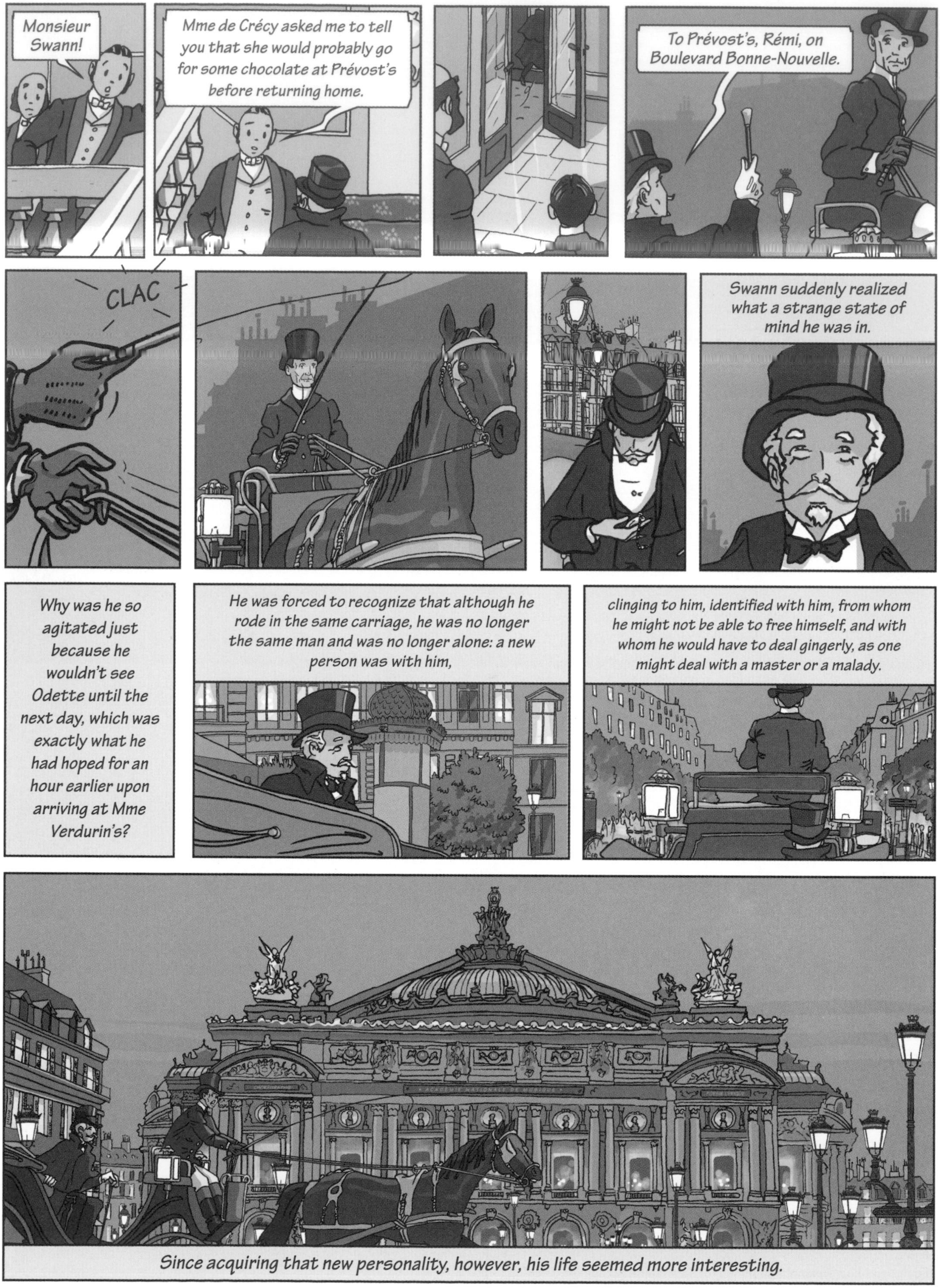

Monsieur Swann!
Mme de Crécy asked me to tell you that she would probably go for some chocolate at Prévost's before returning home.
To Prévost's, Rémi, on Boulevard Bonne-Nouvelle.
CLAC
Swann suddenly realized what a strange state of mind he was in.
Why was he so agitated just because he wouldn't see Odette until the next day, which was exactly what he had hoped for an hour earlier upon arriving at Mme Verdurin's?
He was forced to recognize that although he rode in the same carriage, he was no longer the same man and was no longer alone: a new person was with him,
clinging to him, identified with him, from whom he might not be able to free himself, and with whom he would have to deal gingerly, as one might deal with a master or a malady.
Since acquiring that new personality, however, his life seemed more interesting.

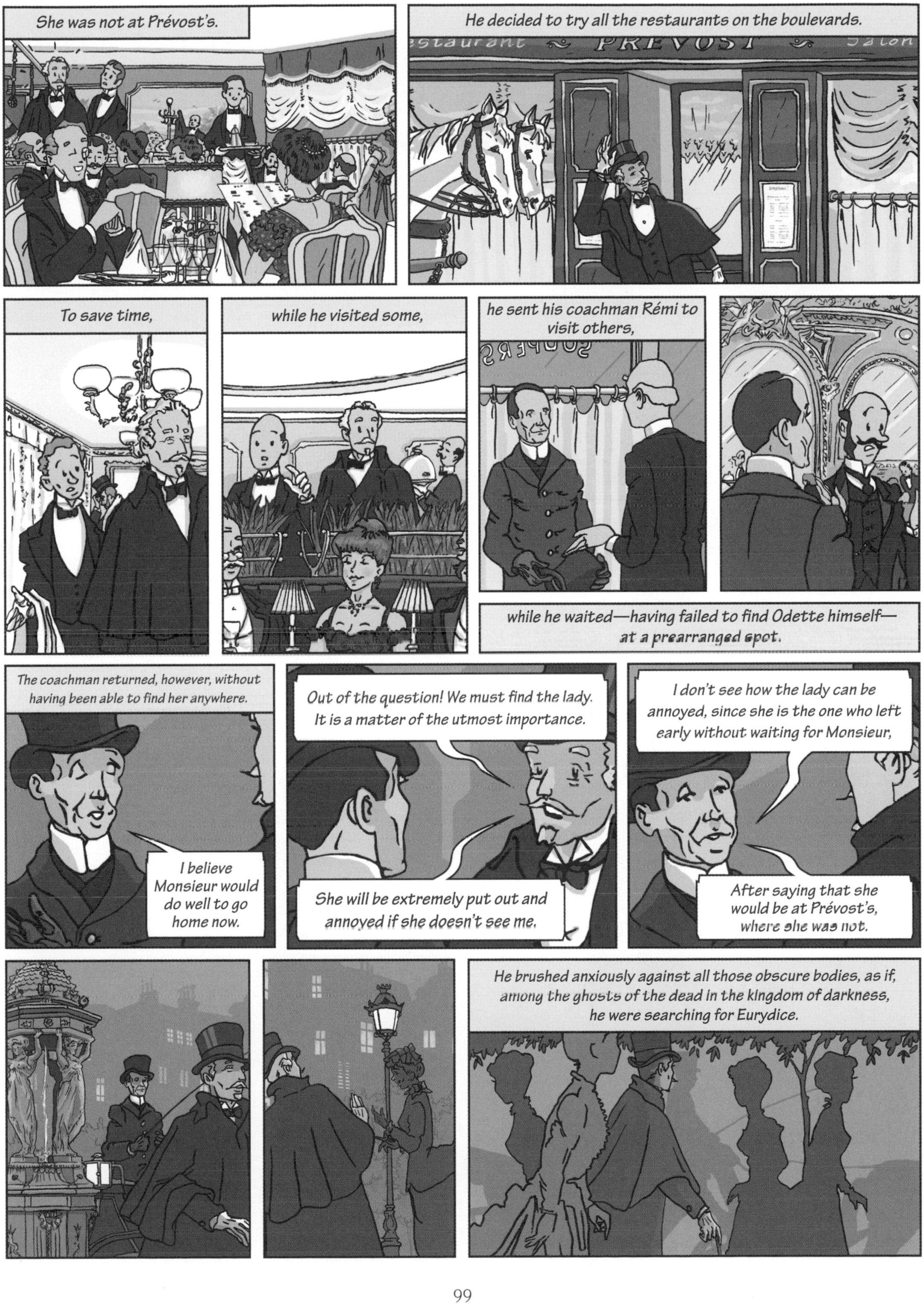

She was not at Prévost's.
He decided to try all the restaurants on the boulevards.
Restaurant PREVOST Salon
To save time,
while he visited some,
he sent his coachman Rémi to visit others,
SOUPERS
while he waited—having failed to find Odette himself—at a prearranged spot.
The coachman returned, however, without having been able to find her anywhere.
I believe Monsieur would do well to go home now.
Out of the question! We must find the lady. It is a matter of the utmost importance.
She will be extremely put out and annoyed if she doesn't see me.
I don't see how the lady can be annoyed, since she is the one who left early without waiting for Monsieur,
After saying that she would be at Prévost's, where she was not.
He brushed anxiously against all those obscure bodies, as if, among the ghosts of the dead in the kingdom of darkness, he were searching for Eurydice.

Of all the ways in which love comes to pass, one of the most effective is to be submerged by a great wave of agitation. The die is then cast in favor of the person who pleases us at that moment: she is the one we will love. Instead of the pleasures we once sought in her company, we suddenly feel an anxious need, the object of which is the person herself— an absurd need, impossible to satisfy and difficult to cure, a senseless and painful need to possess.

Swann ordered his coachman to drive to the remaining restaurants . . .

He no longer concealed his agitation or how urgently he wished to find her, and he promised his coachman a reward if they succeeded.

And there was Odette.

She explained later that because there was no room at Prévost's, she had gone to the Maison Dorée for a late meal, which she had taken in a hidden alcove he must have overlooked, and now she was searching for her carriage.

Rémi! Follow us!

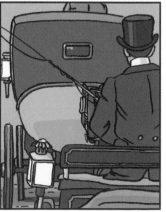

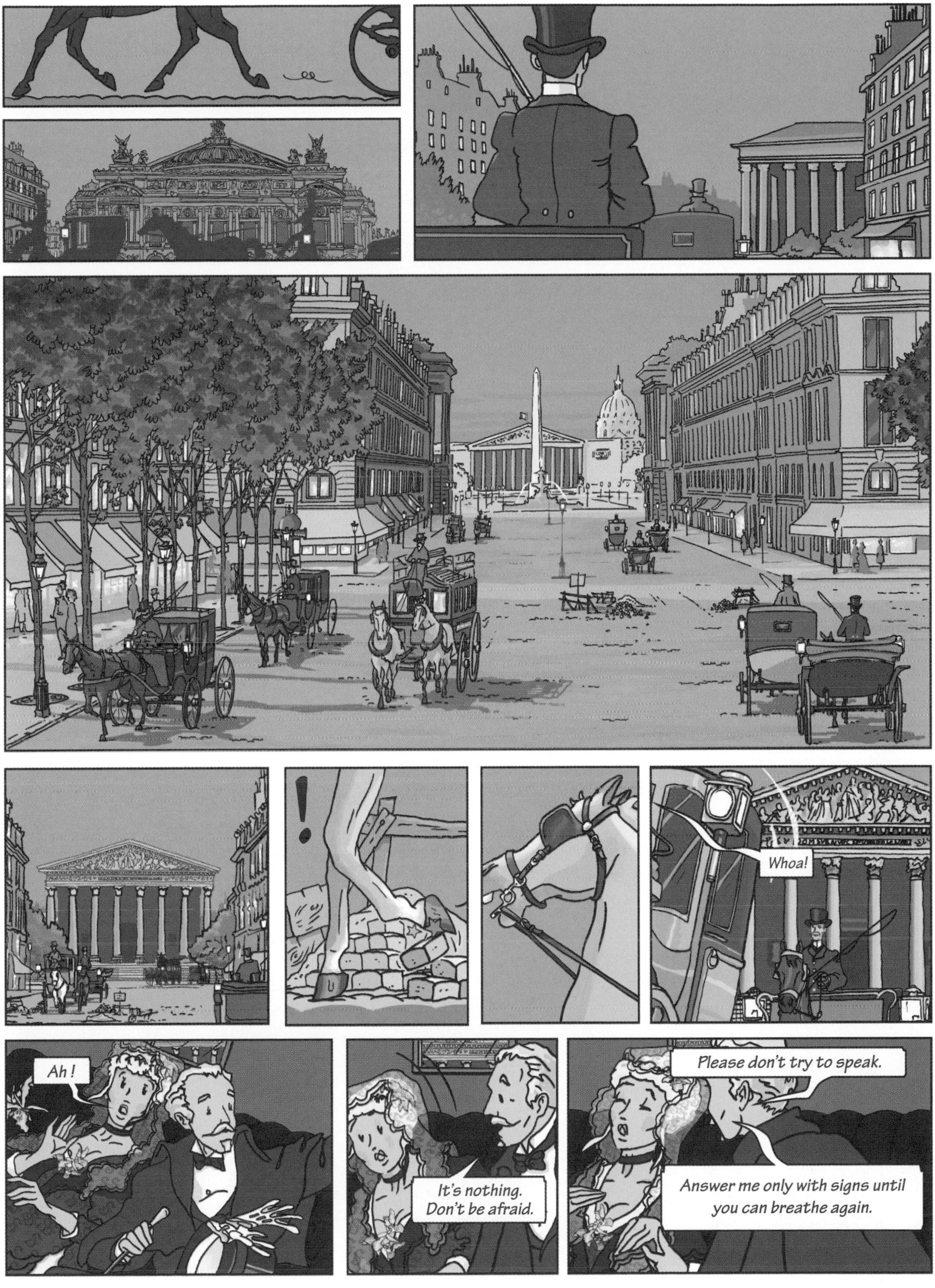

!
Whoa!
Ah !
It's nothing. Don't be afraid.
Please don't try to speak.
Answer me only with signs until you can breathe again.

Will it upset you if I straighten your corsage, which the accident put awry?

I'm afraid you'll lose it. I just want to put it back a little more securely.

She wasn't used to men being so careful with her:

No, it wouldn't bother me at all.

Oh, no, please don't try to speak, it will be even harder for you to catch your breath.

You can respond with gestures. I'll understand you quite well.

Honestly, this doesn't bother you?

Look, there's some . . . I think you've gotten some pollen on you.

May I caress it with my hand.

I hope I'm not being too bold. Am I too brusque?

Might I be tickling you a little? I wouldn't want to touch your velvet gown for fear of wrinkling it.

It was really essential, you see, to reattach your corsage, otherwise it would have fallen off.

So I just pushed it down a little.

Seriously, you don't find me unpleasant?

Even when I sniff the flowers to see if they've really lost their fragrance?

I've never touched there. May I? Tell me honestly.

Striking a pose she knew to be suitable in such moments, she seemed to need all her strength to hold her face back, as if an invisible force were drawing her toward Swann.

Before Swann let go of her face, he held it for a moment at some distance between his two hands. He had wanted to allow his thoughts time to catch up, to recognize the dream he had harbored in his mind for so long.

Perhaps Swann stared at Odette's face, which he had yet to possess or even to kiss, for the last time, the way a departing traveler might stare for the last time at a landscape he was about to leave forever.

102

But he was so hesitant with her that, although he eventually took her that evening, he used the same pretext in the days that followed.

If she wore a corsage of cattleyas:

It's too bad . . .

. . . tonight, there's no need to rearrange the cattleyas. They're not out of place as they were the other night:

Still, your corsage seems not quite straight to me.

May I see if these are more fragrant than the others?

Or, if she wasn't wearing a corsage:

Oh! No cattleyas this evening.

No way for me to arrange them.

And much later, long after there was no further need to arrange cattleyas, the metaphor "making cattleya" was the phrase they instinctively used to refer to "making love," the act of physical possession, in which in any case nothing is possessed. This forgotten habit lived on in their language, commemorating that first instance.

From then on, when he drove her home every evening,

What does it matter to me . . .

what others think?

On evenings when he didn't go to the Verdurins' (because he could now see her in other ways), on those increasingly rare evenings when he ventured into society, she would ask him to come to her before returning home, no matter what the hour.

If he arrived after Odette had dismissed her servants for the night, before ringing at the gate of her little garden he would first go into the street, onto which her first-floor window looked out, the only lighted window among the similar but darkened windows of the adjacent houses.

tac
tac   tac

And awakened,

she would wait for him inside the gate.

He would ask her to play . . .

Play me instead our little phrase from Vinteuil's sonata.

LES ROSES
VALSE.
Pauvres Fous!   D. TAGLIAFICO

. . . even though Odette played very badly.

He would have her play it ten or twenty times while insisting that she kiss him all the while.

Kiss me . . .
kiss me . . .

What exactly do you want? Should I play the phrase or nuzzle with you?

Each kiss called forth another.

In the early stages of love, kisses come so naturally!

He saw her only in the evening and had no idea what she did with her time during the day,

any more than he knew about her past,

including the sort of preliminary information that,

by allowing us to imagine what we do not know, makes us eager to know it.

He merely smiled at times, when it occurred to him that a few years ago,

someone had spoken to him about a woman who surely must have been Odette, as a prostitute, a kept woman, one of those women to whom he attributed the fundamentally perverse character that certain novelists had long associated with such creatures. He contrasted that image with the Odette he knew, a good, naïve woman taken with the ideal . . .

. . . incapable of not telling the truth . . .

Rarely, she came to him in the afternoon.

Mme. de Crécy is in the small salon.

Since he knew nothing of the rest of Odette's life, he saw it as a drawing on a neutral, colorless background, like Watteau's studies, filled with countless smiles placed every which way and drawn on laid paper with three pencils.

Occasionally, however, a friend of his would describe Odette's silhouette, which he had seen walking up the Rue d'Abbattucci wearing a light "wrap" trimmed with skunk.

This simple sketch upset Swann, because it abruptly revealed to him that Odette had a life that didn't belong exclusively to him.

Swann did not try to correct her poor taste in music any more than in literature. He was well aware that she was not intelligent.

. . . Did this Vermeer from Delft suffer because of a woman? Was it a woman who inspired him?

About poetry, you know, nothing would be more beautiful if it were true, if poets believed everything they said. But many of them are awfully materialistic.

I know what I'm talking about. I had a friend who loved a poet of sorts. His poems were all about love, the heavens, and the stars. Was she ever taken in!

He took her for more than 300,000 francs.

If Swann attempted to teach her what artistic beauty was, she quickly stopped listening.

She was amazed by his indifference to money, his kindness to everyone, and his tact.

Odette respected Swann's social standing, but she didn't want him to exert himself to get her invited anywhere. She may have been afraid that the mere mention of her name would lead to unwanted revelations.

If Swann read a list of dinner guests in a newspaper, he could immediately tell you precisely how exclusive the dinner was, much as a connoisseur of literature can judge the quality of an author from a single sentence. But Odette was a person without such abilities.

About one person Odette said:

He never goes to the chic places.

What do you mean by that?

Why, the chic places, for Heaven's sake! If I have to tell you at your age what the chic places are, what can I say? On Sunday mornings, for example, the Avenue de l'Impératirce.

. . . at five o'clock, a turn around the lake, on Thursdays, the Eden Theater,

. . . on Fridays, the Hippodrome, and then there are the balls . . .

Which balls?

Why, the balls people throw in Paris, the chic balls, of course.

You know Herbinger? But you must know him, he's one of the men most in view in Paris, that tall, blond fellow who's such a snob. Well, he threw a ball the other night, and every fashionable person in Paris was there.

How I would have liked to go!

Swann did not try to alter her conception of chic, because he thought that his was no truer than hers, that it was just as foolish and unimportant.

She could not understand why Swann lived on the Quai d'Orléans, which, though she dared not tell him, she thought unworthy of him.

To be sure, she claimed to love "antiques."

I love to spend days shopping for "bibelots,"

. . . for "old stuff."

She once mentioned to Swann a friend who had invited her.

In her place everything is a "period piece."

Which period?

After thinking about it:

"Middle Age-ish."

By that she meant that the walls were paneled.

He critically remarked that Odette's friend lived among ersatz antiques:

You wouldn't want her to live as you do with broken furniture and threadbare carpets, would you?

Bourgeois respectability took precedence over the dilettantism of the cocotte.

Because Swann's eyesight was somewhat deficient:

That's quite all right, it's very chic! You look like a real gentleman.

All you need is a title.

He loved Odette the way she was, just as, if he had been infatuated with a girl from Brittany, he would have been happy to see her in Breton headdress and hear her say she believed in ghosts.

106

Like everything else that surrounded Odette and in a sense formed the frame in which he saw her, he liked the company of the Verdurins and tried to attribute genuine merit to them.

Truly, the life they lead is the real life. How much more intelligent and artistic their guests are than society people!

Despite a few rather ridiculous exaggerations, Mme Verdurin sincerely loves painting and music.

Perhaps I have no great intellectual need for conversation, but I'm perfectly happy to talk with Cottard, even though he makes those stupid puns.

And as for the painter, while his pretentiousness is unpleasant, when he aims to surprise he's one of the most intelligent people I've ever known.

Mme Verdurin sometimes offered Swann the only thing that really pleased him:

Odette, you'll see M. Swann home, won't you?

He went so far as to say that Mme Verdurin was a woman of great soul

. . . I much prefer the Verdurins.

They are generous people, and in the end generosity is the only thing that matters, the only thing that sets one apart in this fallen world.

He knew other big-hearted people, but they did not know Odette.

Among the Verdurins' friends, there was probably not a single one who liked them, or thought he liked them, as much as Swann.

Yet when M. Verdurin said Swann wasn't to his taste, he not only expressed his own thought but divined his wife's.

They would have forgiven him for spending time with bores had he been willing to set a good example by disavowing them in the presence of the faithful.

But they realized they would never be able to wrest such a disavowal from his lips.

What a difference from the "new" friend Odette asked them to invite, the Comte de Forcheville!

He was in fact Saniette's brother-in-law, which surprised the faithful no end.

To be sure, Forcheville was an outright snob, whereas Swann was not, and he was a long way from placing the Verdurins' salon above all the others, as Swann did.

But he lacked the natural tact that prevented Swann from assenting to the plainly false criticisms that Mme Verdurin leveled at people he knew.

Indeed, the first dinner that Forcheville attended at the Verdurins revealed all these differences and highlighted Forcheville's virtues, thus precipitating Swann's disgrace.

In addition to the usual guests this dinner included a Professor Brichot of the Sorbonne, who had met the Verdurins at a spa.

When he discussed philosophy and history with Mme Verdurin, he made a point of seeking comparisons with contemporary events.

Your white gown is quite original.

Blanche? Blanche de Castille?

What can you say about a scientist who makes such puns?

You can't speak seriously with him for two minutes.

Do you make such puns at your hospital?

If so, I'm sure no one is ever bored. I'll have to arrange to have myself admitted.

I believe I heard Dr. Cottard mention Blanche de Castille, that old chippy, if you'll allow me to put it that way.

Didn't he, Madame?

Ha ha ha.

Dear Madame, I do not wish to alarm any reverent souls, should there be any around this table, *sub rosa*. . . . I recognize, moreover, that our ineffable Athenian republic—how Athenian indeed!— might wish to honor that obscurantist Capetian woman as the first of France's tough-minded chiefs of police.

The Chronicle of Saint-Denis, whose reliability cannot be challenged, leaves no doubt in this respect.

Yes indeed, my dear host, yes indeed.

She saw to it that everyone got what they deserved.

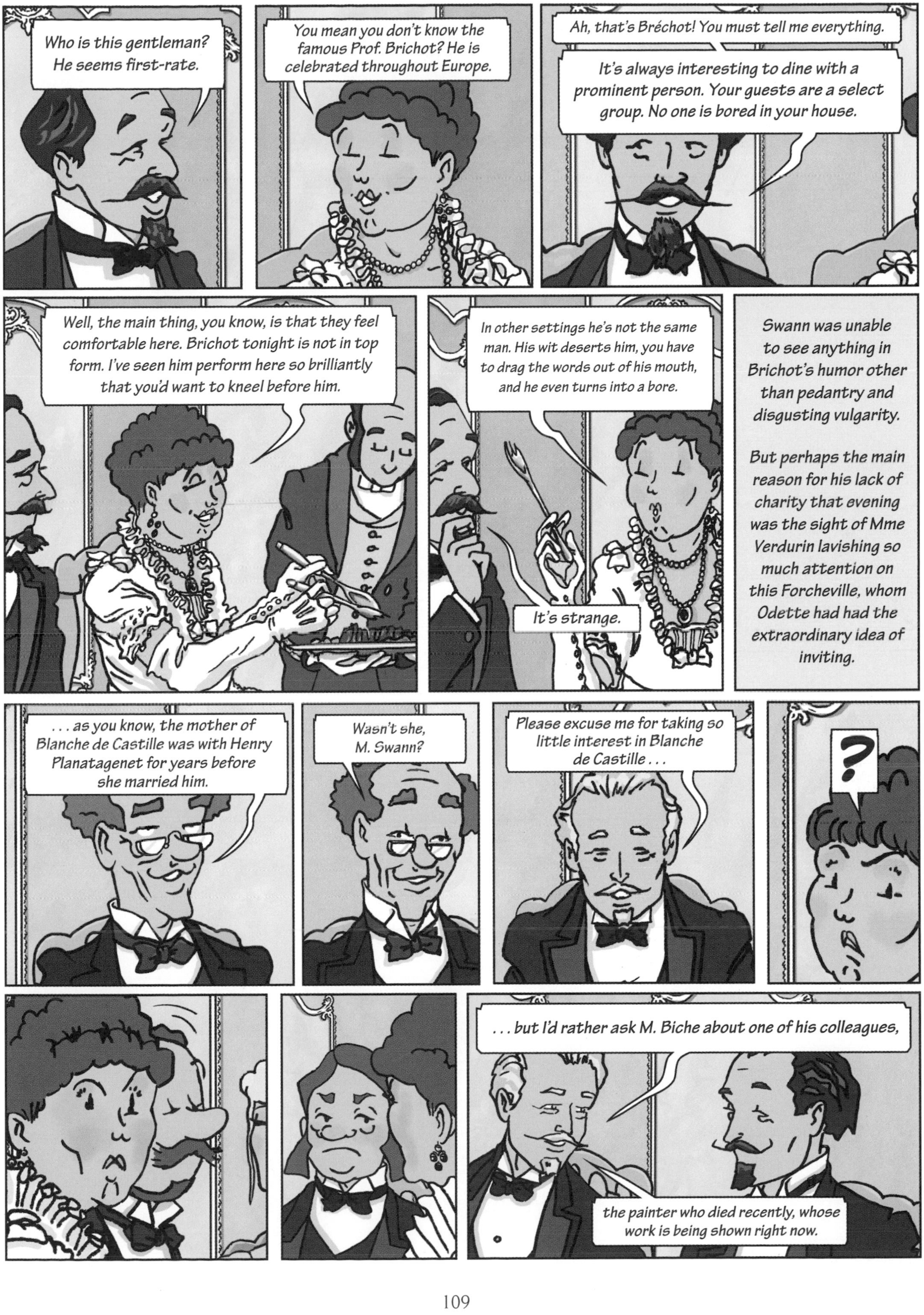
Who is this gentleman? He seems first-rate.
You mean you don't know the famous Prof. Brichot? He is celebrated throughout Europe.
Ah, that's Bréchot! You must tell me everything.
It's always interesting to dine with a prominent person. Your guests are a select group. No one is bored in your house.
Well, the main thing, you know, is that they feel comfortable here. Brichot tonight is not in top form. I've seen him perform here so brilliantly that you'd want to kneel before him.
In other settings he's not the same man. His wit deserts him, you have to drag the words out of his mouth, and he even turns into a bore.
It's strange.
Swann was unable to see anything in Brichot's humor other than pedantry and disgusting vulgarity.
But perhaps the main reason for his lack of charity that evening was the sight of Mme Verdurin lavishing so much attention on this Forcheville, whom Odette had had the extraordinary idea of inviting.
. . . as you know, the mother of Blanche de Castille was with Henry Planatagenet for years before she married him.
Wasn't she, M. Swann?
Please excuse me for taking so little interest in Blanche de Castille . . .
?
. . . but I'd rather ask M. Biche about one of his colleagues,
the painter who died recently, whose work is being shown right now.

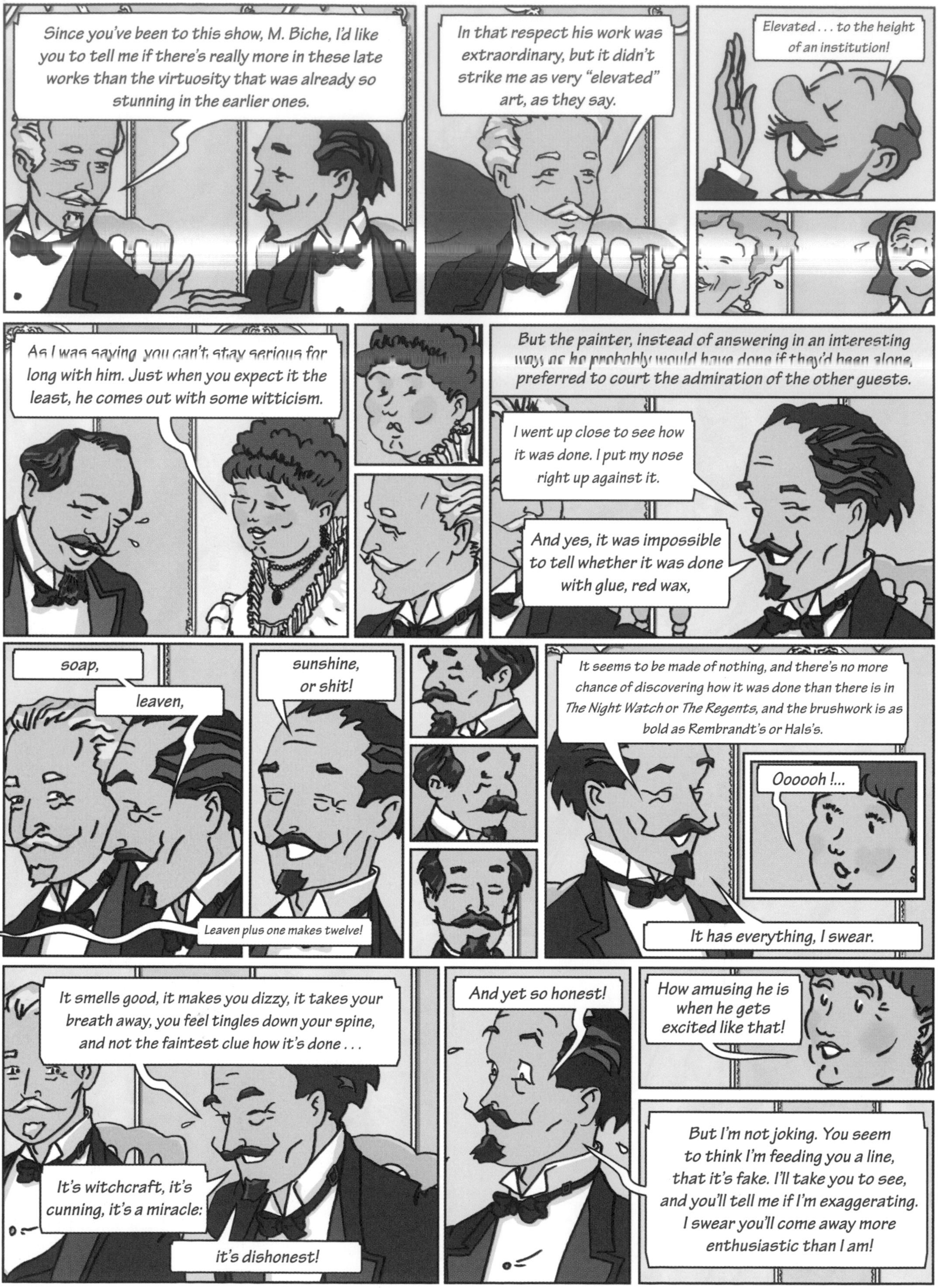
Since you've been to this show, M. Biche, I'd like you to tell me if there's really more in these late works than the virtuosity that was already so stunning in the earlier ones.
In that respect his work was extraordinary, but it didn't strike me as very "elevated" art, as they say.
Elevated . . . to the height of an institution!
As I was saying, you can't stay serious for long with him. Just when you expect it the least, he comes out with some witticism.
But the painter, instead of answering in an interesting way as he probably would have done if they'd been alone, preferred to court the admiration of the other guests.
I went up close to see how it was done. I put my nose right up against it.
And yes, it was impossible to tell whether it was done with glue, red wax,
soap,
leaven,
sunshine, or shit!
Leaven plus one makes twelve!
It seems to be made of nothing, and there's no more chance of discovering how it was done than there is in The Night Watch or The Regents, and the brushwork is as bold as Rembrandt's or Hals's.
Oooooh !...
It has everything, I swear.
It smells good, it makes you dizzy, it takes your breath away, you feel tingles down your spine, and not the faintest clue how it's done . . .
It's witchcraft, it's cunning, it's a miracle:
it's dishonest!
And yet so honest!
How amusing he is when he gets excited like that!
But I'm not joking. You seem to think I'm feeding you a line, that it's fake. I'll take you to see, and you'll tell me if I'm exaggerating. I swear you'll come away more enthusiastic than I am!

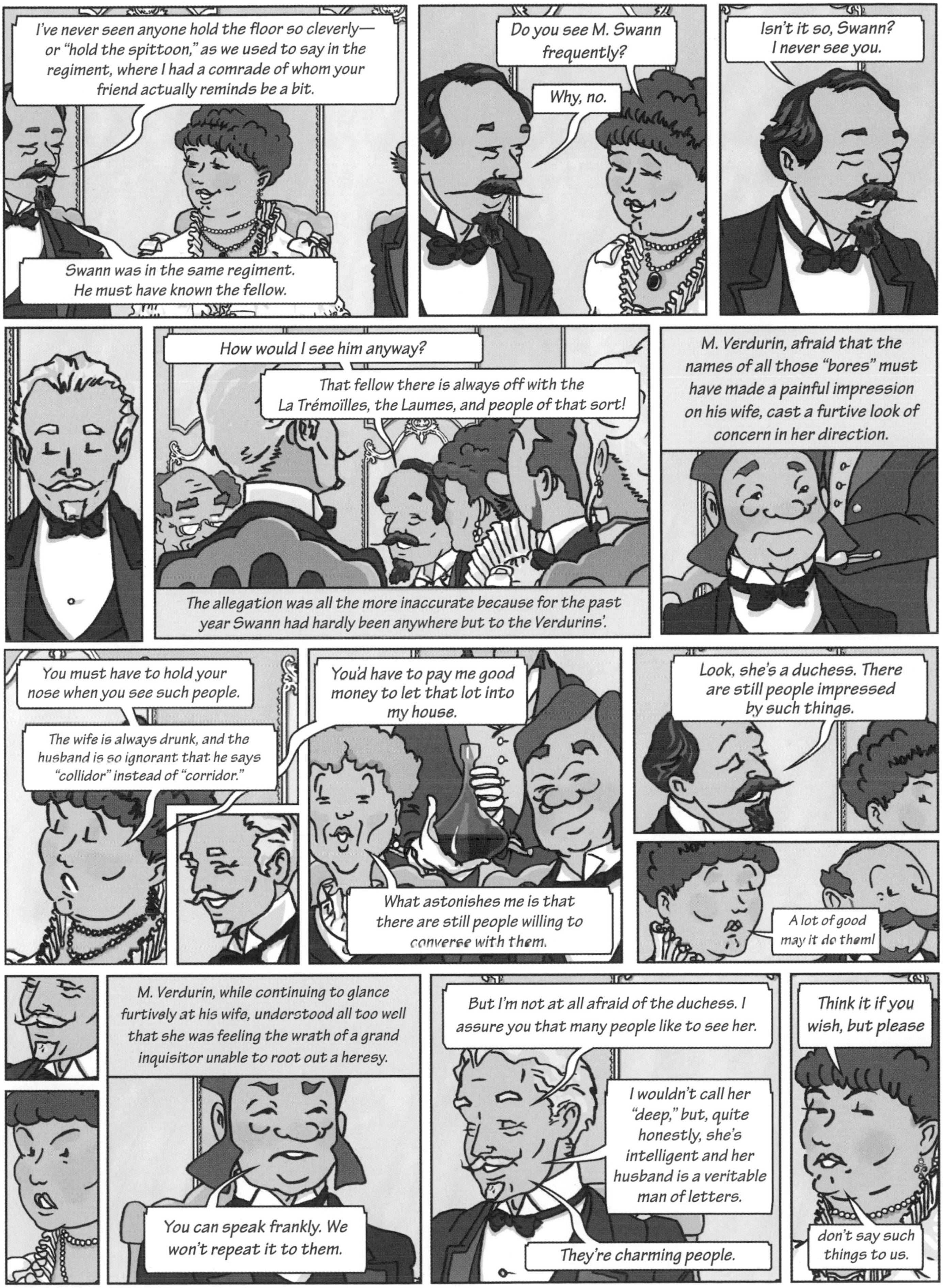

I've never seen anyone hold the floor so cleverly— or "hold the spittoon," as we used to say in the regiment, where I had a comrade of whom your friend actually reminds be a bit.
Swann was in the same regiment. He must have known the fellow.
Do you see M. Swann frequently?
Why, no.
Isn't it so, Swann? I never see you.
How would I see him anyway?
That fellow there is always off with the La Trémoïlles, the Laumes, and people of that sort!
The allegation was all the more inaccurate because for the past year Swann had hardly been anywhere but to the Verdurins'.
M. Verdurin, afraid that the names of all those "bores" must have made a painful impression on his wife, cast a furtive look of concern in her direction.
You must have to hold your nose when you see such people.
The wife is always drunk, and the husband is so ignorant that he says "collidor" instead of "corridor."
You'd have to pay me good money to let that lot into my house.
What astonishes me is that there are still people willing to converse with them.
Look, she's a duchess. There are still people impressed by such things.
A lot of good may it do them!
M. Verdurin, while continuing to glance furtively at his wife, understood all too well that she was feeling the wrath of a grand inquisitor unable to root out a heresy.
You can speak frankly. We won't repeat it to them.
But I'm not at all afraid of the duchess. I assure you that many people like to see her.
I wouldn't call her "deep," but, quite honestly, she's intelligent and her husband is a veritable man of letters.
They're charming people.
Think it if you wish, but please
don't say such things to us.

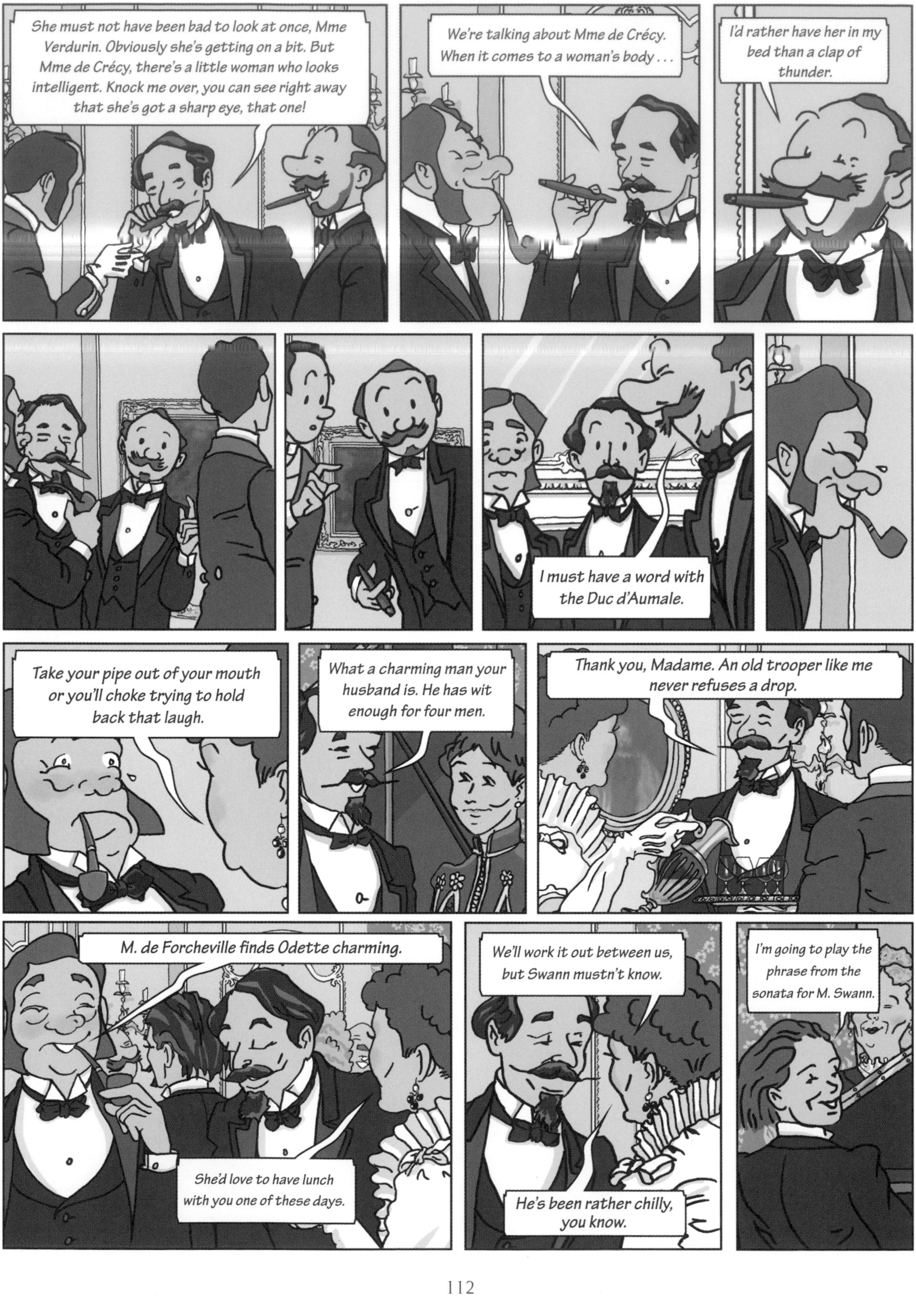
She must not have been bad to look at once, Mme Verdurin. Obviously she's getting on a bit. But Mme de Crécy, there's a little woman who looks intelligent. Knock me over, you can see right away that she's got a sharp eye, that one!
We're talking about Mme de Crécy. When it comes to a woman's body . . .
I'd rather have her in my bed than a clap of thunder.
I must have a word with the Duc d'Aumale.
Take your pipe out of your mouth or you'll choke trying to hold back that laugh.
What a charming man your husband is. He has wit enough for four men.
Thank you, Madame. An old trooper like me never refuses a drop.
M. de Forcheville finds Odette charming.
She'd love to have lunch with you one of these days.
We'll work it out between us, but Swann mustn't know.
He's been rather chilly, you know.
I'm going to play the phrase from the sonata for M. Swann.

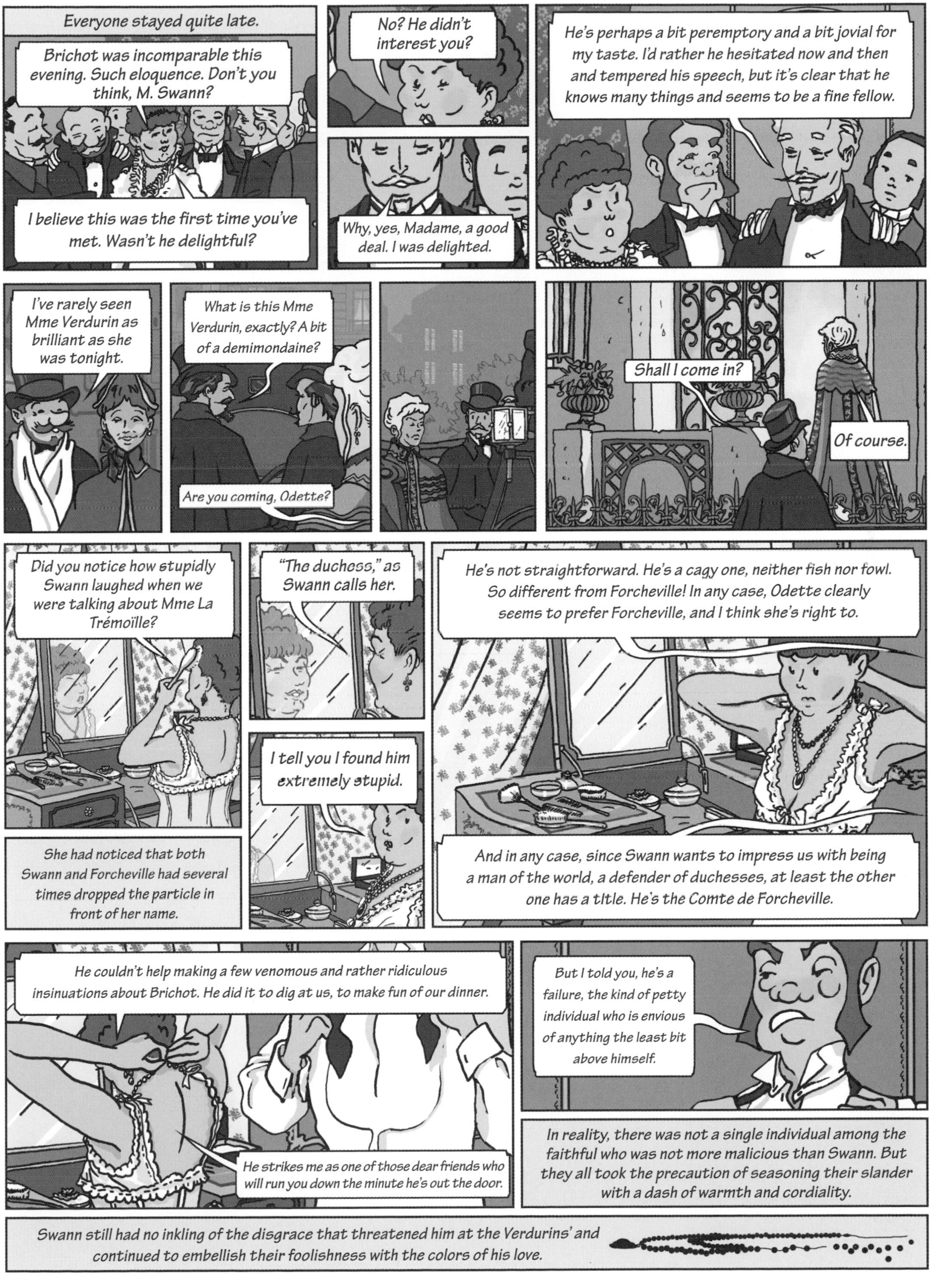

Everyone stayed quite late.
Brichot was incomparable this evening. Such eloquence. Don't you think, M. Swann?
I believe this was the first time you've met. Wasn't he delightful?
No? He didn't interest you?
Why, yes, Madame, a good deal. I was delighted.
He's perhaps a bit peremptory and a bit jovial for my taste. I'd rather he hesitated now and then and tempered his speech, but it's clear that he knows many things and seems to be a fine fellow.
I've rarely seen Mme Verdurin as brilliant as she was tonight.
What is this Mme Verdurin, exactly? A bit of a demimondaine?
Are you coming, Odette?
Shall I come in?
Of course.
Did you notice how stupidly Swann laughed when we were talking about Mme La Trémoïlle?
"The duchess," as Swann calls her.
I tell you I found him extremely stupid.
She had noticed that both Swann and Forcheville had several times dropped the particle in front of her name.
He's not straightforward. He's a cagy one, neither fish nor fowl. So different from Forcheville! In any case, Odette clearly seems to prefer Forcheville, and I think she's right to.
And in any case, since Swann wants to impress us with being a man of the world, a defender of duchesses, at least the other one has a title. He's the Comte de Forcheville.
He couldn't help making a few venomous and rather ridiculous insinuations about Brichot. He did it to dig at us, to make fun of our dinner.
He strikes me as one of those dear friends who will run you down the minute he's out the door.
But I told you, he's a failure, the kind of petty individual who is envious of anything the least bit above himself.
In reality, there was not a single individual among the faithful who was not more malicious than Swann. But they all took the precaution of seasoning their slander with a dash of warmth and cordiality.
Swann still had no inkling of the disgrace that threatened him at the Verdurins' and continued to embellish their foolishness with the colors of his love.

In the evening, when he did not stay home until it was time to meet Odette at the Verdurins' or in one of the open-air restaurants they liked in the Bois or especially in Saint-Cloud,

he would dine in one of the elegant houses where he had formerly been a regular guest.

Because he had felt ill and depressed for some time, especially after Odette had introduced Forcheville to the Verdurins, Swann would have liked to go to the country for some rest. But he could never muster up the courage to leave Paris for as much as a single day while Odette was there.

The weather was hot.

What was always in his mind's eye was a property he owned near Combray . . .

Once, after dinner, he left so quickly that the Princesse de Laumes, with whom he had dined late,

and whom Swann had left before coffee was served in order to join the Verdurins on the island in the Bois, said:

You know, if Swann were thirty years older and had bladder trouble, it would be excusable for him to run off like that.

But he's thumbing his nose at the world.

He told himself that if he could not savor the charm of spring in Combray, he would at least find it on the Île des Cygnes or in Saint-Cloud.

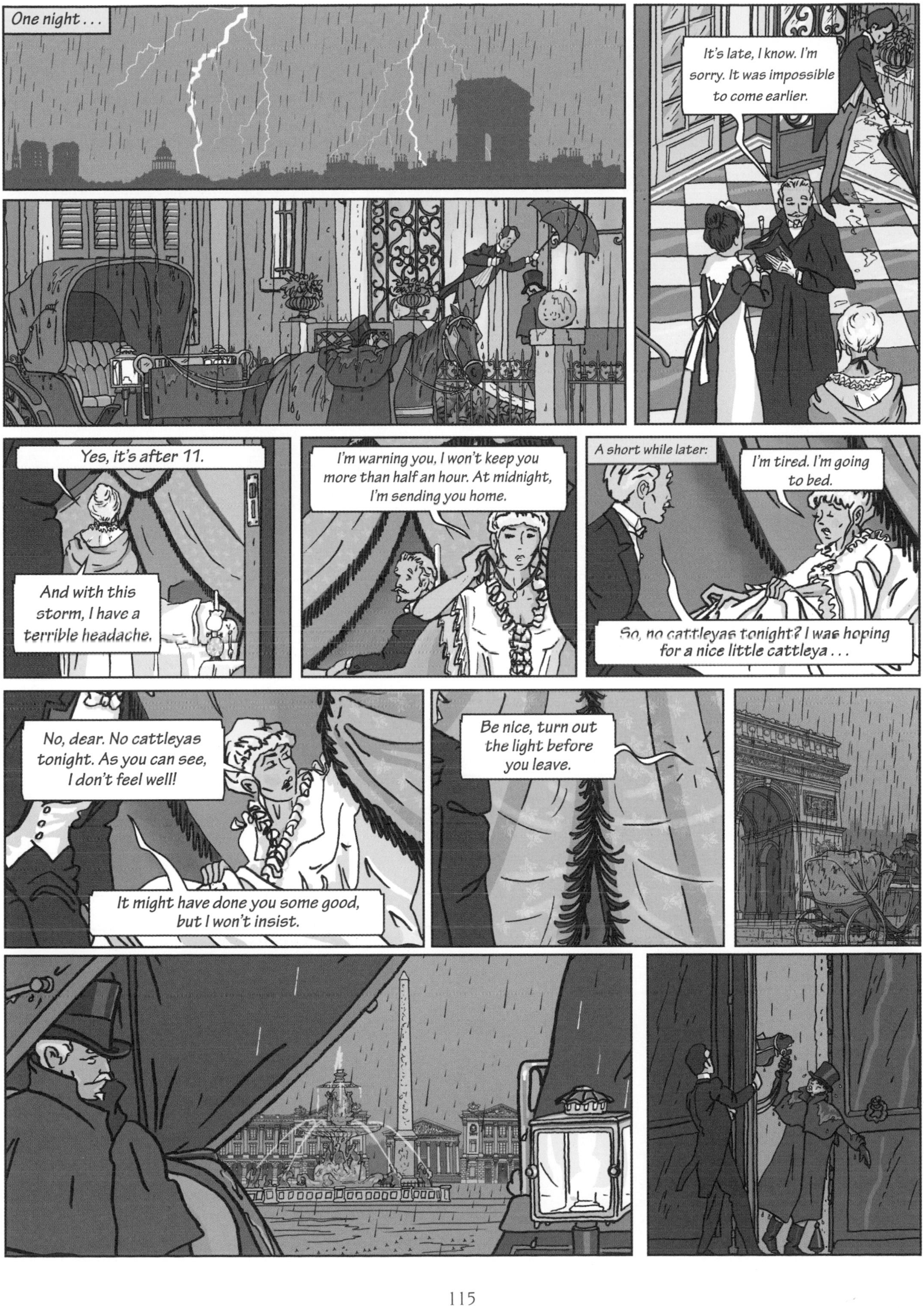
One night . . .
It's late, I know. I'm sorry. It was impossible to come earlier.
Yes, it's after 11.
And with this storm, I have a terrible headache.
I'm warning you, I won't keep you more than half an hour. At midnight, I'm sending you home.
A short while later:
I'm tired. I'm going to bed.
So, no cattleyas tonight? I was hoping for a nice little cattleya . . .
No, dear. No cattleyas tonight. As you can see, I don't feel well!
It might have done you some good, but I won't insist.
Be nice, turn out the light before you leave.

It suddenly occurred to him that Odette might be expecting someone else and had only pretended to be tired and that as soon as he left, she would turn the light back on and welcome whoever was supposed to spend the night with her.

He had left her almost an hour and a half earlier.

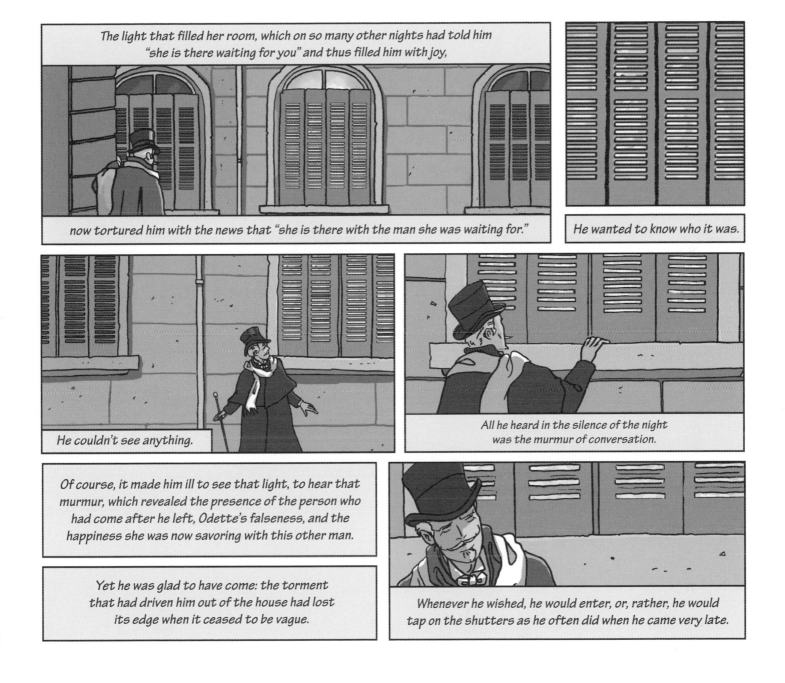

The light that filled her room, which on so many other nights had told him "she is there waiting for you" and thus filled him with joy,

now tortured him with the news that "she is there with the man she was waiting for."

He wanted to know who it was.

He couldn't see anything.

All he heard in the silence of the night was the murmur of conversation.

Of course, it made him ill to see that light, to hear that murmur, which revealed the presence of the person who had come after he left, Odette's falseness, and the happiness she was now savoring with this other man.

Yet he was glad to have come: the torment that had driven him out of the house had lost its edge when it ceased to be vague.

Whenever he wished, he would enter, or, rather, he would tap on the shutters as he often did when he came very late.

That way, at least, Odette would know that he knew, that he had seen the light and heard the conversation, and, having earlier imagined them laughing at his illusions,

he now pictured them as confident in their error, tricked by him, whom they thought far away even as he knew he was about to tap on the shutters.

What he felt at that moment was also something else, something almost pleasant, perhaps: an intellectual pleasure.

His jealousy had revived another faculty: the passion for truth.

A person's everyday actions and behavior had always seemed insignificant to Swann. If someone gossiped with him about such things, he would listen, but at these moments he felt utterly abject.

But during this strange period of love, he felt his old curiosity about history coming back to life. And things of which he previously would have been ashamed—

spying at windows and, who knows? Before long bribing servants and listening at doors—

now seemed to him nothing more than methods of scientific investigation

appropriate to the search for the truth.

For a moment he felt ashamed at the thought that Odette would know he had harbored suspicions about her. She had often spoken of her horror at jealous lovers who resorted to spying.

She would then detest him, whereas for the moment, perhaps, she still loved him even as she cheated on him.

But his desire to know the truth was stronger and in his eyes nobler. He knew that the truth was legible behind that window streaked with light, which was like the gold-illuminated cover of a precious manuscript to whose artistic riches a scholar cannot remain indifferent.

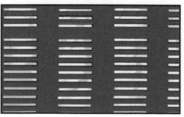

The advantage he felt he had over them, moreover, was perhaps not so much to know

as to be able to show them that he knew.

They didn't hear his tapping.

toc
toc
toc

Who's there?

A man's voice.
He wasn't sure he recognized it.

There was no way to turn back now.

Don't get up. I was passing by,

and saw the light. I wanted to know if you still felt ill.

?

He returned home, happy that the satisfaction of his curiosity had left their love intact and that, after having feigned indifference to Odette for so long,

he had not given her, with his jealousy, the proof that he loved her too much, which, between two lovers, forever dispenses the one who receives it from loving enough.

Being in the habit, when he visited Odette very late at night, of recognizing her window by the fact that it was the only one of all the similar windows in which there was a light, he had made a mistake and tapped on the window of the house next door.

He did not mention his misadventure to her and never gave it another thought.

119

When he left Odette, he was happy, he felt calm.

He remembered her smiles, which showed affection for him as she made fun of other men.

But then, as if his jealousy were the shadow of his love,

it immediately conjured up copies of those smiles, which now made fun of Swann and indicated love for someone else.

He therefore came to rearet every pleasure he savored with her, every grace he discovered in her, because he knew that a moment later they would be added to the instruments of his torture.

His torture was rendered crueler still when he remembered having noticed something in her eyes for the first time a few days earlier. It was after dinner at the Verdurins'.

Either Forcheville, sensing that his brother-in-law Saniette was not in favor with the Verdurins, had sought to attack him in order to shine in their presence at Saniette's expense, or else he had been irritated by a clumsy remark.

Forcheville responded in such a crude way, with insults emboldened by his hapless victim's fright, pain, and pleading,

that the poor wretch, after asking Mme Verdurin if he should stay and receiving no response, left muttering to himself.

Odette had witnessed this scene in silence.

She threw him a complicitous glance.

Matching Forcheville in vileness, her eyes sparkled in a sly smile of congratulation.

Well, you've done for him, unless I miss my guess.

If he'd just been more friendly, he'd still be here. A proper scolding can be useful at any age.

One day, Swann went out in the middle of the afternoon and decided to visit Odette, whom he never saw at that hour although he knew she was always at home.

...yes, I think Mme de Crécy is in.

He thought he heard the sound of footsteps, but no one came to open the door.

Perhaps he hadn't heard footsteps.

An hour later he returned and found her there.

...no, I was here when you rang earlier, but I was sleeping.

The bell woke me and I guessed it was you.

I ran, but you had already left.

I clearly heard the tapping on the window...

Swann immediately recognized one of those fragments of a true story that liars caught in the act like to include in the false stories they invent.

She didn't realize that this true detail didn't mesh with other details of the true story from which she had arbitrarily detached it.

She admits that she heard me ring and then tap and that she thought it was me and she wanted to see me.

But that doesn't jibe with the fact that she didn't send anyone to open the door.

He didn't point out the contradiction in her story. Left to her own devices, Odette might come up with a lie that would hint at the truth. He didn't interrupt her.

When he got up to say goodbye . . .

No, Charles, stay a while longer!

How sad, since you never come in the afternoon, that I've had so little time with you.

He knew she didn't love him enough to feel such regret at missing his visit,

but since she was kind and often felt sad when she vexed him, he found it quite natural that she was sorry to have deprived him of the pleasure of spending an hour together.

When did I see her in similar distress?

It was such a trivial thing, however, that in the end the persistence of her pained air surprised him.

Suddenly, he remembered:

It was when Odette had lied to Mme Verdurin the day after not coming to dinner.

Because she was gripped with fear whenever she lied, she felt an urge to cry.

It occurred to him that it was not merely about what had happened that afternoon but something more current . . .

DING

DONG

What depressing lie was she now telling Swann?

He heard the sound of the front door being closed . . .

Giddyup!

The thought that merely by coming at an unaccustomed hour

he had disturbed so many things she didn't want him to know about made him feel disconsolate and almost distraught.

But since he loved Odette,

Poor darling!

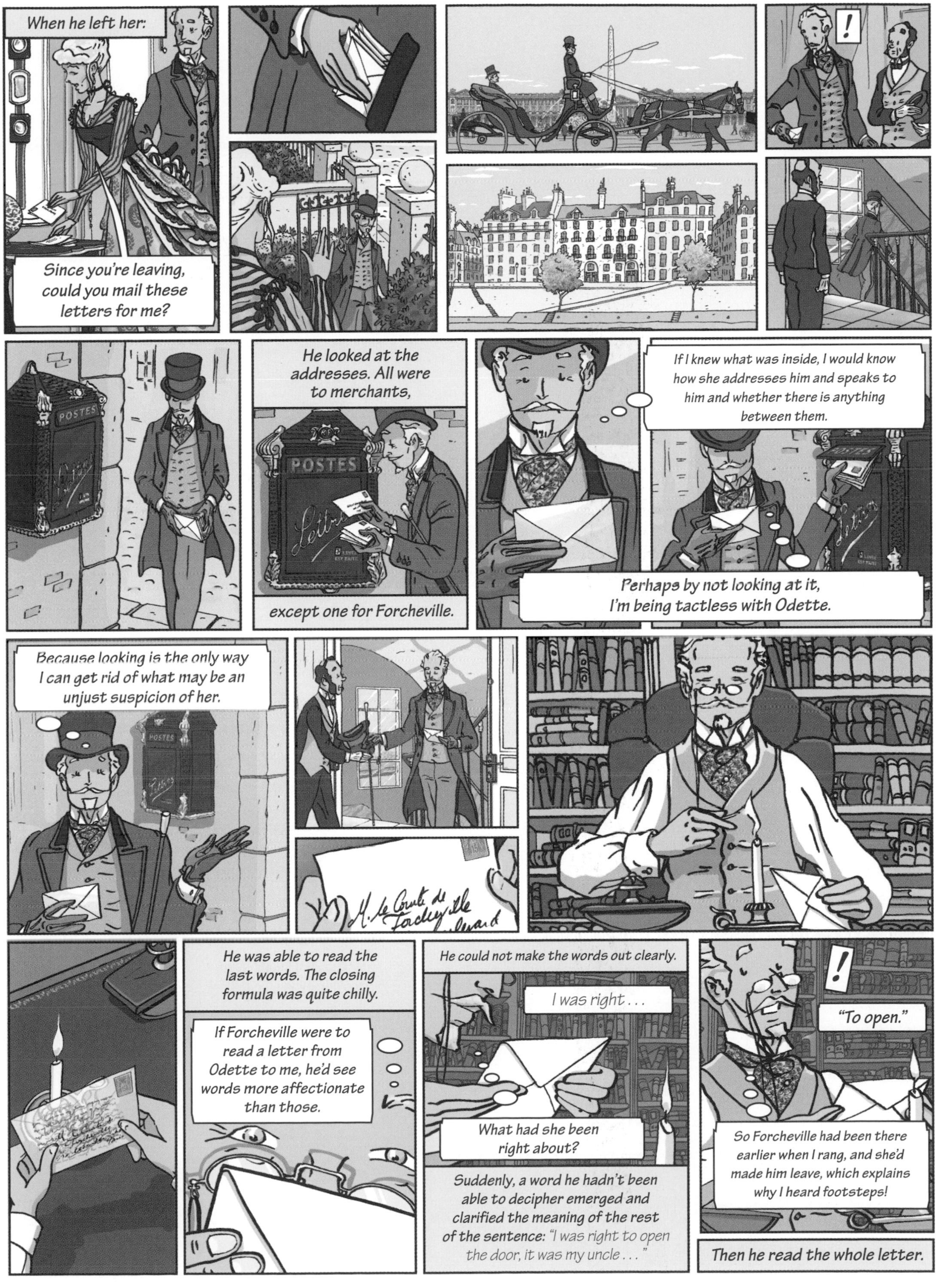

When he left her:
Since you're leaving, could you mail these letters for me?
!
He looked at the addresses. All were to merchants,
except one for Forcheville.
If I knew what was inside, I would know how she addresses him and speaks to him and whether there is anything between them.
Perhaps by not looking at it, I'm being tactless with Odette.
Because looking is the only way I can get rid of what may be an unjust suspicion of her.
He was able to read the last words. The closing formula was quite chilly.
If Forcheville were to read a letter from Odette to me, he'd see words more affectionate than those.
He could not make the words out clearly.
I was right . . .
What had she been right about?
Suddenly, a word he hadn't been able to decipher emerged and clarified the meaning of the rest of the sentence: "I was right to open the door, it was my uncle . . ."
!
"To open."
So Forcheville had been there earlier when I rang, and she'd made him leave, which explains why I heard footsteps!
Then he read the whole letter.

. . . at the end she apologized for having dismissed him so brusquely. There was no allusion that might indicate any intrigue between them.

In any case, Forcheville was even more deceived than he, because Odette had written to make him think that the visitor had been her uncle.

In short, the man she considered important was he himself, Swann, for whom she had dismissed the other.

Yet if there was nothing between Odette and Forcheville, why hadn't she opened the door at once?

Swann stood there abashed and confused yet happy in the presence of the envelope Odette had fearlessly given him, through whose transparent window

a little of her life was revealed, like a thin slice cut from a specimen and illuminated under a microscope.

Then his jealousy rejoiced, as if that jealousy had a life of its own, as if it were a selfish, voracious monster devouring whatever it could at his expense.

Now his jealousy had something to feed on, and Swann began to worry every day about what visitors Odette might be receiving at 5 o'clock.

At first he was not jealous about everything in Odette's life,

but only about episodes or circumstances that led him to think Odette might be deceiving him.

Like an octopus that puts out first one tentacle, then another, and then a third,

his jealousy firmly fastened on the hour of five in the afternoon, then on another, and then still another.

He tried to get Odette away from Forcheville, to take her to the south of France for a few days.

But he believed that every man in the hotel wanted her and that she wanted them.

So he, who once assiduously sought out new people and company while traveling, became fearful and fled the society of others as if they had wounded him.

How could he be anything but a misanthrope when he saw every man as a possible lover for Odette?

Jealousy thus altered Swann's character and completely transformed the external signs by which that character manifested itself to others.

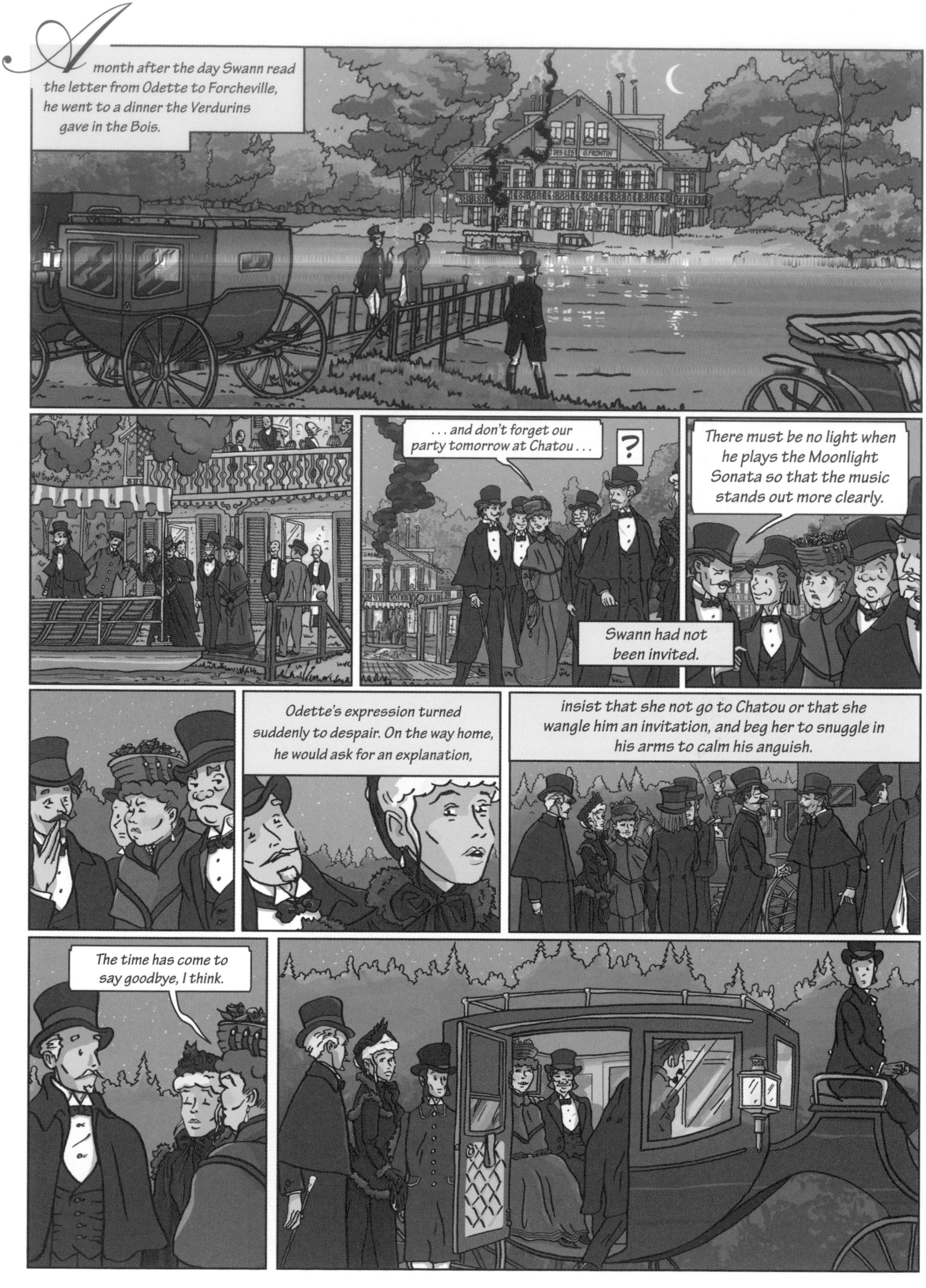
A month after the day Swann read the letter from Odette to Forcheville, he went to a dinner the Verdurins gave in the Bois.
. . . and don't forget our party tomorrow at Chatou . . .
?
Swann had not been invited.
There must be no light when he plays the Moonlight Sonata so that the music stands out more clearly.
Odette's expression turned suddenly to despair. On the way home, he would ask for an explanation,
insist that she not go to Chatou or that she wangle him an invitation, and beg her to snuggle in his arms to calm his anguish.
The time has come to say goodbye, I think.

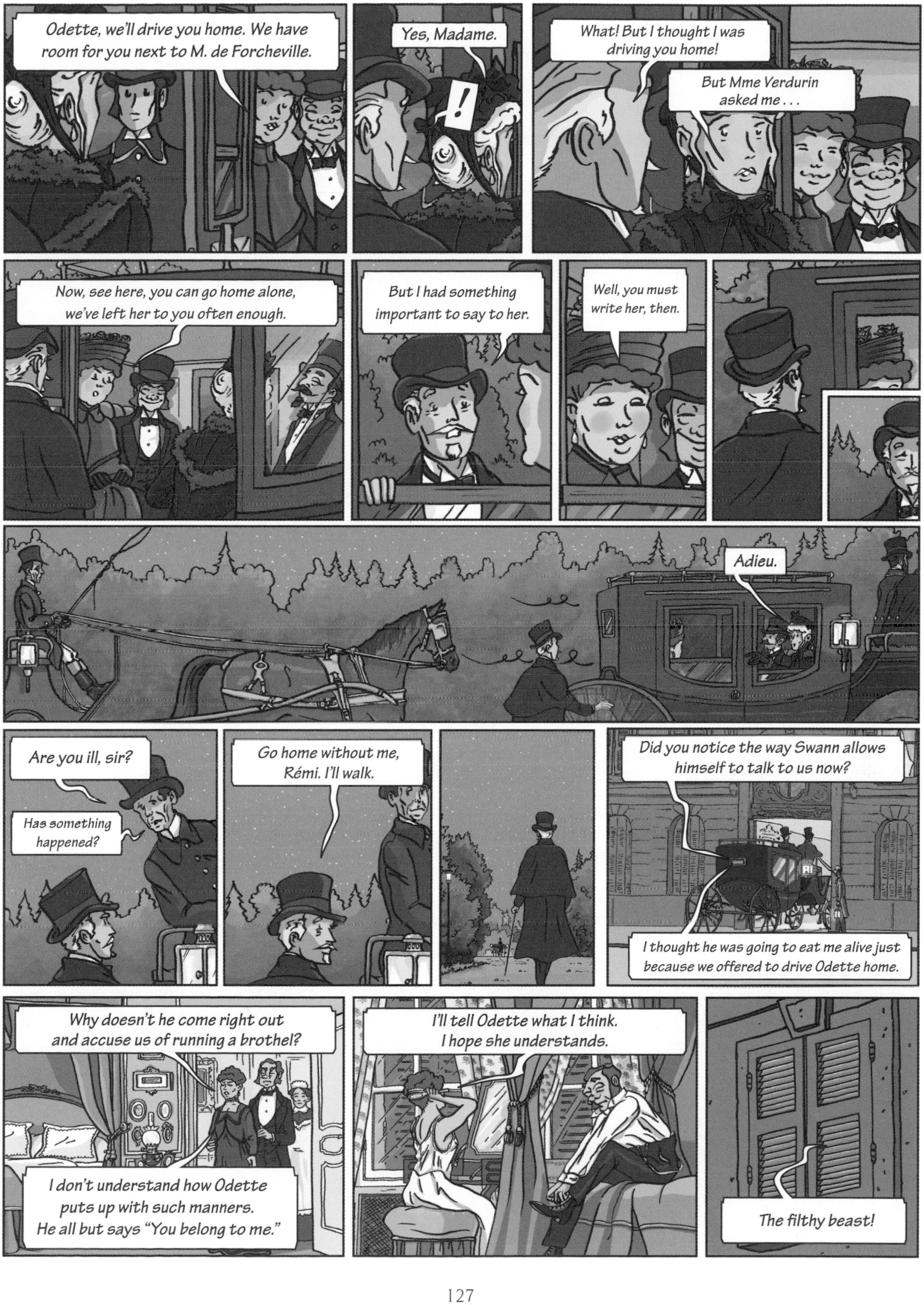

Odette, we'll drive you home. We have room for you next to M. de Forcheville.
Yes, Madame.
!
What! But I thought I was driving you home!
But Mme Verdurin asked me . . .
Now, see here, you can go home alone, we've left her to you often enough.
But I had something important to say to her.
Well, you must write her, then.
Adieu.
Are you ill, sir?
Has something happened?
Go home without me, Rémi. I'll walk.
Did you notice the way Swann allows himself to talk to us now?
I thought he was going to eat me alive just because we offered to drive Odette home.
Why doesn't he come right out and accuse us of running a brothel?
I don't understand how Odette puts up with such manners. He all but says "You belong to me."
I'll tell Odette what I think. I hope she understands.
The filthy beast!

Swann talked to himself out loud in the same somewhat artificial tone he had previously employed when listing the charms of the Verdurins' inner circle and praising their magnanimity.

The idea of going to Chatou to begin with! Like haberdashers who have just closed their shop for the day!

Those people are really sublime examples of philistinism. Surely they don't actually exist. They are right out of a play by Labiche!

The Cottards would be there and perhaps Brichot.

It's rather grotesque the way those nobodies spend all their time together and would feel lost, I swear, if they don't all turn up tomorrow "at Chatou."

Unfortunately, the painter would also be there, the one who likes to "arrange marriages" and who would invite Forcheville to come to his studio with Odette. He imagined Odette somewhat overdressed for such an outing to the country.

Because she's so common and, really, she's an awfully silly thing!

Then he suspected they might try to get Odette to laugh at him.

What disgusting gaiety!

The least sensitive nose would recoil in horror from such foulness.

I live too many thousands of meters above the cesspits in which they spit and spew their vile slander to be smeared by the japes of the Verdurins.

As God is my witness, I sincerely hoped to save Odette from their clutches. But patience has its limits, and I've come to the end of mine.

as if he'd taken on the mission of rescuing Odette from the climate of sarcasm at the Verdurins' more than a few minutes earlier . . .

He imagined the pianist preparing to play the Moonlight Sonata and Mme Verdurin's grimaces . . .

Idiot! Liar!

And that woman thinks of herself as a lover of "Art!"

Make some room next to you for M. de Forcheville...

In the dark! Procuress! Madam!

"Procuress" was also the name he gave to the music that would invite them to sit silently together and dream, to look at each other, to take each other's hand. He thought well of the severe attitude toward art exemplified by Plato, Bosseut, and French education in the good old days.

In short, the life one led at the Verdurins', which he had so often called "the true life," now seemed to him the worst of all lives and their inner circle the worst of all company.

...Dante's last circle. No doubt but that the great poem refers to the Verdurins'!

How wise society is to refuse to admit them.

How perspicacious is the Faubourg Saint-Germain's "Noli me tangere."

Verdurin! What a name! They really take the cake, one of a kind! Thank God, it was about time I stopped condescending to mix with those wretches, with that garbage.

Swann's voice was doubtless more perceptive than Swann himself when it refused to utter these words full of disgust in anything but an artificial tone. Indeed, his mind was probably preoccupied with a very different subject, without his being aware of it,

because when he arrived home:

clac

I think I've found a way to have myself invited to the dinner in Chatou tomorrow!

But he must have been mistaken, because he wasn't invited.

Dr. Cottard, having been summoned to the provinces to attend to a seriously ill patient, had not seen the Verdurins for several days and had not been able to go to Chatou.

On the day after the dinner:

Will we be seeing M. Swann this evening?

He is what you call a personal friend of...

Well, I should hope not! God preserve us.

He is a deadly bore, stupid, and ill-bred.

Ah!
Ah!
Ah!
Ah! Ah!

And Swann was never again mentioned at the Verdurins'.

After that, the salon that had brought Swann and Odette together became an obstacle to their seeing each other.

No longer did she say to him, as in the early days of their love:

We'll see each other tomorrow evening in any case. There's a supper at the Verdurins'.

but rather:

We won't be able to see each other tomorrow evening. There's a supper at the Verdurins'.

Or else the Verdurins were taking her to the Opéra-Comique to see *Une Nuit de Cléopâtre*,

and Swann could read in Odette's eyes her terror that he would ask her not to go, which now exasperated him.

It's not anger I feel, though, when I see her eagerness to pick at such turds of so-called music,

it's sorrow for her.

Sorrow that after six months with me, she hasn't changed sufficiently to purge herself of Victor Massé on her own!

I swear to you that when I ask you not to go out, I would like nothing more, if I were a selfish man, than for you to refuse, because I have a thousand things to do tonight.

But I must think of you.

Don't you see that *Une Nuit de Cléopâtre* has nothing to do with anything.

—what a title!—

The real question

is to find out whether you're really one of those ultimately frivolous and contemptible people who is incapable of forgoing a pleasure.

Her familiarity with men had taught her that once they were in love, there was no point in obeying them; they would only love you more if you didn't.

I'm going to miss the Overture.

Physically, she was in a bad phase: she was putting on weight.

In other words, she had become precious to Swann at precisely the moment he found her distinctly less pretty.

But knowing that within this new chrysalis remained the same old Odette, with the same fickle, elusive, and devious will, was enough to sustain Swann's passion to make her captive.

When the Verdurins took her off to Saint-Germain, Chatou, or Meulan, they often proposed to stay the night. Odette would say that there was no one she needed to notify, because she had told Swann once and for all that she couldn't send him a note in front of everyone without compromising herself.

Sometimes she would stay away for several days, while the Verdurins took her to see the tombs in Dreux or Compiègne and continued on to the Château de Pierrefonds.

To think that she could visit real monuments with me, who studied architecture for ten years,

and instead she goes with those consummate brutes to sigh in ecstasy over the abominations of Louis-Philippe and Viollet-le-Duc!

But when she went to Dreux or Pierrefonds, he would plunge into that most intoxicating of love novels, the railway timetable, for information about the way to join her.

The way?

Perhaps more: the authorization. If it was announced to the public that at 8 o'clock a train destined to arrive in Pierrefonds at 10 would leave the station, then going to Pierrefonds was a lawful act for which Odette's permission was superfluous. Indeed, he felt that he wished to go there and would have done so had he not known Odette.

He had long wanted to learn more about Viollet-le-Duc's restorations.

He briefly considered the idea of going there with one of his friends, the Marquis de Forestelle, who had a château in the vicinity.

But she would have guessed that he had come for her.

And when M. de Forestelle came to pick him up:

He spent his days poring over a map of the forest of Compiègne as if it were a map of the Land of Love.

No, unfortunately, I can't go to Pierrefonds today, because Odette is there.

When the day on which she might return arrived, he went back to the timetable to figure out which train she might have taken. He waited all night, to no avail, because the Verdurins had decided to return earlier, and Odette had been in Paris since noon.

It had not occurred to her to send him word.

This was because she had not so much as given him a thought.

And the times when she forgot that Swann even existed did more to attach him to her than all her coquetry.

Because Swann then experienced the same painful agitation that had caused his love to blossom forth on the night he had tailed to find her at the Verdurins'.

Swann spent his days without Odette. But the thought of the absent woman . . .

mingled inextricably with his simplest actions

owing to the sadness he felt in performing those actions without her.

Some days he went for lunch to a restaurant to which he would not have gone had it not been for what is called a "romantic" reason,

in this case the fact that the name of the restaurant was the same as the name of the street where Odette lived.

Sometimes days passed before she thought of letting him know she was back in Paris.

I just this instant got home after taking the morning train.

This was a lie, at least for Odette.

For Swann, however, her words were false only if he previously suspected they would be. For him to believe she was lying, a prior suspicion was a necessary condition. It was also a sufficient condition. In that case, everything Odette said seemed suspect to him.

If she mentioned a name, it was surely that of one of her lovers. Once he even contacted a detective agency to find out the address and activities of the unknown individual, only to learn that the man was an uncle of Odette's who had died twenty years earlier.

At certain parties to which he was invited, he would run into her. On one or two such occasions he experienced a kind of joy that one is tempted to call tranquil, because it is of a nature to soothe the emotions:

Would you be kind enough to wait five minutes for me. I'll be leaving, we could go together and you can drive me home.

One day, Forcheville asked to be driven home as well . . .

Would you allow me to visit you in your home?

Ah! That depends on this gentleman. Ask him. I warn you: he likes to chat quietly with me. If only you knew this man as well as I know him. Isn't it so, my love? Is there anyone who knows you as well as I do?

Swann was even more touched when she criticized him in certain ways in Forcheville's presence:

Did you leave your essay on Vermeer here just so you could work on it a little tomorrow? What a lazy fellow! I'll make you work!

which proved that they were a couple.

If only fate had allowed him to live with Odette, so that her home would also be his. Then, all the trivialities of Swann's life, which so depressed him,

would have partaken of Odette's life and thus have been infused with overwhelming sweetness and mysterious density.

He suspected, however, that what he really longed for was a calm, peaceful existence, which would not have been a climate favorable to his love. If Odette were no longer an always absent, missed, imaginary figure,

if his feeling for her no longer coincided with the mysterious disturbance the phrase of the sonata occasioned in him, Odette's activities would no doubt cease to hold much interest for him.

Considering his malady with scientific detachment, as if he had inoculated himself in order to study it, he told himself that when he was cured, what Odette did would no longer matter to him. In his morbid state, however, he feared such a cure as he feared death, for it would mean the death of everything he was at that moment.

These tranquil evenings would calm Swann's suspicions, and the next day he would order an exquisite jewel and have it sent to her.

At other times, however, his pain reclaimed him. He imagined that Odette was Forcheville's mistress.

Then Swann detested her.

I'm such a fool. My money pays for other people's pleasures.

Because she said she wanted to attend the season at Bayreuth, I was fool enough to offer to rent one of the King of Bavaria's lovely castles for just the two of us.

Good God, let's hope she refuses!

To spend two weeks listening to Wagner with her, who cares for Wagner as much as a fish cares for apples, would be such fun!

He even imagined he would receive a letter from her asking for money to rent the castle but warning him not come because she had promised to invite Forcheville and the Verdurins. How he would have loved her to be so bold! What joy it would have given him to refuse and draft a vengeful response!

On the following day precisely this came to pass.

"... and if you were willing to send me the money, I would at last have the pleasure of inviting them after so often accepting their hospitality ..."

About him she breathed not a word, it being understood that their presence excluded his.

Hence he had the pleasure of dispatching the devastating response he had contemplated.

Unfortunately, with the money she has or can easily find,

she'll be able to rent in Bayreuth anyway, since that is what she wants,

even though she can't tell the difference between Bach and Clapisson.

In any case, she'll have to live rather frugally there.

And at least I won't be paying for that abominable trip.

If only he could stop her! If only the coachman would agree to drive her to a place where the perfidious woman Odette had become for Swann for the past forty-eight hours could be sequestered for a time!

But she never remained that way for long.

... Ah! If only you knew this man as I know him ...

How could I have written that offensive letter?

If she and Forcheville triumph there in spite of me, I will have brought it on myself.

Whereas if I approve her plans,

which can of course be justified,

she will feel I sent her there and paid for her lodging,

and she'll be grateful to me.

134

So Odette, sure of seeing him come around within a few days, as tender and obedient as before and begging for a reconciliation, ceased to worry about displeasing him and refused, whenever it suited her, to grant the favors that meant the most to him.

She may not have realized how sincere he was when, during their quarrel, he told her he would not send the money.

On other occasions, to prove to Odette that he was perfectly capable of doing without her and that a rupture was always possible, he decided to go for a few days without seeing her.

He imagined her worrying.

If, however, a slight vexation or physical discomfort

led him to look upon the present as a unique moment, an exception to the rule, in which wisdom itself would counsel him

to suppress his will;

or, not even that, the mere memory that he had forgotten to ask Odette for some piece of information, such as whether she had decided what color she wished to repaint her carriage or whether she wished to buy ordinary or preferred stock in a certain company . . .

It's very nice to show her that I can go without seeing her,

but if it means that the paint job must be done over or the shares pay no dividends,

what will I have gained?

He saw no problem with postponing the trial separation he was now certain he could have whenever he liked.

But just as Odette had believed that his refusal to give her money was just a ploy, she saw his request for information as nothing but a pretext.

For she did not reconstruct the various phases of the crises he endured; she believed only in what she already knew in advance, namely, the necessary, inevitable, and always identical end.

Indeed, Swann's love had reached that stage at which even the boldest doctor or surgeon must ask whether it is still reasonable or even possible to deny a patient his vice or relieve his malady.

Of course Swann had no direct knowledge of the extent of his love.

When he tried to measure it, it sometimes seemed that it was diminished, almost shrunk to nothing.

For example, on certain days he recalled that before he loved Odette, he had found her expressions and pallid complexion not much to his taste, not to say downright distasteful.

I'm really making noticeable progress. Considering things carefully, I find that I took almost no pleasure yesterday from being in her bed.

It's strange, but I even found her ugly.

And of course he was sincere, but his love extended well beyond the realm of physical desire.

Odette the individual was no longer an important part of it.

It's Odette.

He found it difficult to relate the sight of her, whether in the flesh or in a photograph, to the constant and painful anxiety that dwelt within him,

as we might find it impossible, when shown the material cause of a disease, to relate it to the suffering we actually endure.

"She": he asked himself what the word meant,

for love and death are alike in that both cause us to interrogate the future in fear that we will never grasp what it really consists of, wherein its mystery lies.

Swann's love was a disease that had so metastasized, that had become so intimately intertwined with all his actions, thoughts, and even his health and what he hoped for after his death, so thoroughly fused with his being, that it would have been impossible to remove it without all but destroying him:

as a surgeon would say, his love was no longer operable.

*S*wann's love had so detached him from all his interests that when he went back into society he felt the same objective pleasure he might have experienced before a painting depicting an idle leisure class. The reason for this newfound pleasure was that he was able to emigrate into those regions of himself that remained foreign to his love and sorrow. In this respect, the personality that my great-aunt ascribed to "the Swann boy," distinct from the personality of Charles Swann, was the one that now pleased him most.

One day, for the birthday of the Princesse de Parme, he decided to send a basket of fruit and asked a cousin of his mother's to take care of it. She wrote him about her efforts:

"...I did not buy all the fruit at the same place..."

"but took the grapes from Crapote..."

"...that's their specialty..."

"...the strawberries from Jauret..."

"...the pears from Chevet..."

"...where they always have the finest..."

"...and I personally inspected and examined each piece of fruit one by one."

The phrase "personally inspected and examined each piece of fruit one by one" alleviated his suffering by transporting his consciousness into a region in which it rarely roamed, although it belonged to him as the heir of a wealthy and respectable bourgeois family that retained, as its hereditary property always available for his use, knowledge of "the best shops" and the proper way to place an order.

He had too long forgotten that he was "the Swann boy" not to feel, when he briefly resumed that role, a greater pleasure than he was capable of feeling the rest of the time;

...and a letter from a prince could not please him more than an invitation to a wedding from old family friends.

But his relationships with society people made them a part of his family as well. And the knowledge that if he succumbed to a stroke, it would be the Duc de Chartres, the Prince de Reuss, the Duc de Luxembourg, and the Baron de Charlus whom his valet would notify first brought him the same consolation that our old maid Françoise felt in knowing that she would be buried in her own fine, monogrammed, and undarned linen.

To the socialites he was obliged to make excuses for not visiting, but to Odette he chose to make excuses precisely so that he would have a reason to visit. He invariably paid the price,

Still, I've rather abused her patience this month.

I've visited her often.

I wonder if sending her 4,000 francs is enough.

and each time he found a pretext, a present to give her or a piece of information she needed . . .

And when no pretext was available, he asked M. de Charlus to call on her and let drop in the course of the conversation that he had just remembered he needed to speak to Swann and would she be good enough to invite him to come to her house at once.

Usually, though, Swann waited in vain, and M. de Charlus would tell him that evening that his stratagem had been unsuccessful.

So that even when she stayed in Paris, he saw little of her.

When she loved him, she used to say:

I'm always free . . .

and:

. . . What does it matter to me what other people think?

. . . now, whenever he wanted to see her, she invoked proprieties or mentioned some engagement as a pretext to refuse. When he mentioned going to a charity ball, art opening, or premiere she planned to attend:

So then,

you treat me as though I were a prostitute!

You want our affair to be public!

Things got so bad that Swann, who knew that Odette was very fond of my great-uncle Adolphe, went to see him one day to ask him to use his influence with her.

You know that Odette stands above all other women and what an adorable angel she is.

But you know what life in Paris is like.

Not everyone knows Odette as you and I know her.

So there are people who think I'm playing a rather ridiculous role.

She won't even allow me to see her in public, at the theater.

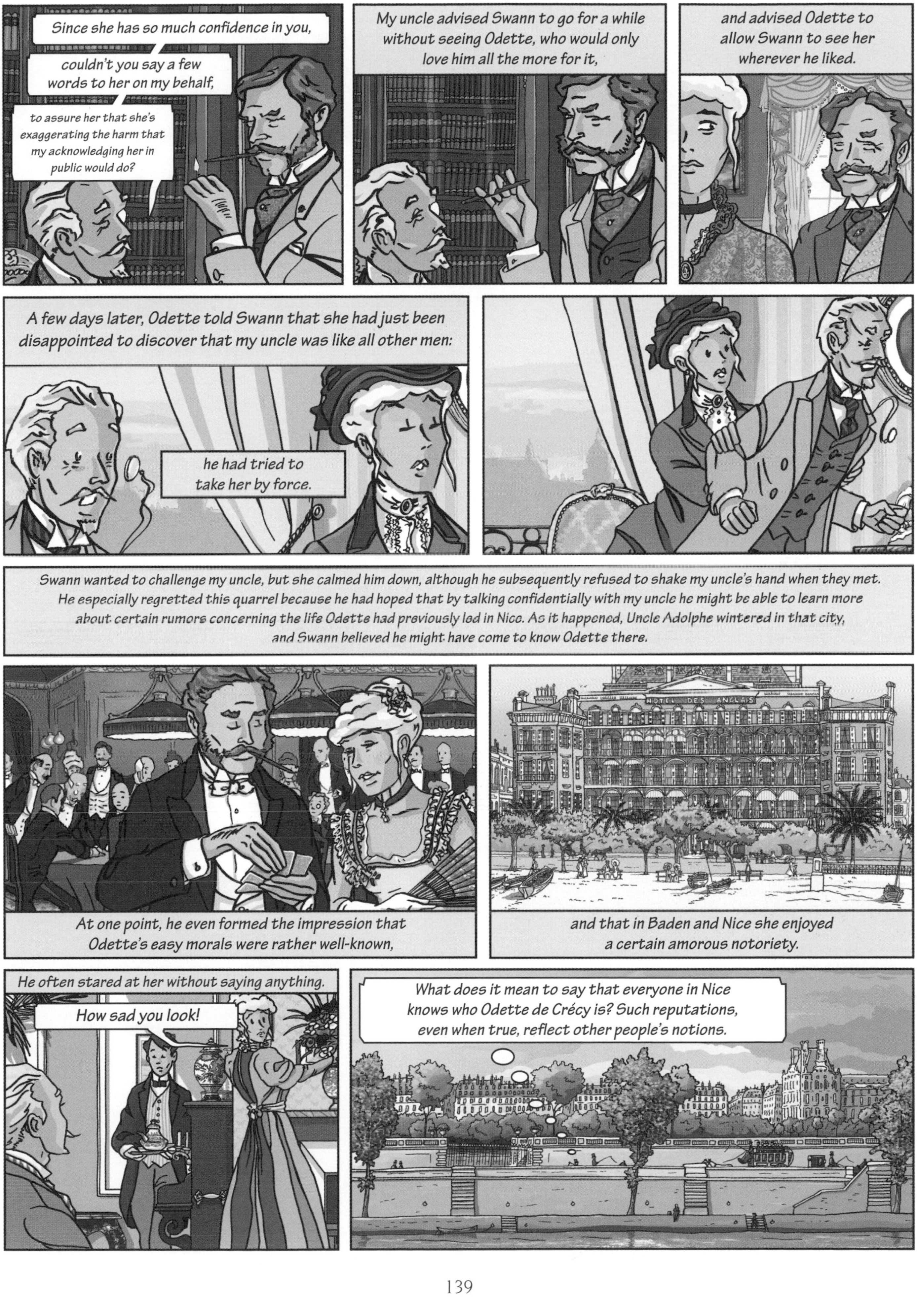
Since she has so much confidence in you,
couldn't you say a few words to her on my behalf,
to assure her that she's exaggerating the harm that my acknowledging her in public would do?
My uncle advised Swann to go for a while without seeing Odette, who would only love him all the more for it,
and advised Odette to allow Swann to see her wherever he liked.
A few days later, Odette told Swann that she had just been disappointed to discover that my uncle was like all other men:
he had tried to take her by force.
Swann wanted to challenge my uncle, but she calmed him down, although he subsequently refused to shake my uncle's hand when they met. He especially regretted this quarrel because he had hoped that by talking confidentially with my uncle he might be able to learn more about certain rumors concerning the life Odette had previously led in Nice. As it happened, Uncle Adolphe wintered in that city, and Swann believed he might have come to know Odette there.
At one point, he even formed the impression that Odette's easy morals were rather well-known,
HOTEL DES ANGLAIS
and that in Baden and Nice she enjoyed a certain amorous notoriety.
He often stared at her without saying anything.
How sad you look!
What does it mean to say that everyone in Nice knows who Odette de Crécy is? Such reputations, even when true, reflect other people's notions.

But now he saw little of her.

And even after she had invited Swann, if friends asked her to join them at the theater or for supper, she would jump for joy and quickly dress.

Even when they were to meet in the evening, she wouldn't tell him until the last minute whether she'd be available, because she could count on his being free and wished first to know for certain whether anyone else would propose to visit.

Swann looked so sad that:

So that's how you thank me for having kept you until the last minute. And I thought I was being so nice.

Next time I'll know better!

Sometimes, at the risk of making her angry, he determined to find out where she had gone.

Of course, obtaining certain kinds of information did little to advance Swann's knowledge. Knowledge of a thing doesn't always allow us to prevent it from happening, but we hold on to the things we know, at least in our minds, where we can do with them as we please, and this gives us the illusion of a sort of power over them.

He was happy whenever M. de Charlus was with Odette.

Swann knew that nothing could happen between her and Charlus and that when Charlus went out with her, it was out of friendship for him,

and he would have no problem telling Swann what she had done.

The next day:

What's that, Mémé my friend, I don't quite understand . . . You didn't go directly to the Musée Grévin after leaving her place?

You went somewhere else first? No? Oh, that's funny!

But what a strange idea to go next to the Chat Noir. That must have been her idea. . . . No? It was yours?

How odd.

But it wasn't a bad idea after all, was it? She must have known a lot of people there?

No? She didn't speak to anyone? How extraordinary!

So you stayed there just like that, both of you, all alone?

I can imagine the scene from here.

You're a good fellow, Mémé.

I'm awfully fond of you.

140

Even when it was impossible to know where she was, he still would have been able to calm his anxiety had he been allowed to wait in her apartment until she returned. But this she would not permit, so he had to return home.

On the way, he forced himself to formulate plans.

He put Odette out of his mind.

EXPOSITION FRAGONARD

INVITATION REMBRANDT

But as he made ready to go to bed and relaxed his grip on himself, a cold shiver went down in his spine, and he began to sob. He didn't even want to know why.

How charming, I'm becoming neurotic!

He didn't understand his malady. The problem was that day by day Odette grew chillier toward him.

This change was his secret wound, and whenever he sensed that his thoughts were pressing too near, he vigorously turned them aside lest he aggravate his suffering.

It fatigued him no end to think that the next day he would once again be faced with the need to find out what Odette had done and somehow contrive to see her.

Abstractedly, he told himself:

There was a time when Odette loved me more.

But he would never see that time again.

Just as he had a commode that he took pains to avoid, detouring around it whenever he entered or exited his apartment because he had placed in one of its drawers . . .

the chrysanthemum she had given him

the first night he had driven her home

and the letters she had written:

Had you also forgotten your heart, I wouldn't have

. . . he also had a place within himself that he never let his mind come near:

it was there that his memories of happier days resided.

But his prudent precautions were defeated one evening when he went into society.

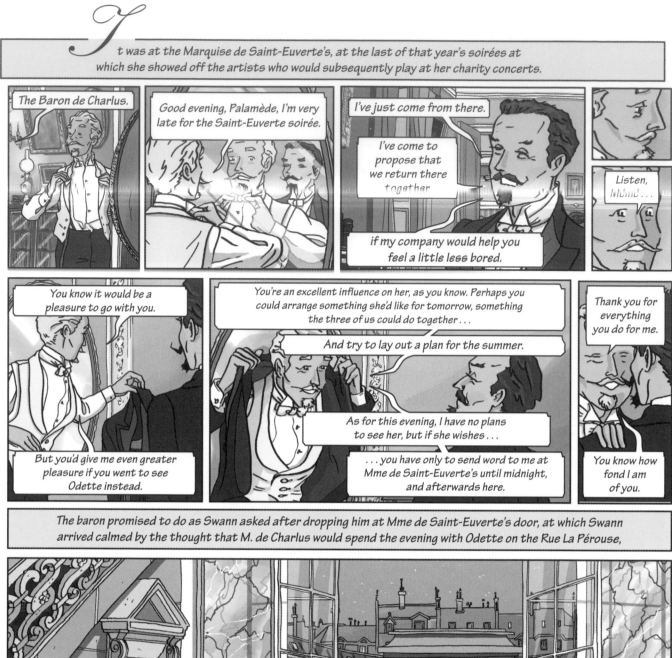

It was at the Marquise de Saint-Euverte's, at the last of that year's soirées at which she showed off the artists who would subsequently play at her charity concerts.

The Baron de Charlus.

Good evening, Palamède, I'm very late for the Saint-Euverte soirée.

I've just come from there.

I've come to propose that we return there together

if my company would help you feel a little less bored.

Listen, Mumu...

You know it would be a pleasure to go with you.

But you'd give me even greater pleasure if you went to see Odette instead.

You're an excellent influence on her, as you know. Perhaps you could arrange something she'd like for tomorrow, something the three of us could do together...

And try to lay out a plan for the summer.

As for this evening, I have no plans to see her, but if she wishes...

...you have only to send word to me at Mme de Saint-Euverte's until midnight, and afterwards here.

Thank you for everything you do for me.

You know how fond I am of you.

The baron promised to do as Swann asked after dropping him at Mme de Saint-Euverte's door, at which Swann arrived calmed by the thought that M. de Charlus would spend the evening with Odette on the Rue La Pérouse,

...but in a state of melancholy indifference to all things unrelated to Odette, and in particular to social things.

For the first time he noticed the sparse, splendid pack of idle footmen, awakened by the unexpected arrival of such a late guest.

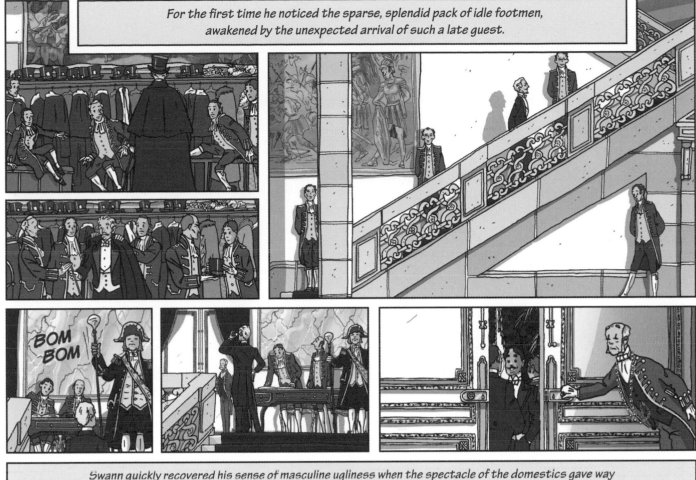

BOM BOM

Swann quickly recovered his sense of masculine ugliness when the spectacle of the domestics gave way to that of the guests. But this ugliness seemed new to him. Even the monocles that many of the men wore seemed endowed with a kind of individuality.

The general's monocle, which he wore in the middle of his forehead so that he looked like a one-eyed cyclops, seemed to Swann a monstrous wound, which might have been glorious to receive in combat but was indecent to exhibit in public,

while M. de Bréauté's revealed, glued to the back of the glass like a natural specimen prepared for a microscope, a tiny eye teeming with amiability.

A society novelist

I am obserrrrving.

had just placed his monocle in the corner of his eye, where it served as the unique instrument of his psychological investigations and analyses.

So, there you are. It's been eons since we last saw you . . .

You look good, you know!

The Marquis de Forestelle's monocle had to be squeezed tightly, thus imparting a melancholy delicacy to his face, making women think he was capable of suffering deeply in love.

M. de Saint-Candé's monocle, surrounded like Saturn by a gigantic ring, was the center of gravity of a face that at every moment organized itself in relation to the lens.

While behind his monocle M. de Palancy, with his great carp's head and round eyes, moved slowly, steadily working his mandibles, so that he seemed to carry with him a shard of glass from his aquarium.

At Mme de Saint-Euverte's insistence, Swann had moved forward to listen to an aria from *Orfeo*

and had placed himself in a corner from which the only people he could see were the Marquise de Cambremer and the Vicomtesse de Franquetot, who, being cousins, always sought each other out at soirées and were never at ease until they had marked out two places next to each other with their fans or handkerchiefs.

Filled with ironic melancholy, Swann watched them listen to the piano intermezzo, *Saint Francis Preaching to the Birds* by Liszt, which followed a flute solo.

On the other side of Mme de Franquetot sat the Marquise de Gallardon, preoccupied with her favorite subject, her connection with the Guermantes, from which she derived much glory along with a certain shame,

since the most illustrious of them kept her at a certain distance, perhaps because she was boring, or nasty, or from an inferior branch of the family, or perhaps for no reason at all.

At that moment she was thinking that she had never received an invitation or a visit from her young cousin, the Princesse des Laumes, in the six years since the princess's marriage.

From having told so many people surprised not to have seen her at Mme des Laumes's receptions that it was because of the risk of meeting Princesse Mathilde there, something her ultra-legitimist family would never have forgiven, she ultimately came to believe that this was in fact the reason.

And furthermore:

In any case, it's not up to me to make the first move. I'm twenty years older than she is.

Had Mme de Gallardon's conversation been subjected to the kind of analysis employed in finding the key to a cipher, the analyst would have discovered that no expressions occurred more often than:

"at the home of my Guermantes cousins"

"at my Guermantes aunt's home"

"the health of Elzéar de Guermantes"

"In the box of my cousin Mme de Guermantes."

As it happens, the Princesse des Laumes, whom one wouldn't have expected to see at Mme de Saint-Euverte's, had actually just arrived.

She had entered without a fuss, deliberately remaining in the back of the room, like a king who stands in line at a theater entrance because the management hasn't been notified that he was coming.

She stood at what she took to be the most modest place (from which she knew full well that a delighted exclamation from Mme de Saint-Euverte would rescue her as soon as she noticed), alongside Mme de Cambremer, whom she did not know.

The pianist finished the piece by Liszt and began playing a Chopin prelude, at which point Mme de Cambremer cast a furtive glance to her rear. She knew that her young daughter-in-law despised Chopin.

But being out of the eye of that Wagnerian, who was with a group of people of her own age, Mme de Cambremer succumbed to her delight at the music.

The Princesse des Laumes felt a similar delight.

Chopin is always ch-charming.

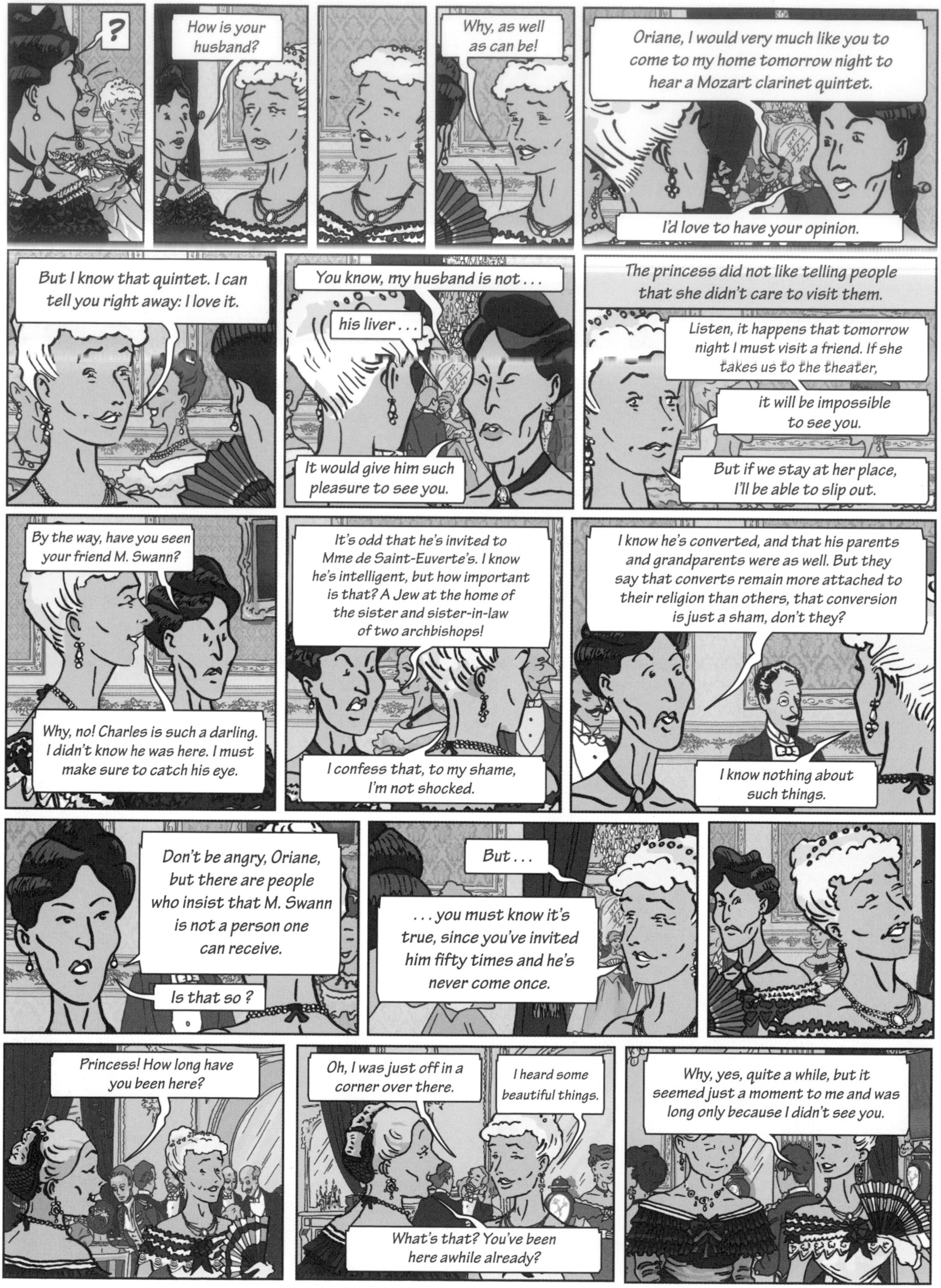
?
How is your husband?
Why, as well as can be!
Oriane, I would very much like you to come to my home tomorrow night to hear a Mozart clarinet quintet.
I'd love to have your opinion.
But I know that quintet. I can tell you right away: I love it.
You know, my husband is not . . .
his liver . . .
It would give him such pleasure to see you.
The princess did not like telling people that she didn't care to visit them.
Listen, it happens that tomorrow night I must visit a friend. If she takes us to the theater,
it will be impossible to see you.
But if we stay at her place, I'll be able to slip out.
By the way, have you seen your friend M. Swann?
Why, no! Charles is such a darling. I didn't know he was here. I must make sure to catch his eye.
It's odd that he's invited to Mme de Saint-Euverte's. I know he's intelligent, but how important is that? A Jew at the home of the sister and sister-in-law of two archbishops!
I confess that, to my shame, I'm not shocked.
I know he's converted, and that his parents and grandparents were as well. But they say that converts remain more attached to their religion than others, that conversion is just a sham, don't they?
I know nothing about such things.
Don't be angry, Oriane, but there are people who insist that M. Swann is not a person one can receive.
Is that so ?
But . . .
. . . you must know it's true, since you've invited him fifty times and he's never come once.
Princess! How long have you been here?
Oh, I was just off in a corner over there.
I heard some beautiful things.
What's that? You've been here awhile already?
Why, yes, quite a while, but it seemed just a moment to me and was long only because I didn't see you.

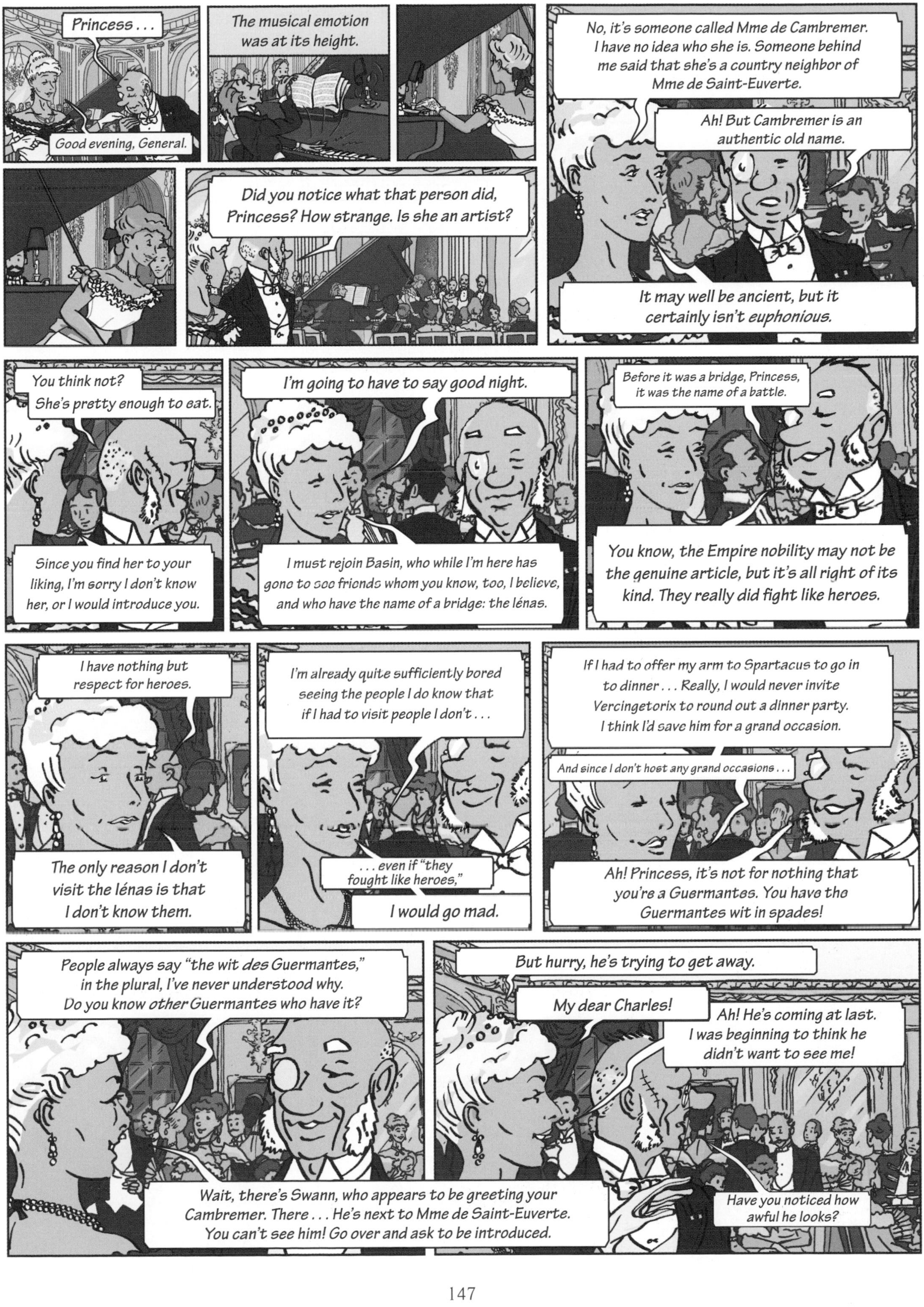

Princess . . .
Good evening, General.
The musical emotion was at its height.
Did you notice what that person did, Princess? How strange. Is she an artist?
No, it's someone called Mme de Cambremer. I have no idea who she is. Someone behind me said that she's a country neighbor of Mme de Saint-Euverte.
Ah! But Cambremer is an authentic old name.
It may well be ancient, but it certainly isn't *euphonious.*
You think not?
She's pretty enough to eat.
Since you find her to your liking, I'm sorry I don't know her, or I would introduce you.
I'm going to have to say good night.
I must rejoin Basin, who while I'm here has gone to see friends whom you know, too, I believe, and who have the name of a bridge: the Iénas.
Before it was a bridge, Princess, it was the name of a battle.
You know, the Empire nobility may not be the genuine article, but it's all right of its kind. They really did fight like heroes.
I have nothing but respect for heroes.
The only reason I don't visit the Iénas is that I don't know them.
I'm already quite sufficiently bored seeing the people I do know that if I had to visit people I don't . . .
. . . even if "they fought like heroes,"
I would go mad.
If I had to offer my arm to Spartacus to go in to dinner . . . Really, I would never invite Vercingetorix to round out a dinner party. I think I'd save him for a grand occasion.
And since I don't host any grand occasions . . .
Ah! Princess, it's not for nothing that you're a Guermantes. You have the Guermantes wit in spades!
People always say "the wit *des Guermantes,*" in the plural, I've never understood why. Do you know *other* Guermantes who have it?
Wait, there's Swann, who appears to be greeting your Cambremer. There . . . He's next to Mme de Saint-Euverte. You can't see him! Go over and ask to be introduced.
But hurry, he's trying to get away.
My dear Charles!
Ah! He's coming at last. I was beginning to think he didn't want to see me!
Have you noticed how awful he looks?

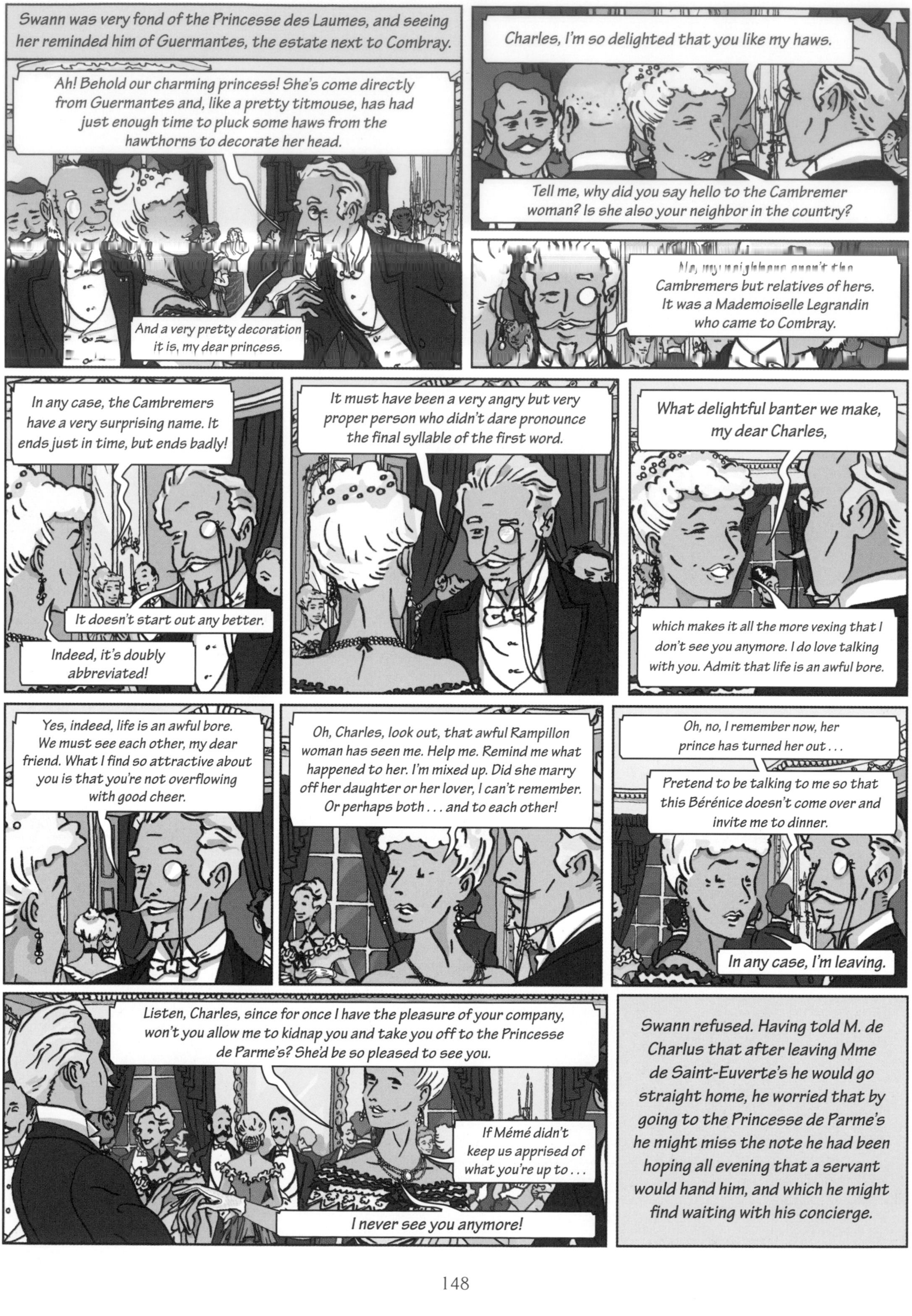

Swann was very fond of the Princesse des Laumes, and seeing her reminded him of Guermantes, the estate next to Combray.
Ah! Behold our charming princess! She's come directly from Guermantes and, like a pretty titmouse, has had just enough time to pluck some haws from the hawthorns to decorate her head.
And a very pretty decoration it is, my dear princess.
Charles, I'm so delighted that you like my haws.
Tell me, why did you say hello to the Cambremer woman? Is she also your neighbor in the country?
Cambremers but relatives of hers. It was a Mademoiselle Legrandin who came to Combray.
In any case, the Cambremers have a very surprising name. It ends just in time, but ends badly!
It doesn't start out any better.
Indeed, it's doubly abbreviated!
It must have been a very angry but very proper person who didn't dare pronounce the final syllable of the first word.
What delightful banter we make, my dear Charles,
which makes it all the more vexing that I don't see you anymore. I do love talking with you. Admit that life is an awful bore.
Yes, indeed, life is an awful bore. We must see each other, my dear friend. What I find so attractive about you is that you're not overflowing with good cheer.
Oh, Charles, look out, that awful Rampillon woman has seen me. Help me. Remind me what happened to her. I'm mixed up. Did she marry off her daughter or her lover, I can't remember. Or perhaps both . . . and to each other!
Oh, no, I remember now, her prince has turned her out . . .
Pretend to be talking to me so that this Bérénice doesn't come over and invite me to dinner.
In any case, I'm leaving.
Listen, Charles, since for once I have the pleasure of your company, won't you allow me to kidnap you and take you off to the Princesse de Parme's? She'd be so pleased to see you.
If Mémé didn't keep us apprised of what you're up to . . .
I never see you anymore!
Swann refused. Having told M. de Charlus that after leaving Mme de Saint-Euverte's he would go straight home, he worried that by going to the Princesse de Parme's he might miss the note he had been hoping all evening that a servant would hand him, and which he might find waiting with his concierge.

Just as he was about to escape, however, General de Froberville asked to be introduced to Mme de Cambremer, and he was obliged to return to the salon to look for her.

You know, Swann, I'd rather be married to that woman than massacred by savages. What do you say?

Many fine men have lost their lives that way . . .

Do you know, for example, the explorer La Pérouse, whose ashes were brought home by Dumont d'Urville . . .

La Pérouse was a fine character and one who interests me greatly.

And Swann was already happy, as if he had spoken of Odette.

Oh, of course, La Pérouse.

It's a well-known name. He has his street.

Do you know anyone on Rue La Pérouse?

Only Mme de Chanlivault, the sister of the excellent Chaussepierre.

She organized a lovely evening at the theater the other day. Her salon will be very elegant someday, you'll see!

So she lives on Rue La Pérouse. That's nice, it's a pretty street, but so depressing.

Not at all. You must not have been there for some time. There's been a lot of construction over there, all around the neighborhood.

At last, Swann introduced M. de Froberville to young Mme de Cambremer.

Her parents-in-law declared she was an angel, especially since, having arranged for their son to marry her, they preferred to be seen as having yielded to her many fine qualities rather than her substantial fortune.

But the concert resumed, and Swann realized that he would not be able to leave before the end of this additional piece of the program. It pained him to be stuck among people whose stupidity and foolishness depressed him no end. He suffered above all from having to prolong his exile in this place where Odette would never set foot.

Suddenly, however, it was as though she had made her entrance.

149

Before Swann could tell himself:

It's the little phrase from Vinteuil's sonata. Don't listen to it!

all his memories of the time when Odette was infatuated with him had been reawakened.

He saw it all again

He remembered the gaslights being out the night he met her among the wandering shades, a night that had seemed almost supernatural and indeed belonged to a mysterious world to which, once the gates have been closed, one can never return.

And Swann perceived, transfixed by this relived happiness, a miserable fellow who filled him with pity, and he had to lower his eyes to hide the tears that had welled up in them. That miserable fellow was himself.

A wave of pity and tenderness transported Swann's thoughts toward Vinteuil, that sublime, fraternal stranger who must also have suffered deeply. What could his life have been like? From what depths of pain had he drawn the godlike strength, . . .

the limitless power to create?

150

The little phrase spoke to him of the vanity of his suffering. It sought to imitate, to re-create, the charms of an intimate sadness, down to their essence, which is to seem frivolous to anyone but the person who feels them. This the little phrase captured and made visible.

Swann took musical motifs to be genuine ideas from another world, ideas veiled in shadow.

He was not wrong to believe that the phrase of the sonata genuinely existed.

Though human in one respect,

it nevertheless belonged to an order of supernatural beings.

At the beginning of the final passage Swann heard a fine dialogue between the piano and the violin.

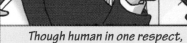

Swann did not dare move. No one even thought of speaking.

The ineffable expression of one man, absent, perhaps dead (for Swann had no idea whether Vinteuil was still alive), made this platform, from which a soul could be evoked in this way, one of the noblest altars for the celebration of a supernatural rite. Thus Swann, who had at first been irritated when the Comtesse de Monteriender, celebrated for her naïveté, leaned toward him to share her impressions even before the sonata was over, could not help detecting in her words a deep meaning, of which she herself was ignorant.

How prodigious! I've never heard anything so powerful . . .

anything so powerful . . . since the table-turning!

From that night on, Swann understood that Odette's feelings for him would never return.

Swann was sure that if he lived far from Odette, he would eventually feel indifferent toward her and would be content to see her leave Paris for good. He would have the courage to stay but lacked the courage to leave.

If he had been poor, humble, destitute, and obliged to accept any job that came his way, or had been tied to relatives or a wife, he might been forced to leave Odette.

No one knows his own happiness. No one is ever as unhappy as he thinks.

But he reckoned that this life had already lasted several years and all he could hope for was that it would last forever, that he would sacrifice his work, his pleasures, his friends, and ultimately his entire existence to the daily expectation of seeing her, and he wondered whether he was not mistaken, whether what had encouraged his affair had not worked against his destiny.

No one knows his own unhappiness. No one is ever as happy as he thinks.

Sometimes he hoped she would die painlessly in an accident.

Swann felt in his heart very close to the Mehmet he admired in Bellini's portrait, who, on discovering that he had fallen madly in love with one of his wives, stabbed her in order to regain his freedom of mind.

Odette had told him:

Forcheville is going to take a nice trip at Pentecost.

He's going to Egypt.

and Swann immediately realized what this meant:

I'm going to Egypt at Pentecost with Forcheville.

And in fact, several days later:

Now, about that trip you told me you'd be taking with Forcheville . . .

Yes, my love, we're leaving on the 19th, we'll send you a postcard of the Pyramids.

He then wanted to know if she was Forcheville's mistress.

One day he received an anonymous letter alleging that Odette had been the mistress of countless men (some of whom, including Forcheville, M. de Bréauté, and the painter, were mentioned by name), that she also loved women, and that she frequented brothels.

None of this worried him, because not one of the accusations against Odette was plausible in the slightest.

Like many people, Swann was mentally lazy and lacked inventiveness. He imagined that the part of a person's life he did not know was identical to the part he did.

Odette arranged her flowers and drank tea. . . . Swann therefore extrapolated those habits to the rest of her life.

But the idea that she visited madams, indulged in orgies with women, and led the dissolute life of an abject woman—what arrant nonsense!

Yet from time to time,

People are nasty. They tell me everything you do!

One day, Swann opened his newspaper . . .

Les Filles de marbre
THÉODORE BARRIÈRE

The word "marble" immediately reminded him of a story Odette had once told him of her visit to the Salon of the Palais de l'Industrie . . .

. . . with Mme Verdurin . . .

. . . watch out, I know how to make you melt: you're not made of marble . . .

Odette had told him this was just a joke.

Yet the anonymous letter had mentioned just this kind of love.

For the first time Swann recalled something Odette had said two years earlier,

At the moment Mme Verdurin has eyes only for me. I'm a love, she kisses me, she wants me to run errands with her,

she wants me to address her familiarly.

He went to Odette's.

He said nothing and watched their love dying.

All at once he made up his mind.

Odette, dear, I know how dreadful I am, but there are things I must ask you.

Do you remember the idea I had about you and Mme Verdurin?

Tell me if it was true, with her or any other woman.

I told you, as you know perfectly well.

Yes, I know, but are you sure? Tell me: "I've never done that sort of thing with any woman."

I've never done that sort of thing with any woman.

Will you swear to me on your medal of Our Lady of Laghet?

Swann knew Odette would not perjure herself with that medal of the Virgin.

You make me so unhappy! Are you quite finished? Just when I hoped to recapture the good times we used to have, and this is how you thank me!

You're quite wrong to think I would hold it against you in any way. I know a great deal more than I'm telling you. My anger is not a consequence of what you've done. I forgive it all because I love you.

My anger comes rather from your absurd deceitfulness, which causes you to go on denying things I already know.

If you're willing, it will all be over in an instant. You'll be free forever. Swear on your medal that you've never done such things.

But I don't know, really. Maybe a long time ago, without realizing what I was doing. Two or three times perhaps.

How strange that the words "two or three times"—mere words—could so lacerate his heart. He understood the madness to which he had succumbed when he had begun desiring to possess another human being—an always impossible thing.

But his jealousy judged that he had not suffered enough.

It's over, my dear. Was it with a person I know?

Why, no, I swear to you! In any case I think I exaggerated.

It's not important. You've already been so kind. It's over. Just one thing: How long ago?

Oh, Charles, can't you see you're killing me? All that is ancient history.

Can't you tell me it happened on a particular evening? . . . So I can imagine what I was doing that night?

I don't know, but I think it was in the Bois one evening when you came looking for us on the island. You'd been to dinner with the Princesse des Laumes.

There was a woman there I hadn't seen for a very long time. She said, "Come with me behind this rock to see the effect of the moonlight on the water."

At first I yawned and said, "No, I'm tired, and I'm fine here." She assured me that she'd never seen such a moon before.

I said to her, "Cut out the nonsense!" I knew what she had in mind.

You're awful. You like to torture me, to force me to tell lies so that you'll leave me alone.

Life is really astonishing. Here is a woman I trusted. I question her, and the little she confesses to reveals far more than I could have suspected.

Poor darling, I see that I'm hurting you. It's over now. I'll not give it another thought.

This second blow was worse than the first. He had never imagined anything so recent, concealed in the nights he had spent with Odette.

He didn't hold it against her. She was only half to blame.

Hadn't someone said that her own mother had handed her over to a wealthy Englishman when she was still practically a child?

What a painful truth these lines from Alfred de Vigny's *Journal d'un Poète* represented for him:

"When seized by love for a woman, ask: With whom does she associate? What kind of life has she led? All your future happiness depends on the answers."

Often it was Odette herself, without realizing it, who spontaneously revealed things he did not know and now dreaded to learn. Indeed, the gap that vice had created between her real life and the relatively innocent life that Swann had imagined his mistress led, was far wider than she knew.

At one point he tried to find out if she had ever been in contact with a procuress. He was actually sure that the answer was no. The anonymous letter had planted the suspicion in his mind, but in a mechanical way, and Swann hoped that Odette would dispel it.

Oh, no! Not that they don't persecute me. One of them waited two hours for me yesterday and invited me to name my own price. I wish you could have seen how I treated her.

I shouted at the top of my lungs: "But I'm telling you I want no part of this! It's a crazy idea, and I don't like it. If I needed money, I would understand."

I wish you'd been hidden somewhere in the apartment. I think you'd have been happy, dear.

There's some good in your little Odette after all, you see.

When she confessed to him, moreover, her confessions served only to arouse new doubts in Swann's mind.

Once, to frighten him:

. . . the Maison d'Or reminds me of something I can't quite remember but knew not to be true.

Yes, I didn't go there the night I told you I had when you went looking for me at Prévost's.

I'd actually gone off with Forcheville.

I'd really been to Prévost's, that wasn't a lie, but he met me there and asked me in to see his etchings.

But someone had come to see him.

I told you I was coming from the Maison d'Or because I was afraid you'd be annoyed.

So you see, I was being rather kind to you. I was wrong, but at least I'm telling you candidly what happened.

So even during the months she'd loved him, she was already lying to him.

In addition to the time (the first night they'd "made cattleya") she'd told him she'd been to the Maison Dorée, how many other times must there have been in which some lie lay concealed? He remembered one day when she'd said:

I'll just tell Mme Verdurin my dress wasn't ready or my cab came late.

There's always a way to arrange things.

She'd probably used similar words to explain a delay or a change in the time of their meeting in order to conceal from him something she'd had to do with someone else, someone to whom she'd said:

I'll just tell Swann that my dress wasn't ready or my cab came late.

There's always a way to arrange things.

Beneath his fondest memories and behind the simplest statements Odette had made to him in the past, Swann sensed the possible subterranean presence of lies that dishonored everything he held dearest, dismantling his entire past stone by stone.

Some nights, she was suddenly kind to him again in a way that she duly warned him he'd better take advantage of right away, lest years go by before she was nice to him again.

Right now, let's go home and "make cattleya."

The desire she pretended to feel for him was so sudden and so inexplicable, and the caresses she dispensed afterwards were so demonstrative and unusual, that this abrupt and implausible tenderness caused Swann as much pain as a lie or an insult.

One night, after returning home at her behest . . .

What's that noise?

Someone's there!

Charles, be reasonable, no one's there. Come here!

There's nothing to be done with you!

He remained unsure whether she might have hidden someone she wished to make miserable with jealousy or inflame with passion.

He would sometimes visit a brothel in the hope of learning something about her, without daring to mention her name.

I have a youngster you'll like.

He would stay for an hour of depressing conversation with a poor girl astonished that he wanted nothing more.

A very young one once said to him:

What I'd like would be to find a friend. I'd never go with anyone else again.

Do you think a woman could be so touched by a man's love that she'd never deceive him?

That would depend on her character!

Swann couldn't prevent himself from talking to these prostitutes in a way that would have pleased the Princesse des Laumes.

How nice, you've worn blue eyes to match your belt.

You, too. You have blue cuffs.

What a pleasant conversation we're having for a place of this sort. I'm not boring you, am I? Perhaps you have something to do?

No, I have all the time in the world.

If you were boring me, I'd tell you.

On the contrary, I love to listen to you talk.

I'm very flattered.

But he got up and said goodbye. She was of no interest to him. She didn't know Odette.

157

The painter was ill, and Dr. Cottard advised him to take a sea voyage. Several of the faithful spoke of going with him. The Verdurins, who could not stand the idea of being left alone, first rented a yacht and then bought it, and after that Odette made frequent cruises.

Each time she left for a short cruise, Swann felt he was beginning to get over her, but the moment he heard she was back, he could not refrain from going to see her.

Once, after leaving for what was supposed to be a month's voyage, the Verdurins and their guests traveled from Algiers to Tunis and then Italy, Greece, Constantinople, and Asia Minor. The voyage lasted almost a year. Swann felt perfectly tranquil and almost happy.

One day, shortly after the travelers returned . . .

Your ears must have been burning, M. Swann. Throughout the voyage with Mme Verdurin,

we talked of nothing but you.

Mme Cottard!

Swann was quite surprised, since he assumed his name was never to be mentioned in the presence of the Verdurins.

In any case, Mme de Crécy was there. Need I say more? When Odette is around, it's never long before the conversation turns to you.

And rest assured that it's not to speak ill.

What? You doubt it?

But she adores you!

She even had what I thought was a nice turn of phrase. M. Verdurin asked her, "But how do you know what he's doing right now since he's a thousand miles away."

And Odette answered: "To a friend's eye nothing is impossible."

158

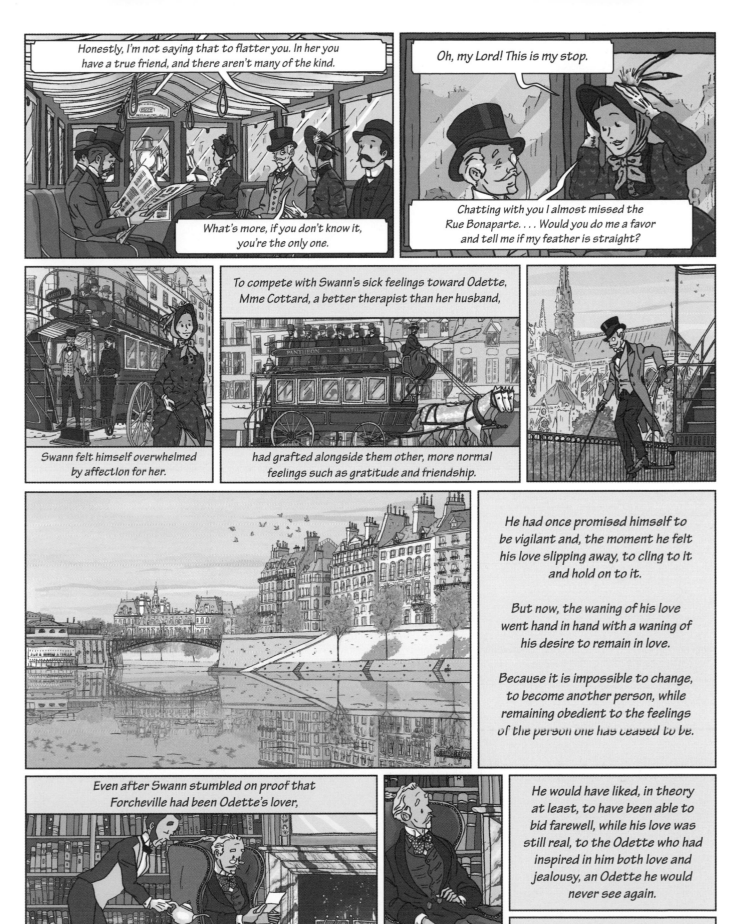

Honestly, I'm not saying that to flatter you. In her you have a true friend, and there aren't many of the kind.

What's more, if you don't know it, you're the only one.

Oh, my Lord! This is my stop.

Chatting with you I almost missed the Rue Bonaparte.... Would you do me a favor and tell me if my feather is straight?

Swann felt himself overwhelmed by affection for her.

To compete with Swann's sick feelings toward Odette, Mme Cottard, a better therapist than her husband, had grafted alongside them other, more normal feelings such as gratitude and friendship.

He had once promised himself to be vigilant and, the moment he felt his love slipping away, to cling to it and hold on to it.

But now, the waning of his love went hand in hand with a waning of his desire to remain in love.

Because it is impossible to change, to become another person, while remaining obedient to the feelings of the person one has ceased to be.

Even after Swann stumbled on proof that Forcheville had been Odette's lover, it caused him no pain, because his love was now so distant, and he regretted not having noticed the moment it had deserted him for good.

He would have liked, in theory at least, to have been able to bid farewell, while his love was still real, to the Odette who had inspired in him both love and jealousy, an Odette he would never see again.

He was wrong. He was to see her one more time, a few weeks later . . .

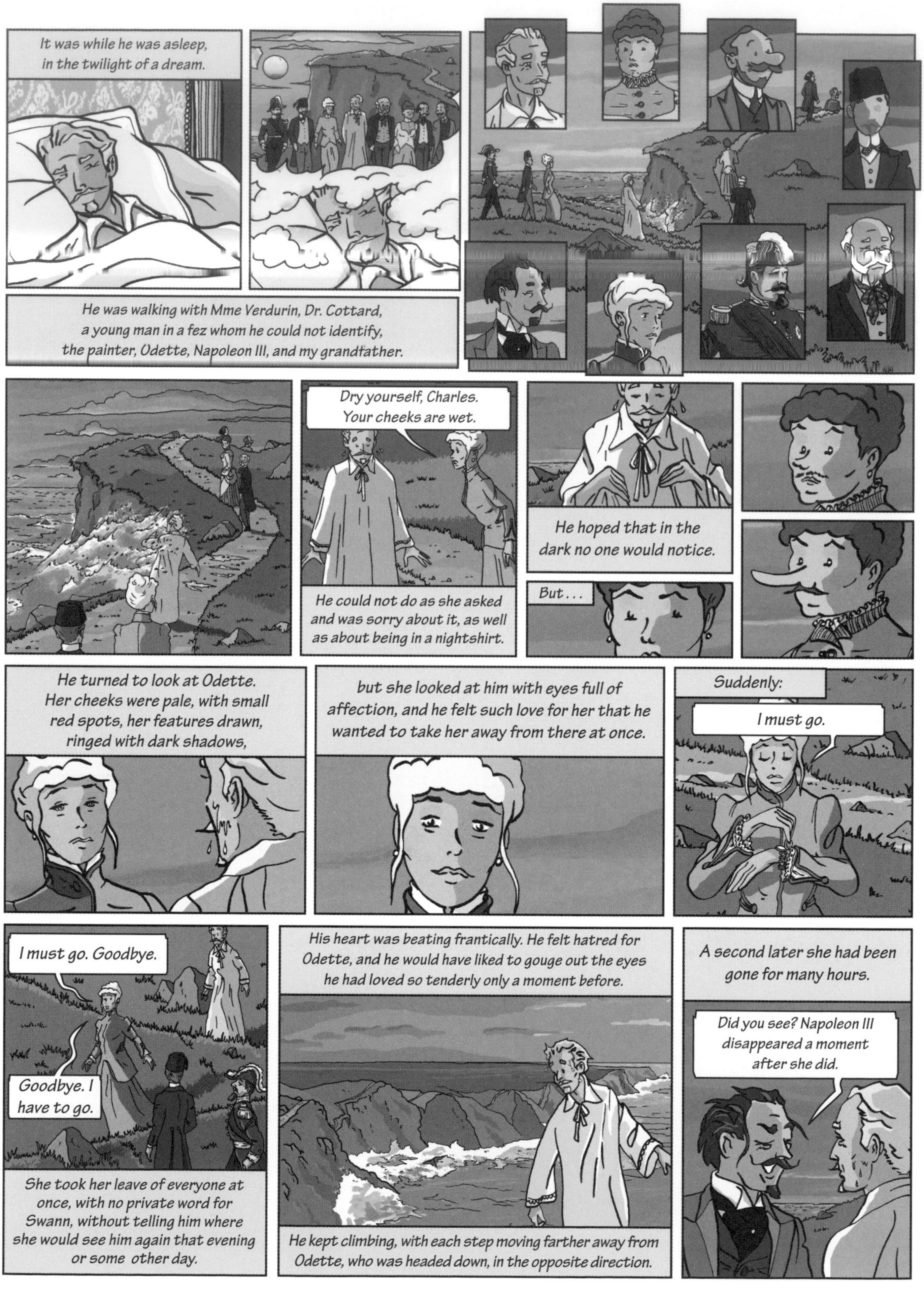

It was while he was asleep, in the twilight of a dream.
He was walking with Mme Verdurin, Dr. Cottard, a young man in a fez whom he could not identify, the painter, Odette, Napoleon III, and my grandfather.
Dry yourself, Charles. Your cheeks are wet.
He could not do as she asked and was sorry about it, as well as about being in a nightshirt.
He hoped that in the dark no one would notice.
But . . .
He turned to look at Odette. Her cheeks were pale, with small red spots, her features drawn, ringed with dark shadows,
but she looked at him with eyes full of affection, and he felt such love for her that he wanted to take her away from there at once.
Suddenly:
I must go.
I must go. Goodbye.
Goodbye. I have to go.
She took her leave of everyone at once, with no private word for Swann, without telling him where she would see him again that evening or some other day.
His heart was beating frantically. He felt hatred for Odette, and he would have liked to gouge out the eyes he had loved so tenderly only a moment before.
He kept climbing, with each step moving farther away from Odette, who was headed down, in the opposite direction.
A second later she had been gone for many hours.
Did you see? Napoleon III disappeared a moment after she did.

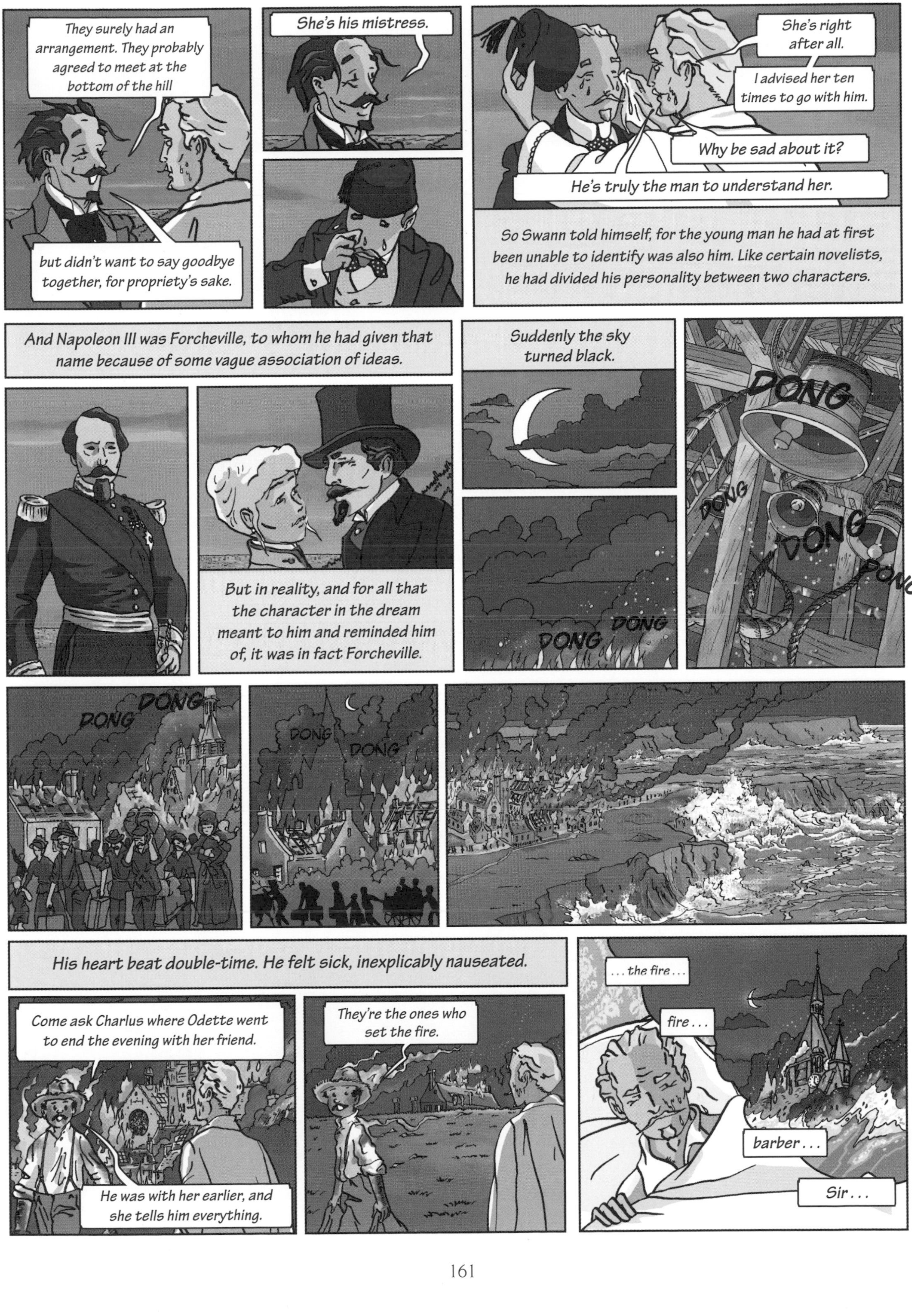
They surely had an arrangement. They probably agreed to meet at the bottom of the hill
but didn't want to say goodbye together, for propriety's sake.
She's his mistress.
She's right after all.
I advised her ten times to go with him.
Why be sad about it?
He's truly the man to understand her.
So Swann told himself, for the young man he had at first been unable to identify was also him. Like certain novelists, he had divided his personality between two characters.
And Napoleon III was Forcheville, to whom he had given that name because of some vague association of ideas.
But in reality, and for all that the character in the dream meant to him and reminded him of, it was in fact Forcheville.
Suddenly the sky turned black.
DONG DONG
DONG DONG DONG DONG
DONG DONG
DONG DONG
His heart beat double-time. He felt sick, inexplicably nauseated.
Come ask Charlus where Odette went to end the evening with her friend.
He was with her earlier, and she tells him everything.
They're the ones who set the fire.
. . . the fire . . .
fire . . .
barber . . .
Sir . . .

And again, as if Odette were once more close beside him, he saw her pale complexion, her excessively thin cheeks. her drawn features, her tired eyes—all things he had ceased to notice since the first days of their affair. And with that intermittent callousness that returned whenever he ceased to feel unhappy, taking his moral level down a notch . . .

Place Names:
The Name

Among the bedrooms I conjured up most frequently during sleepless nights, none resembled the rooms in Combray less than my room in the Grand Hôtel de la Plage at Balbec.

But nothing resembled the real Balbec less than the one I often dreamed of on stormy days . . .

My greatest desire was to witness a storm over the ocean. For me, the greatest spectacles were those I knew had not been artificially staged for my pleasure.

Let's hurry home.

Don't walk so close to the wall. A tile might fall on your head with all this wind.

Holy Virgin!

I've had quite enough of all these catastrophes and shipwrecks the papers are full of.

My God . . .

I was eager to know only those things that had value for me because they showed me an aspect of the thought of a great genius or the force or grace that nature exhibits when left to her own devices, free of man's intervention.

Just as the pleasant sound of a woman's voice reproduced in a recording cannot console a man for the loss of his mother,

so would a mechanically produced tempest have left me as cold as the illuminated fountains of the World's Fair.

To make sure that the ocean storm was absolutely real, I also required a natural coast rather than a jetty recently constructed by the town.

I remembered the name Balbec, which Legrandin had mentioned as the name of a beach very close to...

...those funereal coasts, famous for countless shipwrecks and for six months of the year shrouded in fog and spray.

...there, far more than in the Finistère, you feel beneath your feet the veritable end of French, of European, soil, of the ancient land.

One day in Combray, when I mentioned the beach at Balbec in the presence of M. Swann:

I do indeed know Balbec! The church in Balbec, which dates back to the twelfth and thirteenth centuries and is still half Romanesque, is perhaps the most curious specimen of Norman Gothic,

and most unusual! You might mistake it for a work of Persian inspiration.

...and the Gothic seemed more alive to me now that I could see it apart from the cities in which I had always until then imagined it and see how, in one particular instance on these barren rocks, it had germinated and blossomed into a fine steeple.

I was taken to see reproductions of the most celebrated statues in Balbec,

and I felt such joy that I could scarcely breathe at the thought that I might someday see them set in relief against the eternal briny fog.

On sweet stormy nights in February, the wind mingled my desire for Gothic architecture with my desire to witness an ocean storm.

I would have liked to take, the very next day, the lovely and magnificent 1:22 train.

It stopped at Bayeux, Coutances, Vitré, Questambert, Pontorson, Balbec, Lannion, Lamballe, Benodet, Pont-Aven, and Quimperlé,

Benodet

Pont-Aven

Quimperlé

splendidly freighted with names among which I could not say which pleased me most.

If I dressed quickly, I could even leave Paris that very night and arrive in Balbec as dawn broke over the raging sea, from whose spray I could seek refuge in the Persian-style church.

As Easter vacation approached, however, and my parents promised that I could spend it this time in northern Italy,

my dreams of ocean storms gave way to contrasting dreams of a most iridescent spring among the lilies and anemones that already covered the fields of Fiesole and dazzled Florence with a background of gold such as one sees in the works of Fra Angelico.

These alternating images had shifted the front of my desire and transposed my sensibility to a different key.

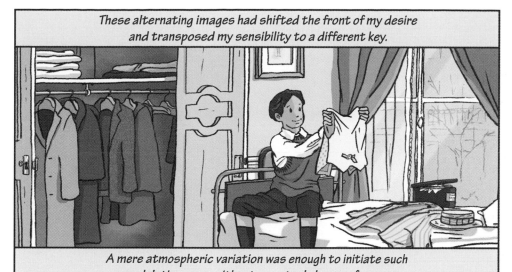

Before long, however, these dreams of the Atlantic and of Italy ceased to depend solely on changes of season and weather.

A mere atmospheric variation was enough to initiate such a modulation, even without an actual change of season.

To bring them to life I needed only to pronounce these names:

Balbec

Venice

Florence

Even in the spring, it was enough to find the name "Balbec" in a book to revive my desire to see ocean storms and Norman Gothic.

Even on a stormy day, the names "Florence" or "Venice" filled me with desire for sunshine, lilies, the Doges' Palace, and Santa Maria del Fiore.

Yet while those names forever shaped my images of those cities, they also transformed them.

They exalted my idea of certain places on this earth by making them more specific and therefore more real.

How much more individual they became by being named with names of their own, like people!

Words present us with a clear, common image of things.

things conceived as similar to all other things of the same kind.

A workbench.

A bird.

An anthill.

But names present a vague image of individuals—or cities—that draw from their bright or dark sonority the color that is uniformly applied to each, as in one of those posters that is entirely blue or red because of some limitation of the process used to print it, or some whim of the designer.

The name "Parma," one of the cities I most wanted to visit after reading Stendhal's *Charterhouse of Parma*, seemed to me compact, smooth, mauve, and soft. If someone mentioned a house I might visit in Parma,

I would experience in my mind the pleasure of inhabiting a house that was smooth, compact, mauve, and soft, bearing no relation at all to the houses

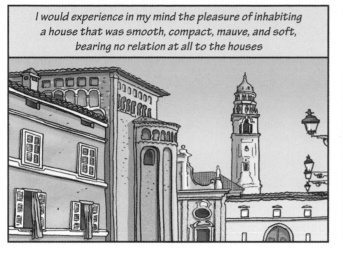

in any Italian city, since I would be imagining it solely with the aid of the ponderous syllable "*Parme*," in which no air circulates, and all the Stendhalian softness and tincture of violet with which I invested it.

And when I thought of Florence, I thought of a city that resembled a corolla, because it was called the city of lilies, and its cathedral was Santa Maria del Fiore.

As for *Balbec*, it was one of those names in which, like an old Norman pot that retains the color of the earth from which it was made,

one could still visualize the image of some abolished custom or obsolete pronunciation I was sure I would find in the innkeeper to whom I assigned the solemn, disputatious, medieval look of a character from a fabliau.

Had my health improved and my parents allowed me, if not to stay in Balbec then at least, just once, to take the 1:22 train

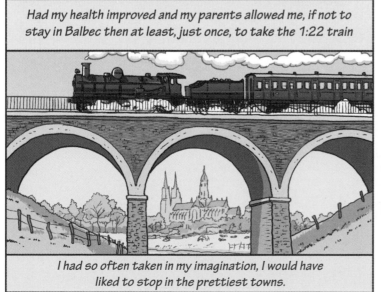

I had so often taken in my imagination, I would have liked to stop in the prettiest towns.

But how would I choose among *Bayeux*, so estimable in its noble reddish lace and with its summit illuminated by the old gold of its final syllable; *Vitré*, whose acute accent framed the old window in dark wood; and gentle *Lamballe*, which, in its whiteness, ranged from eggshell yellow to pearl gray . . .

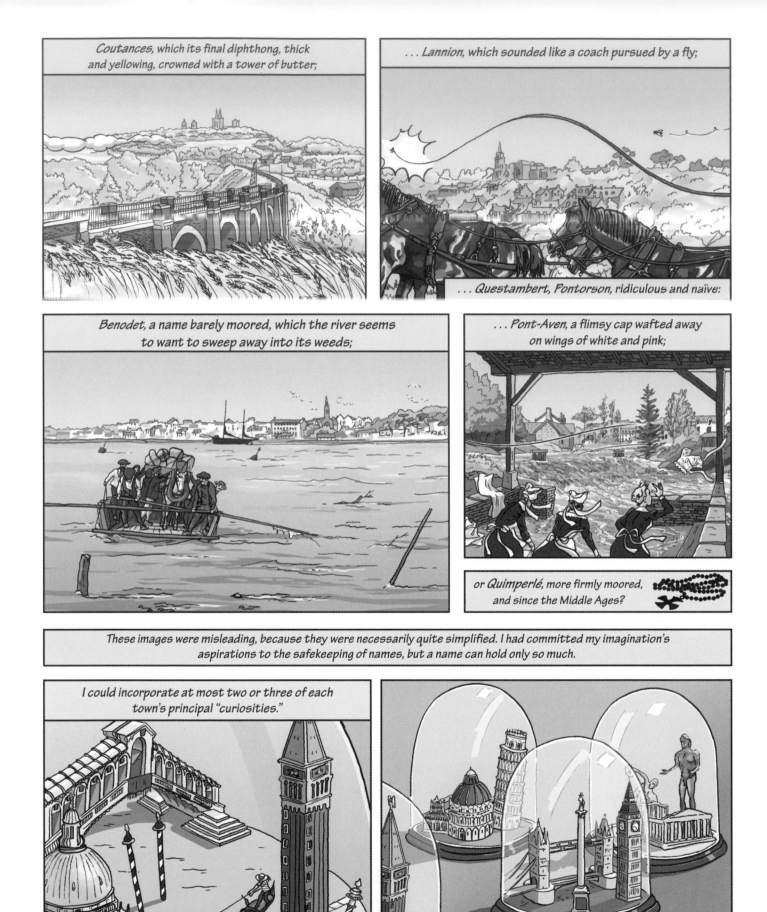

Coutances, which its final diphthong, thick and yellowing, crowned with a tower of butter;

. . . Lannion, which sounded like a coach pursued by a fly;

. . . Questambert, Pontorson, ridiculous and naïve:

Benodet, a name barely moored, which the river seems to want to sweep away into its weeds;

. . . Pont-Aven, a flimsy cap wafted away on wings of white and pink;

or Quimperlé, more firmly moored, and since the Middle Ages?

These images were misleading, because they were necessarily quite simplified. I had committed my imagination's aspirations to the safekeeping of names, but a name can hold only so much.

I could incorporate at most two or three of each town's principal "curiosities."

When my father decided one year that we would spend Easter vacation in Florence and Venice, I found that, unable to fill the name "Florence" with the ingredients that make up a city,

I was forced to extract a supernatural city from the fertilization by certain springtime fragrances of what I believed to be, in its essence, Giotto's genius.

And since a name cannot contain much more of time than of space, in the way that some of Giotto's paintings show the same character in action at two different moments in time, the name "Florence" was divided into two compartments.

In one, beneath an architectural dais, I contemplated a fresco;

in the other, I was rapidly crossing a Ponte Vecchio filled with jonquils, narcissi, and anemones.

Even from a purely realistic point of view, the places we desire take up much more space in our authentic lives at any given moment than do the places in which we actually find ourselves.

I couldn't contain my joy when my father, while consulting the barometer and deploring the cold, began to search for the best train.

Ah, there: Venice!

...if you take the 6:30 overnight train...

I understood that I would be able to wake up the next day in the city of marble and gold. It and the city of lilies were not simply made-up pictures but quite real places.

...In short, you could stay in Venice from April 20 to 29 and arrive in Florence on Easter morning.

But I was still only on my way to the ultimate degree of happiness.

I finally reached it when:

It's probably still cold on the Grand Canal.

You'd better pack your winter coat and heavy sport jacket.

With those words I attained a sort of ecstasy. By a feat of gymnastics beyond my ability, I divested myself of the useless carapace of air in my room

and replaced it with equal parts of Venetian air, with that indescribable marine atmosphere that belonged to my dreams and that my imagination had encapsulated in the name "Venice."

I felt myself undergo a miraculous disincarnation.

It was immediately accompanied by an obscure need to vomit such as one feels with a severe sore throat,

and I had to be put to bed with a fever so stubborn

that the doctor declared not only that I would not be able to go to Florence and Venice but

that even after I recovered, I must give up for at least a year any thought of travel and avoid any possible disturbance.

Unfortunately, he also said I must absolutely not be allowed to go to the theater to see Berma.

Instead, I should be restricted to going every day to the Champs-Elysées under the watchful eye of a caretaker who would see to it that I didn't tire myself out...

...and that caretaker would be none other than Françoise, who had come to work for us after the death of my Aunt Léonie.

I found going to the Champs-Elysées unbearable. Nothing about that public garden matched my dreams.

One day, because I was bored with our usual place, Françoise took me to a nearby spot where the faces were unfamiliar . . .

Goodbye, Gilberte. I'm going home now.

Don't forget we're coming to your house tonight after dinner.

The name "Gilberte" grazed my ears, evoking the existence of the person it designated all the more forcefully in that it identified her not merely as an absent person under discussion but as someone being addressed directly.

It passed by me, in other words, in action, with an impact enhanced by the curve of its trajectory and the proximity of its target.

Come, it's time to go home!

I'm coming, Mademoiselle.

Come, button your coat and let's be on our way.

I noticed for the first time with irritation that Françoise spoke in a vulgar way and unfortunately had no blue feather in her hat.

Would *she* ever return to the Champs-Elysées? The next day she wasn't there, but I saw her there on subsequent days.

One time there were not enough girls for their game of "bars":

Would you like to join our camp?

And from then on I played with her whenever she was there. But she didn't come every day. There were days when she couldn't come

because she had classes, or catechism, or a tea—all the things that separated her life from mine, condensed in the name "Gilberte," which had so painfully grazed my ears twice, once on the sloping path in Combray and again on the lawn of the Champs-Elysées.

If she had to study, she said:

What a bore, I can't come tomorrow. You'll all have your fun without me.

With a sad look that consoled me somewhat.

On the other hand, when she was invited to a friend's party:

Would you like to play tomorrow?

I hope not! I hope Mama will let me go to my friend's!

On those days, at least, I knew I would not see her.

While other days her mother took her shopping without warning, and the next day she would say:

Ah! Yes, I went with Mama.

. . . as if it were a natural thing and not, for another person, the greatest possible misfortune.

There were also days when the weather was bad, and her governess, who was afraid of the rain herself, did not want to take her to the Champs-Elysées.

So when the sky looked doubtful in the morning, I checked the weather constantly and was attentive to all the signs.

That lady is going out, so the weather must be suitable for being outdoors. Why wouldn't Gilberte do the same?

But the weather took a turn for the worse.

Oh, things may still improve. A ray of sunshine is all it would take.

. . . but more likely it will rain.

and if it rained, what was the use of going to the Champs-Elysées?

So after lunch my anxious eyes remained fixed on the changeable, cloudy skies.

Beyond the window the balcony was gray.

All at once:

176

Fleeting ivy, clambering up the wall—for me, the most precious of all plants since that day when it appeared, on our balcony, as the shadow of Gilberte, who was perhaps already at the Champs-Elysées.

Let's play "bars" right away. You'll be on my side!

. . . a promise of immediate pleasure, which the day would either grant or refuse, and thus of pleasure par excellence: the pleasure of love.

And even on days when the skies were too cloudy to hope that Gilberte would come out . . .

Look, the weather is fine now, you might try going to the Champs-Elysées after all.

No one was there that day but a girl on the point of leaving, who assured me that Gilberte would not come.

Sitting alone near the grass was a rather elderly woman, who came no matter what the weather.

Gilberte greeted her every day. She would ask Gilberte for news about "her lovely mother." I felt that if I had known this woman, I would have been someone else entirely for Gilberte. While the woman's grandchildren played nearby, she used to read the Débats.

In an aristocratic way she spoke of

my old Débats.

. . . my old friend the constable . . .

. . . the lady who rents chairs, who is an old friend of mine . . .

177

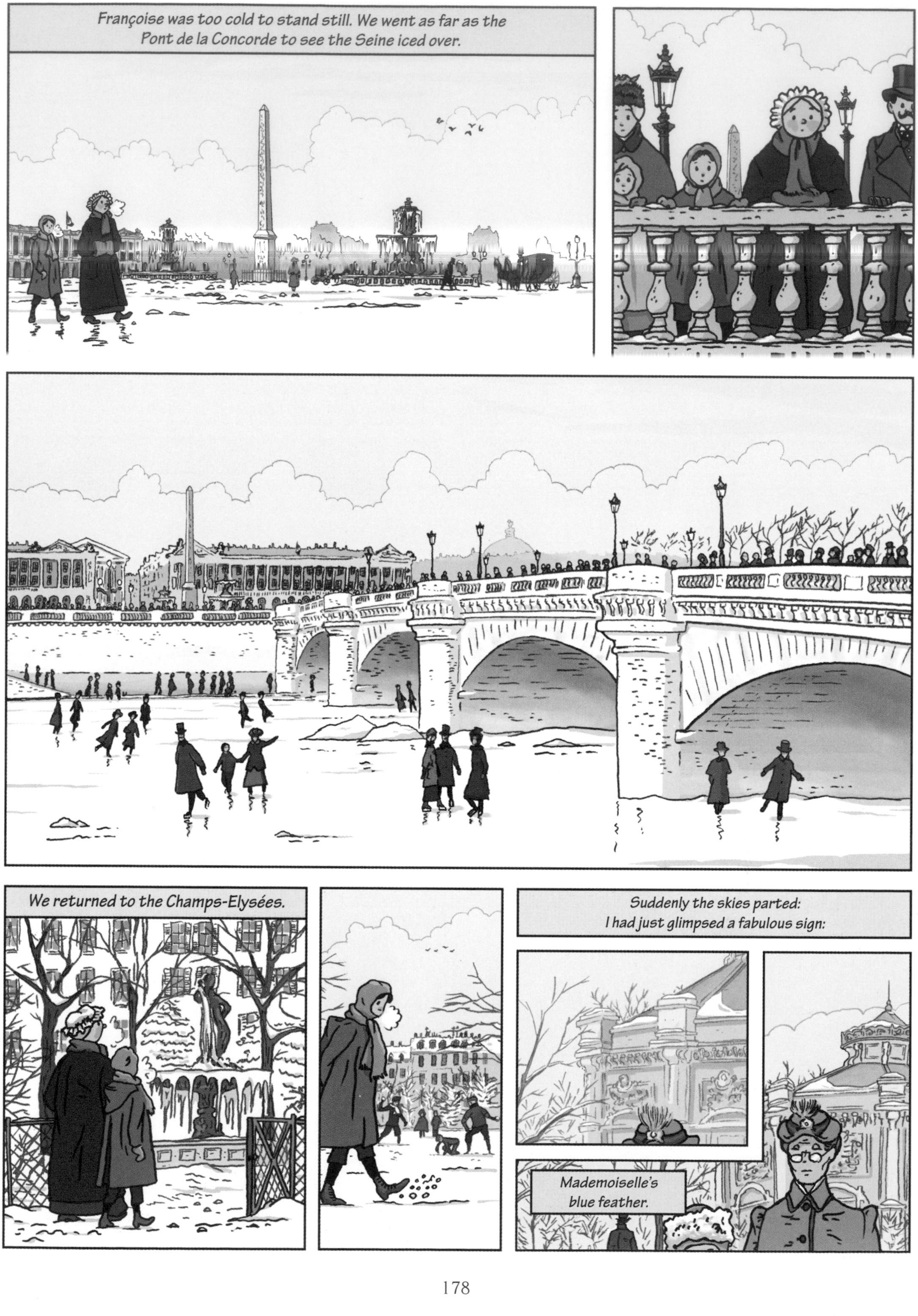
Françoise was too cold to stand still. We went as far as the Pont de la Concorde to see the Seine iced over.
We returned to the Champs-Elysées.
Suddenly the skies parted: I had just glimpsed a fabulous sign:
Mademoiselle's blue feather.

My love progressed that day, for it was the first time she and I shared a sorrow.
We were the only two children from our group.

When you're in love, no one else matters.

Whenever I was away from Gilberte, I felt the need to see her, because after trying so often to conjure up her image, I could no longer imagine her at all, so it was hard to know what the object of my love was.

Of course, she had never yet said that she loved me. On the contrary, she often said she had other friends she preferred.

But I hadn't yet declared my feelings for her either.

It was urgent that Gilberte and I meet so that we could each confess our love for the other, which would not really begin, so to speak, until we had done so.

Of course, the various reasons that made me so impatient to see her would have been less imperious for a grown man.

Later, when we have acquired a certain skill in the cultivation of our pleasures, we make do with the pleasure we have in thinking about a woman without worrying whether our image of her corresponds to reality,

and also with the pleasure of loving her without needing to be sure that she loves us.

But when I reached the Champs-Elysées, the moment I was face-to-face with the Gilberte Swann with whom I had played the day before, it was as if she and the girl who was the object of my dreams were two different people.

As I prepared to study Gilberte's image in order to make sure that she was indeed the person I remembered,

the same self urged me to catch the ball she had thrown,

...as if she were a friend with whom I had simply come to play and not a kindred spirit I had come to join,

thus preventing me from saying the words that might have advanced our love decisively,

and each time I was obliged to defer my hope of progress until the next afternoon.

Progress did occur, however. One day . . .

I can buy two marbles for a penny.

I stared admiringly at the bright agate marbles, captive in their wooden bowl.

Which do you think the prettiest?

I didn't want her to sacrifice any of them. I would have liked her to buy them all, to deliver them all. But I pointed to one the color of her eyes.

Here, it's for you. I'm giving it to you. Keep it as a souvenir.

Another time, when I was still obsessed with my desire to see Berma in a classic play, I asked Gilberte if she owned a small book in which Bergotte discussed Racine.

It's impossible to find in bookstores.

Yes, I think I have it, but you'll need to give me the exact title.

That evening, I sent her a brief telegram, on the envelope of which I wrote the name "Gilberte Swann," which I had written so often in my notebooks.

(Ce côté est exclusivement réservé à l'adresse.)
SERVICE TÉLÉGRAPHIQUE
TÉLÉGRAMME
mademoiselle Gilberte Swann
6, rue de Traktir
seizième arrondissement
(Étoile)
PARIS
LE PORT EST GRATUIT

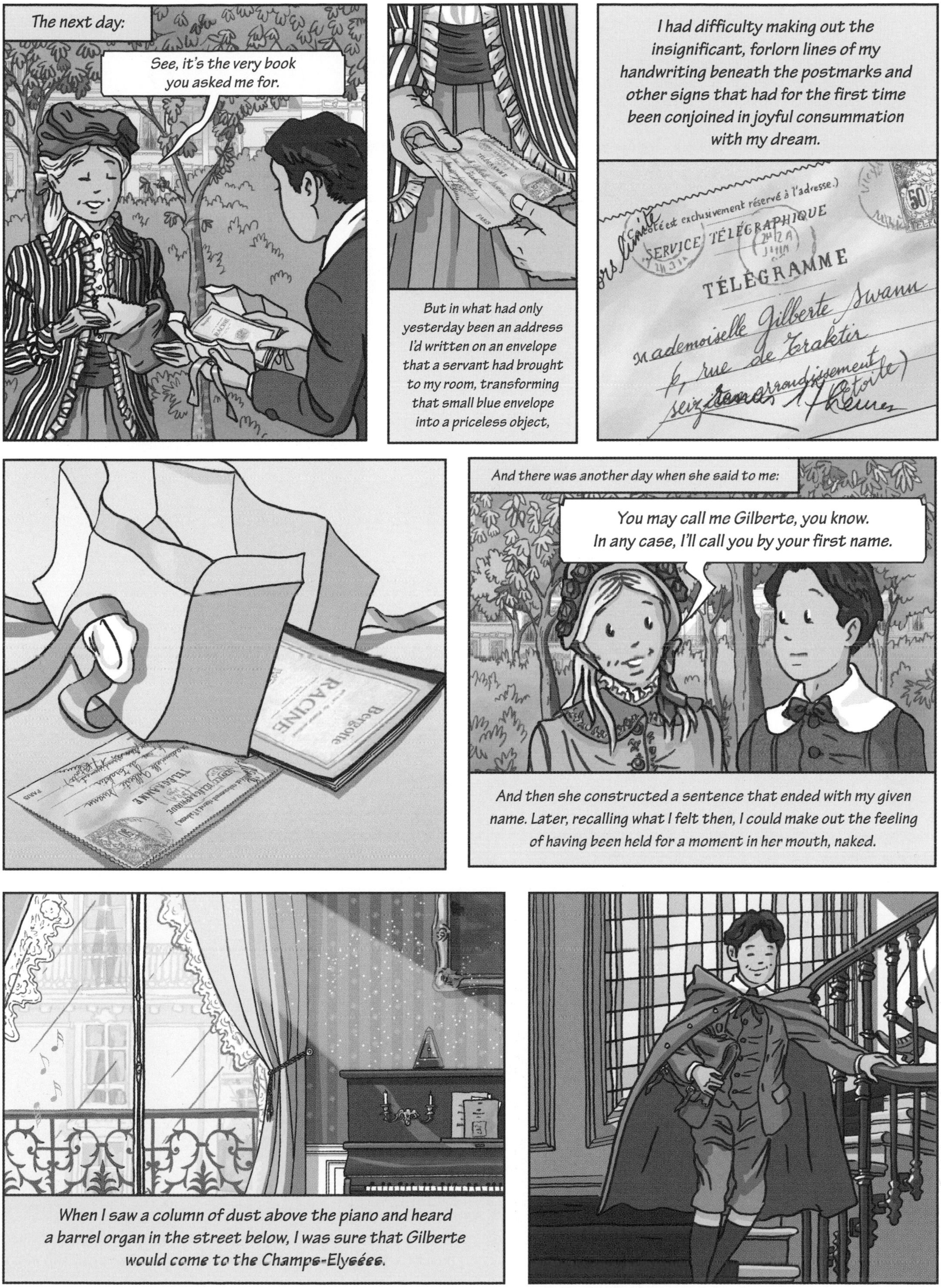

The next day:
See, it's the very book you asked me for.
But in what had only yesterday been an address I'd written on an envelope that a servant had brought to my room, transforming that small blue envelope into a priceless object,
I had difficulty making out the insignificant, forlorn lines of my handwriting beneath the postmarks and other signs that had for the first time been conjoined in joyful consummation with my dream.
SERVICE TÉLÉGRAPHIQUE
TÉLÉGRAMME
Mademoiselle Gilberte Swann
RACINE
Bergotte
And there was another day when she said to me:
You may call me Gilberte, you know. In any case, I'll call you by your first name.
And then she constructed a sentence that ended with my given name. Later, recalling what I felt then, I could make out the feeling of having been held for a moment in her mouth, naked.
When I saw a column of dust above the piano and heard a barrel organ in the street below, I was sure that Gilberte would come to the Champs-Elysées.

At school, in my one o'clock class, the sun made me squirm with impatience and boredom awaiting the moment when Françoise would meet me at the schoolhouse door.

Unfortunately, I didn't find Gilberte on the Champs-Elysées. She hadn't yet arrived.

What fine weather!

I expected to see Gilberte appear at any moment, trailing behind her governess.

I led Françoise off in the direction from which I expected Gilberte to come.

We didn't see her,

Let's turn back. She's not coming.

I was heading back toward the grass when:

Quickly, quickly. Gilberte has been here for fifteen minutes. She'll be leaving soon.

We've been waiting for you to play "bars."

We could never be sure from which direction Gilberte would come.

I guessed some of the things Gilberte did when she was out of sight. I was in contact with the mystery of her unknown life. That mystery troubled me when I saw Gilberte, who could be sharp and peremptory or abrupt with us, addressing the lady with the *Débats* in quite a different tone . . .

What a lovely sun! It's like fire.

. . . with a timid smile or in a stiff manner that hinted at the different girl Gilberte must have been in her other life, which eluded me.

No one revealed that other life to me as fully as M. Swann, who came a short while later to fetch his daughter.

This was because he and Mme Swann, being gods who held all power over her, cast over me, perhaps even more than Gilberte herself did, a painful spell.

His appearance still impressed me as that of a historical personage, whose smallest peculiarities become the focus of our passions.

When I heard his relations with the Comte de Paris discussed in Combray, they meant nothing to me, but now they seemed marvelous.

He responded politely to the greetings of Gilberte's friends and even to mine, although he was not speaking to my family, but he gave no sign of knowing me, although he had often seen me in the country. I held on to this memory, but in the shadows, as it were, because after I saw Gilberte again, Swann became for me her father above all and no longer the Swann of Combray.

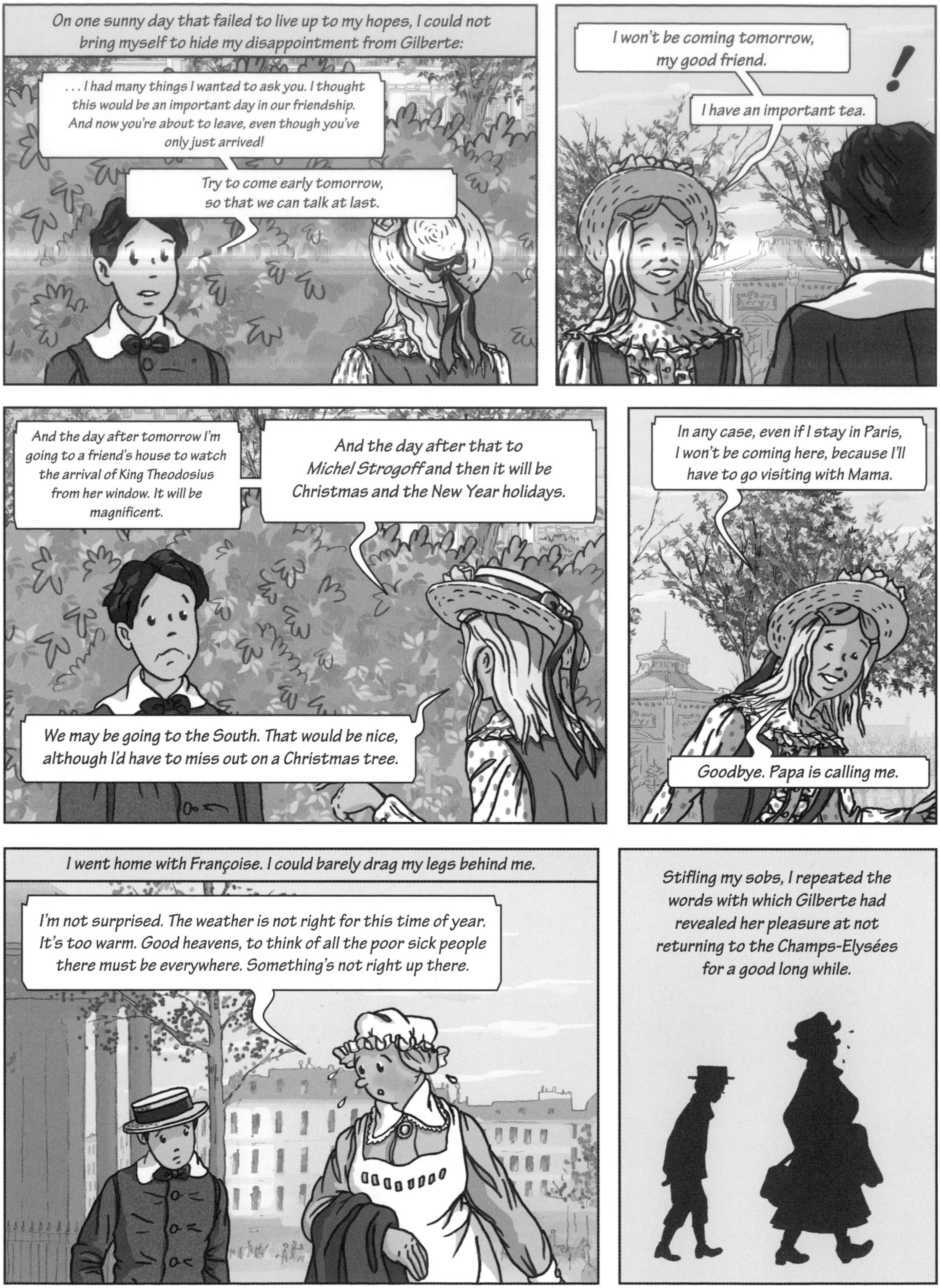
On one sunny day that failed to live up to my hopes, I could not bring myself to hide my disappointment from Gilberte:
. . . I had many things I wanted to ask you. I thought this would be an important day in our friendship. And now you're about to leave, even though you've only just arrived!
Try to come early tomorrow, so that we can talk at last.
I won't be coming tomorrow, my good friend.
I have an important tea.
!
And the day after tomorrow I'm going to a friend's house to watch the arrival of King Theodosius from her window. It will be magnificent.
And the day after that to *Michel Strogoff* and then it will be Christmas and the New Year holidays.
We may be going to the South. That would be nice, although I'd have to miss out on a Christmas tree.
In any case, even if I stay in Paris, I won't be coming here, because I'll have to go visiting with Mama.
Goodbye. Papa is calling me.
I went home with Françoise. I could barely drag my legs behind me.
I'm not surprised. The weather is not right for this time of year. It's too warm. Good heavens, to think of all the poor sick people there must be everywhere. Something's not right up there.
Stifling my sobs, I repeated the words with which Gilberte had revealed her pleasure at not returning to the Champs-Elysées for a good long while.

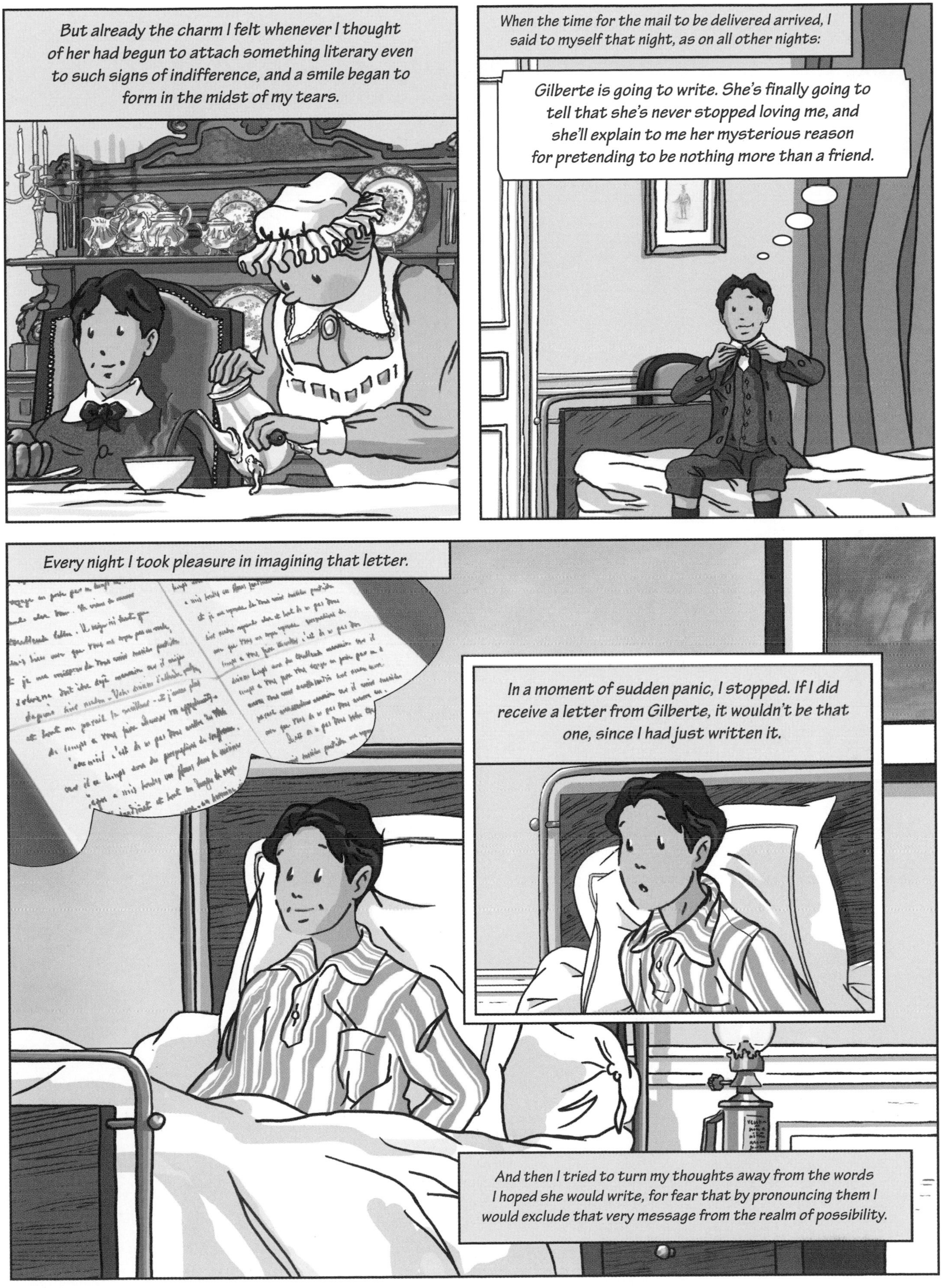

But already the charm I felt whenever I thought of her had begun to attach something literary even to such signs of indifference, and a smile began to form in the midst of my tears.
When the time for the mail to be delivered arrived, I said to myself that night, as on all other nights:
Gilberte is going to write. She's finally going to tell that she's never stopped loving me, and she'll explain to me her mysterious reason for pretending to be nothing more than a friend.
Every night I took pleasure in imagining that letter.
In a moment of sudden panic, I stopped. If I did receive a letter from Gilberte, it wouldn't be that one, since I had just written it.
And then I tried to turn my thoughts away from the words I hoped she would write, for fear that by pronouncing them I would exclude that very message from the realm of possibility.

Meanwhile, I read a page that Gilberte had not written but which at least came from her.

. . . the page by Bergotte about the beauty of the old myths from which Racine took his inspiration and which,

along with the agate marble, I always kept near me.

Bergotte, the infinitely wise and almost divine old man because of whom I had first fallen in love with Gilberte before I ever saw her, I now loved primarily because of Gilberte.

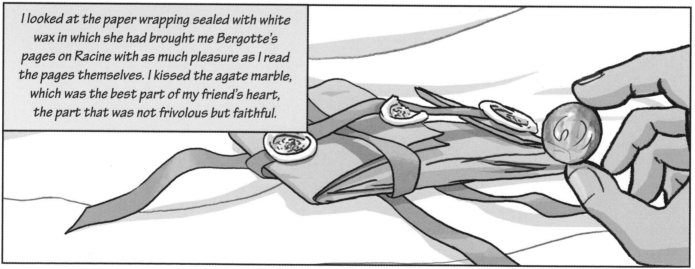

I looked at the paper wrapping sealed with white wax in which she had brought me Bergotte's pages on Racine with as much pleasure as I read the pages themselves. I kissed the agate marble, which was the best part of my friend's heart, the part that was not frivolous but faithful.

But I realized that the beauty of that stone, and of Bergotte's pages, preceded my love, that their elements had been determined by the writer's talent or the laws of mineralogy before Gilberte ever knew me.

When I saw Gilberte go to a party or run errands with her governess and prepare for Christmas vacation, I was wrong to think:

She's doing this because she's frivolous or docile...

...Because she would have ceased to be either if she had loved me, and if she had been forced to obey, it would have been with the same despair I felt on days when I didn't see her.

The next day would be no different from all the other days. Gilberte's feeling for me was already too longstanding to change: it was one of indifference: in my friendship with Gilberte, only I was in love.

It's true. There's nothing to be done about this friendship. It won't change.

But the very next day, I asked Gilberte to give up our old friendship and lay the foundation of a new one.

I always kept close at hand a map of Paris, which, because it showed the street on which M. and Mme Swann lived, seemed to me to contain a treasure. For pleasure, in connection with anything at all, I used to pronounce the name of the street, so that my father asked:

But why are you always talking about that street? There's nothing special about it. It's a very pleasant street to live on because it's just a short distance from the Bois, but there are a dozen others like it.

I contrived constantly to pronounce the name "Swann" in front of my parents. The pleasure I felt in hearing it made me feel so guilty that I thought they could guess what was on my mind and therefore change the subject whenever I tried to bring it up.

I would then turn to other subjects that also had some connection to Gilberte. I thought that by mixing and combining all things associated with her, I might concoct something that would make me happy.

I repeated to my parents that Gilberte was quite fond of her governess, as if this statement would at last cause Gilberte to burst into the room or come live with us for good.

I often praised the old woman who read Débats (I had insinuated to my parents that she was an ambassador's wife or perhaps an aristocrat) and continued to celebrate her beauty, splendor, and nobility until the day I mentioned that from what I gathered from Gilberte, her name was Mme Blatin . . .

Oh! But I know who she is. On guard! On guard! as your poor grandfather would say. And you think she's beautiful! Why, she's horrid and always has been. She's a bailiff's widow.

You were too small to remember the lengths I went to avoid her.

She was always mad to meet people. I always thought she was out of her mind, and she must be if she really does know Mme Swann. Though there's nothing remarkable about her background, I've never heard a bad word about her character.

But she was always eager to be introduced people.

She's horrid, terribly common, and a troublemaker.

As for Swann, I tried to imitate him while dining by constantly pulling at my nose and rubbing my eyes.

The boy is an idiot. How dreadful he'll be when he's grown up.

Once, in the midst of recounting the errands she had run during the day, as she did every evening at dinner, my mother said:

. . . By the way, guess who I ran into at the umbrella counter of the Trois Quartiers:

Swann.

How depressingly delightful to learn that Swann, that afternoon, had insinuated his supernatural form into a crowd of shoppers in order to purchase an umbrella.

Among a series of events great and small, none of which meant anything to me, that one alone stirred in me the special tremors associated with my love for Gilberte.

Does nothing interest you, my boy? I was speaking of King Theodosius, an ally whose visit to France may have considerable political repercussions, and you weren't even listening!

Did you say hello?

Of course.

He came over to greet me. I hadn't even seen him.

My mother always seemed to worry that if she admitted that our relations with Swann had grown chilly, someone might try to patch things up more than she could tolerate, because she did not care to know Mme Swann.

So you haven't quarreled?

Quarreled? Why would you think we'd quarreled?

. . . as if I had questioned the fiction of our good relations with Swann and tried to effect some kind of "rapprochement."

He might resent not being invited anymore.

We're not obliged to invite everyone. Does he invite me? I don't know his wife.

But he used to come to Combray.

Yes, indeed, he used to come to Combray, and then in Paris he had other things to do, and so did I.

But I assure you we did not look like two people who had quarreled.

We chatted for quite a while because he had to wait for his package. He asked me about you and told me you played with his daughter. . . .

. . . apprising me of the amazing fact that I existed in Swann's mind.

To my parents, the Swann family was much like any number of other families of stockbrokers. They lacked what my love had given me, the special sense needed to perceive the unique quality of everything that surrounded Gilberte, the analogue in the universe of emotions of what infrared is in the universe of colors.

It seems she is a big believer in religious medals.

She won't go anywhere if she hears an owl hoot

or a ticking sound inside a wall.

or if she sees a cat in the middle of the night or the furniture creaks.

She's a very religious person.

I was so in love with Gilberte that if I saw their old butler walking the dog, emotion would stop me in my tracks.

What's the matter now, child?

We continued on our way until we came to their carriage entrance, where the concierge seemed to know that I was one of those people forever banned from penetrating the mysteries of the life he was charged with guarding.

On other occasions we walked down the boulevards, and I would take up my station at the corner of the Rue Duphot, where someone had told me Swann often passed on the way to his dentist.

In my imagination, Gilberte's father was so unlike the rest of humanity that even before arriving at the Madeleine,

I became agitated at the thought that a supernatural being might suddenly appear in the street.

192

Usually, though, on days when I was not supposed to see Gilberte, I directed Françoise toward the Bois de Boulogne, because I had learned that Mme Swann went almost every day to the Allée des Acacias around the big lake or to the Allée de la Reine-Marguerite.

It was the Garden of Women. And like the alley of myrtles in the Aeneid, the Allée des Acacias was frequented by celebrated beauties.

I was told that if I went there, I would see certain elegant women who were regularly mentioned along with Mme Swann, but usually by their *noms de guerre*.

But it was Mme Swann I wanted to see, and I waited for her to pass, as excited as if she were Gilberte herself, for her parents, steeped, like everything else connected with her, in her charm, aroused as much love in me as she did.

I can't take any more. We've been walking up and down here for an hour.

. . . My legs are killing me from so much walking!

At last I saw entering the avenue from the Porte Dauphine . . .

. . . an incomparable victoria drawn by two spirited horses, as lean and shapely as in the drawings of Constantin Guys,

in the back of which Mme Swann sat nonchalantly,

... with an ambiguous smile on her lips, in which I saw only the benevolence of a queen, although what it contained was mainly the provocation of a *cocotte*.

In reality, her smile said to some:

I remember very well, it was exquisite.

and to others:

How I would have liked to! What rotten luck!

and to still others:

If you wish!

I'm going to follow the line for a while, but as soon as I can, I'll break away.

How beautiful she is!

For certain men only, she had a tight, bitter, timid, cold smile that meant:

Yes, you swine, I know you have a viper's tongue and can't keep your mouth shut.

Why would I care what you say?

Coquelin passed by, in conversation with a group of friends.

But my only thoughts were for Mme Swann, and I pretended not to see her, because I knew that when she reached the shooting range she would tell her coachman to break out of line and stop so she could continue on foot.

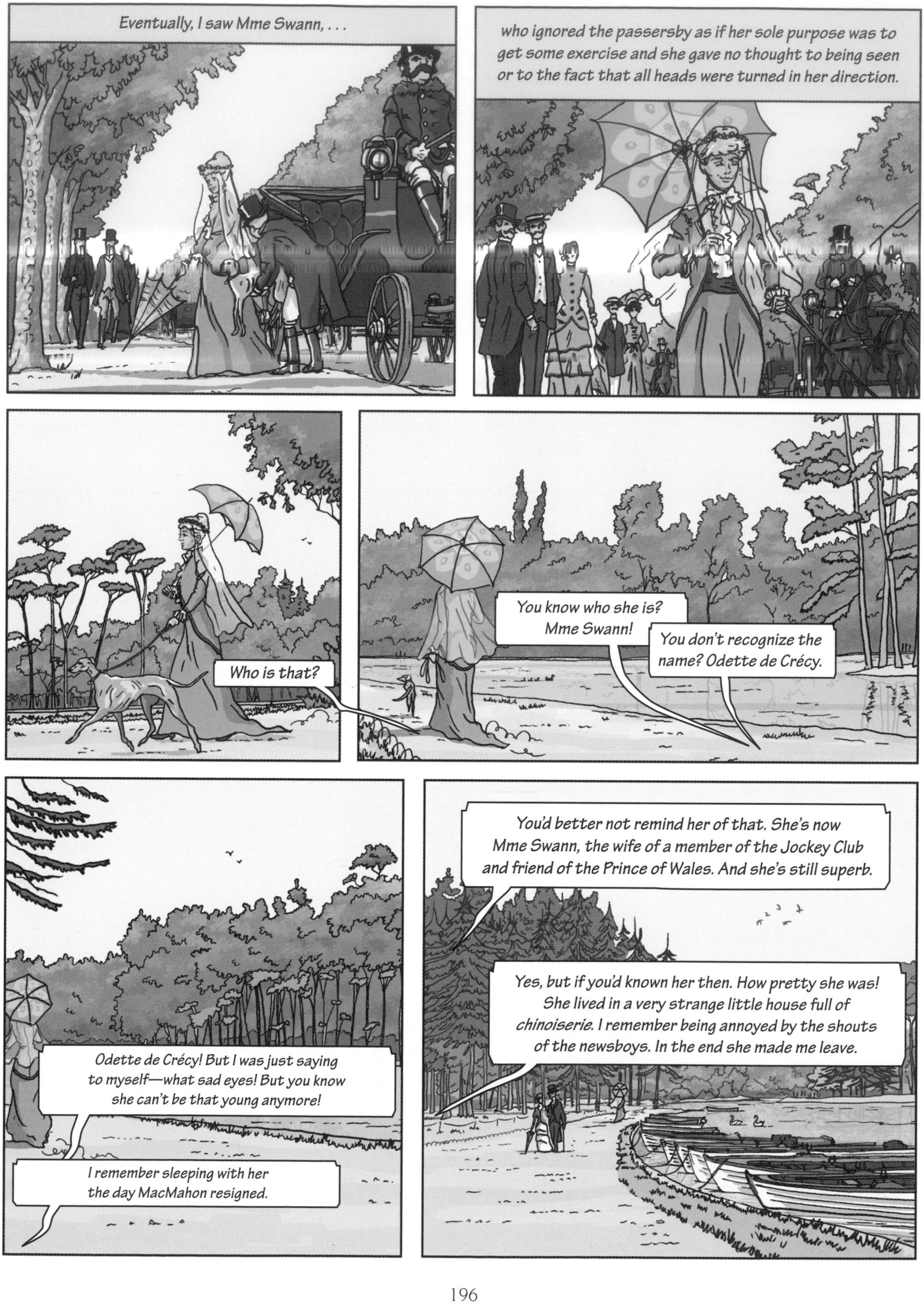
Eventually, I saw Mme Swann, . . .
who ignored the passersby as if her sole purpose was to get some exercise and she gave no thought to being seen or to the fact that all heads were turned in her direction.
Who is that?
You know who she is? Mme Swann!
You don't recognize the name? Odette de Crécy.
Odette de Crécy! But I was just saying to myself—what sad eyes! But you know she can't be that young anymore!
I remember sleeping with her the day MacMahon resigned.
You'd better not remind her of that. She's now Mme Swann, the wife of a member of the Jockey Club and friend of the Prince of Wales. And she's still superb.
Yes, but if you'd known her then. How pretty she was! She lived in a very strange little house full of chinoiserie. I remember being annoyed by the shouts of the newsboys. In the end she made me leave.

Although I couldn't hear these comments, I could see the indistinct murmur of celebrity around her. My heart beat with impatience when I reflected that it would be but another moment before all these people saw the unknown young man, to whom they paid no heed, greet this woman universally renowned for beauty, mischief, and elegance.

But I was already quite close to Mme Swann...

She couldn't help smiling.

People laughed.

She had never seen me with Gilberte and didn't know my name, but for her I was rather like the watchmen in the Bois or the boatmen or the ducks on the lake, one of the familiar, anonymous minor characters who played supporting roles when she took her walks.

On days when I didn't see her in the Allée des Acacias, I sometimes went looking for her in the Allée de la Reine-Marguerite, where women went who wanted to be alone, or to seem to want to be alone.

She didn't stay alone for long.

The complexity of the Bois de Boulogne makes it an artificial place—a garden in the zoological or mythological sense of the term—as I discovered this year while passing through on my way to Trianon.

The Bois had the provisional, artificial look of a nursery or park.

It was the season in which the Bois de Boulogne displays the widest variety of species

and combines in an intricate composition the greatest number of distinct elements.

One felt that the Bois was not merely a wood,
that it embodied a destiny that had nothing
to do with the life of its trees.

So I looked at the trees with unsatisfied longing, which transcended them and was directed without my knowledge toward that masterpiece of beautiful strolling women that they framed for several hours each day.

Having been forced by a kind of graft to share their habitat with women for so many years, they called to mind the dryad, the quick and colorful worldly beauty whom they cover with their branches and oblige to feel as they do the power of the season.

They reminded me of happy times, of my believing youth, when I used to come eagerly to the places where these masterpieces of feminine elegance would briefly appear beneath the unconscious, complicitous boughs.

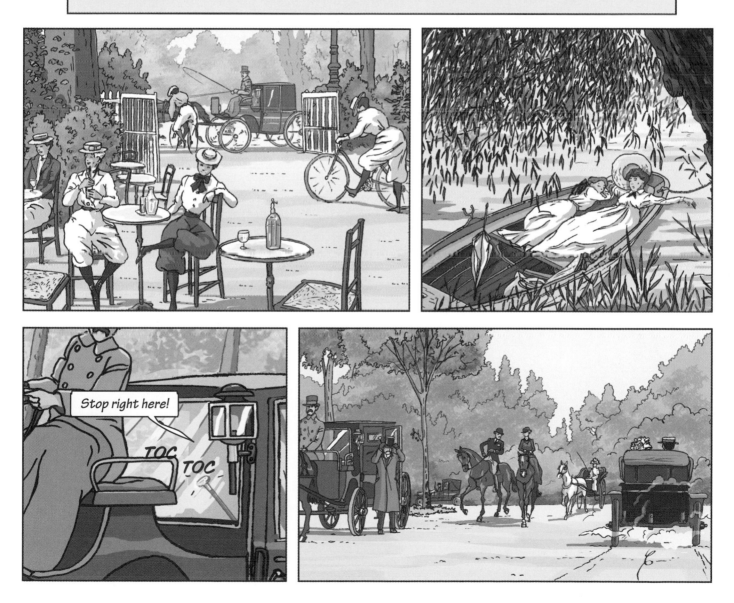

I had bestowed the idea of perfection I carried within me on the height of a victoria, on the leanness of those horses as spirited and weightless as wasps, their eyes as bloodshot as those of Diomedes' cruel chargers, which, now that I was gripped by desire to revisit what I had loved, I wished to see again before my eyes at precisely the moment when Mme Swann's hulking coachman sought to master their wings of steel . . .

Alas! There were only automobiles.

I wanted to see again, with the eyes in my head, the little hats women used to wear, hats so flat that they seemed mere wreaths, to see whether they were as charming as they appeared in the eyes of memory.

But all the hats were now immense and covered with fruits and flowers and all manner of birds.

On the heads of the gentlemen who might have gone walking with Mme Swann in the Allée de la Reine-Marguerite I saw neither the gray hats of yesteryear nor any other kind of hat.

They were bare-headed.

To these new features of the spectacle I no longer had any faith to bring. They appeared before me helter skelter, containing none of the intrinsic beauty that in the past my eyes might have sought to work into an artful composition.

These were just women, in whose elegance I had no faith and whose dress seemed without importance.

But when a belief disappears, a fetishistic attachment to the things it once animated remains, as if the divine resided in them rather than in us, and as if our current disbelief were the effect of a contingent cause, the death of the gods.

How awful! How can anyone think of automobiles as elegant in the way that horses and carriages used to be?

I'm no doubt already too old, but I'm not made for a world in which women hobble themselves in dresses that aren't even made of fabric.

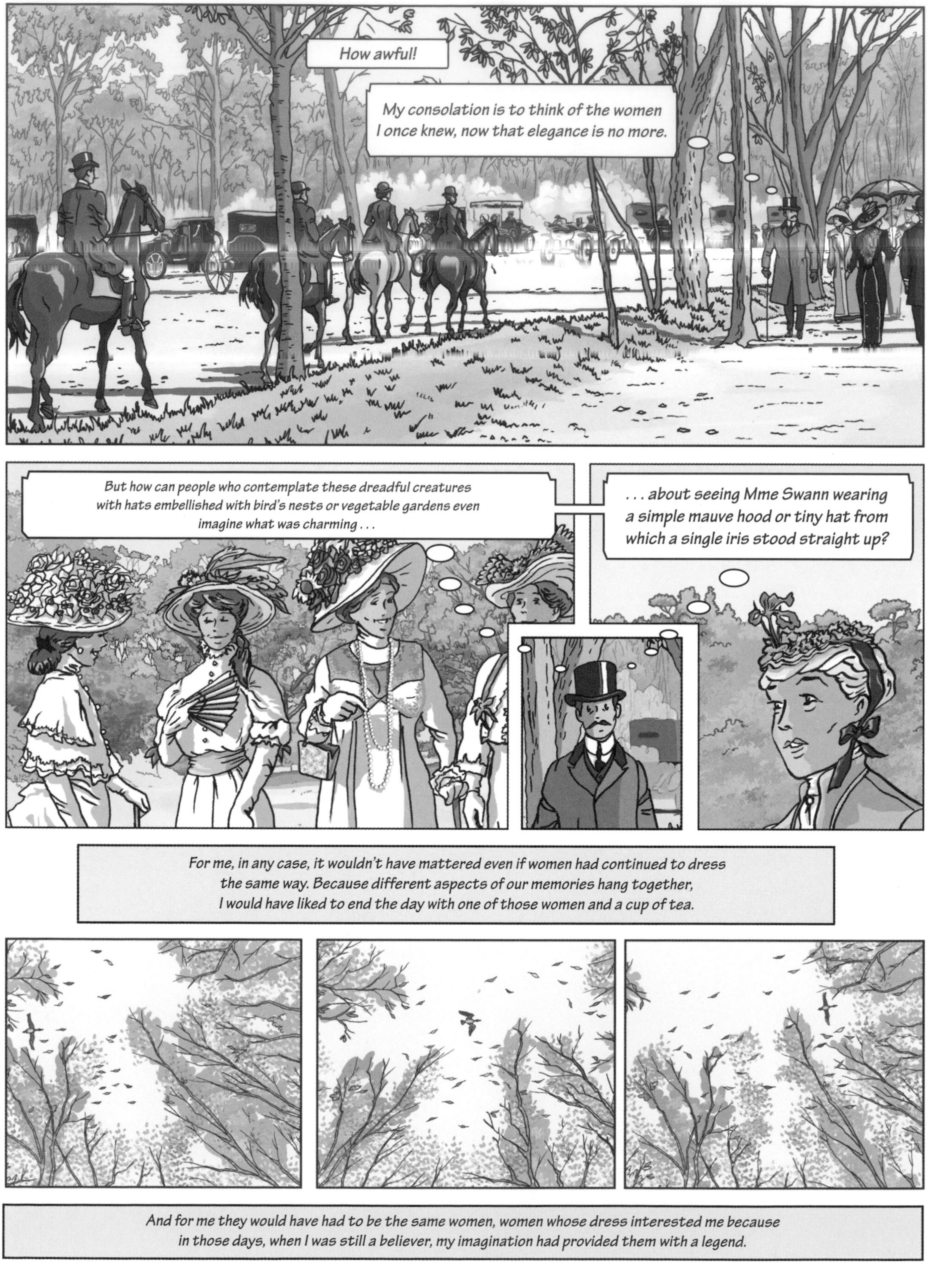
How awful!
My consolation is to think of the women I once knew, now that elegance is no more.
But how can people who contemplate these dreadful creatures with hats embellished with bird's nests or vegetable gardens even imagine what was charming . . .
. . . about seeing Mme Swann wearing a simple mauve hood or tiny hat from which a single iris stood straight up?
For me, in any case, it wouldn't have mattered even if women had continued to dress the same way. Because different aspects of our memories hang together, I would have liked to end the day with one of those women and a cup of tea.
And for me they would have had to be the same women, women whose dress interested me because in those days, when I was still a believer, my imagination had provided them with a legend.

Alas! In the Allée des Acacias—the alley of myrtles—I saw some of them, now old, mere shadows of what they had been, wandering about, desperately searching for who knows what in the Virgilian groves.

Nature resumed its reign in the Bois, from which had vanished the idea that it was the Elysian Garden of Women.

Large birds flew swiftly over the Bois and, squawking loudly, landed one after another on the tall oaks . . .

. . . which, with Dodonian majesty beneath their druidic crowns, seemed to proclaim the inhuman void of the deconsecrated forest, and helped me to better understand how futile it is to search for remembered scenes in reality, which will always lack the charm they derive from memory and from not being perceived through the senses.

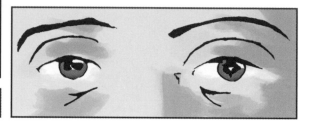

The reality I had known no longer existed.

The places we have known do not belong only to the spatial world in which we conveniently place them: the memory of a particular image is merely the longing for a certain moment.

And houses, roads, and avenues are as fleeting, alas, as the years.

GLOSSARY

COMBRAY
p. 1

Doncières: Doncières, located near the fictional seaside resort of Balbec, is an equally imaginary town where Robert de Saint-Loup, a character in a later volume of the novel is stationed in the military.

p. 2

Magic lantern: the magic lantern is a primitive type of projector consisting of a light source, a painted glass slide, and a lens.

Legend of Geneviève de Brabant: on going off to war, Siffroi, the husband of Geneviève de Brabant, leaves her in the protection of his steward, Golo. She discovers that she is pregnant by her husband, but Golo, irritated at having failed to seduce her, claims that the child is the fruit of adultery. Siffroi sends Golo word that Geneviève and her child are to be drowned. But the henchmen charged with carrying out the murder take pity on the pair and abandon them in a forest, where they take refuge in a cave and manage to survive with the help of milk from a doe. Years later, while out hunting, Siffroi finds them, realizes the truth, and has Golo executed.

p. 5

Jockey Club: founded in 1834, the Jockey was one of the most aristocratic of French clubs. Proust mentions it several times as one of the most exclusive clubs in the world, the sanctuary of the elite. It was located at 1, rue Scribe, in the Hôtel Scribe, near the Place de l'Opéra.

Prince of Wales: before becoming king and reigning for nine years, Edward VII bore the title Prince of Wales for nearly sixty years. Throughout the long reign of his mother Queen Victoria, he personified the wealthy British elite as a world traveler and influence on fashion. An ardent Francophile who spoke fluent French, he visited Paris frequently and knew everyone who was anyone in the Belle Époque. He was instrumental in achieving the second Entente Cordiale (1904) and was a friend of Charles Haas, the principal model for Swann.

p. 6

Pasquier: Gaston d'Audiffret-Pasquier (1823–1905), was president of the Senate and a member of the Academy, who was adopted by his great-uncle, the president of the Chamber of Peers, and thus became the Duc de Pasquier. He published his great-uncle's memoires, which are mentioned by the narrator's grandfather.

p. 7

Asti wine: a sweet wine from the Italian Piedmont. The sparkling wine Asti spumante is made from the Asti muscat.

Saint-Simon: Louis de Rouvroy, Duc de Saint-Simon (1675–1755), is celebrated for his *Memoirs,* a detailed chronicle of court life during the reign of Louis XIV and the Regency.

Maulévrier: in the full text, Swann quotes Saint-Simon on Maulévrier: "He wanted to *donner la main* to my children. I saw this soon enough to stop him." Aunt Céline is outraged that Saint-Simon prevented her children from what she believed was shaking Maulévrier's hand because she doesn't know that *donner la main* is an old expression that doesn't mean to extend one's hand to another person but rather to stand aside for that person, to grant him priority.

p. 8

"Lord, what virtues you make us hate!" Exasperated by Céline and Flora's inopportune compliments and friendly words, which prevent him from savoring Swann's anecdotes, the narrator's grandfather quotes a line from Corneille's *La Mort de Pompée,* which in fact reads, "O heaven! What virtues you make me hate!"

45, rue de Courcelles: the address of the Proust family, which lived on the third floor from 1900 to 1906.

Madeleine: a small pastry in the shape of a cockle shell, invented in the eighteenth century in Commercy by Madeleine Paulmier, the Marquise de Baumont's cook.

According to some, the cockle shell shape dates back to the origins of the pilgrimage of Saint James of Compostella, whose emblem is the cockle shell. The scene with the madeleine is the origin of the expression "Proust's madeleine."

Water lilies, Vivonne: nénuphars are yellow water lilies a couple of inches in diameter. Nymphéas are more impressive and decorative water lilies with white, pink, or red flowers of four to five inches in diameter.

"Madame Octave": Aunt Léonie is the widow of Octave. As was common at the time, Françoise calls her Madame Octave.

Elevation, death knell: in the Catholic liturgy, the priest shows the bread and wine as they are consecrated in the Eucharist: this is the elevation. The death knell is sounded when a member of the parish dies.

Pepsin is an enzyme found in animals. Aunt Léonie uses a medication based on this enzyme and used as a digestive aid.

Tapestry of the Legend of Esther: seven cartoons painted by Jean-François de Troy between 1737 and 1742 served the Royal Factory of the Gobelins as models for the seven panels of the "Legend of Esther."

The Legend: King Ahasuerus of Persia searches his kingdom for a wife, and his eye falls on Esther, whom her Uncle Mordecai asks to conceal the fact that she is a member of the Jewish community, of which he is the head.

The king's grand vizier Haman, jealous of Mordecai's growing influence, learns that he is Jewish and tries to rid the kingdom of all its Jews. Risking her life, Esther begs Ahasuerus to spare her people. Moved by his wife's despair, the king grants her request, and Haman is hanged.

Cardoons: a vegetable similar to the artichoke, it used to be eaten with white meat. Cardoons can be served raw with hazelnut butter, au gratin, in donuts, marinated, or, for gourmets, with marrow, as Françoise serves them.

Marzipan: made of egg white, almond paste, and sugar, originally from Venice (marci panis), and a specialty of the French town of Saint-Léonard-de-Noblat in Haute-Vienne.

Actors: Got, Delaunay, Febvre, Thiron, Maubant, Coquelin (illustrated to the right), Sarah Bernhardt, Bartet, Madeline Brohan, and Jeanne Samary were actors of the day to whom Proust adds the name of the fictitious actress Berma, inspired by Réjane and Sarah Bernhardt.

A "blue": a kind of telegram sent through pneumatic tubes connecting Paris post offices, so called because of the blue paper on which messages were written.

Vaulabelle: Achille Tenaille de Vaulabelle (1799–1879), minister of public education. Uncle Adolphe mentions his name together with Victor Hugo, and Odette mistakes him for an artist.

pp. 32–33

Giotto: Giotto di Bondone (1267–1337), an Italian painter, sculptor, and artist whose influence on the history of Christian art was considerable and whose work inspired the next generation of artists. In his pre-Renaissance paintings, figures are no longer frozen, dress is natural, and perspective is taken into account.

p. 36

"The troops marched through Combray": when Proust vacationed in Illiers (Combray) as a child, the troops he saw marching through the city behind his aunt's house belonged to the Seventh Light Cavalry Brigade, which was stationed in Châteaudun.

p. 39

Mehmet II: In Combray, Swann compares Bloch to the portrait of Mehmet II by Bellini. Mehmet II, known as "the Conqueror" (1532–1481), was the seventh sultan of the Ottoman Empire. He took Constantinople in 1453 and began construction of the Topkapi palace. An adept of literature and art, he wrote poems and songs, took an interest in science, and invited Italian artists such as Gentile Bellini, who painted the best-known portrait of him.

In Swann in Love, however, Swann is interested in him for a different reason: "Swann felt close to Mehmet II, whose portrait by Bellini he loved, and who, when he realized he had fallen madly in love with one of his wives, stabbed her, as his Venetian biographer naively wrote, in order to regain his freedom of mind."

p. 45

Hawthorns and Mary's month: Catholics have referred to the month of May as "Mary's month" since the eighteenth century. In many parishes, one recites the rosary and says prayers to the Virgin during this period. The narrator and his parents join in these prayers one evening after dinner.

The hawthorn was associated with Mary's month because its white petals symbolized the purity of the Virgin and its thorns the crown of Christ. The month of May therefore became the month of chastity, and a tenacious superstition insists that one must not marry during May or the woman will be sterile. In the past, May was therefore reserved for communions and baptisms. As is often the case, this superstition derived from another, which dates back to the Romans, who forbade weddings in May, the month in which they celebrated their dead.

p. 47

Paul Desjardins (1859–1940) was a French journalist and professor who for more than 22 years organized annual gatherings of intellectuals known as the Décades de Pontigny.

p. 56

"Skinfolk": Françoise confuses parenthèse (parenthesis) with parentèle, the kin of the narrator. This solecism has been rendered in English as "skinfolk" for "kinfolk."

p. 71

Planté: the French pianist Francis Planté (1839–1934) was known as "the god of the piano." He is the only pianist who saw and heard Chopin play of whom recordings exist.

Rubinstein: Anton Rubinstein (1829–1894) was a Russian pianist, composer, and conductor and one of the most important musicians of his time. He knew Liszt and Chopin and was one of Tchaikovsky's teachers.

Potain: Pierre Charles Édouard Potain (1825–1901) was an important French cardiologist. Potain's aspirator, Potain's disease, Potain's solution, and Potain's syndrome are all terms still in use. It is unlikely that he was a less capable diagnostician than Cottard.

p. 74

Faubourg Saint-Germain: one of the most chic and prestigious neighborhoods in Paris. Although the term was extended well beyond its literal meaning, so much so that leading figures of the Faubourg Saint-Germain such as Geneviève Straus and Comtesse Greffulhe actually lived on the right bank, the Faubourg proper was bounded by the Rues de Lille, Constantine, Babylone, and Bonaparte.

p. 78

Vermeer of Delft: Johannes Vermeer or Vermeer of Delft (1632–1675) was a Dutch painter. Proust discovered his "View of Delft," which he judged "the most beautiful painting in the world," in The Hague. He saw it again at the Jeu de Paume in 1921. Swann is writing a study of Vermeer that he will never finish, while the writer Bergotte falls dead before the "View of Delft."

p. 80

"Blue-blooded": aristocratic. Nobles did not work, so their skin was never exposed to the weather and was therefore supposed to remain white, delicate, and so transparent that one could see their veins.

p. 84

"The Ninth": Beethoven's Ninth Symphony.

"The Bear and the Grapes": "The Fox and the Grapes" was a fable by La Fontaine and "The Bear and the Fox" was a fable by Aesop, but "The Bear and the Grapes" is an invention of Proust's.

p. 88

The sonata for piano and violin, like its composer Vinteuil, is an invention of Proust's.

p. 90

Châtelet: a theater built in 1862 on the Place du Châtelet opposite the Théâtre de la Ville (built in the same period and on the same plan on the other side of the square), at the head of the Point-au-Change.

Gambetta's funeral: Léon Gambetta (1838–1882) played a key role in the Third Republic. His funeral on January 6, 1883, was a major public event.

Les Danicheff was a four-act play by Alexandre Dumas Jr., written in collaboration with Pierre Corvin and signed with the pseudonym Pierre Newsky. Performed for the first time in 1876, it was revived in 1884 at the Théâtre de la Porte Saint-Martin.

Jules Grévy (1807–1891) was the fourth president of the Third Republic from 1879 to 1887. He resigned in the wake of a scandal involving his son-in-law, who was selling nominations for the Legion of Honor.

Rue La Pérouse: the street where Odette lives, named for the explorer Jean-François de Galaup, Comte de La Pérouse, who vanished in 1788 on an expedition whose exoticism resonated with the "Oriental" décor of Odette's home ("a very odd small house with *chinoiseries*").

Odette's bedroom looks out on the Rue Dumont-d'Urville, which runs parallel to the Rue de La Pérouse. The buildings that separate the two streets were built where the Wall of the Farmers General once marked the Paris city limits. Having front and rear entrances suited Odette's life as a "demimondaine."

The Rue La Pérouse was located near the Arc de Triomphe in what was then a new bourgeois neighborhood of west Paris, in contrast to Swann's residence on the noble but unfashionable Quai d'Orléans, farther to the east.

In "Place Names: The Name," the Swann family resides nearby, in a small street off the Avenue du Bois (now Avenue Foch), and the Arc de Triomphe marks a sort of boundary between Swann's world, which stretches to the east (he sees his dentist on Rue Duphot, shops at Trois Quartiers, and goes to pick up his daughter at the Garden of the Champs-Elysées) and Odette's world, which stretches to the west, toward the Bois de Boulogne, the site of her indiscretions and of Swann's suffering.

Cattleya: from the scientific term for the orchid named in honor of the English botanist William Cattley. The cattleya, with its large white or mauve flower in the shape of a horn, is native to tropical America.

"And much later, long after there was no further need to arrange cattleyas, the metaphor 'making cattleya' was the phrase they used without thinking about it to refer to 'making love,' the act of physical possession, in which in any case nothing is possessed. This forgotten habit lived on in their language, commemorating that first instance." The phrases "faire catleya" and "arranger les catleyas," meaning to make love, have survived Proust and entered the vocabulary of love.

Our Lady of Laghet: Laghet, a hamlet located between Nice and Monaco, where the Virgin Mary is supposed to have performed several miracles n 1652. A church commemorating these events, Notre-Dame de Laghet, is still a popular pilgrimage site today. The medal to which Odette is so attached (Swann: "Will you swear to me on your medal of Our Lady of Laghet?"; Françoise: "She apparently has great confidence in medals") depicts the miracle-working Virgin.

Zipporah: Swann likes to find the faces of people he knows in famous masterpieces.

Although Odette at first inspires almost physical revulsion in him, he comes to love her after noticing that she resembles Zipporah, the daughter of Jethro, in a painting by Botticelli. A woman whom he himself says "was not [his] type" then becomes "a priceless masterpiece." He even places a reproduction of the painting on his desk as if it were a portrait of Odette.

Doge Loredan: Leonardo Loredan was elected doge of Venice in 1501. Swann sees a striking resemblance between his coachman Rémi and a bust of the doge by Antonio Bregno, known as Rizzo.

Antonio Rizzo had to flee Venice after being accused of embezzlement in 1598, and since he died between 1499 and 1500 he could not have sculpted the doge after 1501. Proust may have been thinking of the sculptor Briosco, known as Riccio.

Ghirlandaio: Swann sees M. de Palancy's nose in a painting by Ghirlandaio (1448–1494), an Italian painter of the Florentine school (opposite: detail from *The Old Man and the Child*).

Tintoretto: in a portrait by Jacopo Robusti, known as Tintoretto, (1518–1594), Swann sees the sideburns, eyes, and nose of Dr. du Boulbon.

p. 98

Prévost: a café-restaurant once located at 39, Boulevard Bonne-Nouvelle.

p. 99

Eurydice: in mythology, the dryad (nymph) Eurydice is fatally bitten on her foot by a snake after marrying Orpheus, who descends to the Underworld to bring her back to the world of the living. Hades, the master of the Underworld, allows him to take Eurydice on condition that he not look at her until he reaches the surface of the Earth. Worried when he can no longer hear her footsteps, Orpheus turns around and Eurydice vanishes.

p. 100

Tortoni: a café-restaurant formerly located at 10, Boulevard des Italiens.

Maison Dorée: a café-restaurant with private rooms formerly located at 20, Boulevard des Italiens. The façade and balcony with gilded railings remain. The building today houses a bank. Also referred to in the text as the Maison d'Or.

Café Anglais: a café-restaurant formerly located at 13, Boulevard des Italiens.

p. 103

Joseph Tagliafico, Olivier Métra: Odette has a taste for the popular music of her day such as the ballad "Pauvres Fous!" by Joseph Tagliafico (1821–1900) and "La Valse des Roses" by Olivier Métra (1830–1889), a very popular composer and band leader also celebrated for his "Quadrille des Lanciers."

p. 104

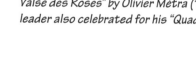

Watteau's three-pencil studies: Antoine Watteau (1684–1721) was celebrated for his paintings "Embarkation for Cythera" and "Pierrot" and also well-known for his three-pencil drawings. The three-pencil technique involved drawing on beige or blue-gray tinted paper with three different pencils or chalks: black for the outline and shadows, sanguine for color, and white chalk for highlights. The technique was much admired in the 18th century. If Swann's identification of Odette with Botticelli's Zipporah represents the illusion created by his passion for art, the allusion to Watteau's three-pencil studies shows that in his unconscious mind Swann associates Odette's life with debauch.

p. 105

Rue d'Abbattucci: the part of Rue La Boétie between the Rue du Faubourg-Saint-Honoré and the Place Saint-Augustin was called Rue d'Abbattucci from 1868 to 1879.

Odette's short, fur-trimmed cape was known as a *une visite.*

p. 106

Avenue de l'Impératrice: became Avenue du Bois after the fall of the Second Empire, then Avenue Foch in 1929.

The lake: the lower lake, the largest in the Bois de Boulogne, into which the upper lake flows.

Eden Theater: built in 1882 at 7, Rue Boudreau, where the Théâtre de l'Athénée is now located.

Hippodrome: a stone and iron track where horse shows and other performances were held. Odette speaks to Swann about the Hippodrome de l'Alma (or Hippodrome of Paris), a huge venue capable of accommodating 6,000 spectators, built in 1877 at the corner of the Avenue de l'Alma (later Avenue George-V) and Avenue Marceau. The owner of the land refused to renew the lease, and the Hippodrome closed in 1892.

Quai d'Orléans: Swann lived on the Ile Saint-Louis, an unfashionable place at the time.

p. 108

Sorbonne: prestigious university, seat of the Rectorate of the Academy of Paris, classified as a historic monument.

p. 110

The Night Watch is a painting by Rembrandt and *The Regents of the Saint Elizabeth Hospital* is by Frans Hals.

p. 112

"a sharp eye," in French *l'oeil américain,* a quick gaze that takes in everything, even to the side, associated with American Indians as portrayed in novels like *The Last of the Mohicans.*

"Converse with the Duc d'Aumale": a jocular expression meaning "to go to the bathroom" (a typical Cottard pun on the words *eau* and *mâle,* water and male). Henri d'Orléans, the son of King Louis-Philippe, Duc d'Aumale (1822-1897), was the pretender to the French throne and as such subject to jokes and mockery in poor taste by republicans, of which this is one example.

p. 126

Chatou: a town 6 miles west of Paris in which the Maison Fournaise restaurant, frequented by the painters Caillebotte, Degas, Monet, Renoir, Sisley, etc., was located.

"Moonlight Sonata": Beethoven's piano sonata no. 14, opus 27, no. 2, in C# minor. The name was given to the piece after Beethoven's death, in 1832, by the German poet Ludwig Rellstab, who saw the sonata's first movement as an evocation of a "bark by moonlight on the Lake of the Four Cantons."

p. 128

Labiche's plays: Eugène Labiche was a playwright who wrote satires of bourgeois manners.

p. 129

Last circle of hell: In Dante's Inferno, the ninth circle of Hell is reserved for traitors.

p. 130

Une Nuit de Cléopâtre: 1885 opera in three acts by Victor Massé, with libretto by Jules Barbier.

Château de Pierrefonds: Impressive 12th-century castle 45 miles northeast of Paris, rebuilt under Napoleon III by the architect Viollet-le-Duc in the style of an idealized medieval castle, taking liberties that many critics found unacceptable. Viollet-le-Duc applied his method to many other restoration projects, including Notre-Dame de Paris and Carcassonne.

The map of the Land of Love, in French called the Carte du Tendre: the map of an imaginary country created in the 17th century by Madeleine de Scudéry, representing the stages of love (village Billet-doux, river Inclination, sea of Passions, Lake of Indifference, etc.).

Restaurant Lapérouse: a great restaurant that has been located on the Quai des Grands-Augustins since 1766. In 1878, one of the owners, Jules Lapérouse, gave his name to the establishment, and its resemblance to the name of the explorer, the Comte de La Pérouse, led Swann to eat lunch there from time to time since it made him feel closer to Odette.

Bayreuth: a German town that is the site of an annual summer music festival inaugurated by Richard Wagner (1813–1883) and devoted to the performance of his ten operas. It is prestigious event, and tickets are much sought after.

Clapisson: Louis Clapisson (1808–1866) was a successful composer of comic operas.

Crapotte (23, Rue Le Peletier) and Jauret (14, Place du Marché-Saint-Honoré) were renowned fruit suppliers. Chevet (16, Galerie de Chartres in the Palais-Royal) was an elegant grocer.

Legitimists: the Legitimists sought the restoration of the Bourbon monarchy, as opposed to the Orleanists, who favored the house of Orléans, and the Bonapartists, who preferred an empire headed by a member of the Bonaparte family. Princesse Mathilde was a niece of Napoleon Bonaparte.

Cambremer: the Princesse des Laumes and Charles Swann engage in a bit of double-entendre word play. In French, the "mot de Cambronne" is merde (shit), which is assonant with the final syllable of Cambremer.

Bérénice (as Odette calls "the dreadful Rampillon") is a tragedy by Racine in which Titus, the Roman emperor, is obliged for political reasons to abandon Queen Bérénice, with whom he is in love, and his best friend Antiochus.

"Les Filles de Marbre," a play in five acts by Théodore Barrière (1823–1877), in which courtesans and actresses are portrayed as hardhearted women who distract artists from their work.

Palais de l'Industrie: a gigantic palace built near the Champs-Elysées for the World's Fair of 1855. It was destroyed in 1897 to clear access to the new Gare des Invalides by way of the Avenue Alexandre-III (now Avenue Winston-Churchill), along which the Grand Palais and Petit Palais were built. This street was extended by the Pont Alexandre-III. The sculpture that decorated the monumental entry (France distributing wreaths to Commerce and Industry) can still be seen in the lower portion of the Parc de Saint-Cloud.

p. 162

Bright fountains of the Fair: The 1889 World's Fair was held in Paris in the centennial year of the French Revolution. In addition to the Eiffel Tower, built for the occasion, the illuminated fountains were also a major attraction, including one representing "France enlightening the world." One of the fountains was decorated with electric lights that changed color with the sound of music played by a military band.

p. 166

Gold background: a gold fill applied in leaf or powder form covering the background of a panel, canvas, or parchment. Very common in Byzantine painting, these gold backgrounds were not replaced by landscapes until the first half of the fifteenth century. The fields of Fiesole: Fiesole is famous for its panoramic view of the city of Florence.

p. 169

City of lilies: the red lily is the symbol of Florence, known in literature as "the city of the red lily"

"Bayeux": the noble reddish lace is probably the celebrated tapestry of Bayeux, whose tones are ochre and brownish red on very fragile cloth. The peak is that of the city's cathedral, and its final "yeux" sound is reminiscent of "vieil or" (old gold).

"Vitré": the acute accent symbolizes the frame of an old church window.

"Lamballe": the word, softened by the letters "l," contains the phonemes of the word "blanc."

p. 170

"Coutances": the final diphthong of Coutances is reminiscent of rance, rancid, and thus of a mound of butter.

"Questambert": an imaginary town phonetically linked to a lascivious allusion to camembert.

"Pontorson": for the narrator, the name probably evokes the contortions of laughter.

"Lannion": the narrator is no doubt thinking of the lanière or lash of a whip, and the coachman is driving him to La Fontaine's fable "The Coach and the Fly."

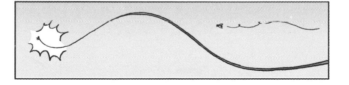

"Benodet": the name Benodet is reminiscent of the aquatic plant élodée (elodea, or waterweed).
"Pont-Aven": Proust was familiar with Pont-Aven, "the city of painters." He may have seen the headdress worn by women there and immortalized by Gauguin, consisting of two light strips of lace. "Aven" recalls the Latin for bird, avis.
"Quimperlé": like an oyster, this name contains a "pearl," which the narrator may associate with a necklace.

p. 191

"Trois Quartiers": a department store that opened in 1825 opposite the Eglise de la Madeleine.

p. 192

Corner of Traktir and Eylau: until 1881, Avenue Victor-Hugo was called Avenue d'Eylau.

p. 193

The alley of myrtles in the Aeneid*: the allée Longchamp was called the Allée des Acacias because it was lined with locust trees (acacias in French). In Virgil's* Aeneid*, Aeneas descends to the Underworld. His path takes him through a forest of myrtles (consecrated to Venus, the goddess of love), where he sees women known to have died for love: Phaedra, Procris, Eriphyle, Evadne, Pasiphae, Laodamia, Caenis, Dido . . .*

p. 194

Constantin Guys (1802–1892) was a French artist. He painted from memory, mainly with ink washes and watercolors, lending a forceful expressiveness to his stylized portraits. Baudelaire baptized him "the painter of modern life . . . of the transient, fugitive beauty of the present." His paintings are recognizable, especially those featuring spirited horses with spidery hoofs.

p. 200

Dryads: in Greek and Roman mythology, nymphs that watched over trees and forests.

p. 202

Diomedes' horses: for the narrator, the horses drawing Odette's victoria, "furious and weightless as wasps, with bloodshot eyes," evoked Diomedes' cruel horses from Greek mythology. Diomedes, the king of Thrace, fed his mares human flesh. One of the dozen labors of Hercules was to tame the mares, who in the end devour Diomedes himself.

According to legend, Alexander the Great's horse Bucephalus descended from one of Diomedes' mares.

p. 206

Dodonian majesty: in ancient Greece, the priests of Dodona (Epirus, today Albany) interpreted Zeus's oracles from the sound of the wind in the foliage of the sacred oaks.

The Narrator's Family Tree

AUNT
CÉLINE

AUNT
FLORA

GRANDMOTHER
(BATHILDE)

GRANDFATHER
(AMÉDÉE)

UNCLE
ADOLPHE

GREAT-
AUNT

FATHER

MOTHER

AUNT LÉONIE
OR "MADAME
OCTAVE"
(OCTAVE'S
WIDOW)

THE
NARRATOR

FRANÇOISE

CHARLES
SWANN

LEGRANDIN

ODETTE DE CRÉCY
(FUTURE MME SWANN)

GILBERTE SWANN
DAUGHTER OF SWANN AND ODETTE

DOCTOR PERCEPIED

CURÉ OF
COMBRAY

EULALIE

KITCHEN GIRL

ALBERT BLOCH

MME
SAZERAT

ORIANE, PRINCESSE DES LAUMES, LATER DUCHESSE DE GUERMANTES

PALAMÈDE DE GUERMANTES, BARON DE CHARLUS, KNOWN AS "MÉMÉ"

THE PRINCE OF WALES

SIDONIE VERDURIN

GUSTAVE (OR AUGUSTE) VERDURIN

NAPOLÉON III

COMTE DE FORCHEVILLE

THE YOUNG PIANIST

SANIETTE

DOCTOR COTTARD

MME COTTARD

PROFESSEUR
BRICHOT

THE PAINTER BICHE (IN "SWANN IN LOVE,"
ELSTIR IN A LATER VOLUME)

THE WRITER
BERGOTTE

THE COMPOSER
VINTEUIL

MLLE VINTEUIL

MLLE VINTEUIL'S
FRIEND

GENERAL DE
FROBERVILLE

M. DE
PALANCY

M. DE SAINT-CANDÉ

M. DE
BRÉAUTÉ

SOCIETY
NOVELIST

M. DE
FORESTELLE

MME DE SAINT-EUVERTE

MME DE CAMBREMER'S DAUGHTER-IN-LAW

MARQUISE DE CAMBREMER

VICOMTESSE DE FRANQUETOT

MARQUISE DE GALLARDON

COMTESSE DE MONTERIENDER

DOCTOR DU BOULBON

ODETTE'S NEIGHBORS

SWANN'S FACTORY GIRL

PIANIST'S AUNT

GILBERTE'S GOVERNESS

MME BLATIN

ODETTE'S COACHMAN

ODETTE'S GROOM

SWANN'S COACHMAN

ODETTE'S SERVANT

ODETTE'S MAID

UNCLE ADOLPHE'S VALET

SWANN'S VALET

SWANN'S CONCIERGE

PROSTITUTES

Marcel Proust was born on July 10, 1871, at 96, Rue La Fontaine in the 16th Arrondissement of Paris (Auteuil district) and died at the age of 51 on November 18, 1922, at 44, Rue Hamelin, Paris XVI.

His family belonged to the wealthy upper middle class. His father, Adrien Proust, was a respected physician and professor of medicine and inspector general of international health. Marcel began frequenting aristocratic salons at a young age and led the life of a society dilettante, in the course of which he met numerous artists and writers.

He wrote articles, poems, and short stories (collected as *Les Plaisirs et les Jours*), as well as pastiches and essays (collected as *Pastiches et Mélanges*) and translated John Ruskin's *Bible of Amiens*. In 1895 he began a first novel, *Jean Santeuil*, which he abandoned and which was not published until 1952. Then, in 1907, he began writing *In Search of Lost Time*, of which seven volumes appeared between 1913 and 1927.

The first of these volumes, *Swann's Way*, is composed of three parts: "Combray," "Swann in Love," and "Place Names: The Name."

The second volume, *In the Shadow of Young Girls in Flower*, won the Prix Goncourt in 1919, and the final three volumes were published posthumously.

All of the *Search* is told in the first person, except for "Swann in Love," which takes place in the Paris of the 1880s, before the narrator is born.

Of fragile health, Proust suffered all his life from severe asthma. In October 1922, on his way to visit Comte Etienne de Beaumont, he became chilled and died of a poorly treated bronchitis on November 18. He is buried in the Père-Lachaise Cemetery in Paris (Division 85).

The "Proust questionnaire"

Like "Proust's madeleine" in Combray and "faire catleya" (in "Swann in Love"), the "Proust questionnaire" has become part of the French vocabulary. Proust was not the author, however. The questionnaire comes from an English game called "Confessions," in which Proust took part at least twice: at age thirteen in the album of Antoinette Faure and again at age twenty. The questions (and answers) were similar both times but not identical. Both versions can be consulted in the Kolb Proust archives at http://www.library.illinois.edu/kolbp/proust/qst.html.

PROUST'S FAMILY TREE

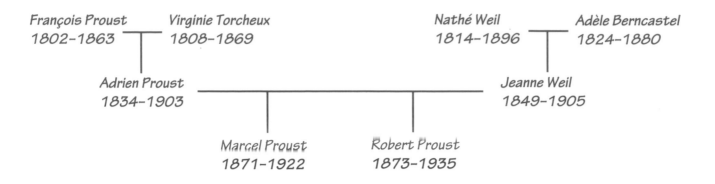

François Proust
1802–1863

Virginie Torcheux
1808–1869

Nathé Weil
1814–1896

Adèle Berncastel
1824–1880

Adrien Proust
1834–1903

Jeanne Weil
1849–1905

Marcel Proust
1871–1922

Robert Proust
1873–1935

Marcel's father was originally from Illiers in Eure-et-Loir, where "little Marcel" spent vacations with his aunt Élisabeth Amiot. She became Aunt Léonie in the *Search*, and Illiers inspired the fictive Combray.

In 1971, the centenary of the writer's birth, Illiers paid homage by changing its name to Iliers-Combray. It is the only village in France to have taken its name from a work of literature.

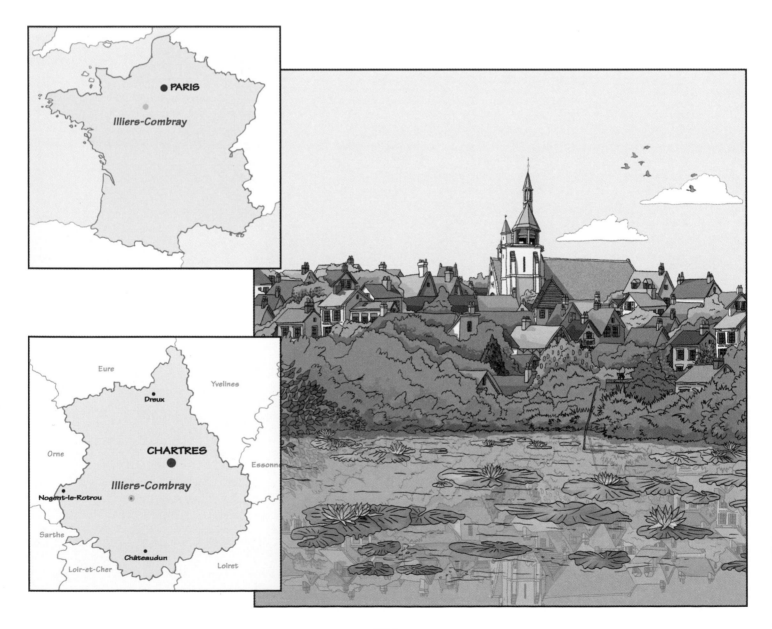

224